KAI KAGO

A NOVEL BY
SOVINA SEY

Visit our website at www.StillwaterPress.com for more information.

First Stillwater River Publications Edition

ISBN-13: 978-1-950339-65-5

1 2 3 4 5 6 7 8 9

Written by Sovina Sey
Cover design by Emma St. Jean
Published by Stillwater River Publications, Pawtucket, RI, USA.

"One moment can change a day,
one day can change a life,
and one life can change the world."

-Buddha

ACKNOWLEDGMENTS

To my closest friends who always support me when life becomes tough. Having an amazing group of friends who can make me smile and forget all the negative things in my life are the type of friends who are close to my heart.

To my mom and dad who love and support me in every single way. It seems impossible to find a way to fully repay all the things the two of you had done and sacrificed for me. Thank you for everything.

CHAPTER 1

I woke up to a hand on my shoulder, slowly shaking me back and forth. "Hey, kiddo wake up!" said a familiar male voice.

"Uhh, w-what time is it?" I let out a lazy groan. I could feel my brain becoming foggy as on other mornings. I tried to open my eyes, but they were unable to flutter even the slightest.

"It's time for you to get ready for school, that's what time it is," repeated the voice.

My whole body was numb and I kept my eyes shut. Unable to move my body, I couldn't do much of anything.

"Oh come on! It's just high school; you're always like this in the morning. Don't be lazy Kai, wake up!" said the voice as he attempted to take my blankets away and kept shaking my shoulders.

I lazily opened my eyes. Beside me sat my Uncle Rick, who awkwardly smiled, pursing his lips inwards. The button-up white shirt tucked into his black suit pants, topped off with a single color tie, screamed "ready-for-the-day." I looked like I was recently hit by a tornado.

I let out a yawn as I rose up from the bed and rubbed my eyes. "It's a Monday, isn't it? I wish it was Friday already. Rick, can you imagine the disappointment that I'm feeling because today's a Monday? I was starting to feel happy for a second, but then my hopes were crushed."

Rick got up from the bed and strolled towards my closet. After a bit of searching, he had chosen a white t-shirt with a sunset centered on it and a pair of blue skinny jeans, placing them on my desk chair.

"Go wash up," he said before leaving the room.

I swung my legs onto the side of the bed. My feet touched the cold wooden floor as I let out another yawn. Walking up to the desk where my backpack was slung on the chair, I began to pack everything I needed for school.

Afterward, I took my newly picked outfit and stumbled out of the room and into the bathroom.

As I walked down the stairs I can instantly smell the aroma of cooked eggs. Inside the kitchen plates of scrambled eggs, toast, and a glass of orange juice was set on the table. Grabbing the toast with my left hand, I took out my phone with my right. I have gotten a few notifications from Ronnell, my guess is that she wants to tell me something about her boyfriend Kyle.

I let out a sigh. Kyle is not…bad, per se, it's just this wasn't the best time for Ronnell to start dating. We're just sophomores and I don't want her to be involved in something that she'll regret in the future; it's very common in today's world that a relationship wouldn't last longer than two months. Most people in my high school knew that couples would eventually break up because either they were cheating, making up fake reasons to break up with them, or had enough of their drama and ended the relationship completely.

Ronnell said that I could be more of a supportive best friend. I've tried to be more supportive in her relationship with Kyle, but I'm just worried that something might happen to her. Ronnell and I have been best friends since third grade, and we have been through a lot during our years together. It just seems odd for me to see that Ronnell is dating someone who she just met two weeks ago.

I took a bite out of my toast, my eyes quickly skimmed through Ronnell's texts. Right about then, Rick entered the kitchen, wearing his gun holster around his torso. I don't know that much about guns but what I do know is to stay away from them. I always wondered what it's like to be a lieutenant detective for the Boston police department; I guess it's a difficult job because of the huge responsibility of handling crimes and bad guys. Oh, and god knows how much paperwork the position involves.

"Good morning Sleeping Beauty," he told me as he poured coffee into a mug that I made for him when I was seven. It was very rigid, and wasn't nearly big enough to hold the amount of coffee any human needed to survive their mornings. I've seen Rick refill the thing at least three times on normal days. But he always drinks out of that mug in the mornings.

I smiled and pointed at the mug with my toast in my hand. "You still have that?" The mug might've been oddly shaped, but it was still stable. I could see the messy seven-year-old writing that read "World's Greatest Uncle" scribbled on the side.

"Of course I still have it! You made it just for me, plus I am the greatest uncle in the world!" he said with a sly smirk edging on the corner of his lips.

He took a sip of coffee and placed the mug on the table. He walked towards me and pulled out a jar of cover-up from his pants pocket and held it out to me.

I placed my phone in my back pants pocket and took the makeup as I read the label out loud, "Tattoo concealer." I looked up at Rick, raising an eyebrow as I finished my toast.

"Is this from Stella? Or someone else?" I said with a straight face, not looking surprised.

"It's from Stella, I told her to get the concealer for you since the weather is getting warmer. Plus you're wearing a t-shirt so you can use it now without worrying about people looking at your... tattoo."

Only a few people knew about my tattoo; Rick, Stella, and my two close friends Ronnell and Owen. Back when I was a little kid I had to put on the concealer to hide my tattoo from everyone. Luckily this one was waterproof so I wouldn't have to worry about "accidentally" wiping it off.

I lifted my left arm to show my tattoo. It was a symbol of a lotus flower, with small shapes around it in red ink. I don't know how or even when I got it. A few years ago I asked Rick about it; he said he didn't know when or where my tattoo had appeared from. At that time his answer to my question sounded off; maybe it was the nonchalant tone of his voice, or maybe it was the fact that he never closely examined the tattoo. My unanswered question about my tattoo still makes me feel strange about it, even to this day. Of all people, I thought that Rick would know something about it; possibly he could be hiding something from me, or not.

I put some of the concealer on my tattoo and rubbed it in. At least it matched my skin tone perfectly.

"Is Stella your girlfriend now?" I asked in a relaxed tone without looking up.

"What? No, she's just a close friend," Rick said awkwardly.

I looked up; his cheeks were slightly pink. He glanced at his expensive black Rolex watch. "Hey, it's almost time to go, I don't want you to be late again."

I walked into the hallway and took my jacket off the wall coatrack. Wearing my jacket and backpack I looked at Rick, who walked up to me.

"Tell Stella thanks for the concealer," I told him as we hugged.

"I will, now you better hurry up and get on the bus. I love you." He kissed me on the head.

"Love you too," I replied.

"Oh Kai! Don't forget to watch out for yourself and do not cause any trouble," he said in a concerned tone, giving me his usual serious look.

"Yeah I promise." I paused for my comedic timing, then added, "Promise not to get caught. See you later!" I ran through the door and out of the house, down the steps, and across the long street, all with a smile on my face. A smile that could be read as I couldn't be stopped.

Once I was on the sidewalk where my bus stop is, my smile faded. "Oh shit," I said to myself. My eyes narrowed as I looked down at the long street. My school bus had already started to drive down the street and took a sharp left.

I started to feel worried; the next bus stop is six blocks away from here. I knew that I wouldn't make it with the time I had left. I didn't want Rick to know that I missed the bus again.

I frantically looked around my surroundings, hoping no one would see me. I took a deep breath as my body felt slightly numb, before I instantly disappeared into thin air.

I reappeared behind a guy who was holding a cup of coffee from a nearby coffee shop on the block. I turned my head towards the guy and realized it was Owen. Owen and I are neighbors, so he should have been on the bus by now.

Owen turned around and jumped when he saw me standing behind him; this kid is on edge sometimes. He bumped into a girl who was in front of him.

"OH MY LORD!" he exclaimed, with his eyes growing wide open with shock. "It's only you," he said, slowly calming down. Then he turned to look at the girl. "Sorry," he apologized. I'd never seen her before, maybe she was a new student.

"It's okay," she said in a quiet voice.

Owen turned his head towards me. "You used your powers didn't you?" he whispered, leaning his head towards mine.

"Yeah, but no one saw me so it's all good. I don't want to miss the bus again; this would be my fourth time missing the bus this month and I don't want Rick to know about this."

Owen made a frown. "What happens if someone sees you using your powers? There's a chance that you'll be taken by the government and be experimented on," he whispered as he looked left and right, searching for anyone listening in to our conversation.

"Come on Owen, that's not going to happen to me, I'll promise you that. If someone did find out about my powers then I would teleport them to some isolated place like the Bermuda Triangle or Antarctica."

"Please don't say that, I don't even want to know the things that you can do with your powers. For all I know, you can make anyone disappear without giving any effort. Just be careful about when and where you use your powers; maybe next time someone else will find out about your secret."

"I'll make sure to limit the use of my powers. What's taking so long?" I said, tilting my head to see a guy with crutches trying to get on the bus. Luckily he did in a few minutes.

Everyone at the bus stop got inside the bus and took a seat. Owen and I sat next to each other. Owen was looking at his phone, playing some shooter games, and I put on my earbuds as I looked through the window, watching the city go by.

"Did you read my texts?" asked Ronnell as we put on our goggles for a chemistry lab.

"I didn't have time to read all of it, we can talk about it right now if you want," I told her as I doodled in my notebook. Ronnell looked up at the front of the lab where there was a large table with multiple sets of beakers and substances for today's lab experiment. Students from our class gathered around the table, collecting the needed materials.

Ronnell pushed her chair back and stood up. I watched her walk to the table and grabbed two beakers and a small colored container.

As she walked back to our table I asked her, "So what did you text to me anyway?"

"I was wondering if you like to hang out with me, Owen, Kyle, and the others at the movies on Friday at seven," she said as she placed a small container of purple food coloring and two beakers of sodium polyacrylate and water on our lab table.

"I have to ask Rick about it, but I would like to go. Hope that Kyle doesn't do…something to you."

"Come on Kai, I can take care of myself. You're my best friend, but don't be too overprotective," Ronnell said as she looked over the lab paper.

"Yeah I know, but don't be surprised that he might do something that you don't like. You know how guys are like in this school, or even in our generation."

"Damn Kai, don't be a pain in the ass, let your friend grow up. Maybe someday you will have a boyfriend too if he actually likes you." Megan turned around from the table in front of us and looked at us with a smug expression on her face.

Ugh, Megan is one of those people who makes me hate people more than I need too. I wish I could teleport her to the bottom of the ocean so she'd get eaten by sharks, but Rick would know something was up, so I can't do it…sadly. I hate how annoying and fake people like her can be in a class like this. This is an honors class and I know that she's completely failing this class big time.

I let out a sigh. I took my lab worksheet and wrote my name down. "At least I don't date every guy in the whole damn school. The last one exposed you in front of everyone, such a shame," I said with a sarcastic tone. "It's a bit funny to be honest, you told me I could have a boyfriend if someone 'actually likes,' me but none of your exes actually like you. So you can piss off and don't talk to me or Ronnell you desperate slut," I said as I continued to answer the pre-lab questions on my paper.

What the hell did I say? If someone snitched on me to the principal, Rick would kill me. I can't believe I said that to her! I feel nervous, but at the same time I feel amazing. She's been bullying me since middle school and I have a grudge against her. I guess I just had enough of her and called her out. I'm a bit happy I did that to be honest. I looked up at Megan, who was giving me a death glare, but who gives a shit anyways? I turned to see Ronnell staring blankly at her paper; I could feel my face getting warm from the tension of what just had happened.

I looked to the side; a few people took a quick glance at me and Megan, but then looked away. A few people whispered something to each other and looked in my direction. I clenched my jaw as I could feel my eyes harden. None of us spoke or made a noise. A few minutes passed that felt like an hour.

Someone said something, but wasn't from the three of us. "Shit gonna get real. Damn Kai, I can't believe you told her off like that. Good girl gone bad,

I like that," said Nick. He was sitting next to Megan, carelessly holding up a beaker of water with two fingers.

Mr. Philips, our chemistry teacher, yelled to the class, "Okay class! Make sure you got all the materials for the lab; we will begin mixing water and sodium polyacrylate to see if they will react with each other…"

As the whole class started to do the lab, I settled back on my seat and looked at the other table, where students poured different beakers into an empty glass container. Once the two reactants came in contact with each other, they created some gel-like substance.

"This is boring," I told Ronnell flatly as she added a few drops of coloring into the sodium polyacrylate and stirred it with a glass rod. The white powder slowly changed to light purple.

"You know what's not boring? Saying all of those stupid things to Megan where people can hear you; you also embarrassed yourself in front of everyone." She gazed at me with concern, but then she looked at her paper and wrote something down.

I closed my eyes and stretched my arms. "At least you're not a part of this. This doesn't concern you at all." I hope that Rick doesn't hear about this mishap or I'll be in trouble.

Later during the lab I got really bored, but I'm always bored and I thought, what if something interesting happened? Maybe someone could use the wrong chemicals in the wrong beaker and something crazy happens. I know who the perfect victims would be: Megan and Nick, well, mostly Megan.

I used all kinds of chemicals from all the beakers that we used in the lab and teleported them into Megan and Nick's beaker. In under a minute the beaker made a weird sizzling noise. I looked in front of me and saw a huge orange blob on their desk.

"What happened? Mr. Philips! Something is going on; I think Meghan used the wrong chemical!" Nick yelled, which made everyone stare at the huge blob on his desk.

Then the breaker made a 'pop' sound and the foam-like blob exploded. Both Nick and Megan got covered with the stuff. Luckily, everyone around them, including Ronnell and I, didn't get a drop of the stuff on us, all thanks to my teleporting powers.

"WHAT THE HELL IS THIS! This is your fault! You're the one who always fucks up everything!" Megan screamed and pointed a finger at Nick, who was trying to wipe up the gooey substance with the lab paper.

"Why do you blame everything on me! It's not my fault that your ex exposed the real you and make you act more of a basic bitch!" yelled Nick, glaring at Megan with furrowed brows.

The stench of the orange substance made me gag; its smell was far worse than rotten food.

The whole class was very quiet. Even Mr. Philips didn't move, or even say anything, which I found to be a bit humorous. I could hear the clock faintly ticking throughout the lab.

"Megan and Nick, the two of you will immediately clean up this mess, once you're done with that clean yourselves up in the emergency showers. I expect the two of you to not make more of the mess than you already have." Mr. Philips said with a composed stern tone that made me shiver.

After the two of them cleaned up the mess, Mr. Philips cancelled the lab and told us to go back to the classroom and to do some classwork with our textbooks.

Not bad for a Monday; it might've even made my day.

"Huh, no wonder everyone was talking about it. I wish I could have seen that happen. I hate Nick, he's such a pain in the ass," said Jake, who was eating an apple as my group of friends and I sat at our usual lunch table. Everyone was eating except me; I don't eat the school's lunch most of the time, except when it's nacho day.

"And you also said that no one else got covered in the smelly foam thing? That's a bit weird right? I thought the foam exploded and it covered half the people in your class, how come no one got hit by it?" asked Kyle, who was sitting between me and Ronnell.

"The explosion wasn't that big; it was big enough to make Megan and Nick get covered by that thing. At least everyone else didn't get hit by it. I'm glad that it didn't touch me, the foam smelled disgusting." I replied.

"I heard that Megan might get suspended," said Tyrone who is sitting across from me. He was also my best friend who I have known since I was a little kid, but I never told him about my powers. I'm afraid that he or my other friends, besides Ronnell and Owen would think I'm a supernatural freak and will stop being friends with me. I even make up scenarios about me exposing my powers in public, and most of the scenarios turn out bad for me.

"Why would she get suspended if it was an accident?" Owen asked Tyrone.

"It's not about that incident. I overheard Megan's friends saying that Megan got caught with a bag of weed by the school cop."

"What can we expect? Most people in this school know that half of the students here are somewhat drug dealers or drug users," Ronnell said sarcastically as she drank her soda, looking at nearby tables throughout the cafeteria.

After lunch was over Ronnell and Owen walked up to me. Since they already knew about my powers, I guess they knew something was up.

"Did you use your powers again? You know that's not right Kai, I thought you wouldn't do something like that," Ronnell said quietly as the three of us walked down the long hallway filled with people.

"It's not a big deal," I told them as I peered at the people around us.

"What happens if someone else discovers your secret? We don't want you to get in trouble, but I wish you'd teleported me to see the look on Nick and Megan's faces when they got covered by that foam though." Owen looked at me with a grin, but got elbowed by Ronnell and made a frown. He blinked continually as he changed his train of thought. "Who cares anyway? We care about you not exposing yourself and getting into something that you can't get out of."

I stop walking and turned back to observed my two friends standing right in front of me with a sad look on their faces. I couldn't help but feel ashamed of myself that I made them become worried.

"I don't really care if I got in trouble; even if I do get in trouble I'll leave everyone out of it. Thank you for being concerned about me, but I can handle my own problems.

Don't be too stressed out because of one minor incident; I can even ask Rick for help." "You know that Rick might not help you if you get into some mess, even if he's a high-ranking personnel in the police department," Ronnell said as she walked into her class.

"I agree with Ronnell, I don't know what to do without you," Owen said, looking into my eyes.

He turned around and walked down the hallway and into a classroom. The crowd of students quickly died down. The only person in the hallway was me. I looked down at the vacant hallway and walked toward the stairway.

Finally, the end of the school day! Owen and I were walking to our neighborhood, which is about a twenty-five to thirty minute walk from school. I'm glad that Owen is my neighbor so I don't have to walk alone.

After about ten minutes of walking, we began to talk about Ronnell asking us to go to the movies on Friday. Owen asked me if I was going with them and I told him that I didn't know yet. I don't really want to go but at the same time I want to go. I don't feel like thinking about this now, my brain is fried from my classes.

We were about three blocks from our street. A few cars and bikers drove through the street as joggers and other people are on the sidewalk. I glanced up at the light blue sky; there were a few fluffy clouds floating peacefully in one direction. The temperature seemed to drop steadily by each hour; I'm glad that I wore a jacket so I don't complain about the weather to Owen.

I looked straight ahead of me; a little kid was chasing his dog in front of us. The kid kept calling the dog to come back, but the dog didn't listen. The dog made a sharp left and ran into the street. Lucky there were only a few cars driving by so the dog didn't get hit. The little kid ran into the street yelling out "Kippy!" I guess it was the dog's name, but there was a car is driving towards him.

I noticed that the car wasn't stopping. Without thinking I took off my backpack and ran toward the kid, who was standing in the middle of the car's way like a deer in headlights. I ran to the kid as fast as I could, grabbed the kid, and ran to the other side of the street. The thing is, the car ran into me, but there's more secrets about my powers. I can go through objects at any time. I had researched my powers and learned that this was called phasing or intangibility. This other power I have is pretty cool, but you know what's not cool? Getting stuck inside an object, and let me tell you the pain is much worse than anything I had felt before.

The car ran through my legs and back, but I pushed the boy out in front of me so he didn't come in contact with the car. I bolted to the other side of the street until I stopped at the sidewalk.

"Oh man. That was close." I let out a deep breath and heard the car make a screeching sound behind me. I looked at the kid, who looked back at me with bulging eyes. The dog, sat in front of me and began barking at me. Seriously? I saved the boy's life and now his dog is barking at me.

I looked back at the kid. "Are you okay kid? You should watch where you're going," I told him. All he could manage was to nod at me and then look at his dog. I put the kid down next to his dog and walked up to the car that almost hit the kid. The inside of my body felt like it is inflamed with anger and annoyance, now I'm pissed off.

Owen ran up to me carrying my backpack with the same terrified look as the kid on his pale face. He was breathing harder than me. I walked to the car and crouched down to look through the driver's side window. The window was rolled down, a blonde woman who was in her mid-twenties sat at the driver's seat. There was no one else inside the car. I noticed that she was staring at me with the same look as Owen and the little boy had. Her lipstick was all over her face, which is probably why she didn't stop the damn car.

I slammed my hand on the roof of the car aggressively. "You should watch where you're going! You almost killed that kid!" I yelled at the dumbfounded lady, who jumped up at my loud voice as she gripped the steering wheel, still staring at me with a startled look.

"Kai, be careful of what you're gonna say, I don't want you to get in trouble," Owen told me as he touched my left shoulder.

I shrugged his hand off, I could feel my brows furrow. "I don't give a shit if I get in trouble with the damn police, or even Rick," I said in a low voice.

"I...I don't know what happen, I...I can't remember what...what happened. It was...It was like a blur I'm so...so sorry! I wish...I wish I could stop it but...but I can't!" the lady said, stuttering with fear, but then, without thinking, my hand forcefully reached into the lady's window. Owen was trying to hold me back, but I was gripping the car door hard with one hand; the other hand was trying to grab the lady who was screaming and yelling at me.

I glanced to the side and saw the mom of the boy running towards him, but she was pregnant so she couldn't run that fast. I could hear her yelling at the boy and hugging him and the dog. I'm just glad that the boy and the dog didn't get hurt, but the lady in the car might be.

After a few minutes yelling and fighting with Owen and the lady I could feel more hands pulling me away from the lady and the car. I looked back again and saw two cops trying to pull me away from the car.

"Let go of the car!" one of the officers said.

"No! Piss off!" I hissed.

"Kai just let go, the lady had enough and the kid is okay now. You're making a scene," Owen told me as I struggled to let go.

Then my sweaty hands slipped off the car door and I bumped my chin on it. At least the window was completely rolled down

CHAPTER 2

I was at the police department in Rick's office. Rick was sitting behind his desk, staring at me with his hands laced together. He silently studied me with his lips pressed together, creating a hard line as he knitted his eyebrows towards each other. I waited for Rick to say something to me, but he didn't move or say anything at all. I let out a sigh. I closed my eyes and lay back in my chair as I pressed a bag of ice on my chin. The ice gave me goosebumps and it also made my chin very numb.

I opened my eyes and looked at Rick, who unlaced his fingers. "Kai." He took a deep breath and exhaled. "You attacked a woman inside her own car! She was so scared of you!" He raised his hands up as his voice got louder. "You're going to be in so much trouble young lady. You're so unbelievable; I can't believe you did that! Owen told me the whole thing and how you used your…you know what." Rick said the last part of his rant quietly; he wanted to keep my powers a secret from the people who could be eavesdropping on our conversation. He literally yelled so loud that some people outside his office were looking at us. I had already known that he was going to talk about my powers; the good thing is that no one had seen me using them, I hope.

"Did Owen tell you that I saved a boy's life?" I said, moving the bag of melted ice away from my chin and shaking it at my side.

"He did, and I'm proud that you did such a heroic thing for someone, but just remember about your powers. I don't want anyone to learn the truth about you, I don't want something bad happen to you," he said softly with a frown.

"I know Rick, but no one actually saw me using my powers, so no one knows about it. Plus that lady didn't even look at the road; she was too busy trying to put on some damn lipstick! And she has the fuc—"

"Don't you say that word in here, especially in my workplace Kai," Rick said in a low, intense voice that made me have goosebumps. "The good thing is that you're only a minor so you can't go to jail, but you already know that you're getting punished. You basically committed a misdemeanor for assault! If you did any real harm to that woman you would have a felony! And you're only fifteen years old! You know what? You're grounded until you graduate from High School; I can't believe you did that! You're so lucky that the woman didn't press charges against you or even put up a fight with you..." He slammed his hands on his desk causing all the objects on his cluttered desk to rattle. He continued to rant loudly about me not being a good role model and all this law stuff that I don't really pay attention to.

I looked behind Rick and looked at all the things that he placed on his walls. Pictures of his police certificates and awards hanging on the wall next to the picture of his friends and me. There is a spot where all my drawings that I made when I was a little were placed; a few drawings were with Rick and me. I could even remember when I made those drawings and remembered how happy Rick was when I showed them to him. There were a few photos of Rick and me at some places and events. I specifically liked the picture of Rick and I at the father-daughter dance at my elementary school; even though Rick and I were not 'father' and 'daughter' I still enjoyed the dance. His office was an average office, but with a lot of filing cabinets.

I slowly faded back into reality. "At least you didn't cause any trouble at school which I'm glad that you didn't. What will people say about you? I don't want them to get the wrong impression about you, you're a good kid and I don't want people to think that you're not. You should at least tolerate people's ignorance, I did and I learned how to handle my emotions, unlike some of my coworkers. Try to set a better example for your—"

"Yeah I know," I told him in the middle of his very long rant.

Rick stopped talking and then ran his hand through his dark brown hair. "What am I going to do with you?" Rick told me, and leaned back in his chair, still keeping his gaze on me.

Since Rick was working on a case, we had to come home late in the evening. He told me that I have to stay with him until it's time to go home. At least I have a lot of time to finish all my classwork and homework and also re-do my notes from class.

The rest of my afternoon was spent in the police department with Rick. He gave me things to do around the building, like organizing papers and some other boring stuff. He was making me do all his office chores while he did his "more important" work.

As I was carrying a box full of papers to an office across the building, I saw Bridget Greenfield. She is one of the department's forensic scientists. She sat at a table inside the break room reading a book.

"What are you reading?" I asked as I walked into the room. Bridget looked up from her book as her lips curved into a smile. She wore her usual white lab coat under her casual outfit. There were a few cops eating their snacks and talking to other cops in the room.

Bridget closed her book. "It's called Smoke Gets in Your Eyes; it's an interesting intake point of view about death. Since I'm someone who works with deceased people, I can relate to this book and the author."

"That book sounds very interesting; maybe I can find some other books for you to read if you like."

Bridget nodded. "I think that would be wonderful, maybe you could come to see me in my lab if Lieutenant Kago lets you go. But you know I'm a doctor who works on dead people every day, so it wouldn't be a good idea for you to go down there."

"We'll see about that," I said, nodding to myself.

I have been inside the morgue, but I have never seen a real dead body before. I hope I won't see one in the near future. I wonder how people get used to seeing something as traumatizing as that or worse every single day. I wonder what is going on in Rick's mind when he seen something like that; does he feel remorse, sympathy, or nothing at all? I shouldn't think that way, I know what he feels is heartbroken about the crime scene, or the victim and his or her family.

"I could hear Rick's loud voice from my lab, what happened?" Bridget asked as she ate a piece of mini pretzel from a plastic container.

Bridget gestured for me to sit with her. I placed my box on the floor next to a chair and took a seat.

"I got in trouble for 'attacking' a lady who almost ran over a little kid, whose life I saved from that close encounter," I said, putting up air quotes with my fingers when I said "attacking."

"Is the kid alright?"

"He didn't get hurt and that's all I care about."

Bridget's eyes widened. "You ran into the street and saved the kid's life? Your uncle should thank you."

"He did, but he went back to talking about how I should be careful and not attack people on the street."

"But overall you should be proud of yourself, you saved someone's life. I'm proud of you Kai, you should be happy about that."

"I know, but I have a weird feeling about that incident," I said, looking down at my hands on my lap. What would happen if I was too late to save that kid? Would the kid still be alive if he was struck by the car or will he be dead? Would the car eventually stopped in time before it hit the kid? All these questions swarmed in my head, it made me feel light-headed

"What kind of feeling?"

I snapped back into reality once again. "I don't know, I just feel odd about something," I said, looking up at her.

"You know what you need? A snack, it will make you feel better. Let's go up to the vending machine, I'll pay for whatever you want," she said, standing up and pushing her chair.

"You don't have to, I don't want you to waste your money," I said, still sitting on my chair.

"Come on, it's my treat. You saved someone's life, you deserve it," she said, holding my shoulders and forcing me up out of my chair.

"Do you want to go out and eat at a restaurant? I don't think we have much food in the fridge, I forgot to go to the grocery store yesterday," Rick said as we were getting ready to leave.

"I want to eat at the Terrells' diner," I said, picking up my backpack and putting it on.

"I was thinking about the same thing," he said as the corners of his mouth lifted up to a smile, but I can tell that he's a bit sad, judging by the look of his eyes. Maybe it's because I got in trouble.

I looked at his desk; there was a cardboard box resting on top. Rick turned around and walked towards one of his filing cabinets, rummaging through all the paperwork and folders until he stopped moving his fingers. He took out a folder that held dozens of papers inside. He opened the folder and looked through its contents as he pushed the cabinet drawer back and walked up to his desk.

He placed the folder inside the cardboard box with one hand and the other was diving into his pants pocket. He took out his set of keys and lifted the box up with both hands.

"Do you have everything?" Rick asked as he walked towards the door.

I stood in front of the door and turn the knob to open it. "Yep I got everything, let's go."

I walked out of the office and turned around, watching Rick following right behind me. He closed the door and inserted his key in the door lock, making sure that his office was locked and secure until tomorrow morning.

The two of us began to walk through the building passing desks, officers, and other office furniture until we were outside the large building.

Rick and I sat at a booth in the corner of the diner with a large window to look out from. I love diners because they have that cool aesthetic feel to them and the food is great, especially at this one. I especially like this diner because Owen's parents own it, and the food is way better than at any other diners and restaurants in the area. Mr. and Mrs. Terrell are Owen's parents and also my neighbors. The Terrells are really nice people; Rick and I have known them for a long time now.

A waitress came to our table and took our orders. I ordered a burger and fries with a vanilla milkshake and Rick ordered a turkey sandwich and onion rings with root beer.

After the waitress took our orders and left, Rick turned his head in my direction. "I'm sorry that I yelled at you today, I never expected you to do something like that. I wish I was a better uncle and took better care of you, I guess you got mad because I was never home because of my crazy job." He looked at me with his sad brown eyes.

I took a deep breath and exhaled. "You don't have to be hard on yourself just because of your important job. You got nothing to do with this. Everyone's not perfect, even the most perfect person you know has some secrets. Also you never yelled at me, you were just saying those things to me with a stern adult tone. You're the last person who would ever yell at me, you're too nice to do that to a kid. It's my fault; I let my emotions get the best of me which caused me to lash out from all my stress and emotions," I said as I leaned back looking at Rick, who made a frown.

Mrs. Terrell came up to our table and served our food, setting it down with a smile. "How was your day you two?"

Rick looked at me and then at Mrs. Terrell. "It's been well, how about you Stacy?"

"The diner is busy as usual," she replied.

Rick and Stacy continued their conversation as I ate my food and looked at them, listening in. After a good three minutes of the conversation, Rick and Stacy said their goodbyes, and I said goodbye as well. Rick started to eat his sandwich as he looked through the window.

After we finished our food we went into our car and drove home in the dark night through the city. The two of us struck up a normal conversation about work and school during the car ride home.

We arrived at our home and I grabbed my keys out of my backpack and walked up to the door. Rick was inside the car, searching for his box of files and papers. I unlocked the house door and walked inside, taking off my shoes and walking up the stairs to my room.

After I took a shower and got in my sleeping clothes I walked down to the living room and watched television. Later Rick came downstairs and sat next to me and watched television; he was also wearing his sleeping clothes.

"Hey kiddo, are you alright?" he asked me as he watched the news channel; more crimes as always in the city.

"I feel the same as always," I said as I hugged the sofa pillow.

"That's good…just make sure you stay out of trouble at school. I don't want you to become one of those kinds of kids at school. I trust you to behave yourself."

"I know Rick, I promise not to get in trouble at school, but I'm not sure of outside of school though."

He gave a light laugh and patted me on the head. "You better go to sleep. I don't want to wake you up again."

"Alright, goodnight Rick." I gave him a hug and got up.

"Goodnight, I love you my little monster."

I climbed up the stairs and open my bedroom door. My room is an average size room with windows that show a part of the city. The walls are decorated with maps, stickers, and polaroid photos of places I have traveled and teleported to. Good thing that Rick doesn't ask about the photos.

I picked up my backpack off the floor and placed it on the desk chair. I looked down at my desk; there were a few blank pieces of lined paper, pens and pencils scattered all over, and my phone laid face-down on the wooden desktop.

I dove into the bed. I rolled over so that my back was pressed against the soft mattress. I stared at the white ceiling while my thoughts drifted away like driftwood, moving with the waves towards an unknown destination.

I woke up lying on the cold floor inside a building. I stood up and looked around the place. There was a huge blurry wall in front of me. I looked behind me and there was another wall, but it wasn't blurred, so I was stuck between two walls, great.

I walked closer to the blurred wall and touched it with my hands but they couldn't go any further. I tried to go through the wall with my powers, but it didn't work. It was like the wall was an invisible force that prevented me from getting through to the other side.

I tried to look through the blurred wall, but everything looked so blurry, the only thing I could see were three silhouettes. Two of them looked like they're adults and the other one looked like a kid, judging by the height of the three of them. I could tell that the young kid was holding something in its arms.

What kind of dream is this? What's going on?

"Please take care of her, we trust you to look after her," said a woman's tense voice. Her voice was quiet and soft, but it was also quivering. I could tell that she's nervous about something.

"Run as fast as you can away from this horrible place, we'll take care of this, just protect our child," said a man's voice.

I could hear other people shouting in the background, I punched the blurry wall, but all it did was make a vibrating sound. I looked around the area where there wasn't a blurred wall; the white wall only had a single painting of a field of white flowers.

As I was walking back and forth I heard a baby crying, the noise seemed to come from the kid carrying something in its arms. The kid was shushing and rocking the baby to make the noise stop.

"Don't worry, she'll be safe with me. I would do anything for her," the kid said, looking at the baby in his arms. I couldn't help but notice that the person's voice seemed familiar but unfamiliar at the same time.

A door or something busted open and I heard yelling. Then I saw bright red light burst on my left side, but it's from the outside of the blurry wall.

"If we're dead can you find our bodies and bury them somewhere nice for me, please brother? Tell our baby that we love her so much; tell her the truth when it's the right time. I love you," said the man he walked up to the kid with the baby, hugging the two of them. Then the lady went up and hugged both of them, crying and saying how much she loves her baby and how she wishes things could be better.

"You're the only person who we can trust, please be safe. I can't thank you enough for doing this for the two of us," the woman said as the three silhouettes still hugged each other.

People's yells and screams in the background became louder. The three of them broke the hug. The man and the woman kissed and hugged like it was the last time they'd ever see each other.

I tried to see who these people were, but that stupid wall was in the way and there's no way it can be broken.

The kid holding the baby said, "You can't fight them all; you need my help I don't wan—"

"No. You make sure the baby is safe. Leave now before it's too late," the man said, looking back at the kid with the baby.

"But-but I can't leave you two to die here, you two are my family. The only family I can trust, I don't want to lose you." I could hear the pain and fear in the kid's innocent voice. He looked down at the baby in his arms making noises. He looked up at the two figures. "Be careful, I love the two of you, don't ever forget that!"

"We love you and our child very much, but we have to end this before it gets worse. Please don't ever come back to this place ever again," said the woman, her voice breaking.

Before the kid said anything he suddenly disappeared into thin air. Everything instantly turned black.

CHAPTER 3

T he next day I was at school, I kept thinking about that odd dream I had last night. Why am I dreaming of something like that? I know I've had a lot of weird and confusing dreams before, but this dream felt somehow real.

During geometry class, I asked Owen if he told anyone about my incident yesterday. He said he didn't even tell anyone, not even Ronnell. I don't want Ronnell to worry about what happened yesterday, or anyone else to know about my secret.

The school day went by a bit faster than I thought, maybe because I was goofing off during my history class as we watched a movie about the Civil War.

In biology class, Ronnell asked me if I told Rick about movie night on Friday. I told her that I was grounded because I got a crappy grade on my biology quiz, which was a lie. Ronnell didn't think much about it and told me that we can hang out someday.

Since I've been grounded, I took the bus home. Owen has tennis practice after school, so I was alone with no one to talk to.

I walked into my house and placed my backpack on the sofa in the living room and went to the kitchen, looking for some snacks to eat.

As I took a bag of chips out of the cabinet, I saw a small piece of paper on the kitchen table. I grabbed the paper and flipped it over. It had the lotus symbols on it, the same exact symbol on my arm. I can feel myself sweat because only a few people know about my tattoo and I know no one will ever do this kind of blackmail, if this is considered blackmail.

I looked around the kitchen to see if anything moved, but it looks like nothing is out of place. I needed to call Rick; I had an odd feeling in my gut. I walked out of the kitchen and into the living room where my phone was on the coffee table.

I took a deep breath and got my phone and dialed Rick's phone number. The phone kept ringing until he picked up after a few minutes.

"Hello Kai? Why are you calling me at this hour? Did you get in trouble again?"

"What no, well maybe I think. I found a piece of paper on the kitchen table with the same lotus symbol as the one on my arm. You want me to meet you at your office or should I wait?"

"Kai, do you really think that I would waste my time on a prank? I'm busy right now. When I come home I'll see this piece of paper myself. I'm sorry Kai, but I have work to do, love you." He hung up.

Seriously? It's not a joke. I let out a frustrated groan, teleported my chips away, and sat on the sofa, taking out my notebook and textbook and trying to finish some of my homework.

I waited until eight at night to show Rick the piece of paper. I kept thinking to myself, is this really important? It's just a piece of paper, but it makes me feel uncomfortable because someone else knows about my secret. I might be jumping to conclusions too quick; I should calm down and wait until Rick gets home.

Finally Rick came home. I was sitting on the sofa in the living room watching a television show.

"So are you going to show me the paper?" Rick asked and sat next to me. He loosened up his navy blue tie as he looked at me.

The piece of paper appeared on my hand and I gave it to him.

He took it and looked at the side the symbol was on and then flipped the paper, but that side was blank. His face changed from normal to concerned.

"When did you find this? Do you know who did this?" he asked me with a tense voice. Finally he now knows that this isn't some stupid prank that I made up.

"I have no idea who would do something like this, I found it after I came home. Do you think someone else knows about my secret?" I was now really worried that someone might expose me because of my powers.

"We have to leave tomorrow morning. Only pack the important things you need. I'll tell you what's going to happen tomorrow, but right now just go to sleep. You're going to need it." I looked at him; I could even feel my eyebrows twitching with confusion.

I let out a sigh and walked up to my room and packed my important belongings. I didn't know if I was going back to school, so I emptied out all the school stuff that was in my backpack and stuffed it with clothes. I teleported Rick's black suitcase and filled it with more clothes and other things I needed.

After an hour packing and thinking about what was going to happen tomorrow, I climbed on my bed and stared at the ceiling until I fell asleep.

Rick woke me up early in the morning, telling me to get ready, so I did just that. My brain felt like it hadn't not fully woken up yet and my body felt like it had just been hit by a bus. I hate when I feel like this in the mornings or in general. I made myself get cleaned up and dressed for the day. I have no idea why Rick is making us leave our house in the middle of the week. I know he wouldn't want me to skip school without a valid reason to do that, maybe there's something more to that mysterious paper from yesterday.

I dragged my feet into the kitchen where Rick's suitcase was next to the kitchen table. I rubbed my eyes, opened the fridge door, and grabbed a bottle of water. My backpack and suitcase appeared next to Rick's suitcase.

"Where are we going? Do I have to go to school?" I shouted so that Rick could hear me from another room.

"I don't know when it's safe to go back to school. We're going to the police department first; I need to tell them to find a temporary person to replace me for a while. After that we'll be staying at Stella's apartment for the night. I need time to plan out what I'm going to do during the week." I could hear him in the living room. I walked into the room and saw him dressed in a casual outfit; t-shirt and jeans.

"You sure that Stella would be fine letting us stay at her place with no good reason?"

"I have a good reason why we're going to her house. I called Stella yesterday and she said that she was glad to let us stay for as long as we like." He took a deep breath and looked at me. "Don't worry about this, I'll tell you what's going on when the time is right." He got up and walked past me, grabbing his luggage and walking to the door where the car was parked outside.

"When the time is right?" I said to myself, looking at Rick walking through the door and down the porch stairs.

Trying not to use my powers I carried my bags to the car. I almost tripped over the house steps, but luckily I didn't.

As I got to the car Rick lifted my luggage and put it in the trunk. He walked back to the house to get something that he forgot and to make sure that the door was locked.

I suddenly remembered that I left my phone charger in my room so I walked up to the house. A piece of paper was taped on the door window from the inside of the house, it said that Rick and I were traveling for an unexpected trip and might not come back to the city for a couple of weeks.

Good thing was that I still could see through the door window and saw Rick standing in the hallway near the stairs kneeling on the floor. Rick's body was surrounded by a red glow which made me have shivers. The crazy thing that scared me most was his eyes, his eyes were glowing purple, but I couldn't really tell that much because he was facing sideways.

I heard a slight vibration inside the house like it's coming alive. Rick placed his right hand on the floor and the floor made a weird circle like those crazy black magic summoning circles. The shapes in the circle were black, but the edges of the black outline were white. The circle was getting bigger as seconds flew by, I had no idea what was happening or what would happen after Rick's ritual.

Is my uncle those demon worshipers or a Satanist? This felt like a crazy dream that I wanted to get out of, why was he doing this? Maybe Rick was hiding his powers from me for the past fifteen years, he didn't even say anything about his powers but he knew about mine. I felt both angry and scared because Rick was doing some crazy black magic ritual, he never told me about his powers, and he was doing some voodoo shit in my own home.

I didn't take my eyes off of Rick until he stood up and I just booked it to the car. I hope he didn't see me running like a little kid that was chasing an ice cream truck.

What did I just witness in my own home? How did he hide this from me? I don't know what to do anymore, everything is starting to get crazy because of some stupid paper.

I was sitting in the passenger seat looking at my phone, waiting for Rick to drive us to the police department. I just blankly stared at my phone processing what had just happened. I can't believe he has been hiding his secret from me, I don't know why he would do that to me. He already knew about my powers why can't he tell me about his?

I looked out my passenger window. Rick came out of the house carrying a box of files from last night. He placed the box in the trunk and sat in the driver's seat.

"You ready?" He looked at me and turned on the car.

"Ready as I'll ever be," I said, not looking at him as my heart started to beat faster.

First we had to go to the police department to deliver Rick's stuff to Chief Gray, who was Tyrone's granddad. Rick and I have known the Grays for a long time and I usually call Chief Gray Fred because we're like family, and Chief Gray's first name is Fred, obviously.

Rick was carrying a box of folders as the two of us walked towards the building. I guess Rick's going to tell Fred about this situation and not me, I'm just wondering what is going on in his head that would make him do this.

As we got inside Rick's office he placed the box on top of his desk, and he told me to walk around because he had to talk to Fred about something. So I did what he told me to do, I talked to Bridget in the morgue; at least there were no dead bodies on the lab table. We basically talked about my situation, about how I might be gone for a while. Bridget told me about this new bookstore that her friend just started, which was also a cafe. I actually want to go there but I don't think I can, I'm not sure if I can go there at all. At least Bridget gave me the cafe/bookstore's business card so I can visit it any time.

It's been at least twenty minutes since I got here. I walked out of the morgue and saw Rick and Fred still talking inside the office. I wonder how long they're going to talk. Rick saw me looking through the office and he gives me a thumbs-up and I gave a shoulder shrug and walked away. I didn't know where to walk so I was looking for a snack from a vending machine that was in the break room, luckily no one was there.

I walked up to the vending machine and got myself a chocolate candy bar. I sat on an empty seat in the room and unwrapped my treat.

Detective Alejo walked into the room and walked to a table where there's a box of donuts on top of it. He opened the lid and took out a glazed donut, closed the lid, and walked back towards the door.

He slightly glanced at me and jumped back. "Geez kid you scared me, I didn't know that you're in the room," Alejo said as he walked up to me, taking a bite of his donut.

"I'm just sitting here in an empty room quietly eating my chocolate bar, alone with my thoughts."

Alejo raised an eyebrow. "I still don't understand you kids these days, but anyway how is life Kai?"

"I could be better," I said, taking a bite of my candy bar.

"I feel you, but that's how things happen. We just have to deal with it or go with the flow. Hey, aren't you supposed to be in school?" he asked as he waved his half bitten donut in the air.

"Yeah, but Rick and I have something to do, so I get to miss a day of school."

"If you don't mind me asking, did you guys get in some trouble?" He leaned closer to me; his eyes searched my face.

"I don't think so, it's very confusing for me. Rick never says anything about what is going on. You shouldn't be worried about us; Rick said that he'll handle whatever is going on."

"Well if you or Rick need any help I'm always here for you guys, just to let you know," he said, pointing at me with his donut.

"Thanks I appreciate that," I said, smiling at him as I finished my candy bar.

"Hello Detective Alejo, I guess you two were fighting over food again?" he said, nodding at us.

"Not this time Lieutenant." Alejo walked out of the room as he gave Rick and I a wave with his donut.

Rick glanced at me. "It's time to go." I walked up to the trash bin and tossed the candy wrapper inside it.

I walk up to Rick who put his hands on my shoulders. The two of us walked out of the break room in silence.

Later, we arrived at an apartment complex outside the city; at least the neighborhood is nice and quiet. We got out of the car and carried our luggage up to Stella's apartment. A few little kids played around an area where there was a small playground at one side of the complex. Residents sat at their porches or balconies, watching people walk up and down the sidewalks or observing life around them.

I knocked on Stella's door, I could hear her footsteps walking up to it. The locks on the door clicked, the door opens. Stella opened the door and smiled at the two of us as her eyes lit up.

"Hey guys come in!" Stella said to us as we walked into her house.

I put my bags next to the sofa, which her dog Tobi was sitting on. Tobi is a Rottweiler and he's really friendly, but sometimes scary.

I'm always petting Tobi whenever I see him. I could hear Rick and Stella talking in the kitchen about our stay here and some other things. I couldn't hear that much of what they were saying because they were talking quietly and I couldn't make out the words.

"What am I going to do now Tobi?" I asked him, even though he can't talk back to me.

Stella's apartment is a nice place to live, in my opinion. The house was decorated with stylish furniture which was decent. A few framed photos were hanging on the walls. One of them was a drawing of a weird looking cat that was drawn by a little kid; maybe it's by one of Stella's vet patient owners. I thought it was cool that she is a veterinarian and that she helped make animals feel better. I consider veterinarians as doctors, but instead of humans it's animals. The house isn't that big and that's a good thing, unlike my large house that makes me feel scared whenever I'm alone at night.

After a few minutes Stella showed me my room which was next to her room. My temporary room was like any other room with a bed, a desk, and thank God a large closet. I began to unpack my things and place them inside the closet.

There's only two bedrooms in her apartment, so Rick had to sleep on the sofa in the living room. I told them that I wanted to sleep on the sofa, but Rick refused to give it up. His loss, the sofa is smaller than him so he might have some trouble getting any sleep.

The whole day was dull because it's basically what I do at my own home, most of the time I just use my phone or watch television. This sucks because I was told not to text or call my friends besides Rick or Stella. Rick strictly told me what to do and what not to do and I did what I was told. It makes me feel weird because I missed a day of school which never happens. I wonder what my friends would say about my absence. Would they care if I'm gone for God knows how long?

During dinner Stella cooked a few Spanish dishes that she told me she learned from her mom and grandma. The food that she cooked was way better than any restaurant or takeout food Home cooked food always has a special place in my heart. The three of us talked about work, school, and other things that were going on in the world. I just wished that I got to know why I had to stay at Stella's home, not that I didn't like the place, it's just that I wanted to go home or know the truth about why Rick was doing this.

After an hour of eating and talking, I finally got to go to my room and relax. I turned on my phone, and I looked at my notifications from my friends asking where I am or what happened to me. It was irritating for me because I couldn't text them back and tell them about this weird and confusing situation that I'm in. I lay face down on my bed, I kept thinking about how Rick was making that large satanic symbol inside our home.

Rick and Stella sat on the living room sofa watching television.

"Stella we need to talk if that's okay," Rick said as he took a drink of water from his water bottle.

"You can tell me anything, I think Kai is asleep." Tobi jumped up on the sofa and lay on Stella's lap.

"The reason why Kai and I came here is because I think we're being watched by my siblings and my father. This is the only place I know where Kai and I can be safe," he said quietly, his eyes observing Stella's face.

Stella tilted her head and made a frown. "Siblings? You never told me that you have siblings, you never talk about your family other than Kai. How do you know that... they are watching you?"

Rick let out a sigh, looked at Stella, and moved closer to her before whispering, "Kai isn't the only one who has supernatural powers." He moved back and rolled up his left sweatshirt sleeve, revealing his left forearm. He moved his right hand and held it over his left forearm. His right hand glowed crimson red. Stella's eyes grew wide as she held Tobi. Rick pulled his right hand back, making the glow on his hand disappear., On his left forearm was a lotus symbol marked in red ink just like the one that Kai has.

"Please don't tell anyone, you and Fred are the only ones who I can trust knowing about my secret." Rick looked at Stella once again. Stella opened her mouth, but only managed a shocked noise. He took her hand. "Don't tell Kai. I have been keeping this a secret from her for her whole life; I'm waiting for the right time to tell her this. I trust you not to tell her." Rick reached into his pants pocket and took a piece of paper that had the lotus symbol on it. He turned the paper to the blank side. "When a normal person sees this paper they think it was just a regular blank paper, but for me and my…father, we see things that no other human being can see. This paper," Rick shook the paper softly, "is a warning for me and Kai."

Stella's cheeks turned slightly pink as she looked at him. "You better tell her about this," she said quietly, still looking at Rick with her eyebrows knitted together. "I don't care if it's the right time or not, you have to tell her the truth. She has to know what's going on, she has the right to know the truth no matter what." Tobi got up and walked into the hallway.

Stella let go of Rick's hand to stand up with her back towards him. "You better not let her get hurt," she told him, and walked through the hallway and into her room, leaving Rick sitting on the sofa looking down at the paper.

CHAPTER 4

I spent the rest of the week living in Stella's apartment without going outside. This felt like a prison and I was slowly going insane. I was lying in bed, looking at the ceiling, thinking about how this is a waste of time.

Then someone knocks on the door, making me more irritated than before.

I let out a huge sigh. "Come in."

Rick opened the door, closing it as he walked up to my bed and sat on the edge. I got up my back against the wall. He looked at me with a smile. "We're going out to the mall! Isn't that fun?"

I know I made a pissed face because Rick's smile faded a bit. "When are we going back home?" I asked quietly.

My guess is that Rick thought that my reaction was going to be like 'Oh really? We're going out for once? Thanks Ricky you're the best!' But this pointless thing that he did made me overwhelmingly agitated.

Rick looked down at his hands. "I know this is tough, but I did this because there's something I have been keeping a secret from you for a long time now." He patted the bed next to him, gesturing me to sit there.

I swung my legs over the edge of the bed and scooted next to Rick.

"I'm going to show you something that might make you...um angry and or confused. Please don't yell because I don't want the neighbors to call the police or get us in trouble."

I gave him a nod, what is he going to do anyway? I hope it's nothing too weird or ridiculous. Maybe it's about that time before we left our house and I saw him in his crazy demon form making that circle on our floors.

He held his right hand over his left forearm as his hand began to glow red. I stared at his glowing hand as my thoughts suddenly blanked out. He lifted his glowing hand to reveal a red lotus symbol on his left forearm. Rick looked at me with a shy smile. "Yeah there's a lot of explaining to do." He gave an awkward laugh.

I was still for a couple of minutes trying to process what was happening; my brain was still messed up. Then my body boiled with anger. I made a fist with my right hand and thrust it towards Rick's face without thinking. When my fist was about to hit him, something weird happened. My fist was about two inches away from his face, but some sort of invisible force field was blocking my way. I could feel the air from the force field made a light breeze around me; I could even feel my knuckles going numb. How hard did I hit? Why did I do that? I don't want to hurt Rick for any reason, what's wrong with me?

I move my hand away still maintaining a tight fist, I stood up and looked Rick in the eyes. I could see a purple light flashing in his eyes. I felt the blood in my veins turn cold.

I deeply inhaled as I got up from the bed. "What the hell is going on? You have been keeping your little secret from me for what? Fifteen years already? Well guess what? We both have the same fucking problem then!" I lifted my hands up and made a pity laugh. "And you have the fucking balls to show me that you have powers too? I feel a bit betrayed. You knew I have powers, but you never told me you have them too. I wasn't going to snitch on you because of your powers you know," I said in a low, bitter voice. I took another deep breath, my eyes stinging from my watery eyes. "What other deep dark secrets have you've been hiding from me? Maybe my parents are alive or that I'm not your niece? Maybe you're just doing this for the fun for it!" I said loudly as I stared at Rick's hurt face. His eyes bore into mine as he fought back tears.

"Kai don't say that, you are my niece. I wouldn't do this to hurt you, it-it just..." Rick's voice quietly faded away.

"Just what? The truth is too hard to handle? Well you know what? Screw it! Just fucking tell me the whole God damn truth!" I felt my heart prick with a sharp pain as I let all my feelings out. I couldn't bottle up my emotions inside of me anymore, I had enough of it. I'd had enough of everything.

"I'm sorry," Rick whispered as his voice broke.

"Don't be, we both know that I won't forgive you for that. I thought I can trust you but it doesn't seem like you trust me." I let out a shaky sigh. "I hope you're happy with yourself," I said, turning my head away from him. I didn't even want to look at him.

I disappeared without looking at Rick.

I appeared in some place outside the city. I looked around and saw a sign that read 'Coughlin Park.' Luckily no one was there since it was early in the morning. I'm glad I wore a long sleeve shirt; it's always chilly in the morning especially when I'm near the ocean.

As I was walking I noticed that I only had socks on and I teleported a pair of sneakers next to me and put them on. I found a bench near a playground and started walking towards it. I wiped my tears from my eyes and sat on the bench, thinking about what just happened.

It was a while since I sat on the bench, looking at the city of Boston from afar. I wondered what Rick was doing. At least Stella was at work so she didn't have to hear me yell at Rick.

I closed my eyes and lay back, fighting the urge to cry out in public.

"Hello Kai, it's been a very long time, I never thought I would see you look so grown up," said a male voice.

I quickly opened my eyes to see a man and a woman. I peered at the man who looked like he was in his late thirties, peering back at me. There was a pretty lady standing next to the man with a smile, she looked like she was in her early to mid-thirties. The two of them looked like siblings and a bit similar to Rick. I sat up straight, not letting my guard down.

"Who are you guys?" I asked suspiciously.

I looked at the two of them. Both were dressed in formal but office-like outfits. I looked at the guy; his sleeves were folded up so I could see his forearms. His left arm had the same red inked symbol as Rick and I. Somehow we all are in some weird Asian gang that I didn't know about.

"May we sit with you?" the man asked me; he sounded just like Rick but his voice was much deeper. I gave him a nod, and both of them sat beside me, looking at me, and it made me feel very awkward.

"I know this is unexpected, but I just want to tell you that Rick isn't just your only uncle, I'm Sean and this is Chrissy." He gestured with his hand at the lady, who waved at me. "We're also your uncle and aunt," he said as he turned his head, looking at Boston like he expected something to happen.

I didn't say anything, the fact that I just learned that I have an aunt and uncle shocked me. Why would Rick never have told me about his siblings? Everything that happened this week had been weird for me. What I just witnessed made my head hurt.

I could even feel myself make a weird face when I heard this. Chrissy looked at me with her lips moved to the side as she saw me making it. What the hell is happening? Is this like an episode of the Twilight Zone? I think I'm slowly losing my shit right now.

Chrissy looked at me. "I know this is weird. I bet Rick never told you about us, his own siblings, not even telling you about your own mother and father." I perked up with surprise when I heard her say that. This means they knew my mom and dad, well obviously since they're my "uncle and aunt." I need to know more about them but first I need to know what I'm going to do next.

"So why are you here? Are you going to kidnap me or what?" I said, looking left and right at Sean and Chrissy.

"No, we're not going to do that. We just want you to come with us and meet your grandfather so we all can tell you everything in New York," said Sean, nodding his head.

I have a living grandad too? God, I don't want to go with them to New York. I wish Rick was here, I don't know what to do. I wish that everything goes back to normal so I wouldn't be stressed out.

"I don't know, going to New York with you two." I took a deep breath. "Just tell me who my mom and dad are and I'll consider going."

Sean and Chrissy looked at each other, Sean looked directly at me. "The thing is, we need you to see your grandfather so he can formally meet you and tell you about your mother and father."

My stomach started to feel weird; I needed to get out of here. I was getting lightheaded; I massaged my temples at the sides my head.

"Are you okay Kai?" asked Chrissy.

"I'm just a little lightheaded. I need to get out of here," I said breathlessly, anxiety rising as I stood up with my back facing the two of them.

There was a moment of silence between the three of us. I kept my eyes shut as my headache slowly died down.

"Get her," Chrissy said quietly.

I immediately turned around and saw that the two of them were leaping towards me. My eyes grew wide as I stared at them with surprise.

I crossed my arms in front of my face as I teleported back to Stella's apartment. I moved my arms away from my face. I stood in the middle of the kitchen. I can't believe this is happening, I'm going to be sick.

I speed walked to the bedroom. I opened the doors and saw Rick was lying on the bed with his face pressed onto the pillow. I made another fist but it's not because I'm angry, it's because I'm terrified. I tried not to cry but couldn't help it. What have I done? Sean and Chrissy know that I'm here; they might come for me at any time.

I began to sob and Rick lifted his head up to look at me; I could tell he'd been crying too. I ran into him and hugged him tightly. He sat up and hugged me back. We both didn't say anything for a while. I let all my sadness drain away and cried for what felt like hours.

"I'm so sorry, I should have told you," Rick sniffed, "about everything sooner. I'm such a shitty uncle." He let out a shivery breath. I could feel his tears soaking my head.

I let out a weird crying noise, my heart feeling like it had been tightly squeezed. My throat became dry and scratchy and my eyes felt like they were pricked my needles.

"No, you're not a shitty uncle. I'm the shitty niece. I need to tell you something important." I turned my head so I could breathe, my hot tears streaming down my cheeks. "I think I met your brother and sister."

I heard Rick breathing hard, hugging me tightly as he placed his chin on top of my head. "They're getting on to us. We need to leave now okay? I'll protect you."

"Okay," I whispered as hot tears streamed down my face.

Rick and I were getting ready to leave. Rick left a note for Stella that we're going somewhere to hang out so she doesn't have to worry about us. Rick and I changed our clothes so that we were ready to go outside and be ready for what will happen in the day.

"Where are we going?" I asked, wiping my damp eyes so people wouldn't think that I was crying.

"We're going to the police department; Fred will help us out. I know he would do anything for you, and he still owes me a favor." He placed his hands on my shoulders with a frown. "I'm sorry about everything Kai, I should have told you sooner about my powers and about our… family." His eyes were becoming watery once again.

I took a deep breath. "You shouldn't apologize to me. I should be the one apologizing to you since I almost punched you in the face and said those stupid things to you."

"We can both apologize to each other, but that can wait until we're at the police department," he said as he opened the door. We both ran out of the apartment.

It'd been a long time since I was outside and everything looked the same. I was a bit nervous about Sean and Chrissy finding us. I thought about how they found me even though they're from New York, maybe they looked me up on the internet and thought they might talk to me or something. I wonder why they only want me and not Rick.

Rick and I are in his car driving to the police department. I turned on the radio; it actually relieved my anxiety just a little bit. I looked out through the window to watch out for Sean and Chrissy.

Then up comes traffic as always. Rick's car slowed down to a stop. Oh great, it's going to be a while sitting in traffic since I'm being targeted by my other uncle and aunt.

"You think that Sean and Chrissy will find us?" I asked, looking at Rick. He clenched his jaw when I said those names.

"Maybe, but I'll try to use my powers to protect you and everyone else who might get hurt by them." Rick gripped the steering wheel until it made a tight squeaking noise.

"Do they have powers too?" I know asking a lot of questions can annoy people, including myself, but I needed to know all these things that I didn't know before.

"Yes they do, they both have powers just like us. Sean has fire powers which I think suits him since he has a fiery personality. Chrissy has electricity powers, but she doesn't have a temper like Sean. Back then, when we were kids, Sean always overused his powers because he's an angry person in general. I still think that he still has some anger issues to this day," Rick said with a stern face. "But that's a bad thing. Sean is more powerful than Chrissy so you should watch out for him."

"They both sound like the type of people you shouldn't mess with. I can't even fight them since my powers are not meant for combat fighting. When I talked to them, they sounded like normal people. I guess I didn't see their true colors yet."

"Huh," Rick said, looking at the cars in front of us.

I looked around; we weren't moving at all. "Wait why aren't we moving?" I looked at the right wing mirror. There was a long line of cars behind us honking their horns with irritation.

"I have no idea, let me check it out." I thought he was going to get out of the car, but he didn't move.

In the corner of my eyes I saw a shadow figure slowly appearing out from under the car seat. It sat in the backseat of the car behind Rick.

"What the fuck is that?!" I yelled, staring at the shadow.

"Language Kai," Rick said, looking at me.

I kept looking at the black shadow with purple eyes just like Rick's demon mode eyes, that's just creepy.

I turned away from it and looked at Rick. "I mean whom the fuck is that?" I said quietly, hoping that it wouldn't hear me.

"It's just one of my…um, helpers that I use for work purposes and other means. I use my shadows to help me with difficult cases that I don't want to waste my time with, they're very useful when solving many cases," he told me with a confident nod.

I looked back at the shadow. The shadow slowly sank through the car. It reminded me of my own intangibility powers and it made me realize how creepy it looked from someone else's perspective.

"Wait, don't you have to tell it what to do or does it have some telepathy thing with you?" I asked, my eyes glued to the back seat.

"It's the telepathy thing, they come in handy for a lot of things like searching or doing some actual fighting," he said as he looked through the front window.

It's been at least two or three minutes since that shadow left and we're not moving, not even an inch. Now I started to hear people in other cars beeping their horns and shouting. God, sometimes I hate living in a big busy city like this.

Rick made a 'hmm' sound. "I guess Sean is searching for us, there's a big explosion all the way in the front of the street and I know it was him. That bastard doesn't even care if anyone got hurt. It makes me irritated when someone doesn't care about others' well-being." He gripped the steering wheel again, his knuckles turned pale.

Instantly there was a huge explosion up the street, causing one of the cars to ignite in black flames. There were a few people screaming and yelling as they got out of their cars trying to get away from the fire.

A car that was at least four cars away from us suddenly burst into black flames. I let out a gasp as I looked at Rick who didn't seem fazed by the flames. Lucky the man in the car got out before it was completely engulfed in flames.

I took a deep breath and turn on the AC at full blast. I was starting to sweat continuously with anxiety. I had no idea what was going to happen next.

CHAPTER 5

"We need to get out of here," Rick said as he unbuckled his seatbelt.

"Where you want me to teleport us to?" I asked as I unbuckled my seatbelt.

He looked at me with a frown. "I'm going to fight my brother and save those people who might get in the way of this mess," he said in a very serious tone.

I felt my eyebrow twitching. "You're not going to fight him, what would happen if he seriously hurt you or worse?" I needed to help him in any way I could.

"No, you're going to stay with Fred, he knows about my powers and you'll be safe with him at the police department with all the other cops."

"Wait what happens if someone else who has powers might come and find me?" I looked at the window in front of us. "Did the shadow you sent see Chrissy anywhere? She could be hiding somewhere." I looked out the windows to see if she's coming for us.

"My shadow senses that Chrissy is somewhere near Sean, so you don't have to worry about them. I'll handle them myself." Rick moved closer towards me and hugged me tight. "Remember, I love you so much. I want you to be safe, don't forget about that."

I tried not to cry again. "So maybe this is our last goodbye." My voice quivered, I looked at Rick who made a frown.

"Don't say that, once I'm done with them I'll find you no matter what," he said, nodding as his eyes searched my face.

"Please be careful."

He smiled and kissed me on the head. Then I appeared in Fred's office, Fred jumped as he saw me appear from nowhere. I didn't teleport myself there, possibly Rick had done that.

I looked at him. "Fred, I think Rick might need help."

He looked at me with a straight face. "He told you about his powers right?"

"He did, but you need to help him," I pleaded to Fred as he looked back at me.

"Remember when you two came into this building? Rick and I were talking in my office when you were talking to Doctor Greenfield. Your uncle told me not to send any officers if he didn't come in this building with you. His scary shadow demons or whatever you call them came to my office about five minutes ago and gave me a message from Rick, saying that he's going to use his powers to fight his brother and sister, I guess who are coming after you."

I glanced at the tattoo on his right hand of a similar summoning circle that Rick made in the house right before we left, but his tattoo has a white flower inside the circle. I wondered why Fred had that tattoo; in my opinion he's the type of person who wouldn't get a flower tattoo.

I was annoyed that Rick had told his boss not to send help. I didn't want him to die or get seriously injured. I don't know what to do if that ever happens, my life wouldn't be the same without him.

"You gotta be kidding me. Rick might get himself killed by his own brother and sister; we consider you our good family friend. Why can't you do something?" This seriously can't be happening; this feels like a very screwed up nightmare.

Fred gestured me to sit on a chair that was in front of his desk. I took a seat, waiting for him to say something.

"There's nothing I can do Kai, Rick specifically said not to interfere with whatever he's doing. I know he can handle this on his own since he has powers, I even saw him use them a few times. This is for your own—"

A woman officer burst into the office with a terrified look on her face. "There's someone here who is attacking officers and citizens in the building."

There was a loud 'thud' that came from the entrance of the building. I heard cops yelling and multiple gunshots fired.

Fred stood up. "Get everyone to surround this intruder. I will see this for myself." He walked towards his cabinets and opened the door, taking out his bulletproof vest and putting it on.

He looked at me. "Kai, I need you to stay here and hide, I don't want you or anyone to get hurt." Then he walked out and locked the door.

I stood up and walked to the office windows and shut all the curtains inside the office. I hid behind Fred's desk, anticipating something bad would happen to me.

I was afraid to look out and see what's going on so I just sat completely still and kept quiet. During the attack loud screams and yelling can be heard throughout the whole building, the sounds of multiple gunshots and banging sounds were nonstop. The sound of these noises made me have a tight feeling in my stomach.

All the noise had suddenly stopped, all I could hear was a pair of footsteps. I heard the doorknob turn. I didn't move at all, everything went quiet. The only thing I heard was my shallow breath. I can't believe this is happening, I wish this was a dream.

"You can come out now, I'm not gonna hurt you Kai," said an unfamiliar male voice. When the person said that, I instantly had goosebumps.

It took a couple of minutes to compose my anxiety. "Who are you?" I said as my eyes widened.

"Go look for yourself granddaughter."

What? This is becoming very strange. I clenched my hands into fists with overwhelming nervousness and fear. I worked up my nerve and slowly stood up, my back towards the person.

I turned around. The older man who was standing in front of me had neatly combed salt and peppered hair and an oval like face with a broad fore-head. He had almond shaped eyes and a round nose, similar nose and eye features as myself.

We didn't say anything for a couple of minutes. My heart was beating fast. I looked through the window of the office; one of the blinds wasn't covering the window. I saw blood everywhere and people lying on the ground and on top of the desk. My eyes grew wide. He just massacred everyone right in front of my eyes.

"I guess there's a lot of explaining for me to do huh?" he said as he looked at me and then around the room, placing hands in his pants pocket.

I wondered what's going to happen to me. "Yeah… there's a lot of things you need to tell me," I said, not letting my guard down.

"I should properly introduce myself first. I'm Ken Tep, your grandfather. I guess you already met your uncle and aunt, Sean and Chrissy."

"I met them, I guess one of them told you that I left before any of them got me."

"Don't worry about that, I understand why you teleported yourself away from them and I'm sorry that they frightened you. My apologies, I know this is all unexpected for you and Rick," Ken said, placing his right hand over his heart.

"How do you know I have powers and how did you know where to find me?" I asked as I tapped my foot on the floor.

"I have to tell you this. You know that Rick, my youngest son, has this black magic power that can only be described as the devil's touch?"

"I recently learned he had powers earlier today," I said as I remembered how angry I was when he told me the news.

"Oh really? It seems like he didn't have the courage to tell you sooner, such a shame. I also have powers similar to Rick's, but my powers are the exact opposite. As you know Rick has dark elemental powers, but I have light elemental powers, you could perhaps say that I gained heaven's power and Rick gained hell's power."

This took me a while to process another strange information given to me, I can't believe my entire family has freaking superpowers.

"What do you want from me?"

"I want to see my granddaughter grow up just like any other grandfather would want to witness. I also want to see the potential powers you might develop, if you willingly come with me to New York," Ken said in a matter-of-fact tone which made him sound so sophisticated like a doctor or scientist.

"What are you going to do to me if I come with you? Are you going to take Rick too?"

"I'm leaving Rick here in Boston so I wouldn't... repeat a particular... situation from the past. If you come with me, I will tell you everything about us. I can get you anything you want if you choose to do something for me." Ken looked at me and gave me a smile. "Please come closer to me, I want to see you up close." He gestured his hand for me to come close to him.

I wasn't sure what he'd do to me if I did get close to him, it felt like I was getting pulled towards him. I resisted the urge to walk towards him, but it was too late. If I go with him he can somehow make all the people he killed come back to life and everything will be okay for now.

I walked up to him and I look at him straight in the eye. "If I go with you then you have to fix the mess that you, Sean, and Chrissy made. You have to make sure that only Rick and Chief Gray know about this mess. For everyone else, make sure that they don't remember this awful event that you caused. After that I'll come with you." My eyes narrowed as I observed every detail on Ken's face.

Ken made another smile and held out his right hand. "Deal."

I lifted my right hand and slowly shook his. Bright yellow light started to appear between Ken's palm and my own.

"What is this?" I looked at Ken, I tried to let go but Ken held onto my hand.

"It's a seal to make sure that you wouldn't use your powers." Finally I let go of Ken's grip and see a circle that had a strange symbol inside of it in black ink.

"See you when you wake up," Ken said as I fell onto the floor, blacking out.

Rick was running towards the loud noise in front of him. People were running away from the explosion, but as he looked around his surroundings, everyone was gone in thin air. Rick's eyes change to purple as he was running, and he teleported himself to the spot where the loud explosion occurred.

At the location he saw his older brother Sean shooting fire out of his hands and into nearby buildings. Sean made black flames on his hand and thrust his hands at a car that instantly ignited with them.

Rick clenched his jaw, a red aura surrounding his body. He made a red ball on the palm of his hand and threw it at Sean, who had his back toward Rick. Sean turned his head; he instantly dodged the attack and shot a black ball of flame at Rick. The flame was stopped a few inches from Rick by an invisible force.

"There's the traitor of the family. I hope I can burn you alive!" Sean yelled as his arms were surrounded by fire. getting ready to strike.

Rick clenched his fist. "What are you doing here?" he yelled back.

"I'm here to get our niece and see how we can develop her true potential powers. Since we created a substance that can make anyone more powerful, we can use it on her and see if she can gain her other power from her father," Sean said as fire surrounded him. "And use her as our secret weapon."

Rick's eyes narrowed as he listened. "So you're experimenting on Kai like a guinea pig."

"If she's alive after the substance is in her blood system. Maybe she might be more powerful than you, seeing how you…fight. She might even kill you if she even has the right mindset."

"She will never do that to me and I'll bet she will never listen to you or Ken."

"You sure about that?" Sean smiled and threw a fireball at Rick, who dodged it.

"Quit talking you bastard and fight me if you're not a coward." Rick's red aura grew brighter, the ground started to shake.

He looked around the street to see if anyone else was in the area. Only Rick and Sean were in there.

"I guess I'll make the first move," Sean said, moving towards Rick.

Sean thrust both of his flame-covered arms. Black flames burst out of his hands, rapidly moving at Rick. Rick held out his hand, as the flames moved towards him the flames hit his invisible force field. The black flames spread all around the force field, not touching Rick at all.

"Is that all you got? I thought you would be better than that!" Rick yelled.

Rick teleported behind Sean and curled his fist, landing a punch towards the back of Sean's head. Sean turned around and punched back, making a huge explosion of red and black light. The force of the punch made a strong breeze that broke the car windows that were near them.

Sean jump back, his fists clenched together. "Remember how I told you that Dad made a substance that makes anyone more powerful? Well, I was one of the few people who got injected with this substance. I have enough power to fight anyone without losing my energy." Sean smirked.

Sean unbuttoned half of his shirt to show a tiger tattoo in red and black ink on his upper left chest. He rolled up his sleeves and looked at Rick.

"I can fight you all day if I have too, but it doesn't seem like you'll last long," Sean said as Rick studied the revealed part of Sean's tattoo. He didn't say anything. Sean noticed that Rick was observing his chest tattoo. "I know right, isn't my tattoo badass? I got it when I got injected with that substance, Dad made everyone who took that special substance get a tattoo. I don't mind getting one, but I think you will when Kai gets one," Sean said. waiting for Rick's response; he didn't say anything, just glared at Sean. "I guess you're giving me the silent treatment huh." A black wall of fire appeared around Rick and Sean, blocking any exit.

Cracks from the road rose up and fiercely shot at Sean who swiped his arms in front of him making a black fire wall.

"Do you really think this will hurt me? Oh little brother you don't know how much I've grown to become powerful." The flames in front of Sean died down; he gave a cold glare at Rick.

Multiple bright red lights formed in front of Rick, making a spear like objects. Instantly, all the spears quickly shot at Sean. Sean held up his hand, making another black fire wall and ran towards Rick. All the spears that touched the black flames instantly disintegrated.

Rick ran towards Sean preparing to punch him. Sean was getting ready to punch Rick but then there was a blast of lightning that was in the way of both of the brothers.

"Our goal is complete Sean. Don't waste your time on him," said a female voice that was walking toward Sean and Rick. Both men stopped running and looked at the direction where the voice came from.

"Finally you showed up Chrissy." Sean's fire disappeared as Chrissy walked next to him. Sean kept his gaze on Rick as he quietly talked to Chrissy. Sean nodded and looked back at Chrissy and then looked at Rick.

"I guess you're lucky today brother, I'm not going to kill you." Sean turned around and walked away.

"It's good to see you all grown up Rick, maybe someday we'll meet again, but not like this," Chrissy said looking at Rick, who didn't say anything. She turned around and walked toward the direction where Sean was walking.

Rick stood at the same spot for a couple of minutes, not moving or saying anything. The red aura around his body disappeared and his purple eyes went back to normal.

All the objects that were either destroyed or moved suddenly moved on their own, repairing all the broken objects with a powerful force. Multiple people instantly reappeared on the street and inside nearby buildings.

"What is happening?" he said to himself, frowning.

Everyone was looking around with a confused look, but then they continued with their task like nothing happened to them. Rick's eyes grew wide, he instantly ran towards his car as his face turned pale.

CHAPTER 6

Rick parked his car in the police department parking lot and quickly speed walked toward the building. His co-workers give him a nod once Rick got inside the building, he walked past them without acknowledging their gestures. Some of his co-workers gave a concerned look as they watched him walked towards Fred's office.

Rick opened the door and see Fred sitting at his desk, staring blankly through his office door that was made out of glass.

"Where is Kai?" Rick said, voice breaking as he put his hands on Fred's desk.

Fred never looked up. "They took her. I-I tried to stop him, but he has powers like you, I couldn't do anything about it. He killed every single one of my officers within a second. It's like he didn't even care if anyone died." Fred's voice sounded hoarse; his eyes filled with fear. "He massacred all of them like they were nothing. I can't believe I saw all of that happened right in front of me."

"Shit!" Rick yelled as he slammed his fist against the desk, causing all the desk supplies to shake or to fall over.

Multiple people outside the office jolted, they looked through Fred's office to see Rick in distress. After they saw him kneel on the floor they continued to do their task in silence with troubled looks.

Fred snapped out of his trance and look down at Rick, who had tears streaming down his face. He made a frown and got up from his chair. He walked next to Rick and knelt onto the floor, rubbing Rick's back.

Rick looked up at Fred and leaned his head against Fred's chest, sobbing.

"My child is gone. My child got taken away from me," Rick said, his voice breaking as he kept sobbing into Fred's chest. "I should have been here for the two of you. I should have been here, it's all my fault."

Fred made a sad frown and gently wrapped his arms around Rick.

"Don't say that son, we'll find her. I know we will," Fred whispered.

In a laboratory Ken sat at a desk looking through a small stack of papers as Sean stood next to him. Other scientists wearing lab coats were in the laboratory mixing different chemicals and substances into various beakers. A scientist walked through the double doors that is on the other side of the lab, escorting a patient into another room.

"Is Kai resting in her room? Is anyone looking after her?" Sean asked, his arms crossed.

"She's resting at this moment, I told Ashton to look after her during her time here," Ken said without looking up at Sean.

Sean made a frown. "Are you sure you trust him? You know how teenagers are these days."

Ken took out a piece of paper from the stack. "I'm fully aware, he's one of the few people who I honestly can trust, including you son." Ken took a pen from his coat pocket and wrote something on the paper. "I need her to be with someone who's around the same age as her so she can at least be comfortable, and also to have someone to be with. I need her to trust us because I want to see if she can gain her father's power. It's vital to me to complete this experiment and see how she can handle having more than one power."

Sean looked at Ken. "What will happen if Ashton disobeys our orders? He can easily kill most of the people in this building. I should know, I trained him."

"What are you inferring?" Ken stopped writing and looked at Sean.

"He could possibly help Kai escape from us and this building. What will happen if she exposes the organization out to the public? How will everyone handle the fact that there's people with superhuman powers roaming around the world?"

"I won't let that happen. I placed a seal that prevents her from using her powers and from getting out of this building. She isn't going to be a problem to the public or our organization. If anything happens I'll take care of it," Ken said as he looked down at his papers and continued writing.

"How about Rick? He could be searching for us."

"Then if he ever steps foot in this building, then I'll have to kill him, simple as that. Rick isn't my son anymore; he's just someone who turned his back on me. He's just another dead body," Ken said coldly.

Sean pressed his lips together and walked away from Ken. As he was walking through the lab he looked at a clear container that was on the side of the lab. It had multiple syringe racks that held a few large syringes with different colored substances in them.

I finally opened my eyes. It took me awhile to adjust to the light; the good thing was that I could move my body a bit. I turned my head to the side and I jolted up, banging my head against the headboard.

There was a cute guy sitting on a chair next to a desk looking at his phone. The guy had slightly wavy blonde hair, green eyes, and very light tan colored skin which makes his eyes pop. I see on his right forearm that he has the same lotus tattoo as me but his tattoo is in black ink, and my tattoo is on my left arm and in red ink.

"Did you sleep well?" he asked, not looking at me.

"Not really. Where am I and what time is it?" I tried to move my fingers, but they were a bit numb.

"We're in New York City, it's about three in the afternoon, and this building we're in is owned by your grandfather Ken. My name is Ashton, I'm the person who will look after you," he said looking up at me with his emerald green eyes. He looked like he was about my age.

"So you're like my…nanny or a bodyguard. Cool," I said in a tired voice as I sat up, my back pressed against the headboard.

I look around the small room. There was a desk and chair, a nightstand, a large window on the wall beside me, and a bed that I'm lying on. There was a door that was next to the desk that led to another room or a hallway.

Ashton stood up and walked towards me; I panicked. "Did you do anything to me when I was asleep? Like something freaky or weird?" I demanded, pointing at him. I read a few articles earlier this month about women being taken advantage of by men and going through unpleasant things while they are unconscious, I hope that I'm not one of them.

"I didn't do anything to you, don't worry," he said, his eyes looking into mine.

I got out of the bed; my legs were wobbly but I could manage to walk. Ashton held my shoulders and helped me stand up straight; it was nice of him to do that even though I accused him of being a rapist. I noticed as I was trying to get up that Ashton was at least six inches taller than me, which is nothing new since I'm short.

When I finally could stand up without falling, I noticed that my clothes had been changed, but it wasn't anything bad like a hospital gown. I was wearing an outfit that I would usually wear, which is t-shirt and jeans. I also noticed that my hair wasn't tied so it was all over my face.

I slowly stumbled out of the bedroom and into what it seemed like a hallway, decorated with a wide black and white photograph of a random landscape. I walked through the hallway and into a living room area that had a sofa, coffee table, and a television stand with a large flat screen television mounted on the wall. I looked to my side; there was a closet next to a door that led into the bathroom. This room felt like one of those luxury rooms in a hotel for rich people. I opened the closet door but there was nothing in it, which was a letdown. I closed the door.

I turned my head, looking through the window at the end of the hallway. It looked like the building was far from the city, but the view was amazing.

"Are you looking for these?" Ashton said. I turned around to see him holding up black and white high top shoes. I slowly walked up to him; he moved his mouth to the side, making a smirk as I took the shoes.

I sat down on the sofa attempting to put on my shoes. "What are you guys going to do to me?" I asked.

"First I have to take you to Ken and he'll figure out something for you," he said as I was struggling to tie my shoelaces. Ashton walked up to me and crouched to tie my shoes. "I guess Ken used his powers to make you pass out huh?"

"You're right, my fingers are still numb." I had butterflies in my stomach because some cute guy just tied my shoes for me.

I reached down to unfold my pant hems so it could cover my ankles and the top part of my shoes. As I lowered my head I felt my hair sweeping in front of my face, but Ashton caught it just in time.

"I'm sorry about that, I wish my hair wasn't so...irritating," I said as I looked straight down finishing unfolding my pants. I felt my cheeks becoming warm.

"No worries, are you ready to meet your grandfather?" I looked to the left to see Ashton staring at me. He had really pretty eyes, unlike mine; I could see flecks of gold surrounding his pupils.

I turned my head, looking at a photograph of a wave in the ocean that hung on the wall that connects to the bedroom. I took a deep breath and sighed. I needed to see Rick again so I could tell him how I'm sorry for everything.

"I guess I'm ready as I'll ever be," I replied to Ashton's question.

The two of us stood up and walked out of the room.

CHAPTER 7

A•s I was walking down a long corridor with Ashton, I kept wondering about what Ken might do or say to me when I met him for the second time. Was he going to tell me about our family history, tell me more about my powers or even tell me about this building and the people in it? I wondered if the people in this building also had superpowers like me; the thought of that made me somewhat excited and nervous.

I walked behind Ashton and I looked at my surroundings. All the doors on my left looks the same, but each door had different set of numbers on it. Some of the walls had abstract paintings between a few doors. At my right side there was a long window with a view of everything, including tall buildings, people walking, birds flying, and cars driving on the street. I could have looked at this for the whole day, but I had to do something much more important first.

Ashton was a few feet ahead of me. I quickly walked up to him as I looked through the window at the amazing view.

As I walked next to Ashton he looked through the window. "I will never get tired of this view. I'm glad that I get to see something like this."

"You know that if we ever get out of here, or if Ken gets rid of this seal," I raised my right palm to show Ashton my seal, "I would be happy to show you or teleport you to see the whole world with me. By the way I'm a good tour guide, depends if I have already been to the place."

Ashton made a smile. "I would like that Kai, thanks." Then he continued walking and I followed him.

After walking through long hallways and big rooms we finally reached Ken's office. Ashton knocked on the door firmly.

"Come in," said a voice from behind the door.

Ashton opened the door and I walked in, examining the room. Typical office setup, artwork hanging on the walls, tables and chairs in one corner of the room near a big bookshelf, a black colored desk and a big window behind it overlooking everything outside the city.

"Welcome Kai, sorry that I used my powers on you, I hope you understand. Please have a seat." Ken gestured to one of the two chairs in front of his desk. I took a seat. Ashton took a seat next to me, not saying anything.

Ken was wearing a short sleeved button-up shirt that made his snake tattoo visible for anyone to see. The snake was in black and red ink, the body coiled around his arm until the snake's head reached his lower arm. The scales of the snake had some designs on them; there were also a few flowers on and around the snake's body. I looked at his left forearm. He had a red lotus tattoo like me, which was obvious; only our family has this tattoo.

Ken looked at me and at Ashton then gave a smile, throwing his hands up, but not moving his elbows from the desk. "I'm so happy that I get to see you all grown up Kai. I predicted that you must have a lot of questions about us right?" I nodded at him. "You can ask me anything, anything at all, and I will tell you the answer right away."

I took a deep breath. "Why am I here? Why do you only want me and not Rick? What exactly is this place? How long am I going to stay here?"

Ken let out a quiet chuckle. "I didn't expect you to say all those questions all at once, but I'll answer them anyway. You're here because we want you to learn the real truth about your family, and maybe you can work with us and help us reach our goal. We came only for you because Rick is a traitor to our family who had done some things in our organization. This building is run by my organization, which develops these special substances that can make someone gain powers or abilities; we use it for all sorts of purposes. I don't know how long you will be with us; it depends if you're willing to work with us." Ken laced his fingers together.

I looked down on my lap where my fingers were curled together. That's so much information to process, but I'm the one who was asking all those questions. I might not see Rick or any of my friends again if I work with this organization which I definitely will not do.

"What are you going to do to me?" I said, locking eyes with Ken.

Ken held out his hand towards me, I hesitated a bit but I gave him my hand. "I was wondering if you would willingly let us know more about you by learning how you use your powers and by doing all sorts of tasks so we can create data on your process. I created this hypothesis that if a child who has parents with two different powers, we can learn if that child could possibly gain both of his or her parents' powers. That's where you come in. We'll test you to see if you can gain your father's superhuman strength and invincible body, we already know that you have your mother's teleporting and intangibility powers. We can give you this special power enhancement substance that I just created a few weeks ago that has your father's DNA in it and inject the substance into you, then we'll see what will happen." He held my hand and softly squeezed it.

I glanced at Ashton who was looking through the window behind Ken, not making any facial expression, his elbow resting on armrest, his hand on his mouth.

"Do the people in this building have powers like us?" I asked, wondering if Ashton had any cool powers like mind reading or mind control.

Ken let go of my hand. "My team of scientists and I created many different types of substances for many different reasons. To my knowledge everyone in this organization got injected with a normal type of substance that gave them either abilities or powers. There's this special power enhancement substance that helps improve someone's powers or abilities tremendously, and even develop new powers or abilities. Only a few people get the chance to use this substance. For example, Ashton was injected with the special enhancement substance. The amazing outcomes after he got injected—his ability to read people's moves a few minutes ahead of real time was one hundred percent accurate, his agility and senses became much more superior to any being on earth. He also gained a few other beneficial abilities, but I couldn't name them all. He's one of the people who gained only abilities and got injected with the special substance, and I must say that I'm proud of him. He even fights better and much quicker than anyone that I know, except when he's fighting with me." Ken let out a laugh, Ashton and I didn't laugh. "He is what I call a super soldier." He looked at Ashton and noticed that he didn't seem amused. "Oh I'm sorry to embarrass you Ashton. I'm just proud of what you have become; you're my right hand man after all. Please forgive me."

Ashton avoided Ken's eyes. "No need to apologize," he said in a low, quiet voice.

"I understand." Ken made an apologetic smile. "Now back to talking about you Kai. Do you want to become more powerful and unleash your other powers that you never knew you had? Or should you take some time and learn about everything that Rick had never told you about your other family?" I perked up as Ken said Rick's name.

I nodded. "I would like to know more about this place and our family first and then I will let you experiment on me."

Was this really a good idea? Getting injected with this mysterious substance that makes you…different? It's like selling your soul to the devil, it's scary and I didn't even know the consequences of it.

"I got another question, why do I have this tattoo on me?" I pulled up my left sleeve to show my lotus tattoo.

Ken leaned towards me looking closely at my tattoo, he let out a hum. "This lotus symbol means in Buddhism and Hinduism respectively purity, beauty, and spiritual awakening. I branded all the people who are my colleagues and acquaintances within the organization to represent how people who had bad personal experiences can make something of themselves when no one believes in them. I want to help them reach their full potential and see them grow into the people who they are now, as a lotus bud blooms with beautiful petals."

"That sounds like you're really into symbolism and religion huh?" I said lightly.

Ken made a humorous smile. "It seems like it, doesn't it? I like how the simplest things in nature can mean something so deep and meaningful."

"I know what you mean." I said placing my arms on the armrest.

Ken looked at the side of his office and then back at me. "Remember the time not too long ago a lady driving her car almost hit a young boy who was chasing his dog?

"I remember that, what about it?" I answered.

In the end you saved that boy's life in time by using your powers. You barely escaped the car; you could have gotten hit and had major injuries. Instead you used your powers to go through the car in order to save the boy's life without getting yourself hurt." Ken laced his fingers together and leaned forward. "I would never have thought you would try to save that boy but I was wrong. You used your powers to save a stranger; you didn't have to think about it, you just jumped right in. I'm proud of you Kai, I'm truly am." He made a sad smile. "You remind me of your father, he would go through all the trouble to help people and he wouldn't care what happened to him. This is the reason why many people admired him." His smile slightly changed into a dark frown.

My eyes were getting watery, I took a deep breath. "So you watch me save that boy, but what if I didn't save him in time?" Maybe Ken was the one who didn't make the lady stop her car.

"I have the power to bring anyone back to life if they died, so there's nothing to worry about. The good thing was I didn't have to use my powers on the boy since you saved his life."

"Did you make that lady become unconscious so she wouldn't stop the car?" I can't believe he did that, and just to see how I'd react to this situation.

"Yes I did, I used my powers to control her movements. At the end both the lady and the boy didn't get injured and I make sure that no one died."

Ken turned his chair around, looking out the window.

I stretched my arms. "Why does Ashton have the same tattoo but in different colored ink and on a different arm?"

Ken never turned back to face Ashton and me. "It's because those who have the lotus symbol in red ink are in the bloodline. The many people in the organization who aren't in the bloodline have the same tattoo in black ink and on the different arm. I branded everyone who works for me to represent this organization that I worked so hard to build. I and this organization have a reputation that I don't want to alter."

"Why did you kidnap me now and not all these years ago?" I asked, getting slightly suspicious.

"We didn't kidnap you if you're willing to come with us. We came to get you now because we wanted you to grow up to a mature age and to see if you're comfortable using your powers. It's all about time and patience. I knew when you reached a mature age you would have the chance to fully understand everything that is going on within our family and this organization."

I hesitated for a second, but then I asked another question. "Can you tell me about our family past?" I wanted to know if something happened to my parents here.

"It's better if we can talk privately. We can talk about this later in the week, I must continue my work. You two may leave," Ken said without turning around to look at us. Ashton finally looked at me and motioned me to go.

We both got up and walked towards the door. "By the way Kai, you are welcome to walk around the building if you like, but the seal I place on you forbids you to walk out of the building. It's better if you just stay inside the building with Ashton who I assigned to look out for you. Don't give him a hard time."

The two of us exchanged glances. "I'll remember that," I said.

Ashton opened the door for me and we walked out of Ken's office, not saying anything about this conversation.

As we walked down the hall Ashton asked if I wanted to get something to eat. I was too busy dealing with all the things that were going on today to even realize that I was hungry. I told Ashton that we should grab something to eat.

The two of us walked through the hall as we talked about the building and the city of New York; I was really interested about everything here. I had never seen a building like this before, everything from the decor to the architecture of the building was well put together. I had seen the inside of many buildings in Boston but nothing like this, the appearance of this building was so stylish and modern.

The two of us stopped in front of two large double doors. Ashton walked up and opened one, waiting for me to get inside. As I walked into the large room, I realized that it was some kind of fancy cafeteria. Everything in this large room was sophisticated and modern. There were wooden tables and chairs with gold legs on them and a large window in front of the cafeteria that displayed the city of New York. A large handful of people walked around the cafeteria carrying trays of food or talking to other people. On the right side of the room there was a place where people were in lines tapping on a touchscreen that was next to a built-in box inside the wall.

I followed Ashton to the right side of the room where the boxes were; I noticed that's where people got their food. The two of us walked behind a guy who was ordering his food on the touchscreen. I looked at the line next to me and saw a woman tap on the screen and close the slit in front of the box. In a couple of minutes she opened the slit. Inside the large box her food had appeared, it reminded me of an appearing magic trick or even my own teleportation powers. There's no words to describe how amazing this place was, I'd never seen anything like it. I thought that talking robots are cool, but this place beat talking robots by a landslide. This place was futuristic and amazing; I wish my school would have something like this.

The person was done ordering their food so Ashton and I walked up to the wall. I was hesitant with this because I didn't know what to do. At least Ashton was with me so he could help me with this.

"So this screen is where you can pick your meal but each day has a different menu, so just pick one that you like the most," Ashton said casually.

"What happens if I want to eat more?" I know that's a stupid question, but sometimes I eat a lot depending on the day.

Ashton smiled; I bet he thought that was a joke. "You can order as many foods as you like, so don't worry about that."

I walked closer to the screen and look at it. There were tabs that said 'Breakfast,' 'Lunch,' 'Dinner,' 'Drinks/beverages,' 'Snacks,' 'Desserts,' etc. I chose lunch since I missed lunch today with this crazy situation. I clicked on the 'Lunch' tab and it loaded other tabs showing what food was available, I picked a sandwich wrap with lemon tea.

When I was done ordering my food Ashton shut the slit, blocking the view inside the box. There was a screen on the slit that showed the timer that said two minutes. After that Ashton pulled up the slit, and inside the box there was all the stuff that I ordered.

"Woah. This is so cool," I said out loud. I grabbed the food and looked at Ashton. "Are you gonna get any food?"

"No, I ate lunch a few hours ago. Let's find a table for the two of us," he said, walking towards center of the cafeteria.

I looked around to see that not much people were here, a good thing because I don't like how random people look at me while I'm eating. Ashton and I walked up to the wide window with a long row of tables and chairs against it. I saw many different buildings through the window, people walking and cars driving in the street. I realized how people don't give a second thought that this building is filled with people who have superpowers.

I placed my food on the wooden table and took a seat right next to the window. Ashton sat across the table from me looking through the window with me.

I took a bite of my wrap and looked out the window again, wondering how Rick was handling my 'kidnapping.' I slowly went through my own little world thinking about my friends and Rick and how much I missed all of them.

Ashton poked me on the shoulder. I turned my head to look at Ashton who had his cheek resting on his hand. "Are you okay? You seemed a bit zoned out," he said looking at me with curious eyes.

I let out a sigh and took a sip of my tea. "Today could have been better," I said quietly.

"I can relate to that. If you need some alone time in your room you can tell me, my room is three doors down if you need anything."

"Thanks Ashton, I appreciate it. What kind of things do you like to do in your free time?" I asked, finishing my wrap. I should learn more about him since he has to be with me in this place.

"I usually go to the building's training room and train for my next mission or just for fun. What do you do in your free time?"

"I like to travel around the world and explore new things by using my teleportation powers. I sometimes like to draw or read if I'm too lazy to go out into the world."

"Whenever I'm on a mission I often travel to many different countries around the world, just like you. I just wish that I could enjoy seeing the world and not focus on completing my mission," he said, smiling sadly to himself.

I felt bad for him, Ken didn't allow him to enjoy his life and it made me feel annoyed. I hoped someday Ashton and some of the people here could at least enjoy their lives and not get worried about the organization's responsibilities.

I glanced at my empty tray. "We still have the whole afternoon to ourselves, what do you want to do?" I asked him as we walked out of the cafeteria.

"There's a place that I want to show you, but I don't think you would enjoy it."

I looked at him; I could feel my eyebrows rise up. "I guess we have to go to that place that I 'won't enjoy' huh."

Ashton looked at me with a slight smile. "I guess there's no choice."

CHAPTER 8

"So this is the place you want to show me," I said, looking at the training room. There's basically everything that a training center has, but some of the equipment looked very high tech.

"It's the only training room where not many people go to, there's a few floors in this building that are dedicated for training purposes. I hope you like this place."

"I do, this place seems really cool." I looked at the middle of the room; there was a large boxing ring. "Do you want to box?" I asked.

"Sure, why not?"

Ashton walked towards the boxing ring, and I followed him. He picked up boxing gloves on the ring floor. He gave me a pair of blue colored boxing gloves and put on his red ones.

"You sure you want to do this?" he asked me with a challenging look as he helped me put on my gloves.

"I'm positive that I want to do this, I always want to box," I said, climbing through the ropes of the ring.

"You know that no one had ever beat me in hand-to-hand combat? You even heard it from Ken, but I'll go easy on you," he said standing in front of me, his hands ready to strike.

"Whatever buddy, you do you." I swung my right hand at him, making the first move.

He blocked my hand and tapped me on the shoulder with his other hand. As I stepped back I noticed that I didn't tie my hair back and it was going to get in the way.

A few strands of my hair fell in front of my face; I blew it away. Ashton held his fist up in front of his chest, getting ready to make his next move.

"Is that hair going get in the way?" he said, making a smirk.

I rolled my eyes. "My hair is the least of our problems." This is why I always like to tie my hair back.

"You seem very determined even though you're gonna lose." Ashton ran up to me so fast that I didn't know what to do, so I dodged him.

I felt the ring ropes pressed against my back. I looked up and saw Ashton charging at me. I quickly ran to the other side, avoiding his collision.

"So you're just gonna avoid me all the time? What are you? A chicken?" he said as he walked to the center of the ring.

I clenched my fist. "I'm not a chicken." I needed to find a way to hit him, there's no way I could win since he was an advanced fighter and has those abilities.

I walked up to Ashton and my arms crossed in front of my face, trying to cover it in case he punched me in the face, I hoped not. He struck a punch on my arms; I moved my right hand and thrust it toward his shoulder. He dodged my attack; I moved up closer to him and tried to hit him near the chest area or the stomach.

I kept throwing punches at him, but he kept dodging and blocking them, he didn't even attempt to attack me. My guess in a guy perspective is that I'm a girl, so that means that he couldn't even punch or hurt me. To be honest I can handle a punch or two, I just have to suck it up.

"Are you going to throw some punches or not?" I asked as I swung at him.

Ashton blocked my fist with his arm. "You sure? I don't want to hurt you."

"I don't want a boring pity fight; I want a real interesting one. Show me what you got."

Ashton raised an eyebrow. "Okay, that's what you asked for." He walked up to me with his hands up to his chest.

He thrust his hand at me but I took a step back, barely missing his punch. The two of us kept throwing punches, dodging, or blocking our attacks. I held up my left arm beside my face and kept punching with my right hand.

I swung my right hand at him but he moved to the left, I looked to my side to see Ashton's glove coming closer to my face.

"Oh shit," I said out loud and covered my face with my left hand. I felt Ashton's fist moving my hand towards my face. I could feel my left cheek burning as he pushed my hand onto my face.

I fell on the ground, but my hand cushioned my fall. This is embarrassing. I closed my eyes and lay on the floor, letting myself rest for a moment.

"Hey Kai, you alright?" I can hear him say, but I was too lazy to answer him. I felt a jab on my arm. "Hey Kai, are you hurt? I'm sorry I did that. I-It wasn't a hard punch, please open your eyes." I can feel him gently shaking my shoulders as he breathes heavily in front of my face."

"Kai. Kai open your eyes please I'm sor—" I unexpectedly struck my fist at Ashton's face, but his hand blocked my attack.

"You gotta be kidding me." I opened my eyes; Ashton was staring at me. I let my hand fall to my side and I slowly lay on the ground.

"Seriously? You know you can't do any sneak attacks on me; I know your every move." He came a bit closer to me. "Since I got that substance in my system I can clearly see someone's movements beforehand." Ashton took off his gloves. I sat up, my back against the ring's ropes.

"You know that punch doesn't hurt me," I told Ashton even though it was a lie, it hurt just a little bit. But seriously, what kind of guy punches a girl in the face?

Ashton knelt in front of me and took off my gloves. He sat next to me; our backs pressed against the ropes. He placed our gloves on the floor next to him.

"I was going easy on you just to see how you would react. It's obvious that this is your first time fighting," Ashton said, looking at me.

"Can you tell me more about this organization in your point of view?"

I was very curious about what that substance could do to me, or anyone else, and also what this organization actually did. I wanted to know what this organization was like from the people in it. I felt like Ken was telling me one side of the story about this place to make it more appealing for me, but there's a darker side to it.

"Ken already told you the important part about this organization, so you know the gist of it. All the members of this organization have to accomplish this challenging training to see if we somehow improve physically and mentally with our abilities or powers. He also tests us in his laboratory with other scientists who experiment on you; they stick pins and needles in us like we're lab rats. I thought I was just getting this substance in me and that's it, but I was wrong. I have to train most of the day and go on missions all the time. I don't have any freedom at all because of my reputation in this organization."

He looked down and gripped his hands. "Ken raised me since my parents died in an incident a long time ago. I thought he cared about me, but I later learned that he was using me, manipulating me for his selfish reasons just like everyone else." I was really bothered how Ashton said all of those things, and how he sounded sad.

"Why can't you just leave this place if you don't enjoy being here?" I asked.

"It's not as simple as you think. I know many people who attempted to escape the organization, but they never made it. At the end they either die or get brought back here and get brainwashed by Ken."

"I'm sorry that I made you sad, I shouldn't have asked you that question."

"No it's alright, it's been a long time since I had a real conversation with someone. Thank you for listening to me Kai."

"It's no problem, I'm your friend. I will listen to everything that you have to say," I said, smiling at him.

Ashton looked up at me and smiled back. "You seem like a person who can be trusted. I don't trust anyone in here anymore. The people who I work with think that they're my friends, but in reality they're not. I have trouble trusting any of them. I wish you could meet my best friend who had powers just like you; he died two years ago under difficult circumstances. I think the two of you would've become great friends."

The two of us had been through a lot, especially Ashton. I'm glad that Ashton had someone to talk to so he wouldn't be alone with his thoughts.

"I'm sorry for you loss, it sounds like your friend was a great person. But why do you trust me? It's not that I'm being rude, but we just met." I felt bad for him, his best friend and parents died and he had no one who he could trust.

"You remind me of my best friend and I don't want you to go through the pain and torture that I went through in this hell. That's why I want to help you escape from this place; I want to do something that I can be proud of for once. We need to get out of here, but I don't think it's possible to escape when Ken is here." I heard the fear in his voice, his eyes desperate like he longed to get out of this place, and I was going to help him.

"We need to find a way to get Rick here and the police too, maybe we can text or email him our location. I know if we did that he'll be here, but I don't know what's going to happen after that. He already fought Sean and Chrissy, but he has to fight his dad too? I don't think this will turn out well," I said as I moved my knees up and put my chin on them.

"If we did that Ken will know something is up, but there's a chance that your uncle Rick might be here in time if we did contact him at the right time.

This is risky, everyone in here has powers and Ken will kill you if he knows what's truly going on. I don't want you—"

Someone opened the door. I looked back, there was a guy who was in his twenties, and he was with another guy who was about the same age. Both of the guys had the same lotus tattoo just like Ashton's, both in black ink and on the right forearm. In my opinion, they both looked like total douchebags.

One of the guys who had brown hair looked at us and stopped walking. "Hey look who it is! Ken's servant and he finally got a girlfriend." I cringed as he said 'girlfriend.' I already hated this guy.

Ashton gave a sigh. "Why can't you leave us alone Ben?" The two guys chuckled.

"I really can't, since you embarrassed me in front of everyone. I still want to get my revenge on you," Ben said as he walked closer to us. I side glanced at Ashton, who calmly looked at Ben.

"It's not my fault that you're weak and ignorant. You almost killed that innocent person and I had to stop you before you made matters worse."

Ben was behind me and I didn't turn around to look at him. "Who's this new kid?"

I heard the other guy walking towards us. "Maybe some other worthless kid Ken picked up."

I clenched my jaw. "This worthless kid's got a name!" I said through my teeth.

"What did you just say kid?!" the other guy yelled.

"Do you need a hearing aid?" I turned around to see both guys looking at me. They both looked very annoyed and it annoyed me. "What are you looking at?" I could feel my face getting hot.

"I'm lookin' at you punk," said the other guy with black hair.

"You should back off or else." I shouldn't have made this situation any worse but it's too late. My stomach was feeling weird again and my cheeks were burning hot.

A hand gripped my right wrist. I looked to my right and saw Ben, his grip so tight that it cut off my blood circulation to my hand. He turned my hand and saw my seal that I got from Ken. He yanked my sleeve up to expose my forearm.

Ashton attempted to land a punch on Ben, but he flicked his hand to the side. Ashton suddenly flew to the side of the ring, his arms tangled between the ropes.

"Get the other arm Greg," Ben said.

Greg attempted to grab my other arm, but I moved it away from him. Ben gripped my wrist tighter. I let out a yell and gave in.

Greg snatched my left arm and pulled my sleeves up, exposing the lotus tattoo on my forearm.

The two glanced at each other, not saying anything. I looked to the side and saw that Ashton wasn't in the ring with me. I hoped he was trying to find a way to stop these guys from harassing the two of us even more.

I could feel Ben moving closer to me. "You don't deserve to be here," he said coldly.

"I never wanted to be here in the first place!" I said, struggling to move.

All of a sudden I heard a loud metal clang from the side of me as Greg's hands released my arm. I glanced to the side. Greg fell, making a thud sound.

"Get your hands off her!" Ashton yelled, holding an iron dumbbell, his eyes fierce.

"Or what? You're going to kill me? As if, you can't even touch me!" Ben said, smirking.

Ashton's fingers gripped tightly to the dumbbell as he moved his hand back, preparing to strike. As Ashton was getting ready to hit Ben, he instead fell on to the floor, letting go of the dumbbell and making a loud metal clang.

I tried to slip away from Ben's grip but he wouldn't budge, he only made his grip tighter.

I looked down where Ashton fell. Greg got up; his whole face looked metal like. Part of his face was badly dented from the dumbbell. He tried to grab Ashton by the back of his shirt, but Ashton swiftly rolled away from Greg's grasp.

"I'll handle him, you take care of the girl!" Greg said as his entire skin transformed to metal.

"Hey! I'm related to Ken, the person who runs this organization that you two assholes are in. If you hurt Ashton or me then you're going to regret it!" I shouted into Ben's ear.

"Like I give a shit that you're related to that old man. I can do whatever I want; you and blondie can't do anything about it!" Ben said as he forcefully dragged me out of the ring.

My body lay on the floor. I tried to catch my breath, but I somehow flew against the gym ball racks. The balls floated up as Ben raised his hand and swiped down, all the balls dropped as I clumsily moved away, barely escaping the attack.

I wished my hair was tied back because my long hair fell in front of my face and I couldn't see anything. I moved strands of hair out of my face and saw Ashton and Greg having a fistfight. Every time Greg attacked Ashton he always blocked Greg's attacks or dodged them. I already knew that Ashton could deal with Greg, I just had to put up with Ben.

Just as I got up Ben hurled himself at me and wrapped his hand around my neck. I tried to move my hands but couldn't do it. I let out a sore yell, but Ben squeezed my neck, making me gasp for air.

"You really think that you're so important just because you're Ken's grandkid huh? Well I tried to make something of myself but he never acknowledges it, he doesn't know that I'm better than most people here." He looked at me. My eyes were giving up on me, my vision went blurry.

Then Ben let go of my neck and I fell down. I lay on the floor catching my breath. My vision went back to normal. I could feel a pair of hands touching me on the shoulders.

"Kai are you alright? Ken can heal your injuries, I'm sorry that this happened to you. I should have done a better job protecting you," Ashton said heavily as he helped me get up.

I slumped against Ashton who held onto me. I let out a dry cough, my head aching. He led me towards Ken, who looked at me and made a disappointed frown. I looked to the side where I saw Ben and Greg with their heads down, pinned onto the wall by multiple glowing yellow arrows inside of them. There was blood dripping down from their wounds, the two of them didn't move or make a noise.

"I wish these men would have some respect for the both of you, I'm deeply disappointed in them. I thought that they had some dignity, especially towards children. I'm truly sorry that this happened to you and Ashton, especially when it's your first day here." Ken quickly glanced at Ben and Greg and then looked back at me. "I will handle Ben and Greg after I heal you from your injuries."

Ken's glowing yellow hands hovered over my head. I could feel my arms losing their numbness and my neck slowly losing its tension. I watched my arms returning back to their natural color as he moved his hands towards Ben and Greg, still pinned to the wall. In a couple of seconds both of them disappeared out of thin air. Ken's hands stopped glowing.

"How did you know that we're in trouble?" I asked Ken as I flexed my fingers.

"I heard yelling in the room as I was walking through the building. I overheard Ben and Greg say some unpleasant things towards you two."

I looked back at where Ben and Greg were on the wall to see blood dripping down it, looking at it gave me chills.

Ken raise his hand toward the ball racks and all the balls were back in place within a few seconds. Then he moved his hand to the wall Ben and Greg were pinned against, and the blood stains disappeared. Ken looked at both of us and held out his hands, high. I thought he was gonna teleport us to some place, but he just rubbed both of our heads and gave us a smile.

"Don't need to worry anymore, Ben and Greg will receive a punishment for what they've done. I hope this doesn't happen again. I need to leave and do my work. I hope you two will be safe for now. If anything else happens, just tell me." Suddenly Ken disappeared, leaving Ashton and I inside the gym alone.

CHAPTER 9

Ashton and I were sitting outside of my room in the hallway, looking through the wide window, late in the afternoon. I always liked watching the sunset and this was the perfect view to enjoy it. We didn't say anything for a while, still processing what happened earlier in the training room.

"Do you want something to drink? I think I have something for us in my room, let me go get them," Ashton said to me. I gave him a nod, not looking away from the view as he got up and walked away.

In a couple of minutes Ashton got back with two cans of soda and a bag of chips. He sat down and handed me a can.

We didn't say anything else, just sipping our sodas, eating chips, and looking at the amazing view. A few people were walking down the hall to get to their rooms, but luckily they didn't say anything to us, just glancing at us as they went by.

It's actually nice to relax with a new friend. It made me think about my other friends that I left when I got 'kidnapped.' I wondered how all my friends were handling my absence.

"So…you actually saved someone's life huh?" Ashton said, taking a sip of his drink.

I tilted my drink back and forth. "I did, but Ken didn't tell you what happened after I saved the kid. I got in trouble because I was 'attacking' that lady and then I got scolded by Rick because of it, but he also said that I did a good thing saving that boy's life."

"I'm glad you did that Kai."

I looked at him. "Did you ever save someone before?"

"Yes, but I killed more people than I've saved."

I didn't want to be nosey and ask a ton of questions about this so I kept quiet. I moved my can, feeling the liquid inside the can swishing around.

"I can't believe that Ben and Greg did that to us, I'm glad that Ken came in time. I wish I'd saved you sooner," Ashton said as he kept his gaze at the window.

"Don't beat yourself up because of it, we're alright now since Ken healed us and took care of them." I took a chip and ate it. "I wonder how we're gonna get out of here before anything serious happens."

There was a long pause then Ashton spoke. "Do you really want to get injected with the substance?"

It took me a couple of minutes to come up with an answer. "I actually want to, maybe there's more to just my teleporting power. I might develop better powers so I can do something with them, you know, help people. Like you said in the gym, Ken only wants me to do this just so he can use me as a human weapon. I'm ready to take the risk." I took a deep breath and exhaled. "Ken said that he'll tell me about the past and the rest of our family, I will go to him later during the week to learn what actually happened to my parents. Maybe after that I will willingly get injected with the power substance then we can contact Rick to help us. It's not a good plan, but we got some time to figure things out." I doubted this plan myself, one part of me wanted to see what'd happen if I got that substance in me, but the other part didn't.

Ashton made a 'hmm' sound. "We still have time to think this through, but we have to be careful, we don't want anyone to be suspicious about us. I'm afraid that Ken or anyone else will learn about our plan, I don't want anything to happen to you."

"You don't have to worry about me, I can handle anything. It's you I'm worried about; you've been stuck in this organization for your whole life. I want you to have the life that you wanted without looking back to the past."

"Do you mean that? You don't know everything about me; you'll be surprised at what kind of person I am."

"I only care about who you are and not what you are. Ken made you become a hit man, or whatever he made you become, but that's not the real you. I care about the real you, I conclude that you're just a guy who was forced to become someone you don't want to be and you want to be better than that.

I want to help you to become the person you always wanted to be," I said, turning my head to Ashton who was staring at me with those sad eyes.

"You don't need to do that. I don't deserve your hospitality; I just need you to escape from Ken and be with Rick. I don't care what will happen to me."

"Hey, don't say that, we'll make it out of here no matter what!" I said, trying to be confident and brave.

Ashton had already told me about the consequences of leaving the organization and I had seen Ken using his powers on Ben and Greg. I don't even want to know what Ken will be like when he gets very angry. I still felt doubtful about escaping, Ken was already the main problem and I didn't want Ashton to get hurt because of me.

The sun slowly died down behind the buildings and trees, the sky faded in different shades of blue. I had mixed feelings about everything that was going on, everything seemed to go by really fast. The more I thought about my situation, the more I missed Rick, if only he were here he would help Ashton and I escape from this place.

"I guess it's getting late, I should go to my room." I got up, grabbing my soda and finishing it.

Ashton got up. "I should head to my room too, goodnight Kai," he said, looking at me with a shy smile.

I smiled back. "Goodnight Ashton." I turned around to walk to my room.

"Oh wait I forgot to give you something." Ashton grabbed me by my wrist, I turned back to look at him. He was getting something in his back pants pocket. He took out a card and handed it to me. "This is your room card." The card has a number, 216, on it.

"So the building is like a hotel, but for people with powers." I laughed as I took my room card.

Ashton gave a chuckle. "Yeah I guess so, goodnight." He turned around and walked down the hall.

I inserted my card on the door handle slot and turned the knob, and the cool breeze softly touched my face. I dumped my empty can into the trash bin and walked towards the closet.

I open the closet doors, hoping some clothes might've appeared on the racks. To my surprise, there were a lot of clothes in my closet. I picked a simple sleeping outfit, t-shirt and sweatpants. I looked inside the closet to see what kinds of clothes I had; they were all the same kind of clothes I usually wear.

I walked inside the bathroom, placing my new clothes on the sink counter. Everything in the bathroom was very nice and stylish, just like the building. I turned on the knob of the shower, I kept thinking about what happened today and how unreal it felt, even though it was all one hundred percent real.

After my shower I placed my old clothes in the clothes basket in the corner of the bathroom and searched for an elastic to tie my hair. I eventually found a pack of them in one of the cabinets. I tied my hair and walked out.

I walked around my large room, trying to become familiar with the place. I walked into the room's kitchen area; there was a table with two chairs, a mini fridge, sink, a counter, and cabinets. I opened the cabinet doors, and after seeing a set of dining ware and nothing else, I closed them.

I looked to the left to see the mini fridge that was next to the kitchen sink. I opened the mini fridge; there were a few bottles of soda, juice, and water neatly placed inside. I closed the fridge door and walked up to the sofa.

I sat on the sofa and turned on the television. I was glad to have a television so I wouldn't be bored to death, but I wished that I had a phone to use. I watched the news channel to see what goes on in the city of New York, it seems like the city has more crimes than in Boston.

I watched television until I felt sleepy and passed out on the sofa.

CHAPTER 10

I woke up to a knock on my door, half my body was drooping down off the sofa, but the other half was still on it. I made an annoyed 'grr' noise as I slowly let myself fall onto the floor.

I rolled to my side and sluggishly got up as my bare feet touched the cold tile floor. My lungs tightened as I took a deep breath. I gripped onto the sofa armrest and shuffled towards the door, my whole body aching with fatigue.

I unlocked the door and slowly opened it. Ashton was on the other side, his body leaning against the door frame. He made an amused smile, his eyes observing my face.

I opened the door wide and moved to the side so Ashton could get into my room.

"You look like shit." He laughed as he walked into the room.

"Shut up," I mumbled as I closed the door.

Ashton sat on the sofa picking up the television remote, he turned on the television and scrolled to different channels. He stopped at a basketball channel, placing the remote on the coffee table in front of him and laying back on the sofa.

I sat next to him, my legs crossed. I took a white and gold throw pillow and hugged it as I watched the basketball game with Ashton.

"Shouldn't you get cleaned up and get dressed?"

"Oh come on, it's the morning, we should relax for now. Do you have something better to do?" I asked, looking at him.

"No I don't, the only thing I have to do is to look after you," Ashton said, turning his head to look at me.

"Then for now we should just relax, I want to meet Chrissy or Sean later if that's okay with you."

"Yeah it's fine, just to let you know Chrissy is much nicer than Sean."

"Why, Sean is not the nice one."

"Sean is one of the people who looks over the experiments and trains the most skilled people in the whole organization. I was one of the people who had to train with Sean and it was one of the most challenging things I have ever done. Sean is a very skilled mentor, but he has a big temper; one time he almost burned down the whole training room. Chrissy on the other hand is more caring and less extreme as him, at least she doesn't make people feel intimidated."

"I could relate to Sean, sometimes I have a temper, but not extreme. Did Sean go easy on you because you got injected with that enhancement substance?"

"The funny thing is he pushed me even more because I got injected with that substance. Sean had already made high expectations for me and I had already matched them. I'm Ken's right hand man and have a known reputation for a reason. I don't think Ken told you that Sean, Chrissy, and Ken himself got injected with the same power enhancement substance as me."

"He hadn't. Did they gain any powers or abilities from the substance?"

"Before we talk about that, did you already know about Sean and Chrissy's powers?" he asked.

"I knew about their powers since I got here," I said, remembering the time where Rick and I were in his car and he was explaining his siblings' powers to me.

"That's good. After they took the substance Sean gained a new ability, black flames that can't be put out by anything, which makes them indestructible. Chrissy's powers improved and became more effective; she can manipulate any source of electricity and use it in any way. Ken, on the other hand, his powers become more superior than ever. The three of them became more powerful and you don't want to piss any of them off."

"Geez, that substance does really make someone become crazy powerful!" I said as I made up multiple scenarios in my head about what would happen after I got injected with the substance.

"It does, that's why Ken only picks a few handfuls of people who he fully trusts to get that substance. The people who do get injected with the enhancement substance will have to go on more missions and do a lot of intense training, it's a price to pay but in my opinion it's worth it."

"I guess that settles my decision on getting injected with that enhancement substance. I'm going to do it," I said as I looked back at the television.

"Are you sure? I'll support you decision either way, but don't overthink this too much."

"I know, I'm just excited at what kind of powers or abilities I might develop. Ken already told me that I have a chance to gain my dad's invincible skin or his super strength."

"If you don't mind me asking, do you miss your parents?" Ashton turned his head back to the television.

"I do miss them even though I never met them. I wish that I could meet them and talk to them, even if it's only once in my lifetime. Do you know my parents?" I asked, maybe Ashton had heard of them or even knew them, but I couldn't be too sure.

"I knew about them from Ken, remember that time at the training room I told you that my parents died in an incident?"

"I remember, can you tell me more about the incident?" I needed to learn more about this 'incident' that happened within this organization.

"The incident was about fourteen years ago in an old building where the organization was originally located. From Ken's view the incident started when your parents, Rick, and a few other people, teamed up to destroy the organization, by attempting to stop all experiments from happening. My guess is that they aimed to completely end the organization. The group destroyed most of the substance that Ken and his team made. They tried to burn the whole building, but they only manage to burn two-thirds of it. Only one person managed to escape from this organization, everyone else was either killed or brainwashed by Ken."

"And I already know who that one person is. Are my parents some of the people who died from that incident?"

"Yes, they were killed by Ken." He made a short pause and turned his head to look at me, I didn't look back at him because I didn't want him to pity me. "I'm sorry to tell you that, I don't want to ruin your morning telling you all about this."

"No need to apologize, I would rather hear the truth than hear a lie about what really happened to my parents. Thank you for telling me this," I said quietly as I blankly stared at the television.

When I learned that Ken killed both of my parents and the people who fought to become free from this place, it made me want to finish what my parents had started. Once I was injected with that substance and gained some new powers, I would stop this organization for good.

Inside a bedroom, a person slept on a bed covered by blankets. Sunlight shone through the sheer dark blue curtains and onto the wooden floors. A phone rang on the nightstand; the person inside the blankets made a tired groan as the phone suddenly turned off.

The person moved around under the blankets. Rick's head peeked out of the blankets, his head lying on the side of the pillow. His hair was messy, his eyes bloodshot and puffy, his face was pale tan, and his nose slightly red.

He moved his arm on the edge of the bed and let it dangle over the side. He closed his eyes and made a sick sniffing sound as he rolled onto his back.

His phone rang again. On his phone screen it said 'Stella,' the background picture was a picture of her, Rick, and Kai. Rick made another groan as his eyebrows knitted together. He opened his eyes and inhaled.

His arms moved on top of the nightstand, his hands patting around until finding his phone. Once he grabbed his phone he took it and rolled onto his side, moving the phone in front of his face.

He stared at the incoming call screen and tapped the answer button. He tapped the speaker button and placed his phone on the pillow next to him.

"Hello?" he said sleepily.

"Rick, I'm outside your home, can you unlock the doors? I need to talk to you," Stella said from the other line.

"Okay," he said. At the front door of the home the two locks suddenly clicked, unlocking the door. "You can come in, I'm in my room."

"Okay I'll be there," Stella said as she hung up the phone.

Rick's phone turned off, he lay on his bed looking off to the distance, waiting for Stella to come up to his room. Inside the home there's a faint sound of the door opening and closing. A pair of footsteps climbed up the stairs and then there was a knock on Rick's door.

"Come in," Rick said, not moving out of his bed.

The door opened. Stella walked through the door and stood in front of Rick with a frown, her eyes searching Rick's gloomy face.

"Where's Kai?" she asked quietly as she sat down on the edge of the bed.

Rick didn't say anything or even glance at her. He only stared at nothing in particular.

"Rick, please tell me that Kai is okay."

"I'm not sure anymore, they took her," he whispered, closing his eyes.

"Who took her?"

Rick didn't answer her question right away. Slightly opening his eyes, tears immediately streamed down the side of his face. Stella made a worried look as she moved closer to Rick, patting him on his arm.

"If you need a shoulder to cry on, I'm here for you."

Rick wiped his eyes with his blanket. "Thanks Stella," he said, still lying on the bed.

The two didn't say anything else. Stella stared at Rick making a frown.

"You know what? If you keep moping around like that you won't have enough time to find your niece. I can help you find her, even the whole police force and Chief Gray can help you find her. You're Lieutenant Rick Kago, the person who solved almost all cold cases in the city of Boston. You can find her within days, you just have to get up and do it. You have your powers; you can use them to help you find Kai and her kidnappers!" Stella said confidently as she locked eyes with Rick.

"My father and siblings took her. I'm too weak to fight the three of them and I can't let you or anyone else get into my personal business," he said densely.

"I don't care if you want me to help you or not, I want Kai to come back home. Do you know where they are?"

"Somewhere in New York City, it's my problem to deal with this, not yours. I just hope my child isn't hurt," he said as tears started to fall down his face once again.

"I know she can handle this herself, she's a tough cookie just like you. Now get up and do what you need to do, find Kai," she said as she pulled the blankets off of Rick.

Rick still lay on the bed. Stella grabbed his shoulders and attempted to hoist him up. She managed to make Rick sit up, his back against the bed's headboard. Rick looked at Stella with an empty look in his eyes, his chest rising up and down. Rick was wearing the clothes that he wore yesterday. His red lotus tattoo was visible on his left forearm.

Stella sat next to Rick in the bed. She wrapped her arms around Rick's waist and laid her head on his shoulder, hugging him.

Rick pressed his head onto Stella's head. "Thank you for being here with me," he said, his tears streaming down his cheeks.

CHAPTER 11

After I got changed I walked out of the bathroom. Ashton sat on the sofa looking through his phone. I went up to the closet and took out a pair of black slip-on shoes. I closed the closet door and walked up to Ashton.

"Hey Kai, can you tell me more about your Uncle Rick? I want to learn more about him," he asked as I sat down next to him.

"Sure thing. Rick is a lieutenant detective of the Boston Police Department, he's close friends with Chief Gray, but Rick and I just call him Fred. His favorite food is loaded fries with extra bacon and a can of cold root beer to go with it. His favorite type of music to listen to is indie rock music or jazz. His favorite thing to do in his free time is to travel with me and explore new things in the world. He hates when people are being rude to nice people, or when people don't pick up their trash. Rick is really friendly and cares about everyone's wellbeing," I said, smiling to myself as I looked back at the times when Rick and I were hanging out in the city park when I was just a little kid.

Ashton made a pleasant smile as I talked about Rick. The more I talked about him, the more I wanted to get out of there and live my life as it was. I wondered where Rick was and what he was doing.

"He sounds like a wonderful person, maybe someday I will meet him," Ashton said as he placed his phone on the coffee table.

"He is, I know that the two of you will become great friends," I said, nodding to myself. "Do you want to go see Chrissy or do you want to go someplace else?"

"I have nothing better to do; I'll lead you to Chrissy's office. Let's go," Ashton said, standing up.

I stood up and walked through the hallway and into my bedroom. I looked around the room and saw my room card on top of my desk. I took my room card and walked back into the living room where Ashton was standing by the door, waiting for me.

"Let's go," I said as Ashton opened the door for me.

I walked out of my room and into the hallway. I looked back at Ashton who closed the door and tugged the doorknob, making sure it was locked. I placed my room card in my back pants pocket.

Ashton and I walked side by side down the hall as I looked through the wide window once again. I wondered what Chrissy and Sean were like; I already learned that Sean is more intense than Chrissy, but anyone can be intimidating.

As we walked through long hallways and through large rooms, we got inside an elevator. Ashton pressed a button that went up to the fifteenth floor, the highest floor to go on was the seventeenth floor and we were on the ninth. The elevator doors closed and I felt the pressure of the elevator going up. I looked up at the screen that shows what floor we're on as the numbers on the screen increased.

Ashton lay back against the metal walls, his arms crossed, looking up at the screen counting up. I looked at the door, staring at it as I zoned out. What will Chrissy say to me, what will happen if she doesn't like me? The first time I met her I teleported myself away from her and Sean, I had no choice because they were about to capture me. I wondered how she or Sean felt about that little incident.

Ashton touched me on my arm and I snapped back into reality. I looked at him and then at the screen. We were already on the fifteenth floor; that was quick.

"Are you okay? You look zoned out sometimes," Ashton said as the two of us walked out of the elevator.

Many people were walking left and right in the main area of the floor, I moved closer to Ashton so I wouldn't lose him in the crowd. Ashton noticed that I was getting closer to him; he held me by the shoulder and led me through the crowd.

"Sorry about the crowd, it's always busy here. This floor is where people get assigned to do a task or go on missions."

"Huh, it's like a superhero headquarters in those hero comics or movies," I said, amazed, as I look at the passersby.

The two of us squeezed through the crowd until we were in a long and less crowded hallway. The hallway was decorated with flowerpots, benches, and abstract paintings hanging on the walls.

Ashton removed his hand off of my shoulder and looked at me. "Chrissy's office is a few doors down, follow me."

Ashton begin walking down the hall, I quickly followed behind him. As we walked a few people glanced at me, and then at my left forearm. I only took a quick glance at them and could tell that they're surprised at my tattoo. I chose to ignore their stares and continued following Ashton.

He stopped in front of a door with a clear plaque that said 'Chrissy Tep' on the side of the door in black text. He looked back at me and I nodded at him, I actually wanted to know more about my aunt, uncle, and granddad.

Ashton knocked on the door. "Come in," said the person from inside the room.

Ashton opened the door and held it open for me. I nodded at him as I got inside the room. I looked around the room, everything was nicely put together. There was a black bookshelf on the side of the room that was in front of a small table with two chairs, the white walls were decorated with picture frames that each had a quote or a saying.

I looked in front of me. Chrissy was sitting behind her black desk, typing on her desktop computer. Two black and white chairs were placed in front of her desk, and a large window was right behind Chrissy that overlooked the nearby buildings behind her.

Chrissy looked up from her computer and smiled at the two of us. "Welcome, please take a seat." She gestured her hand toward the two chairs in front of her.

I walked up to the chairs and sat on one. I could hear Ashton close the office door and walk up to me, sitting on the other chair.

"What brings the two of you here?" she asked, looking at the both of us with interest.

"I wanted to talk to you about our family, I want to learn more about the family that I never knew I had. Maybe you knew my mom and dad back then," I said, looking at Chrissy.

Chrissy tilted her head to the side as she studied my face. "I would be happy to tell you everything about our family, but I want Sean to come here and talk about this too. Just hold on for a few minutes, I have to make a call to Sean."

I nodded as Chrissy took out her cell phone and scrolled through it. She placed her phone against her ear and waited for a few seconds.

"Hey Sean, it's me Chrissy, do you have time to come to my office right now? I'm with Kai and Ashton, I want to tell her about our family with you here." There was a pause; she laid her hand on top of the desk and tapped it with her finger. "Okay, see you in a few minutes," she said before she hung up.

She placed her phone on the table and looked at Ashton. "How was training with Sean? I know that he's very stubborn and a serious type of person, I apologize for my brother's behavior to you and to everyone who has to bear with him."

"No need to apologize, I got used to him within a week. He's a good trainer and he made me become very skillful person," Ashton said, making a comforting smile.

"That's good to hear, you're the type of kid who doesn't give up when something hard hits you. You're a hard working kid and that's the type of person this organization needs," Chrissy said, smiling at him.

"Thank you for the compliment." Ashton turned his head to me. "Are you comfortable that I'm here listening to your family personal stories?" he asked me.

"It's fine with me," I looked at Chrissy, "is it fine with you?" I asked her.

"It's no problem at all; you're one of Ken's most trusted people. As long as you never tell anyone else besides the four of us about our conversation, it's all good."

"Chrissy, are you the youngest sibling in your family?" I asked, looking around her office once more.

"I'm the second youngest. I'm ordering our ages from youngest to oldest: Rick, myself, Sean, and then your father Veha." Chrissy leaned closer to me, looking at me. "The more I look at you, the more you look equally alike to both of your parents. You even have the same eye shape and lips as your mom, and you have a similar nose shape as your dad." She leaned back into her chair. "How is Rick doing these days? Can you tell me more about him, like does he have a job or a girlfriend?" she asked, her eyebrow raised in curiosity.

I crossed my legs on my chair. "At this moment I think he's not doing so good because you guys took me."

Chrissy made a light laugh. "I would've guessed that you have a sense of humor from your dad, but I understand what my little brother is going through. Sorry if I interrupted you."

"No it's alright, Rick is a lieutenant detective of the Boston Police Department so his job is very important. He doesn't have a girlfriend, but he has a friend and I feel like the two of them have some chemistry together. He's a good uncle; he always takes good care of me. He's like a normal person, but with superpowers, you know," I said, scratching my head.

Chrissy nodded as she looked at something in the room. "It seems like he's enjoying his life. It feels somewhat unbelievable that my little brother has grown up, the last time I ever saw him was when he was at least fourteen years old. Isn't Rick at least in his late twenties now?"

"You're right, he's twenty-eight years old," I said as I placed my arms on the armrest.

"He's quite young to become the lieutenant, but I guess he has his powers to use," she said, slightly nodding to herself as she looked off into the distance.

There was a hard knock on the door, Ashton and I looked back at the door. The door opened and Sean stepped into the room, eyeing the three of us.

"Did I interrupt your conversation?" he asked, closing the door and walking up to us.

"No you haven't, we're just killing time by talking about Rick," Chrissy said, looking up at Sean.

Sean lightly patted me on the right shoulder as he walked up to Chrissy's desk and sat on top of it. He placed his hand on his lap and studied me quietly, his lips pressed together as he looked at my face.

"You certainly do look like your parents Kai," Sean said while looking at me. He looked at Ashton. "Did she give you a hard time?" he asked.

I looked at Ashton, who had his right elbow on the armrest, his fist pressed against his cheek. "She didn't give me a hard time at all; everything seems to be going well."

Sean nodded. "That's good to hear."

"Remember the time when you two first met me at that beach park?" I asked.

"Yes, what about it?" Sean asked.

"I would like to apologize to both of you for teleporting myself away from you guys, I was really nervous and got scared," I said, remembering the feeling of terror when the two of them were trying to grab me.

Sean made a slight nod. "It's okay, Chrissy and I felt bad because we scared you and tried to detain you. But now we can get to know each other better. What brings the two of you into Chrissy's office?"

I glanced at Chrissy and then back at Sean. "Since Rick hasn't told me much about our family I want to learn everything about it and this organization."

Sean and Chrissy looked at each other, exchanging glances. Chrissy raised an eyebrow at Sean, wanting him to say something first. Sean let out a sigh and turned his head to look at Ashton and me.

"We'll talk about this organization first. This organization is called The Lotus. Our father Ken created this organization right here in New York City. He used to work at a prestigious laboratory along with a few skilled scientists. One day our mother, your grandmother, developed pancreatic cancer which is a rare disease. Ken tried to find a cure to stop the cancer from spreading by creating multiple substances and testing them on people to see their reactions to it. He discovered that a substance that he created makes someone develop some kind of abilities. Shortly after he created that substance our mother died a peaceful death." Sean paused and took a deep breath. "Our father was devastated and so was I and your own father, Chris and Rick were too young to understand all of this. Ken decided to move on from our mother's death within a year or two. He left his job to create an underground business where he could make more of this substance and improve on it to sell it to many underground buyers. As the years went by his organization had increased significantly. He and his group of scientists created many substances that can make a person develop abilities, powers, or cure them from a few diseases," Sean said, crossing his arms. "He also tests people with all different kinds of substances to see which substance is acceptable to use or sell. The people who were injected with the substance work as personnel in the organization who complete tasks or missions, depending on their rank or powers."

"I'm sorry about what happened to Grandma, at least she's in a better place," I said somberly.

Chrissy nodded. "Everyone lives and dies, it's part of life. I wonder if mother looks down at us from above and see how we've all grown up to be."

Sean looked back at Chrissy and patted her on the shoulder. "Life can be cruel sometimes, but we have to be strong and move on," he said, closing his eyes like he was remembering something in the past.

"Ken is a very smart man, he must have a very well-known reputation within the underground community," I said, trying to change the depressing subject about my grandma and death.

"He and this organization are very well known to many underground businesses all around the world. That's why we have many long time reliable customers to buy our products," Chrissy said factually.

"What exactly do you do here? Are the two of you like the co-CEOs of the whole organization?" I asked, observing Sean and Chrissy. They both have dark brown hair, and oval shaped heads. Chrissy had plump cheeks, unlike Sean who had sunken cheeks.

"We are the co-CEOs of the organization. I'm in charge of looking after the people who got injected with the substance and training them. I mostly train people who are more skilled and stronger than an average person here. Chrissy is in charge of taking care of the demands from our clients, tracking our money, making sure that people in here are doing what they need to do, and all that business crap that I don't look into that much," Sean said, looking straight at me.

"It seems like the two of you have a lot of responsibility on your shoulders," I said.

Chrissy nodded. "We sure do, but that's what it's like to be an adult. My advice to you and Ashton is don't grow up too quick, enjoy your innocent lives."

Sean made a 'pfft' sound as he looked down onto the floor. "No one is innocent Chris, even kids like them. Sooner or later you guys will learn the hard truth about life."

Chrissy looks up at Sean and slapped him on the arm; he looked back at Chrissy with a raised eyebrow. "What? I'm warning them about life." He looked up at Ashton and me. "You'll go through a lot of tough challenges in life no matter how old or young you are. Even though it may seem impossible to face your problems, it's not. When you have the right motive it makes you push forward to do it no matter what it takes. Remember my advice kids, you might be in that type of situation someday," Sean said as he uncrossed his arms.

"Sean is right, everyone will go through some tough times, but you have to push forward and be strong for yourself and the people you love," Chrissy said, lacing her fingers together on top of her desk.

"I will remember that advice thanks," I said, taking it in.

"Do you want to learn more about our family? Sean and I are happy to answer all your questions if we can answer them," Chrissy said.

I made a pause, thinking about all the questions I have about my family. I asked about my parents first since I longed to know more about them.

"Do you know anything about my mom and dad?" I asked. I knew that the two of them knew something about my parents.

"We know a lot about your mom and dad. I can tell you that your dad Veha was a friendly person and always helping out people whenever he could. Veha had powers just like us, super strength and an indestructible body. Your mom Jenna, she was a very kind and caring person, just like your dad, always helping people whenever they could. Jenna's powers were the exact powers you have, teleportation and the power to move through objects, called intangibility. Both of your parents were wonderful people and I wish that you could have met them before..." Chrissy's voice faded as she looked down at her desk, avoiding eye contact with me.

"Before what?" I asked, wanting to learn more about my mom and dad.

"It's better if you talked to your grandfather Ken about their deaths. Do you have any more questions about your parents?" Sean asked quietly.

"How did my parents meet?" I already knew that Ken was involved with their deaths so I tried to ask a question that could be answered in a less depressing way.

"I can tell her," Chrissy said quickly before Sean began to answer my question. From what Veha told me he said that he and Jenna first met on a mission that they were on. They were in a train ride from France to Sweden. Somehow the train had stopped and everyone in the train was stuck inside. Veha and Jenna struck up a conversation with each other to kill some time; once they got to know each other they quickly became friends, and the rest was history."

I could feel myself smile as I imagined my parents talking inside the train booth, looking into each other's eyes as a city from afar can be seen through the train window. It would be a lovely place to meet your soul mate, it now seems sad that my parents are gone and they won't experience that same heartfelt moment anymore.

"Do you know anything about Rick when he was young?" I asked. I had already learned enough about my parents and wanted to change the subject.

Chrissy made a sad smile. "Rick back then was like any other young boy at his age; he would always follow his older brothers and always cause trouble. He was a nice kid, he sometimes played with me or stayed in my room when he was sad or scared." Chrissy's voice softened, she looked up at Sean. "You can add more detail about Rick if you like."

Sean looked back at her and, nodding, he turned his head to look at me. "Rick was a crazy little brother, he always wanted to cause trouble just like Chris said. There's nothing much to add, we and our father never talk about him or your parents after an awful incident that happened a long time ago. I'm sorry if you're not satisfied with our response," Sean said as his lips moved into a frown.

I shook my head. "It's alright, I have learned enough about my parents and I would like to thank you for spending your time to tell me all of this."

Chrissy made a pleased smile and Sean nodded his head. "Thank you for coming here, but I have a few questions to ask you. Did Rick tell you about us or keep it a secret from you?" Chrissy asked.

"He never told me about you, Sean, and Ken until yesterday when he had to fight the two of you. He only told me about who you are to him and your powers, that's all," I replied.

Sean looked off into the distance silently thinking, his lips pressed together into a thin line. His eyes narrowed as he was thinking hard about something, I could see his jaw clenched tight. He looked very tense right then, I was a bit worried he was going to do something crazy.

"Did he even tell you about his own powers?" Sean asked without looking at me.

"Not until yesterday, he told me right before I first met the two of you at the park," I said, thinking back to that time when I lashed out at Rick right after he showed me his powers.

"It seems like he's too afraid to tell his own niece the truth." Sean glanced at me. "At least now you know the truth about everything."

CHAPTER 12

I sat on the edge of my bed staring through the window, it was already nighttime. The city was bright against the dark sky. An airplane over flew a building, streetlamps randomly turned on as the night sky got darker.

I told Ashton that I wanted to be left alone in my room, he obeyed my request and went off the do his own thing. I sat on my bed alone in my room with no lights on, only my hurricane of thoughts swirling in my head. I'm still stunned that all of this is happening. How can I escape from this place? I know that Ashton will help escape with me but I can't risk the two of us getting hurt. I just need to find a non-harmful way to get out of here. But I have to face reality, Ken has unlimited powers, he can kill people within seconds.

The more I thought about this as the last time I'd ever see my friends and Rick, the more I felt empty inside. I couldn't escape from this place. Ken wanted me to be part of this organization that I didn't want to be a part of. What the hell was I going to do?

"Shit," I said quietly as hot tears streamed down my face. I wiped my tears with my shaking hands, quietly crying in the dark.

My eyes stung from my tears, my nose was becoming runny. I sniffed up the snot and wiped my nose with the bottom of my shirt. There's no way I can ever leave Ken's sight, I'm stuck here.

I let out a quiet chuckle as I fell back onto the bed, staring at the white ceiling. I place my hands on my damp face and continued to chuckle thinking about the crazy situation that I'm in. I've only been in this building for about two days and I'm slowly losing it.

"What am I going to do?" I said to myself as my chuckle faded.

I rest on my bed listening to the noise outside the building, what will happen to me?

I opened my eyes. I was blinded by a light that went through the leaves above me. I closed my eyes and sat up; I opened my eyes again. It seemed like I was somewhere in a park with benches, trees, shrubs, flowers, fences, and one large walkway. The strange thing about this place was that there was a white mist that surrounded about twenty feet around and above me.

I moved my legs over the edge of the bench. I looked up at the leaves and the white mist above me. The leaves swayed calmly as the light breeze blew through the area. I looked down at my clothes.

I let out a gasp and immediately stood up looking down at myself. I was wearing a knee length white dress with elbow length sleeves. I looked down at my feet, I was barefoot.

I looked up at the trees, running my hands through my long hair as I was preparing for what might happen next. I looked left and right, both directions looked exactly the same.

I walk to the left, my bare feet patting against the cold pavement of the walkway. I realized that the mist still surrounded me when I walked. I looked to the side where the fence was placed at the edge of the walkway. Behind the fence were a few bushes of different types of colorful flowers.

I walked up to the fence and place my right hand over the bushes, my hand brushing against the flowers as I kept walking into nowhere. Is something going to happen? How long am I going to be here?

I kept walking for about a few minutes. It felt like I was walking in circles, everything I passed through looked the same. What kind of dream is this? I wish something much more interesting would happen.

As I was walking, I looked at the mist in front of me. There was a slight silhouette of a person walking towards me. I suddenly felt afraid of who that person was, was it a person I knew or a random stranger?

I built up the courage to walk toward that mysterious person. The silhouette of the person became clearer; I could tell that the person was a man but I couldn't see anything else about that person.

As the man's silhouette came closer I realized that the man was Rick and stopped walking. He was wearing an untucked white button-up shirt, black dress pants, and black shoes. Rick stopped walking; he was ten feet away from me.

The three top buttons of his shirt were undone, his sleeves folded up to expose his forearms. I could see his lotus tattoo on his right forearm. He seemed to dress in a lazy way but look stylish at the same time.

I looked down at my left forearm and saw that I still had my lotus tattoo. I looked at my right palm; I still had that tattoo seal from Ken. I looked up at Rick, who looked back at me.

Rick made a cheerful smile. "Hey kiddo, what are you doing?"

"I-I… um, just strolling around," I said nervously. I need to be calm; this is not the time to freak out.

Rick nodded, still maintaining his smile. "Do you want to come home?"

I smiled, feeling relieved. "I've been wanting to come home for a while." But then my smile faded, realizing that this was all a dream.

Rick's smile turned into a frown; he tilted his head. "What's wrong honey?"

My eyes became watery. "This is all a dream, I can't come home even if I want to," I whispered, my voice slightly breaking.

"Don't say that. Home is where the heart is, isn't it? Whenever you're with me I feel happy, don't you want to be happy too?" he asked, his eyes searching my face.

"I do, but I have to face reality—"

"And what is that reality?" Rick asked, his hands placed inside his pants pockets as his smile slightly fades.

"That I will never see you, my friends, or anyone else ever again because of this insane mess that I'm in!" I said loudly as my tears dripped down my face. I let out a bitter laugh. "I will never get out of here. All this crap happened so suddenly; I feel like I'm going insane."

Rick uncrossed arms and walked up to me. We were standing face to face. He looked down on me, his eyes staring into mine. He moved his arms and wrapped them around me.

He placed his chin against the top of my head. "You're not going insane; you're just having trouble processing everything all at once. Let's go someplace else, someplace where the two of us will be happy," he said as he broke up our hug, his hands holding onto my shoulders.

"Let's go Rick," I said. If I went with him through this strange walkway then there's a chance that this dream will end. I want to see Rick again but not like this, not in a dream.

Rick made a relieved smile and removed his hands from my shoulders. He began walking down the walkway into the mist. I walked right behind him. I looked to my side; nothing looks out of place.

As the two of us were walking I felt a sharp pain in my chest. I looked down at my chest.

I let out a yell and stopped walking. I was impaled by a yellow arrow that was similar to Ken's arrows. The blood from the wound swept onto the white material of my dress, making a large bloodstain on my chest.

I instantly felt lightheaded as my vision became blurry. I looked at Rick, who kept walking without turning back to look at me. I slightly touched the arrow, my chest started to feel like multiple needles pricked it. I stopped touching the arrow and looked behind me. There was only that white mist.

I turned back and saw that Rick was still walking away from me; I stumbled forward to catch up with him. Another arrow struck me on the abdomen. I began to taste blood and spat the blood out. My torso felt hot and painful as I tried to get Rick's attention, but another arrow stuck me once more, preventing me from yelling for help.

I knelt down and fell onto the pavement, the front of my body lying against the ground. There was a burning sensation all over my body and I couldn't yell out for help or say anything. I let out a painful cough, blood leaked out of the corner of my mouth and onto the ground.

I sluggishly moved my head so I faced the direction where Rick was walking to. I watched him walk away from me and into the white mist as I gave into the pain.

I could feel my mouth slightly open from my sleep, and my saliva dripping down from the edge of my mouth. I opened my eyes; the only thing I saw was Ashton's face close to mine.

My eyes grew wide as I moved away from him. Ashton grabbed me by the arm, preventing me from moving away.

Ashton looked down at me. "Calm down, it's just me."

I stopped moving and looked back at him and let out a tired groan. I closed my eyes and sat up; Ashton helped me by holding onto my shoulders.

I opened my eyes, looking at Ashton. I wiped the corner of my mouth with the back of my hand. The two of us sat on top of my bed, the room was bright from the sunlight through the window.

"How did you get into my room?" I asked, remembering that I locked my door last night.

Ashton took out a room card from his pants pocket; the card had my room number on it. "Ken gave me a copy of your room card on the first day you were here. I knocked on your door but you didn't answer it, so I let myself in," he said, putting the card back into his pocket.

"Did you do anything else while I was asleep other than staring at me like a weirdo?" I asked as I scratched my head.

Ashton looked to the side, avoiding my stare. "I didn't stare at you; I was checking that you're not dead or something."

"What time is it?" I asked as I moved my legs to the edge of the bed.

"It's about nine in the morning, I got you breakfast if you're hungry," Ashton said, looking at me.

"Thanks Ashton, did you eat yet?" I asked him.

"I haven't yet, I was waiting for you," he said as he got up and looked through the window.

I stood up and untangled my hair with my hands. "You don't have to wait for me; if you're hungry then you should eat when you want to." It was nice that he waited for me so that we could eat together.

"It's alright, I'm just glad that you're awake now. Let's go to the kitchen area," he said as he walked out of the room.

I followed him out of the bedroom through the hallway and into the living room and kitchen area. I looked at the kitchen table to see a few black containers on the center of it.

I sat on a chair as Ashton went to the mini fridge to take out some drinks. He closed the fridge door and turned around holding one bottle of orange juice and another bottle of some kind of green smoothie.

Ashton placed the bottles on the tabletop and took a seat. "I got you pancakes, an omelet, fruit parfait, and a bottle of orange juice. I hope you like it," he said as he handed me a few containers of food.

I took the containers and placed one of them in front of me and the other one to the side. I opened the lid of the container in front of me. It was the pancakes, drizzled in maple syrup and butter.

"You shouldn't have brought me this much food, but thank you anyway. What did you get for yourself?" I asked Ashton as I took my fork and knife and began cutting my fluffy pancakes.

Ashton opened his container's lid and looked up at me. "I got myself avocado toast with some seasoning on it, a bowl of mixed berries, and a bottle of green smoothie."

"You're really into healthy stuff huh?" I said as I took a bite of my pancake. This was one of the best pancakes I'd ever eaten, buttery and sweet, but it didn't taste too overpowering. The food in this building was the highlight of my stay.

"I always have to stay in top shape for missions and work I have to do. I like to stay healthy in general, how about you? Do you exercise or eat healthy?"

I almost choked on my food because I was laughing. "I wish, the only exercise I do is walking or running away from something. If you see me running that means that you should start running too."

Ashton laughed. "You're quite a funny person you know that? I wish people here were more like you; everyone's always serious because of this organization. It's nice to laugh with someone once in a while."

"One day you'll meet my other friends, they will make you laugh your ass off I guarantee it." I smiled as I took another bite of my pancake.

Ashton smiled back, his eyes looked lively and happy. "I would love to meet them someday."

The two of us continued to eat our breakfast as we talked and laughed together.

I sat on the floor; my arms spread out on the coffee table as I watched the television. Ashton was sitting on the sofa behind me watching a game show with me. I had already changed my clothes and took a shower so I was ready to do anything today.

I tapped my fingers on the table. "Hey Ash, can we go to Ken's office today if you don't mind? I want to ask him a few questions about the incident and my parents' deaths."

"I don't mind, I would happily take you anywhere."

"Before we go I just have to get my room card and put on some shoes." I stood up and walked to my bedroom to get my room card on my desk.

I got out of the bedroom and walked up to the closet, grabbing a pair of sneakers. I closed the closet door and sat next to Ashton on the sofa, putting my shoes on.

"Are you going to tell Ken that you want to get injected with the enhancement substance?" Ashton asked.

"I will, don't worry about it. Once I get that substance into me, I will develop some powers that will help us escape from this place," I said, tying my shoes.

"You have high hopes about this plan, but what happens if it doesn't go as planned?"

"Then we'll figure something else out, we have to try at least." I could tell that Ashton doubted this plan and though I felt the same, we'd never know if this plan will work if we didn't try.

I finished tying my shoes and looked up at Ashton, the two of us locked eyes. I could sense he was worried. I didn't know what would happen after I talked to Ken or took that substance, except that I had to be ready for anything.

CHAPTER 13

Ashton and I were standing in front of Ken's office as I knocked on his door. "Come in," Ken said behind the door. Ashton opened the door for me and I walked in.

"Good morning you two, what brings you to my office?" Ken asked as he wrote something on a piece of paper without looking up at us. Ashton closed the door and walked next to me and gave me a nod.

"I want to learn more about our family history and then I will accept your offer to get injected with that enhancement substance." I could hear my voice slightly quiver. I had to man up or woman up and do this for better or worse. I closed my eyes and took a deep breath, forcing myself to be calm. "I'm ready to learn the truth about our family."

Ken looked up at me. "Okay then, I will get Sean and Chrissy in here so we can talk about this together as a family." Ken grabbed his office phone to dial a phone number, calling Sean or Chrissy. Ken looked at Ashton and then at me. "Do you want Ashton to say here or leave?"

"Ashton can stay here with me if you don't mind." I sat down on the chair in front of Ken's desk as Ashton sat on a chair next to mine. "I already talked to Sean and Chrissy about the organization and our family. I want to talk to you about the incident a long time ago and the deaths of my parents since you know much more about this subject than them."

"Oh I understand, then I should talk about the incident and your parents." Ken turned his attention to his phone. "Sean, I want you and Chrissy to come to my office. Kai and Ashton are with me, Kai wants to learn more about the incident and I consider you and Chrissy should be here for this." Ken paused, listening to what Sean was saying. "Okay see you soon," he said and hung up the phone.

"We'll have to wait for Sean and Chrissy to come here, how do you like your stay here?" Ken asked.

I side glanced at Ashton who looked back at me. He lay back onto his chair with his arms crossed. "This place is nothing that I have seen before, it's very futuristic and stylish," I said, looking back at Ken. "I have a great time here with Ashton."

Ken smiled when he heard my comments. "I'm pleased that you liked the building and your stay here, I worked very hard to make this building and this organization as they are. I specifically chose Ashton to look after you so you won't be alone in this large building. I'm glad that the two of you got along and became friends."

"I'm glad that I made a new friend," I said, looking off to the side of the room. I started thinking about our family and how Sean or Chrissy told me about my grandma's death. I wondered what my grandma was like, she could be the type of person who's always friendly and likes to cook a lot.

When the office door opened I looked behind me. Chrissy walked into the room and closed the door behind her. "Hello, how are you two?" she asked, looking at Ashton and me.

"We're doing well, how about you?" Ashton replied.

"I'm doing well, thank you," she replied as she walked to the corner of the room and sat on the sofa. In the corner of the room there was an area where there were two large sofas and a clear glass table in between that had a single chair in front of it. There was also a large bookshelf behind the single chair that was against the wall.

Chrissy was wearing a yellow sweater and black jeans with high heeled boots. To be honest, she's the type of person who I would love to go shopping with, she had a great sense of fashion, just like the people in our family.

It was a couple of minutes before Sean came into the room. "Sorry that I was late, I was working on the subjects." He sat down on the sofa next Chrissy, the two exchanged glances.

Ken stood up and pushed his deck chair into the desk. "You two kids can sit on the sofa on the other side where Sean and Chrissy are sitting." Ken walked to the area where Sean and Chrissy were sitting, but he sat on the single chair that was behind his bookshelf.

I followed Ashton to the sofa and sat at the end of it, in front of Sean and next to Ken. A large brown-colored book appeared on the table. Ken opened the book to the first page; the book was a large photo collection.

I looked to my side and saw Ashton looking at the book with an interesting look in his eyes. In the book there were a lot of pictures neatly placed on the pages, the pictures were mostly full of people and were taken in different locations. In most of the pictures there were people who looked like they're the same nationality as my family. I noticed that most of the people didn't have the lotus symbol on their arm.

Ken quickly explained to me who those people were and who they were in the family. He also told me that some of these pictures were taken all over Asia. It was actually nice to learn about my ancestors and see how our family has grown up to be.

We spent a long time just looking at the pictures, but near the end of the book Ken stopped talking as he saw a picture of two people, a man and woman holding hands on the beach, smiling at each other. I couldn't help staring at the couple looking at each other like they're the only thing that they saw.

I looked up and saw Sean, Chrissy, and Ken looking down at the photo. The three of them had a sad look on their faces, I could tell that they missed someone who was close to them.

Ken broke the silence. "This picture is my younger self and my wife Vanna when we first arrived in America. She was the love of my life, my children and I still miss her to this day." My heart ached as I heard Ken say that, it reminded me of when I was really young and I cried because I'd never met or seen my parents. I remember that Rick was there to take care of me and always there for me when no one else was.

"What happened to her when she got cancer?" I asked. Ken looked at me with a surprised look. I was slightly sweating because I don't want to be annoying and ask a lot of questions, especially when it's about something very personal.

"I see that you have already learned about your grandmother's illness, I'll tell you the whole story." Ken laid his arms on the armrest. "Five years after Rick was born Vanna got pancreatic cancer. Pancreatic cancer is very rare and the survival rate is very low." Ken took a deep breath and exhaled. "I tried to find a way to prevent the cancer from spreading all over her body, but it never worked. One time when I was experimenting with different chemicals, I injected one of my new substances into a person to see how they reacted. I learned that the substance makes them develop supernatural powers and the more I improved the substance, the more powerfully the substance worked.

But when injected with the substance, each subject developed a different variety of power, the power or ability itself is random. I kept trying to find a cure for Vanna's cancer but I was too late, she died a few months after my discovery. It broke my heart when I had to experience that, but I still have my children to take care of. I know that Vanna would have wanted me to raise them without her." Ken raised his right hand, his palm facing up. A yellow light appeared floating on his palm; everyone look at Ken's ball of light. "I injected myself with the substance and gained this power, I injected my children with different substances too. I thought it would be better if my children developed powers or had immunity from different kinds of diseases. I want what's best for them to survive in the real world; their powers will benefit them in so many ways. I injected all the members of my organization with the substances to do many tasks or for other reasons." Ken's ball disappeared; he rested his hand on his lap.

"By 'other reasons' what do you mean by that?" I asked.

"This organization is underground; the public doesn't know what we do here. We work with other underground organizations who want to use people with supernatural powers for their personal reasons. Some organizations use them as people who help heal or save people, some use them as soldiers or agents, but there's a lot more that they can do with their powers. It's too complicated for you to understand." Ken laced his fingers together. "Back to the family story, long after you and Ashton were born, both of your parents, Veha and Jenna, and your Uncle Rick wanted to end my organization. They thought it was wrong to use people for experiments, use them as weapons and other outrageous things, so they attacked us. They destroyed most of the building, they killed people who were fighting back against them, but most importantly they lost my trust. As I think back, at the time your parents were afraid that I might use and experiment on you, which is not true, the only thing I did to you is brand you as you can tell," he said, gesturing at my left forearm with his eyes. "During the attack your parents and uncle created a secret group that was against me and the whole organization. Both of your parents died during the attack, along with some other people in that group. After the attack I learned that only one person escaped, that person was your Uncle Rick who took you away from us, but now," Ken grabbed my hand and we both looked at each other. I felt my forehead sweat with anxiety. "I finally get to see my granddaughter at last."

"At least we get to see you grow up to become a wonderful young woman," Chrissy said as she put her head against Sean's shoulder. Sean looked at Chrissy and nodded at me, agreeing with her.

Ken laughed as he flipped a page. There were a few pictures of Ken and Vanna with four little kids. I knew those kids were my uncles, aunt, and my dad. One of the pictures was taken at a park. Vanna was sitting on a picnic mat, holding a baby who was smiling at her. Behind them in the background there was one boy who was blowing bubbles and another boy who was playing with his sister, crawling on the grass.

Ken made a sad smile as he looked at the photo. "I remember that day; all six of us were just having fun like any other family. I miss those days."

We looked at a few pages with pictures of Ken, Vanna, and their family, but one of the pictures was Vanna lying on a hospital bed holding hands with Ken. The other kids were there with him. I could tell they had been growing up; the four kids were huddled together on the bedside looking at their mother. I felt bad because they had to see their mom slowly dying in front of them. I looked at the kid who was the youngest of the three. I know that was Rick. Young Rick was crying as his older brother, my father, held him in his arms. My heart ached as I looked at the photo, closely examining every detail.

"This picture was taken before Vanna died; it took me a while to move on but I have to stay strong for my children. It's sad that two of them disappointed me," Ken said without looking up. Wow, throwing Rick and my dad under the bus, that felt nice to hear.

I turned to look at Sean and Chrissy. Sean looked at the window behind Ken's desk and Chrissy looked down at the ground, her eyes watery.

Ken slowly turned the page. The first photo was a couple smiling at the baby that was sitting on the man's lap. I instantly knew they were my mom and dad. I gripped my hands, trying not to get emotional in front of everyone. Chrissy and Sean were right, I do look similar to both of my parents.

I built up my courage to speak. "They're my mom and dad right?" I said, my eyes becoming watery. I pressed my lips together, holding back the tears.

"Yes they are; I was happy that your father found someone to start a family with. Later on your parents wanted to end this organization and things didn't end well after that," Ken said, looking at me. I kept looking at the picture, avoiding Ken's gaze.

Ken took out the picture of me and my parents from the book. He took my right hand and pressed the picture on my palm, covering my seal. "I want you to have it."

I felt mixed emotions inside me, but I tried to keep myself composed. "Thank you," I said quietly.

All I was thinking is how I wanted to talk to my parents even for an hour; they wanted to destroy this organization for a reason. I was going to end this organization; that's what my parents would have wanted in the first place.

I carefully folded the picture and put it in my back pants pocket. I looked up to see Sean smiling at me. This was the first time I ever saw him smile; it was something new. My eyes darted to Chrissy who wiped her eyes and made a sad smile at me. I turned to Ashton who was my only friend in this place. He looked me in the eyes; his eyes were a soft shade of green that made me have butterflies in my stomach.

I looked at Ken and tried to smile but I couldn't do it, I was nervous about what I was going to say next. "I decided to get injected with your enhancement substance," I said confidently as I looked around and saw that everyone was looking at me, this was awkward.

Ken smiled and laughed lightly. "You sure you want to do it? I support your choices either way Kai." I nodded and Ken shook my hand. "Good, but first we need to get your information and create some data for you. It would take me a day or two to create your substances, I will lead you to the laboratory and get your information." Ken closed the photo book and the book disappeared as he got up, letting go of my hand. Everyone stood up. Ken looked at them. "The rest of you don't have to come, I will do this myself."

"If you need anything you can ask me," Chrissy said as she walked next to me and hugged me. "I'm glad that you finally learned the truth about our family. I hope you have a great time here, see you soon," she said, and walked out of the room.

I had to get tested first and then get injected but that wasn't going to take long, I still had to think about our escape plan. I had to plan every single detail of it so Ashton and I would have a chance to get out of here.

Sean stretched out his hand across the table to me. I grabbed his hand and we both shook hands. "You're not that bad kid, don't cause any trouble," he said, letting go of my hand, and he gave a nod at Ken as he walked out of the room.

I didn't want to be alone with Ken. "Can Ashton stay with me as I get tested in the lab?" I looked at Ashton. He looked at me, his lips pressed together.

"Of course he can, we should go now." Ken walked towards the door and opened it. Ashton and I stood up and walked out the office, following Ken down the halls in silence.

CHAPTER 14

K en, Ashton, and I were standing in front of two double doors of the laboratory. I was wondering what kind of data he'd be collecting. Ken opened the door and let Ashton and I walk inside first.

As the three of us walked inside the lab I looked around the large room. There were a few people in white lab coats doing tasks throughout the room, either testing something with the substance or doing some paperwork. The lab had multiple computer screens, desks, chairs, etc. around the center of the room. I looked at the back corner of the lab; there was another set of double doors that led to another room. There was also a single door on the other side of the lab that was next to the double doors.

Most scientists in the room were busy doing their own thing so I just kept looking around the room. Everything was very high tech and futuristic. I looked at the left corner of the room and saw a clear container that held many different sized syringes in it. From the distance where I was I could see a different colored substance inside each of the syringes.

Ken led us to one of the desks in the center of the room that had a couple of computers on it. He sat down on one of the chairs and turn on one of the computers. He motioned us to sit on the chairs that were at the desk. I sat closer to Ken and Ashton sat next to me.

Ken was typing on the computer. "I will get your information just as a doctor would do, but I'm going to use my powers on you. It's an easy way to upload your data," he said without looking away from the computer screen.

"Alright," I said calmly, this was not that bad because it's just extracting my information to the computer.

Ken turned around facing me, his right hand glowed yellow as he moved his hand and touched my forehead. I felt his power on my forehead and it was a strange feeling that can't be described.

After a few minutes Ken moved his hands away from my forehead, turned around to the computer screen, and touched it. The computer screen started to put in my information and up popped different charts and graphs. I was amazed that he could do all of that by using his powers. I already knew that his powers were much more powerful than anyone else's which was the scary thing about him.

The computer popped up a sign that said 'complete.' Ken turned around and smiled. "I'm finished with your data and it looks very good. I'll make the power enhancement substance for you, but it would take me a few days to make it. I hope you will be patient. I would like to say that I'm happy that you made the right choice. You are now free to do whatever you want until I'm finished with your substance." We both got up. Ken hugged me and I hugged him back.

I looked back at Ashton who also stood up, the three of us said our good-byes as Ashton and I left, leaving Ken inside the laboratory doing what he needed to do.

The two of us walked around the building doing some sightseeing, it's better to remember routes and exits in case I need them. The building was very big so it would take me awhile to know exactly where to go; at least I had Ashton to lead me to the right place.

"I have some place that I want to show you, I think you will like it," Ashton said as the two of us passed by a guy with a lot of face tattoos.

"Is it another training room?" I asked, my eyebrow raised.

Ashton let out a quiet chuckle. "It's not, so don't worry about that. The place is kind of like a relaxing area in the building that has a water fountain and benches, it's really nice. Let me lead the way."

I followed Ashton through long hallways, large rooms, and down the elevator as the two of us talked.

At the end of a long hallway we walked into a big area with a large marble water fountain in the center of the room. There were a lot of flowers in tall pots with golden designs throughout the room. Benches were placed against the walls and had flowerpots at each end. I couldn't forget how amazing and beautiful this place was. I sat on one of the benches and looked at the water fountain in front of me.

Ashton sat next to me, looking at the fountain with me. "Hey, Kai is it okay for you to tell me about your life? It's okay if you don't want to." He sounded shy as he said that, that was new to me because he always looked and sounded straightforward and confident.

"It's no problem, we're friends after all." I stretched my arms and legs; I got a feeling that we'd be here for a long time. "As you already know I'm Kai Kago, I'm fifteen years old and my birthday is on May 18th so my 'special day' is a few months away but, like, I don't really care about my own birthday to be honest," I said, looking at a few people passing by.

"Huh, my birthday is on January 24th so I'm older than you by five months." Ashton let out a smiley laugh.

"Seriously, I thought you would be like two years older than me." I laughed, looking at Ashton making a shocked face.

"Seriously? I'm the same age as you. That hurt my self-confidence just a bit, thinking that I look so old, I'm so hurt," he said dramatically with his hand on his chest. We both laughed. "But I can't help that you look like a twelve year old kid."

I elbowed him in the arm and laughed. "Oh yeah? At least I look innocent and cute. But anyway, back to my life story, my Uncle Rick who actually took care of me, he always cared about me and would do anything for me. The thing is that he never told me what truly happened to my parents or about our past. I guess he's afraid to tell me the truth, just like Sean said before." I paused for a minute, but then continued. "Now I finally learn what happened to my parents and that I have a family that I didn't know I had until now. Rick as you already know is a lieutenant detective of the Boston police department, which means that he has an important job." I changed the subject to make myself feel a bit better. "I'm a sophomore at Edge Grove High School in Boston, I made a good group of friends that I can trust and maybe someday you can meet them too. I have three close friends, Ronnell, Owen, and Tyrone. I've known Tyrone since I was a little kid so the two of us are like family, he's a really chill person to hang with and he's really athletic. I don't know how I became friends with someone as cool as him, I didn't tell him about my powers because I don't want him to think about me in a bad way, you know. Also he's the grandson of the Chief Gray, or Fred, that's what Rick and I call him because we're friends with him. Fred is a close friend of Rick for a long time now. Fred is a really nice and friendly guy to be friends with. Ronnell is a really smart person who always cares for other people. We can be really funny if we're in the same class, but I don't think other people feel the same way. Owen and I would talk for hours about videogames or which shows to watch, he's a very friendly person and always the funny friend of the group.

Owen and I would spend hours playing on his PlayStation at his house; he lives a few houses away from me. We can be weird at times, but that is what makes our friendship special. Most importantly I told Owen and Ronnell about my powers and they never told anyone about it, not even their parents, and that's what true friends are for." I felt myself smile a genuine smile just thinking about my friends and it made me really happy, but it also made me miss my best friends more.

"It seems like your friends really care about you, I find it shocking that they kept your secret for a long time now," Ashton said thoughtfully as he looked at a potted plant next to him.

"I know right? That's how you know what kind of people my friends are, the ones who won't stab me in the back or go against me. It's quite difficult to find people who are not fake or two-faced; I'm very blessed to have friends like that," I said, smiling to myself as I watched a woman walk past the fountain. "You know what? You're like my friends too, you're really nice and caring. Well maybe because you have to look out for me like a nanny, but overall you're the type of person who I can trust in this place. Thank you for being my only friend in this shithole," I said, laughing as I turned my head to look at him.

Ashton looked up at me with an embarrassed smile. "You don't have to thank me. You're the one who randomly showed up here in the first place. I should thank you for being my friend, but you should continue with what you were saying. I want to learn more about Kai Kago," he said cheerfully.

I nodded at him and continued with what I was talking about. "I've also got other good friends but I never told them about my powers, only Ronnell and Owen. Oh, and also Stella knew about my power too but she's Rick veterinarian friend so she's about Rick's age. She's really nice and she kept my powers a secret which is good. She's got a Rottweiler dog named Tobi; sometimes he can be wild, but he's a nice dog if he gets used to you." Talking about my friends and family made me feel homesick. I wonder what my friends are doing right now, do they miss me or not really care? I have been out for at least two or three days, I guess people don't really get bothered or care if I'm gone.

I didn't say anything after my long summary of my life, I kept thinking about if my friends didn't really care about me or they forgot about me. It made me feel awful. I know that isn't true, I was just making myself feel bad. I know that my closest friends will care about me, but they couldn't even help me in this situation that I got into. Plus Rick made that note that said we're going on a trip, so most people knew why we were gone even though that reason was a complete lie.

Ashton laid his hand on my shoulder, I looked at him. "You seemed a bit sad," he said with a concerned look as his eyes bore deep into mine.

"It's not that important, I'm just thinking about some things."

"What kind of things if you don't mind me asking?"

I looked away from Ashton's gaze. "I was wondering if my friends miss me, I've been gone for a while now."

"You're an amazing friend to have of course they miss you. Don't make yourself feel sad by thinking about the negative things, try to be positive and you will feel much better," Ashton said as he patted me on the shoulder.

I turned my head to look at him. "Thank you for your advice Ash. You should tell me more about yourself," I said, changing the subject. I would rather talk about something else besides me. I really wanted to know more about Ashton.

He tapped his foot "Okay. I'm Ashton Schutz, I'm sixteen years old and I never went to school. I was taught by Ken and a few other people so I guess you can call it homeschooled. I didn't have many friends, but I bet not many people have that many friends here. From what Ken had told me my dad was American and my mom was German, so that makes me German American. I never met my parents because during the incident something had happened to my parents and it somehow killed them, but not me." He said the last sentence quietly.

"Do you know who or what killed your parents?" I asked as I placed my hands on my lap.

Ashton shook his head. "Ken had told me he found my parents deceased in the lab, both my parents were killed by some lab equipment that hit them severely in the head and neck. He also told me that he doesn't know who killed my parents, I was about seven years old when I learned what had happened," he said somberly.

"I'm sorry about that. It looks like we have something in common, right?" I asked quietly. I could feel myself cringe when I said that, I could really say something much better than that.

"It seems like we do, but you know I have to learn how to take care of myself and learn things from experience or from other people."

"That sounds depressing," I said. Ashton looked at me with a straight face. "I-I didn't say that to be rude but it sounds overwhelming for a kid, right?"

"It is, but once you experience all these things in life, it gets easier as time goes by."

"You're a very tough guy; I want to appreciate the things you went through."

Ashton's cheeks slightly turned pink. "Thank you for saying that."

"It's no problem bud, you should finish what you were saying."

"Where did I leave off? Oh okay, so after my parents died Ken took care of me and he raised me, he made me become a human weapon that's able to kill without remorse. I killed many people in missions that Ken assigned me to do, and as time went on Ken made me his trusted go-to assassin. I was only twelve years old! I was so naïve, I thought doing these missions would make Ken like me more and help me try to forget who my real family is." Ashton took a deep breath. "But it didn't make me a better person, I'm the person who ended lives and obeys orders. All I am to Ken is his assassin, nothing more, nothing less. I wanted to leave this place and this organization, but the last time someone tried to leave this building that person got tortured by Ken and then killed. I should know because I was there with Ken," he said with a frown. "I speak German, Mandarin, Russian, Spanish, and of course English. I can remember things better than an average person; that means that I can recall anything that I witness or learn. And that's my summary of my life."

"You're quite a smart guy, I wish I could be as smart as you," I said, tapping my foot on the tile floor.

Ashton looked at me. "Don't say that, you're as intelligent as me. Don't look down on yourself; you're an amazing person who doesn't know what she's capable of."

Ashton's life was more extreme than mine. I looked at Ashton and touched his shoulder. "Once we get out of here I will let you live your own life and make choices that only you can decide. You will be free to do anything that you like; no one can force you to do things that you don't want. Someday I might show you the world and you can experience new things that you never learned or did before. You can have the life you always wanted and I promise that you will get out of here. As your friend I will make this happen," I said.

His mouth opened but he didn't say anything for a few minutes, I started to get worried that I said something wrong.

"Uhh, sorry if my little speech sounds awkward," I said, removing my hand from his shoulder.

"No it's fine Kai, you better keep your promise," he said turning to face me as he held up his left fist. "Thank you for being my friend."

I glanced at Ashton's fist and raised my right hand, making a fist. I bumped fists with him. Ashton made a relieved smile as the two of us fist-bumped.

"So do you want to stay here or go somewhere else?" I asked Ashton as he ran his hands through his blonde hair.

"I have no idea." He took out his phone and turned it on. I looked at the phone and it's about three in the afternoon. We still had a lot of time left; maybe we should plan our escape.

"We can go to my room and talk about our plan," I said in a low voice so that no one could hear me.

"That's a good idea but we should go get something to eat."

I nodded and we both stood up to walk through the long hallway.

Ashton and I ate our lunch at the same table next to the windows; I guess this table was our usual spot. We both picked sushi for lunch. As we ate our food we just talked about normal stuff like what kind of music you like, what kind of things you like to do in your free time, and other things that we liked to do. It was really fun just talking to a friend in a situation like this, I'm just happy that I had Ashton with me.

When we were done with lunch we walked up to my 'hotel room' and sat on my sofa and watched television.

I hugged a throw pillow that was on the sofa and rested my face on it. It'd been a hectic few days for me and there were a lot of things that I still needed to process. I instantly remembered that Ken gave me a picture of my parents and I reached into my pocket and took out the folded photo. I unfolded the photo and looked at it once again. I could see the resemblance between me and my parents. I have the nose shape of my dad and I have the same face shape and eyes as my mom.

I stood up and walked into my bedroom to put the photo in my desk drawer. I walked back into the living room and sat back down on the sofa. Ashton sat next to me holding the television remote, flipping through channels. I moved my legs up so my chin could rest on my knees and slowly fell asleep for what felt like a couple of hours.

I woke up and looked to the side, I didn't see Ashton. I looked down at the coffee table, and there's a note on it. I picked up the note which read, 'When you wake up come to my room, it's room 219. -A.S.'

I rubbed my eyes and stretched my arms and back. I heard a crack in my back and it felt nice. I went to the bathroom and washed my face with cold water, then walked out of my room and took a right to where Ashton's room was. I looked at the doors, 217, 218, and 219.

I knocked on the door with 219 on it; it took a minute until someone unlocked the door and opened it.

Ashton opened the door wide. "You have been sleeping for two hours, at least you're awake. Come in."

I walked in and looked around Ashton's room. His room was stylized with many decorations and furniture that fit his style and the room itself. I sat on his sofa and looked around the room once again. I had noticed that he has some exotic souvenirs carefully placed throughout the room.

"You want anything to drink?" he asked as I took his television remote and turned it on.

"No thanks, nice room you got here," I said as I looked at his nice bookcase filled with books of different sizes and colors.

"Thanks, now time to get serious." He stood next to me and opened a can of sparkling water and took a sip as he sat down.

"So our plan is going well. We'll just have to wait for a few days until I get injected with that substance, then we'll get in contact with Rick." I had doubts about this plan, but I needed to end this organization or at least escape from this place. "I want to know what powers I gain from that substance but it will take time, right?"

"It depends on the person. For me it took me about three days to fully develop my abilities, for some other people it might take days or weeks to develop them. Are you sure that we'll go through the plan after you get injected?"

It took a few minutes to think about it. "Yes I'm sure. Maybe my new powers might be helpful for our escape, plus I have only been here for a few days so it wouldn't be that bad." I wondered what Rick was doing. I hoped he was trying to find me wherever he was.

CHAPTER 15

In the city of Boston, Rick drove down the street looking at the buildings that he passed by. The sky was cloudless, the sun shining down at the city. Rick parked in front of a convenience store and got out of his car. The store bell rang as Rick walked into the store. The man sitting behind the counter looked up from his phone and smiled.

"Hey Rick, how are you? It's been a while huh?" said the man from the counter. He was medium build with a buzz cut hairstyle. Rick smiled as he held out his hand to the man and they both hugged each other over the counter. Manny was a few inches shorter than Rick.

"Yeah it's been a while Manny, these past few days have been difficult. How is your family doing?" Rick asked as Manny sat back down onto his chair.

"They are doing well; I even had enough money to buy my wife a nice ring a while back. How's your kid doing?"

Rick smile fades a bit. "I need your help Manny I need to find Liam; do you know where he's at?" He lay his hand on the counter looking at Manny, waiting for him to respond.

Manny looked back at Rick and raised an eyebrow. "You sure you want to talk to him? Since you left the gang to become an officer he became more… whatcha call it?" Manny snapped his fingers. "Unpredictable and scary. He even scares the shit outta me sometimes, but he does the job well."

"I know that Liam has strong feelings about me but I never snitched on the gang. I've known you for a long time now. I need your help, my niece Kai was taken by my father, I know that Liam might have an idea where they're at. Just tell me where to find him and I won't let anything happen to you or your family," Rick said sternly as he searched Manny's face.

Manny looked around the store and took out a piece of paper and pen. He wrote something on it and handed it to Rick. He moved closer to Rick. "Just be careful when you're there and good luck finding your niece. Don't tell Liam that I told you where to find him, I'm still in the gang ya know."

Rick took the piece of paper and touched Manny's shoulders. "Thank you." He walked out of the store. Manny looked at Rick as he left the store with a worried face.

Rick got in his car and turned the car on, looked at the piece of paper, and drove off down the street.

In a quiet street Rick parked his car on one of the parking lots near a quiet building and got out. He looked around his surroundings and walked towards the warehouse on the other side of the street.

The warehouse was surrounded by a few people in black suits. One of them spotted Rick and walked towards him with a straight face.

"You're not allowed to be in the area, this area is for staff personnel only," the man said, standing in front of Rick.

"I'm only here to see Liam who runs the place. I don't want to cause any trouble." Rick tried to walk around the man, but the man blocked his way.

"Only staff personnel are allowed to enter the premises. Leave now or I will shoot you." The man opened the left side of his suit jacket to show a gun holstered on his belt.

Rick glared at the man who didn't move a muscle. He let out a sigh. "Is that a threat? I'm not afraid to hurt someone more than necessary." Rick's eyes glowed purple as the man swiftly took out his gun and pointed it at Rick. The second he looked at Rick his eyes flashed purple. He instantly dropped the gun and fell onto the ground.

Another man in a black suit saw what happened and ran toward Rick with his gun positioned at Rick. Rick gave a side glance at the man running towards him, the man dropped his gun and fell.

Rick walked to the entrance of the building and opened the door. Multiple people in black suits pointed their guns at Rick as he took a step in the building. He raised his glowing red hand and swiped it down, and all the men were suddenly forced on the ground. All of them tried to get up, but the strong force prevented them from moving.

He walked over to one of the men that was on the ground and crouched in front of the man who had light brown hair. Rick held out two red glowing fingers and touched the man's forehead.

After a few seconds Rick removed his hands from the man's head and got up. He looked at the group of men on the floor struggling to move or speak. He held out his hand, his palm facing up, and he slowly closed his hand into a fist. All the men stopped moving, the red glow on Rick's hand and his purple eyes disappeared.

Rick stepped over the men's bodies and looked at one of the wooden crates that were stacked in a pile. The crates were branded with an Ankh symbol on the side. He opened the lid of one of the boxes and inside there was a huge amount of medium-sized packets wrapped in a dark material. He grabbed one of the packages and opened it; there were multiple small bags that all had black powder in them.

He took out one of the little bags and examined it closely. The small bag had the same Ankh logo on it in shiny gold print. He put the small bag in his pocket and put the medium-sized package back inside the crate.

Rick looked around the room, his eyes darting left and right as he started to walk toward the double doors on the other side of the building. As he was walking down the building everything seemed quiet and empty, there were no other men in black suits in sight.

He stopped in front of the rusted metal doors and took a deep breath. He opened the double doors and walked inside the room. Inside the room multiple people wearing white coveralls were standing at different tables doing their assigned jobs. Everyone was also wearing plastic gloves and surgical masks. At the first two tables which were in a row, people put small black rocks in a machine that poured out black powder into a large bowl. In the next row people poured the black powder into a small plastic bag that had the golden Ankh logo on it. The last row was where people packaged the small bags in a big bundle, wrapped in a black material.

As Rick walked in, everyone in the room looked at him and stopped. More men in black suits came rushing in, taking out their guns, while the people who wore masks ran toward the exit, trying not to get hurt.

All the people in masks were gone and the only people in the room were Rick and the men in black suits. The men were pointing their guns directly at him. Rick stared at the men, his eyes glowed purple once again. All the men dropped their guns and fell on the floor, unconscious.

Rick headed toward another door. He opened the door and saw a man who was in his late forties standing in front of a desk, pointing his gun at Rick.

"You know I'm really tired of people pointing their guns at me," Rick told the man. He walked closer to the man. The man didn't move an inch.

"What do you want Kago?" the man said in a cold deep voice.

"I'm here because I thought you would help me find something. I'm not here to cause any more trouble than I need to. Just help me for once Liam." Rick walked a few inches closer to Liam.

Liam made pfft sound. "Why would I help you? You left The Pharaohs to become a fucking cop! You even made quite a reputation for yourself Rick 'devil' Kago, I guess they had already known the real you. Back then I trusted you, but now you betrayed me and the gang." Liam raised his gun up to Rick's forehead.

Rick clenched his jaw. "I did not betray you, I never told anyone about this gang or what we did here. I became an officer because I'm done feeling guilty and ashamed of myself! I didn't snitched on your or the gang, the police already knew about what you do here so it wouldn't matter anyways." Rick moved closer to Liam. Liam's gun touched Rick's forehead. "I'm done pitying myself." Rick glared at Liam.

Both Rick and Liam stared each other down not saying anything. The quiet lasted a few seconds. Liam's finger curled on the trigger.

"I became a different man after you left, I never give second chances. Not anymore." Liam inhaled sharply, his eyes narrowed with silent rage. "See you in hell Rick." Liam pulled the trigger.

The loud gunshot cracked in the air, the sound echoed off the walls. Rick's body stiffly fell back onto the cement ground, making a thud, and lay still. His head tilted to the side, his purple eyes faded into his natural brown color. Blood from the bullet hole slowly leaked down across his forehead, a trail of blood flowing from the edge of his mouth.

Liam coldly watched Rick fall to the ground. The ground and objects behind Rick were splattered in his blood. Liam let out a 'humph' as he walked behind his desk and took a seat behind it, placing his gun on the side of his desk.

He ran his fingers in his hair and looked down at Rick. "It's such a shame that you left the gang. I had high hopes for you, maybe because you have powers and such. But you're just one of my pawns, a useless object."

The men in black suits rushed into Liam's office after Rick was shot. They looked at Rick and then at Liam.

"What do you want us to do boss?" one of the men asked, Liam took out a cigarette from his shirt pocket and lit it.

Liam puffed out a cloud of smoke. "Do whatever you want. I'm done with him."

Two men look at each other and nodded; they grabbed Rick by the shoulders and legs and carried him out of the office. A large pool of blood from Rick's bullet hole slowly spread out on the cement ground.

Liam looked at the pool of blood in repulsion. "Clean the blood off of my floor." The group of men nodded and walked out of the room.

Rick was carried by two men in black suits. They walked through the area where the wooden box crates were stacked. His eyes flashed bright purple, but then turned back to brown. His fingers twitched slightly. One of the men holding Rick's legs saw that his eyes flashed purple and instantly dropped his legs.

The man that was holding Rick's shoulders looked back. "What are you doing? We have a job to do."

The man in the back stared at Rick with alarm. "Look at him Ralph, I don't think he's dead."

Ralph looked at Rick and then up at the man. "He looked dead to me Joe. Just do your job before boss gets mad." Ralph motioned to Rick's feet with his eyes. Joe gingerly picked up Rick's legs and they both carried him down the passageway between the large piles of crates.

Rick's bullet hole started to regenerate, filling the small hole with missing bone fragments and tissues. Rick's head looked like it had never been destroyed. He blinked his eyes and moved his jaw.

Joe dropped Rick's legs again. "I told you he's not dead!" he yelled and took a step back, his hand grabbing his gun. Rick let out a weak groan.

Rick's eyes flared purple as he drew a sharp breath and looked up at Ralph, who was still holding Rick's shoulders. Ralph looked at Rick with surprise, but then his facial expression changed into an emotionless look. He lifted Rick up helping him stand up.

"Stop or I'll get more personnel to take care of this," Joe said, hesitating as he pointed his gun at Rick.

It only took Rick a slight glance at Joe to make him drop his gun. Joe had the same straight expression as Ralph.

As Rick regained consciousness he firmly stood up and looked at the two men. He held out his right hand and closed it. Both men in black suits instantly dropped on the floor; they lay on the floor passed out. He touched his head and winced. He rolled his shoulders and neck. He drew out a deep breath, turned around, and casually headed for the doors.

As he was walking Rick closed and opened his eyes. His pupils dilated, his eyebrows knitted, his facial expression furious. More men ran to Rick, shooting at him and yelling. Rick kept walking, bullets ricocheting off an invisible force that surrounded him. He closed his right hand and every black suited man dropped onto the floor.

Rick forcefully pushed the double doors open so hard that they broke off and slammed into the office, knocking off objects and furniture. A man who was on the floor cleaning up the blood took out his gun, but instantly flew back into the wall.

Liam sat behind his desk watching Rick. He lit another cigarette and put it in his mouth. He reached for his gun that was on the desk, but the gun was knocked from Liam's reach by an invisible force.

White smoke oozed out from Liam's mouth. "I guess this is why people call you a devil, you can never die and you always look sinister when you're angry," he said with a smirk.

Rick walked closer to Liam and slammed his hands on top of his desk. "I'm here to find someone and I know you might have an idea where he is."

Liam looked up at Rick with a nonchalant look. "What happens if I don't?" He swiftly took out a sharp pocketknife and held it to Rick's neck. "I would rather die than to help someone like you." Liam stood up to plunge his knife into Rick.

Rick's hands squeezed on Liam's neck until Liam let go of the knife. "Aren't you going to kill me? Since I already shot you to death," he wheezed, glaring at Rick.

Rick clenched his jaw. He let go of Liam's neck to grab his head and forcefully slam it into the desk, causing the desk to break in half.

Liam's body lay on the ground, blood started to flow from his head and down onto the ground. Rick picked him up and dragged him against the wall. Liam's face was severely scratched and cut. There were bruises on his left cheek, streams of dark red blood oozed out of his cuts, nose, and mouth. His eyes moved left and right, trying to avoid Rick's furious stare.

Rick crouched down, his two fingers glowing red. He touched Liam's forehead with his fingers. Liam made a struggling noise but Rick ignored him. A few seconds passed and Rick moved his hand away from Liam's head.

He gets up and looked down at Liam, who looked back at him with furrowed brows. "You're lucky that I didn't kill you." Rick's eyes faded back to brown. He walked to the door and left the warehouse without turning back.

CHAPTER 16

Ashton and I walked into the building's library; there were not as many people in the library. Ashton thought that I could spend some time exploring the building so I wouldn't be locked up in my room and do nothing.

I looked at the book spines that were facing out as I walked through an area where a few bookshelves were placed in rows. There were multiple wooden round tables and chairs arranged in the center of the library, large bookshelves were placed on the walls and in small areas throughout the library.

Ashton walked next to me. "I thought you would like to just stay in here for a while and relax," he said quietly as he walked up next to me looking at the books. He pulled out a book To Kill a Mockingbird.

I looked at the book. "I read that book before; it's a good book to read." I looked back at the bookshelf to look at some books that I might want to read. He turned to the back cover of the book and read the text that was on it.

"I read it about three times already, it's one of my favorite books," he said, placing the book back on the shelf. He turned around to another bookshelf that was behind me and examined all the books that were in nice neat rows.

I walked around multiple bookshelves until I saw a whole bookshelf that was filled with books about chemistry and science. I instantly looked at the books to see if I wanted to read them; it looked like this library had most of the textbooks that my school has. I found a textbook that I had for my chemistry class, I also looked for some other textbooks that I used in my classes and took them as well. I quickly skimmed through a U.S. history textbook as I walked to one of the tables and took a seat.

I opened the history textbook and read it until Ashton came to the table. He sat down in the chair in front of me and opened a book called *The Science of Good and Evil.* It seemed like a far more interesting book than a textbook, I wondered what kind of book he was reading.

"Hey Ash, what kind of book is that?" I asked, looking up from my book.

"Oh this? This is a philosophy book that is about the origins of morality and ethics based on the book summary. I haven't read this book but it seems interesting, I like philosophy because it gets me thinking about certain things in the world." He looked down at my stack of textbooks. "It seems like you're trying to keep up with your classes while you're away, right?"

"You're right, I know that I'm going to bomb all my classes because of my absence. But whatever, the trimester will end soon so what's the point of reading all of this?"

"It's better to learn something rather than nothing."

"You make a good point, I should just read these books to kill some time or hopefully learn something from them."

We both continued to read our books. I'd become bored with reading the U.S. history book so I got up and walked to the bookshelves to put the book back. I picked out another history book about ancient Asia which made me think about samurais and the Mongols.

As I walked back towards my table I saw a blonde girl with blue eyes who was about my age staring at me. Great, more random people judging me. I ignored her and kept on walking until I was at the table where Ashton sat. Maybe she looked at my tattoo on my forearm; I could care less about what she or others think about me.

I opened the history book about ancient Asia and began reading it. Reading this book in silence makes me feel uncomfortable since I always listen to music while I do anything productive. I wished I had my phone with me, I looked up and saw Ashton on his phone.

I saw the blonde girl again but it looked like she was walking towards my table. I tapped on the table to get Ashton's attention. He looked up from his phone.

"Look behind you," I whispered.

He turned around glancing at her and turned his head back to look at me. "Great it's Bella, she's so annoying," he said rolling his eyes. He looked adorable when he did that even if he looked annoyed.

I was about to ask him more questions about her but she was standing next to us, so I kept quiet and looked at her. She reminded me of those girls in school who think that they're better than most people, but in reality they're not.

"Hey Ash, how are you?" she said to him. She placed her hands on the top rail of his chair, her blue eyes gazing at him.

"Same as always," he said impassively. I could tell that he didn't like her but Bella seemed to want to keep talking to him. She looked like that type of girl who would do anything to have a boyfriend, but then dump him in a week like some other people in my school would do.

Bella turned her head to look at me once again, she made a fake smile. "I thought the bloodline ended with Rick?" she said with a snobby tone in her voice. I clamped my fist trying to compose myself. I hated that fake smile she made, I hated how she looked at me with those judgmental eyes, it made me want to fight her.

"So what? You got a fucking problem?" I said, crossing my arms as I raised an eyebrow. First it was Ben and Greg and now her; some of these people get me on my last nerve.

Bella's smile faded. "I see that you got a temper like Sean. How did you get here in the first place?"

I could feel my eyebrows twitch. "Ken found me in Boston and took me here." I heard my voice deepen.

Bella tilted her head and looked at Ashton. "I guess you and Ashton are friends, huh. I hope he doesn't trouble you, but how can he be troubling? He's such a good boy," Bella said making another fake smile as she reached her hand towards Ashton's hair. He pulled his head away from Bella's reach. "I don't bite," she said in a flirty and weird way.

"Hey, stop flirting with your cousin," I said out loud so that a few people in the tables near me could hear what I said.

Bella's cheeks turned pink as she glared at me, she looked annoyed, but like I care. All I could do is smile and raise my hands. I actually enjoyed watching her reaction.

Ashton looked at me with shock but he suddenly laughed; I had never heard him make a very humorous laugh before. He tried to cover up his mouth with his hand but I could still see his smile.

As I looked at him I began to hold in my laugh, but I couldn't. I began to make weird sounds with my mouth. Ashton had started to laugh harder as I kept making those noises.

"If I wanted a bitch, I would have bought a dog," Ashton said laughing. Bella's eyes grew slightly wide as opened her mouth with complete shock.

I burst out laughing. "Oh my God, this is the first time I heard you make a joke about someone!" I said as I lay my head on my textbook.

"You know what? Someone as fake and unworthy as you shouldn't be in the bloodline of the Tep family," Bella said as she gave me the death stare.

"Oh honey like I care about that, and you dare to call me fake?" I said as I placed my hand on my chest and batted my eyes dramatically. "At least you don't have to look behind your back, you have another face to do that for you," I said boldly.

Bella opened her mouth to say something, but she didn't say anything at all. Ashton turned to the side and made a muffled laugh. No one said anything and Bella still stood there, glaring at me.

I looked at Bella dead in the eyes. "You're excused," I said as I turned my head to the other side motioning my hand at her to leave.

She stood there stunned for a few seconds until she crossed her arms, and made a 'humph' sound as she walked away. I looked at Ashton as I could feel myself smile. Ashton turned his head so that he was facing me.

He made a grin and laughed. "I can't believe you just said that to her!" he said as he lightly patted the table as he continued laughing.

I smiled as I slightly laughed. "I can't believe you said that joke to her! To be honest I didn't see that coming at all, you surprised me!"

Our laughter slowly died down, the two of us looked at each other without saying anything. I was smiling like an idiot as I thought back at what Ashton said that to her, I had no idea he could be that sassy.

"What happened to not drawing attention to us?" Ashton leaned closer to me, still maintaining a smile.

"Well we said, 'not to draw suspicion to ourselves,' suspicion and attention are two different things. Plus she's being weird and touchy with you, so I found a way to get her to leave, which she did. You can just tell her that you don't like her and tell her to leave you alone." It's not the first time I had an encounter with someone like Bella, unfortunately.

"I told her so many times that I don't like her but she keeps talking to me, why can't she just annoy someone else?" Ashton sighed. "I'm just happy that you made that clear to her now."

"No worries, it's not as bad as our encounter with Ben and Greg right? But I did enjoy seeing Bella's and your reaction when I said those things to her. It actually made my day."

"It made my day; I have never heard anyone say such things like that to someone who they just met." Ashton's eyes lit up as he looked into my eyes. "You're something else, you know."

We stayed in the library until we started to get bored then we decided to go to Ashton's room and hang out there. In Ashton's room I sat on the floor in front of the coffee table, while he went to his room to grab something.

Ashton walked out holding a thin laptop with one hand. He sat next to me and opened his laptop and typed on it.

"Do you want to use it?" he asked as he placed the laptop on the coffee table.

"Sure, do you want to watch some funny videos?"

"What kind of funny videos?"

"Funny animal videos. Since you told Bella that dog joke, I kept thinking about animals doing funny things," I said as I searched up a video that had the most views. I clicked the 'play' button on the video and the two of us watched the video.

After the video was done we began to search for more funny videos of people doing dumb stunts. We were watching videos until I began to feel a stinging sensation in my eyes.

I rubbed my eyes and looked next to me. "Hey Ash, do you want to do something else besides looking at videos? My eyes are getting blurry because of it."

He looked back at me. "Sure, we could talk about something if you like."

"What type of music do you listen to?" I asked.

Ashton placed his hands on his chin. "I like any music that sounds good. I mostly listen to any kind of indie music. How about you?"

"I also like to listen to indie music too. I often listen to instrumental music when I need to concentrate on a task."

"I want to listen to some of the songs that you like, I'm always open to new song suggestions." Ashton said as he moved the laptop closer to us.

"Sure thing, I hope you like some of the songs that I listen to," I said as I searched for one of my favorite songs.

The two of us talked as our favorite music played in the background during the rest of the night. It seems like time flies by when I'm talking to Ashton. I didn't notice we stayed up till midnight

CHAPTER 17

I rubbed my eyes as I lay on my back. I opened my eyes and stared at the ceiling. My eyes started to get blurry, so I blinked them a couple of times until my vision got better. I looked to the side at the clock, but it was hard to tell what time it was from where I lay.

I slowly sat up and got out of bed, my feet touching the cold tile floor. As I got closer to the clock I could clearly read it; it's about 7:46 in the morning. I let out a yawn and stretched my body.

I walked to the mini fridge, took out a bottle of orange juice, and drank it. I placed the bottle on the kitchen counter. I walked to the closet and picked my outfit for the day. I went inside the bathroom and got changed, brushing my hair and putting it into a low ponytail, and rinsed my eyes with cold water.

I got out of the bathroom and placed my pajamas on my bed. I grabbed a bottle of orange juice and sat on the sofa, waiting for Ashton. I looked at Ashton's laptop on the table, last night he allowed me to bring his laptop into my room. I took the laptop and pressed the power button, the laptop turned on.

I pressed Ashton's computer account; it was unlocked. I touched the laptop's touchpad and moved the mouse over the photo icon. I know this is wrong but I was curious what kind of photos he had, looking at someone's picture albums says a lot about a person.

I clicked on the pictures icon, there were not many pictures, but I looked at them anyways. Most of the pictures were of people and places that I guess he had been to. I noticed there was one picture that looked much older than the others. I clicked on the picture and it was a family picture of a couple and a baby, a man with brown hair and green eyes and a lady with blonde hair and gray eyes. I looked up to see if Ashton was sneaking behind me but there was no one here besides me. I leaned closer to the screen and noticed that they looked very similar to Ashton. I realized that the couple was Ashton's parents.

I exited out of the picture and looked at another picture of Ashton and a Latino boy, they looked like they're the same age at the time. I looked at the time where the photo was taken or when the photo was loaded into the laptop and it was about two years ago. I looked at the picture again. The two of them were at a pier, there was a long bridge behind them and tall buildings in the background. Both of them seemed really happy, it reminded me of my friends. It made me happy that Ashton looked like a normal teenager in the picture.

I instantly remembered that he said that his best friend died two years ago, maybe that guy in the picture was his best friend. I don't know what I'd do if my best friends left me or even died without me knowing.

Someone knocked on my door. I quickly exited off the photo albums, turned off the laptop, and placed it where it was when I left it. I got up and opened the door; Ashton was standing in front of me with a room card in his hand.

"You don't have to use the room card this time. I woke up early, which is a shocker." I opened the door and let him in.

Ashton flashed a smile and walked in. "I was surprised that you actually woke up before I got to your room, at least I don't have to drag you out of bed." Ashton sat on the sofa and placed the laptop on his lap.

I closed my door and stood behind Ashton who was typing on his laptop. I looked at Ashton and observed him, his hair was a bit messier than usual, but I liked it.

I peered over Ashton's broad shoulders and look at the screen; it's the Boston police department website.

"What are you looking for?" I asked him as I placed both of my hands on the top of the sofa.

"I'm looking at the B.P.D. website to see if I can find anything about Rick, I want to learn what he is like from a professional perspective." He clicked on Rick's profile and read articles about him. Ashton moved to the side so I could get a better look at the articles. I moved a bit closer, interested in what kind of things the articles said about him.

We both read all the articles and reports about Rick, I already knew what he does because I have been to the department all the time so it wasn't something new. I let Ashton do his research as I walked up to the coffee table and I sat on the floor, my torso leaning on top of the table. I grabbed the remote and turned the television on. I clicked on the news channel to see if anything had happened, but in a city like this there's a lot of crime happening.

I lay my face on the table and closed my eyes. In some odd way I got used to living in this place even though I'd lived here for only a few days. This place and the people living here made me feel like I'm not alone, what I mean by that is that I know that other people in the world have powers like me.

"Hey Kai, I have something to tell you that's very important when you get injected with the substance." I moved my head to the side to see Ashton looking at me with a frown.

"What is it?" I asked him, my face still lying on the table.

Ashton took a deep breath. "When you get injected with the substance you will get this animal tattoo that represents yourself, think of it as getting a spirit animal tattoo. Ken will use his powers to give you your tattoo without feeling any pain, unlike getting a regular tattoo with those tattoo machines. I just want to let you know that you will get another but much more... revealing."

I already got a tattoo so why not get another one? This is me being sarcastic, I just looked at Ashton. "As long as my tattoo doesn't look bad I'm fine with it." I paused. "Does Ken let me pick where I want it to be put on my body and why does he do this to us?" Now I was starting to feel concerned because I didn't want a tattoo on my face or worse.

"Ken lets you pick where you want your tattoo and he does this because he wants the people who did get injected put into a group so he can use them to complete important missions. Getting this special tattoo somewhat shows who Ken trusts and who is more…superior."

I raised my head up. "Wait. So we're going to be in some special group with other people who are more powerful than most of the 'normal' people with powers in this building? I just got here and Ken wants me to join some group with experienced fighters? That means that I'm going to possibly kill someone, I don't want to kill anyone innocent."

Ashton's mouth moved into a frown. "Don't panic, things will hopefully get better. I'll be here for you if you need someone to talk to or anything at all."

I stared at him, but I had to face the reality, took a deep breath, and exhaled. "Thanks Ash for being my best friend." Ashton is actually a very good and loyal friend to me and I fully trust him. I knew that he would try to help me get out of this building and away from Ken without thinking about himself.

Ashton gave me a surprised look, his lips moving into a soft smile. "Thank you for being my best friend too," he said awkwardly as he blushed.

My head perked up when I remembered that he got injected with the substance. "Wait, that means that you have a tattoo from getting injected. Can I see your tattoo? It's okay if you don't want to, I know this is a personal matter." I was interested in what kind of tattoo Ashton had, but I didn't want to be nosy about it.

Ashton's cheeks turned a light shade of red. "Uhh my tattoo is on my back. But I can show it to you if you're okay with me taking off…my shirt." God this was going to be awkward, I could feel my cheek turning a shade of red.

"It's fine, I just want to have an idea what kind of tattoo style I might have…" I heard my voice getting weird as I said that sentence. I could tell that Ashton felt weird about this because he volunteered to take off his shirt in front of me and I felt weird about it too.

Ashton stood up, turned around, and took off his shirt. I'm so glad he had his back to me because I was blushing like crazy. I couldn't help but notice his muscular arms and his smooth back, thinking about it makes me have butterflies in my stomach.

I looked at his back and I could tell that his tattoo was a centipede colored in red and black ink. I got up off the floor and slowly examined his tattoo closely, looking at all the shapes and colors. It's a very detailed tattoo and I liked the design of it. I hoped my tattoo was cool looking like Ashton's. The centipede's body was swerving in a loose S form. I could tell that the centipede was moving towards Ashton's head because the tail was at his lower back.

"I like your tattoo, hope mine is as nice as yours," I told him as I sat on the sofa.

"Thanks, I like it too." Ashton turned around. I could feel my cheeks becoming warm once again. I looked at his muscular stomach; he literally could be in some sport team in my school because he looked very fit. It made me feel self-conscious about my body because he's all muscles and I'm not.

We both looked at each other but then we looked away. Why am I best friends with him? I don't even look like the kind of girl who hangs out with someone like him, he's like a popular athlete kind of guy and I'm just an outcast. But who really cares? I'm glad that the two of us became best friends.

I placed my hands on cheeks, my face felt so warm. "I should put my shirt on." He said. My eyes glanced at him as he put his shirt on.

I looked away from him before I could do anything weird. I felt my breathing go back to normal. I looked up to him as he sat next to me, his cheeks still slightly pink.

"My tattoo is a centipede, Ken told me that a centipede represents finding my true self and looking at what my heart really wants. To be honest I don't know exactly what I truly want. The tattoo that Ken picked is meant to represent ourselves as a person and it's a good idea because sometimes I have trouble finding who I am, so I just look at my tattoo as a reminder."

"I understand how you feel, I sometimes want to know who I really am, but I never give much effort on something like that. Sometimes I give up on something that I don't care about or want."

"I think we're too young to find who exactly we are yet, but we have enough time to figure it out eventually."

"You're right, but kids like us are always put to some expectations by adults who want what they think is the best for us. I hate when people don't give us the chance to explore new things and learn more about ourselves. To be honest we're not too young to have an idea of what we want to do, I've known what I wanted to do since I came here," I said, leaning my back against the sofa and looking at Ashton.

"And what is that? Ending the organization and escaping?" Ashton asked.

"That's about it. I don't want anyone else to know about this organization or even be involved with it. My parents and Rick wanted to end this organization for a long time now but they haven't been able to do it, we should try and attempt to end this for good."

"We both know this is very risky, Ken has the power to do anything he wants to do. He can even kill someone on the spot." "I don't want you to die because of him."

"I know and you don't have to be worry about me, I can take care of myself. You should be worried about yourself and how you will escape and find Rick. Your life is much more important than mine."

"Don't say that. We'll get out of here together no matter what."

Once again I began to think of multiple scenarios about our escape and none of them turned out well. I hoped for the better when the time came, I just wished that I knew what Rick was doing. I wondered if he was trying to find me or if he gave up on his search.

CHAPTER 18

Rick arrived at John F. Kennedy Airport carrying a black suitcase and a duffel bag. He walked through the airport doors that lead outside to the streets of New York. He took out his phone from his jacket pocket and turned it on, an address of a hotel was shown on the screen.

Rick looked up and scanned his surroundings, people walking up and down the sidewalk, people walking up to the bus, taxis parked in a parking lot waiting for customers, and trees and shrubs decorating the sidewalk.

Rick looked at one of the taxis that was parked in the parking lot and walked towards it. As he was walking to the parking lot he looked back to where the airport doors were at, but there was nobody suspicious who had followed him.

When he walked up to one of the taxis he knocked on the door and a forty year old man woke up from his nap. The man looked at Rick through the window and nodded as he unlocked his car doors and also opened up the trunk.

Rick lifted his suitcase and bag inside the trunk and closed the lid. He rolled his shoulders and walked to the door on the passenger side. He opened the door and sat on the leather seat.

"Where are you heading?" asked the driver.

Rick put on his seatbelt and looked at the driver. "Orchard Hotel on 230 West 101 Street."

The driver nodded and turned on his car and drove out of the parking lot and into the city.

As the taxi was driving the driver started to make light conversation with Rick, who was looking through the window. "So where are you from if you don't mind me asking?" He adjusted his car mirror and look at Rick through the mirror.

"I'm from Boston," Rick replied.

"Boston huh, I heard that the city is much more toned down than New York. This city has a lot of strange characters in it and a lot of crazy shit happens in here but it happens mostly in the sketchy side of the city, so just be careful where you're at."

Rick looked at the driver through the mirror with a curious look. "What do you mean by 'a lot of crazy shit happens'?"

The taxi stopped at a red light and the driver turned around and looked at Rick, who was looking back at him. "There is this rumor that a group or a gang had kidnapped many young people, most of them were either runaways or homeless. The police never found the missing people or the reason why they had been kidnapped. I'm afraid that my daughter might get kidnapped by that group. I wish the police would do a better job protecting the children, you know?" The driver stared at Rick with a heartbroken look, but he turned around and looked at the traffic lights. Rick looked down at his lap and frowned. "But the shit thing is the police kept this problem quiet like they don't want anyone to find out what really is happening." The driver made a sniffing sound as he wiped his eyes with his arm.

"There's a possibility that the police were hiding this because someone wanted to keep this a secret from the public, or else the police might suffer the consequences if they did leak this information out." Rick looked up at the driver who was driving down the busy street. "Do you know anything else about this group? Like do they have any markings or tattoos?"

"I'm sorry but I'm not sure if they do have them, we've never seen the kidnappers before. But you can ask the police, if they'd ever tell you that information." The driver paused. "By the way, why did you come to New York from Boston?"

Rick took a deep breath and rolled up his left sleeve revealing his lotus tattoo. "I'm visiting my family. Maybe it's the last time I will ever see them again," Rick said with harsh look in his eyes.

"Oh, are they moving somewhere?" the driver asked as he grabbed his cup of coffee from his cup holder and drank it.

"I guess it's something like that." Rick looked at his tattoo and rolled down his sleeve, covering it.

The car slowly stopped at a sidewalk that was in front of a large hotel that said, 'Orchard Hotel' on the front of the building. Rick looked at the building and then at the driver. "Hey thanks for the ride and telling me about the kidnappings, I have an idea who did those kidnappings."

"It's no problem, but just be careful about that group, we don't know what they're capable of. Oh and by the way, here's my card if you need any rides from me." The driver took out a small business card that was from his shirt pocket and handed the card to Rick. The card read 'Mark Simmons taxi driver' and it showed his phone number beneath his name.

Rick looked at Mark and nod. "Thanks Mark, my name is Rick Kago just so you know," he said with a smile as he held out his hand to Mark who took his hand.

"Good luck Rick," Mark said as he and Rick shook hands.

"Can you stay here for a couple of minutes? I want to go to the police station after I get settled in," Rick said as he let go of Mark's hand. Mark nodded.

Rick unlocked his seatbelt and put Mark's card in his jacket pocket. Rick got out of the taxi, got his suitcase and bag from the trunk, and closed the trunk. He carried his belongings into the hotel. Inside the hotel people sitting in the waiting room were talking to one another. Pots with colorful flowers decorated the lobby while the floor tiling was a nice brown wood tone that made the lobby look stylish and clean.

Rick walked to the front desk, the lady who was behind the desk greeting him with a smile. "Hello how are you today?" the lady asked Rick. She was wearing a gray and white outfit and a name tag that said 'Rachel.'

"I'm well. I'm Rick Kago, I booked a single bedroom for the next three days," he said as he looked around the hotel lobby.

Rachel typed on the desk computer, took out a room card, and handed it to Rick. "Okay Mr. Kago here is your room card, your room number is 47 and it is on the third floor. Hope you enjoy your stay in New York," she said with a pleasant smile.

Rick nodded as he took the room card and walk to the elevator and pushed a button. The elevator doors opened; there was no one in the elevator. Rick walked inside the elevator and pressed the button that led up to the third floor. The elevator door closed and it moved up all the way to third floor and opened its doors again.

Rick walks out of the elevator and into the long hallway, he look at the doors that had a number on it. He walked down the hallway until he saw a door that has the number 47 on it, and he slid the card into the red card slot that was under the doorknob. The light in the slot turned green and Rick opened the door.

Inside the room was a desk, a mini fridge, a bathroom, a neatly made bed, and a flat screen television on top of a television stand. Rick lifted his suitcase on top of his bed and opened it, taking out his police badge and his laptop. He turned his laptop on and put his badge in his back pants pocket. As the laptop turned on, he kneeled down and placed his right hand on the floor. His hand glowed red and a circle formed on the floor. The circle grew bigger until it flashed red then it disappeared. Rick's hand stopped glowing; he stood up and sat on top of his bed, placing his laptop on his lap.

Rick searched the New York Police Department and typed the address in his phone. He also searched the kidnapping that Mark told him about, but he couldn't find anything about it. Rick closed the laptop with a sigh then got up and put it on the desk. He looked at his bag and placed it next to his suitcase on top of his bed.

He looked at the clock that was on the wall and walked out of his room. When Rick got outside Mark's taxi was still parked in front of the hotel. Rick knocked on the door and Mark looked at him and smiled.

Rick got in the taxi. "So you're actually gonna solve that kidnapping? Or were you joking about that?" Mark said as he turned his car on.

"Hey Mark, can you look at me for a second?" Rick said as Mark turned around. Rick's eyes flashed purple. Mark's eyes also flashed purple; his face turned emotionless for a few seconds.

Mark's face was back to normal like nothing happened. "Uh okay, why do you want me to look at you?" he said, his eyebrow raised.

"Oh it's nothing, I just don't want to get confused with you to someone else, there's a lot of people in this city and sometimes I get faces mixed up. You know what I mean?" Rick said as Mark smiled at him.

"Oh yeah I know what you mean, I sometimes get my wife confused with someone else." Marked turned around and gave a light laugh.

The taxi started to move into the busy street. After a long ride the taxi arrived at the police department. Rick paid Mark for the taxi ride as they said their goodbyes. Rick got out of the taxi and walked up to the building, opening the door. Officers and citizens were all over the place, the building seemed busy at this time.

A woman officer was typing on the computer at the front desk. She looked up at Rick who walked toward her. "May I help you?" the lady said as Rick looked at her nametag. The name tag read 'M. Lenae.' Officer Lenae studied Rick with an intrigued look in her eyes.

"I'm here to see Chief Nethercutt, I have to ask him something important. Is he here?" Rick said as he placed his hands on top of the desk.

"I'm sorry; I cannot let any citizens talk to him unless they are involved with a case."

Rick took out his police badge and placed it on the desk. "I'm Rick Kago, I'm the lieutenant of the Boston Police Department and I need to talk to Chief Nethercutt. I will look for him myself if you're not allowing me to go inside."

Officer Lenae looked at Rick, surprised. "Oh I didn't know that you're an officer, you can go through that door and you'll find Chief Nethercutt in his office," she said nervously.

"Thank you Officer Lenae." Rick gave her a nod and walked through the door that was next to the desk. Officer Lenae blushed and looked at Rick as he walked through the doors.

Rick opened the doors; police officers and staff members were either busy working on their paperwork or talking to one another about their personal lives and other things. Rick looked around the large building but he couldn't find where the chief's office was located. He looked at an officer who was walking in the opposite direction of him.

Rick touched the officer's shoulder to grab his attention. "Excuse me, do you know where Chief Nethercutt's office is?"

The officer stopped walking and looked at Rick. "His office is over there." The man pointed at the office that was on the right side of the large room. The man took another look at Rick. "Are you Lieutenant Kago of B.P.D?"

Rick nodded slowly. "Yes I am, how do you know?" he said curiously.

The officer made a grin. "You have a really famous reputation. Most people here know how you're one of the best officers in the whole city of Boston, heck even in the whole state. It's a great pleasure that I even met you!" The man held out his hand and Rick took it, shaking hands with the officer. "Hey guys look who's here! It's Rick 'Devil' Kago!"

After the man said that, a few officers looked at Rick and walked up to him, forming a small circle surrounding him. "Welcome to New York Lieutenant Kago, hope you like your stay here," said a man who lay his hand on Rick's left shoulder, smiling at him. "The whole force has heard of your famous reputation and I must say I'm very impressed, you're the youngest person to become lieutenant at age twenty-six. Twenty-six! You must be very proud of yourself," the man said with joy.

Rick smiled in embarrassment. "I should be proud, but you guys don't know about my…unpleasant past. I guess someone changed me for the better huh." His smile turned into a sad smile.

"And that person is Chief Fredrick Gray right?" said another person that was in the group. The other officers looked at the man; Rick looked at the man and nodded.

"You're correct it was Chief Gray; it makes sense if you guys know the whole story." Rick put his hands in his pants pockets.

"Wait you didn't know? Basically everyone knew that you used to be in a notorious gang, you were nicknamed the 'Devil' for a reason. You literally punished people who were in your way and the people who threatened you or the gang. I'm surprised that you turned over a new leaf," a woman said who was standing next to Rick.

Rick looked at everyone in the group. "So I guess everyone knew about my past," he said with a pondering look.

"This is one of the reasons why you're so famous in the police community; a young kid who was in a gang who did some illegal things, but all of a sudden an officer changed his life and that officer discovered that kid's potential. That kid grew up to become a well-known officer who solves every cold case that he ever encounters, and that kid was you, but you know, older now," a man said.

"He can even solve challenging cases that don't have enough evidence, but somehow he manages to find the real suspect. It's like he has some special powers that God gave to him. I even talked to Chief Gray about you but all he said is that you're just a genius." Everyone looked at Rick. Rick turned around and saw a man who was wearing a chief's uniform. The man smiled. "And I finally get to meet the genius Lieutenant Kago. I'm Chief Nethercutt." He held his hand toward Rick and Rick took it, shaking hands with Chief Nethercutt.

"Hello Chief Nethercutt, pleased to meet you. May I talk to you privately?" Rick let go of Nethercutt's grip.

Nethercutt looked at the group of people. "Alright guys, time to get back to work." Everyone moved away from Rick and Chief Nethercutt to finish their work, Nethercutt gestured his head towards his office. Nethercutt turned around and walked to his office, Rick following him.

As the two got inside Nethercutt's office, Rick sat down on a chair that was in front of a desk as Nethercutt sat at his desk. In Nethercutt's office the walls were decorated with multiple medals in frames, framed photos of him with other government officials and friends, and a few awards for his work.

"So what brings you here?" Nethercutt asked as he adjusted his necktie.

"I'm here to solve another case that your department cannot solve. I was hoping that you might give me some clues about a particular case." Rick moved closer to Nethercutt. "Do you know anything about multiple kidnappings of young people?"

Nethercutt leaned back onto his chair. "You know that we have many kidnapping cases in the city alone. I can't help you that much on kidnappings in general, there's too many to remember or to look back to. Is that why you're here? Looking for kidnappers?"

"There's this specific kidnapper that I'm looking for, I have an idea who the kidnapper is but you have to help me." He rolled up his jacket sleeve to reveal his lotus tattoo. He looked at Nethercutt and showed him his tattoo. "Do you know about this tattoo? Does any underground group have this exact tattoo on their members?"

Nethercutt leaned closer to Rick and examine his tattoo, Nethercutt's expression turned to concern. He looked at Rick, his lips pressed together. "I know what you're talking about, there's this underground group that experiments with drugs, but we really don't know much about them." Nethercutt stood up and walked to a tall file cabinet and opened one of its drawers, he dug in the drawer to find a folder. "One time a detective wanted to find out who these people are, but at the end it cost him his life." Nethercutt took out a folder and placed the folder in front of Rick on his desk.

Rick opened the folder, inside the folder there were pictures of a dead detective with a note that was pinned on his chest. Rick took the photo and looked at it closely. The detective was at least fifty years old, he was badly beaten and burned, but the most important clue was that his right hand had a seal on the palm. Rick placed the photo on the desk and looked through the papers and pictures in the folder. Rick came across the note that was from the photo of the deceased. The note read 'Don't try to find who we really are or else you will end up like this detective.' At the bottom of the note there was a lotus symbol that was stamped in red ink.

Rick looked closely at the symbol, the red ink looked like dried blood, possibly the blood from the detective "Chief, is this symbol made from the detective's blood?"

Nethercutt closed his eyes and sigh. "Sadly it is, whoever made that note doesn't want the cops to look more into this group. I'm afraid that's all the information I have on this group, but if you need any help I would be happy to lend you a hand."

Rick looked up at Nethercutt. "I don't want anyone else to get hurt because of this, I'll handle this myself." Rick moved some papers out of the folder until he saw a picture of a tall building from afar.

Rick's eyebrows knitted. "Do you know where this building is?" Rick gave the picture to Nethercutt; he examined the picture.

"I don't have an exact location of this building but it should be on the upper west side of the city." Nethercutt put the picture back in the folder. "Are you really going to solve this case? What happens if you end up dead?" Nethercutt looked at Rick with concern.

Rick looked back at Nethercutt. "I won't let that happen to me. Will you excuse me, I have to pay someone a visit," Rick said bitterly as he got up from his chair and walked out of Nethercutt's office.

CHAPTER 19

Someone shook my shoulders, my sore lungs expanded as I breathed. My fingers twitched as the person kept shaking me. I could tell that I was on the sofa because my neck was killing me.

"Kai wake up, napping all day isn't good for your health. Why do you sleep so much?" Ashton's voice echoed through my head.

I opened my eyes and saw Ashton next to me his hands touching my shoulder. "I sleep cuz I got nothing to do," I said in a low tired voice. I closed my eyes but Ashton kept shaking me, making me open my eyes. "Give me a couple more minutes."

"Sorry Kai but Ken just called me, he said that he's almost finished with the substance so he might be done in the mid or late afternoon and it's," Ashton looked at the clock on the wall, "about two so we should get ready." Ashton looked at me and I stretched my fingers.

I let out a yawn. "What time did Ken called you?"

"He called me about a few minutes ago, I wanted to make sure that you knew about this so I woke you up."

I got up as Ashton moved out of the way. I stood up and I instantly had a headache as my vision went blurry. I hate when this happens, I closed my eyes once again and rubbed my temples with my hands. The pain died down, I took a deep breath and exhaled as I opened my eyes.

"Are you okay?" Ashton asked as he looked at me.

"I'm alright, I just got a headache; I shouldn't have gotten up that quickly."

"Do you want me to grab some pain relief medicine for your headache?"

I shook my head. "That's not necessary, it's just a headache. I feel much better now, we should relax and wait for Ken to call us again."

I turned my head towards the kitchen area and walked to the mini fridge. I opened the mini fridge door and took out a bottle of water. I took a sip and closed my eyes and opened them slowly. Ashton sat on the sofa and opened a bag of chips that were on the coffee table. There was a black container on the corner of the coffee table with a pair of chopsticks on top of it.

"What's in the container?" I asked as I grabbed another bottle for Ashton.

"I got some sushi for you. I thought you might get hungry after you took your nap." I sat next to Ashton and gave him the bottled water.

"I guess I need some energy for what's going to happen later on." I took a container of sushi and opened the lid. I grabbed chopsticks and started eating my lunch. The sushi tasted really good, like it had been made fresh.

"In Boston around the Chinatown area, there's this sushi restaurant that serves deep fried sushi," I said as I took a big bite of my sushi.

"Oh really? There's some places like that in New York as well, maybe someday we can go to the one in Boston," Ashton said as he laid back his head on the sofa headrest.

"Since you already got injected, did the substance make your life better than before?" I wondered what the pros and cons of getting injected with this enhancement substance were.

Ashton looked at me, opened the bottle of water and took a sip. He took a long pause, thinking about my question carefully. "After I got injected my senses were much better than before, better than any normal person. I was faster, stronger, more resilient and so on, it made my life a bit better but that's the only good thing that comes out of this. It took about three days to fully develop my new abilities, after I developed my abilities Ken made me get tested in the laboratory. After that he made me train with other people who also got injected with that enhancement substance. Ken made me train with Sean and it wasn't easy, I can't even describe how challenging Sean can be," he said with a long sigh.

Ashton had a tough time in this place, I can't believe other people had been through the same thing as well. I immediately remembered when Ashton and I were in the gym; he said that he can read someone's moves beforehand. "Didn't you have an ability that can read someone's moves, why can't you use it on Sean and beat him up?"

Ashton looked at the bottle in his hand, his eyes looked dull. "I didn't develop that ability on my own."

I scratched my arm. "What do you mean? Did you get injected again?"

"Ken used his powers on me so I would become more skillful. He wanted me to foresee people's moves when I'm in combat, that's why I have this ability, he just wants to use me."

I didn't know what to say after that. Ken used Ashton for his selfish reasons and he didn't care what might happen to him. I knew that Ken did this to other people and it made me irritated.

"So to answer your question, it depends on the situation, it's good to have these abilities, but when you're training or going on missions. But that's my opinion, maybe you might experience something much more different than what I have been through," Ashton said placing the bottle on the table.

"I guess we'll have to see it for ourselves." I took another bite of my sushi. "I can handle getting injected with that substance, it's like getting a flu shot but more intense." I couldn't handle doing this, but I didn't want Ashton to be uneasy about this. I had to face it like a mature young adult. I knew there'd be no turning back after getting injected with that substance.

I hoped that when we contacted Rick he'd show up and save us before something major happened. I had a weird feeling that something crazy was going to happen after I got injected, maybe it was my anxiety making me feel uncertain about this..

After I finished my lunch, Ashton and I were looking at his laptop. We looked up different shows or movies that I thought he would like to watch. I showed him an episode of one of my favorite anime. In the series, the main character doesn't have superpowers, unlike most people in his world. He has always wanted to become a superhero like his idol, a famous superhero. He somehow met his idol and gained powers from him and they became close friends. The main character got into a school that helps train students to become superheroes themselves. I could continue, but I might end up spoiling the whole anime.

"So everyone in that world has powers like us but they live their lives with powers like it's no big deal. I wonder if in the future most people will have powers like us," he said without taking his eyes off of the screen.

"I never actually thought of that before and if it did happen then life would be a lot more interesting." I would be scared but amazed at the same time if everyone in the world had superpowers.

We watched both seasons one and two for about three hours and it made my eyes burn, I should let my eyes rest for a bit. I looked at the screen where the time is and it's five in the afternoon, meaning that I might go down to the laboratory at any time.

I looked at Ashton who didn't even move from his spot, his eyes fixed on his laptop screen. I poked him in the arm; he turned his head and blinked. He winced and rubbed his eyes.

"How long have we been watching?" he groaned, running his hand through his hair.

"It's been about three hours. I think it's better to do something else because my eyes are becoming dry." I got up and slowly walked to the bathroom.

I leaned on the sink and turned on the faucet as I let my hands touch the cold water. I cupped my hands together and moved them towards my face. The water felt nice on my skin and made me more awake.

I grabbed a small towel on a hook to wipe my face with, after that I placed the towel on the counter. I leaned closer to the mirror, examining the little details of my face. There were lines under my eyes, maybe because I slept too much or too little, it made me look tired which I am already. I took a deep breath and exhaled, I lean back and walked out of the bathroom.

As I walked through the bathroom's doorway I saw Ashton sitting on the sofa with his arms wrapped around a small pillow. He had his eyes closed and he wasn't moving, I thought he fell asleep. I quietly walked back to my room.

I sat on my desk chair and open a drawer, inside were stacks of lined and unlined paper, pencils, pens, scissors, stapler, and other office supplies. I took out a small stack of papers and a pen.

I closed the desk drawer; I took the pen and placed a single sheet of paper in front of me. I began writing all of Rick's information on it such as phone number, email, and home address for Ashton in case anything happened to the two of us.

It'd been at least an hour since I started using Ashton's laptop. I thought Ken would call by now, I guess he wasn't finished yet. Hope that Ken will do this tomorrow because I'm nervous about getting injected. I hate getting poked by sharp objects like needles, I can't even stand seeing someone get stabbed or slashed even if it's fake like in the movies.

I stretched my arms and looked to my side to see Ashton still sleeping. All of a sudden Ashton's phone rang, and I jumped! Ashton moved his arm and grabbed his phone that was next to him and slowly opened his eyes. His eyes instantly looked more awake. He looked at me and gave me a nod, I gave a nod back.

Ashton tapped on his phone and brought his phone to his right ear. "Yes?" I already knew who's on the other line, during a few seconds of the phone call Ashton kept saying 'okay' and 'yes.'

He brought his phone down and tapped on the screen, he didn't say anything for a few seconds. He took a deep breath and looked at me. "It's time."

We locked eyes. "I'm ready." I stood up and stretched my arms again as I walked to the door.

He stood up and looked at me. "Are you going to get your room card?"

I didn't look back at him. "You have my room card, right? So there's no need for me to bring it if you have the same exact card." I opened the door and walked out, looking at the view through the window in front of me.

Ashton walked out and closed the door, we both walked side by side in silence until we reached the laboratory.

I opened the door and we both walked inside the large room, a few people in white lab coats were scattered throughout the room doing their work. I saw Ken sitting at a table, waiting for Ashton and me to join him. I walked to Ken and sat on an empty chair that was closest to him, Ashton sat next to me.

Ken smiled at us. "I called the two of you down here because I'm done with Kai's special substance. Kai are you ready?" His eyes were twinkling with amusement.

"Yes I am," I said calmly. This is it; it's going to happen and I can't turn back. I felt my stomach turning and it made me feel a bit sick.

"Let's go to one of the private rooms in the lab." Ken stood up and nodded to Ashton. "You can come also Ashton."

I looked at Ashton; he nodded at Ken and got up. I got up and followed Ken to the side of the lab where there were double doors in the wall. Ken opened the door and walked in, as I walked in there were multiple rooms on one side. In one of the rooms I passed by I saw a man who was strapped to a chair in the middle of the room. The man wasn't moving. When I saw him it made my stomach turn. I might end up like him, dead or in a coma. I shouldn't think like that, he could be sleeping.

I could feel my forehead sweat with nervousness. I turned my head away from the man and wiped my forehead with my right arm. I looked straight ahead, not looking at Ashton or the man in the room. We walked near the end of the corridor. Ken stopped at the room and opened the door for us.

I was the first to walk inside the room; everything looked the same as the other rooms that I passed. The medical chair was in the middle of the room. To the left of the chair was a small moveable table that had multiple medical tools on it. On the right side of the chair there was another small table, on the table there were two large syringes with a red colored substance in one syringe and the other, yellow. Looking at that made me feel sicker.

Ken closed the door and walked to the chair. "Come and sit here Kai." He gestured his hand to the chair. I nodded and glanced at Ashton; his eyes looked empty, his lips pressed together.

I looked at the chair and sat on it. My heart beat fast as I sat on the chair looking around the empty room. I hate getting shots, I hated that there were two large syringes that I had to get injected with. I took a deep breath and exhaled slowly.

Ken's hand reached down to his lab coat pocket and took out a pair of rubber gloves. He put them on as he looked at the tray with the medical tools on it.

"Why do you have two syringes?" I asked him as he stood beside me next to the table with the syringes.

Ken looked at me and laid his hand on my shoulder. "One of the substances is made from your father's DNA and the other is made from my own DNA, I want you to become powerful like your grandpa. I know this looks scary, but it's worth it. You will have superhuman strength and an indestructible body like your father, and incredible powers and abilities from me. You will be one of the most powerful people in the whole organization," he said with determination.

Ken grabbed a cotton swab from a table on the other of me; he also got a small container that was filled with clear liquid. He dipped the cotton swab in the small container and wiped it on the area where my arm bends.

"Hey Ken, what is the area where my arm bends called?" I asked. I didn't know the name of this area in my arm and I was also testing his knowledge of anatomy. If he's a real scientist then he will answer this question without hesitation and with confidence.

"Oh, the area where I just wiped your arm? It's called the antecubital fossa," he replied, giving me a delighted smile. Yep he's a scientist that's for sure.

He put the cotton swab on the table and took one of the syringes with the red substance in it with one hand, his other hand laying my arm on the armrest. I felt myself breathe hard.

Ken looked at me, noticing that I was slightly panicking. "Are you okay?"

"I'm okay, I just want this to be over with," I said stiffly and quietly. Ken nodded and touched my left arm. I closed my eyes; I didn't want to see this. The needle of the syringe poked me. I let out a muffled yell. I clamped my eyes shut as the pain increased when Ken injected the substance into me. I thought getting a regular shot hurts, but this is one hundred times worse, it made my whole body feel like it was on fire! I could feel my left arm getting numb, I clenched my teeth together.

I could feel the needle move away from my arm. I opened my eyes just a little bit and looked down at my left arm. A bead of blood was now on my arm where Ken put the needle in, I felt sick now, this was much worse than getting a flu shot. He placed the empty syringe on the table next to him.

Ken grabbed the cotton swab and wiped it on the spot the blood was coming out of. As he wiped my arm I could feel a slight sting. Why do I have to have weak arms? Ken took a bandage out of his pocket and placed it on my antecubital fossa.

I looked closer at my arm to see my blue veins turn crimson red. I let out a quivery sigh; it wasn't that bad, it only hurt for a few minutes, but now my arm felt completely numb.

Ken walked to the other side of me and wiped the cotton swab on the same spot as my other arm. Ken held my arm and injected the other syringe with the yellow colored substance in it, this time I didn't close my eyes. Ken slowly injected the needle into my arm, the pain felt much worse than with the other substance. My veins slowly turned yellow from the substance; the pain made my eyes watery. My right arm went numb. Ken pushed the syringe until the substance inside it was completely gone.

When the substance was gone he slowly removed the syringe from my arm and my arm started bleeding again. I looked up and saw Ashton with a sickening look on his face. I wish he wasn't here to see me like this. Ken rubbed the cotton swab on my arm and put a bandage on it. He took off his gloves and put them on the table beside him. He put both of his hands on my shoulders and moved closer to me, hugging me.

"You did well Kai, your arms might be numb for a while but I bet you're going to get better by tomorrow. This is a new beginning for your new self, you should be happy. When you feel much better I'll let you train with Ashton and try to improve your skills for missions and such." He pulled away from our hug. "Oh I forgot to tell you that you'll get a tattoo, everyone who gets injected with this special substance is required to have it. The tattoo that I personally make is an animal that represents you as a person such as a spirit animal, I'm sorry that I didn't tell you the other day." Ken held up two glowing yellow fingers and he touched them to my forehead.

I didn't move an inch as Ken's fingers touched my forehead. It'd been a few minutes and Ken didn't move, maybe he was reading my memories or something. Ken moved his fingers away from my head as he looked down at me.

"You have this power that can change people's lives and make something of yourself, but you didn't seem to know you had it. You have a good heart but your mind is dark, you feel things that make you feel empty and sad, but you choose not to show it. You hide your feelings from people making you feel isolated inside; you never let people see your real self." His hands glowed yellow. "Where do you want your tattoo to be located?"

I looked at his hands then up at his face. "Left arm," I said weakly, both my arms so numb that I couldn't even slightly move them. I felt sick again, I actually wanted another tattoo but it's going to be more noticeable. What will Rick say about my new tattoo, if I ever see him again.

Ken hands reached towards my left arm and touched it, his hands glowing intensely as shapes and lines started to slowly appear on my arm. My head started to hurt but I just ignored it. My eyes started to fade black in the corners, the inside of my body felt hot. My arms started to feel like pins were jabbing everywhere in my arms, but it still felt numb.

That substance did something to me, I felt lightheaded. I looked at Ashton who was gawking helplessly at me. I couldn't help but notice that Ashton looked very ill. I wonder what he's thinking right now. I swallowed saliva from my mouth, but it still felt dry.

I lay back and looked at the white ceiling, everything instantly went black.

CHAPTER 20

I opened my eyes; a beam of light hit my face as my eyes started to burn. I blinked my eyes continuously until they adjusted to the light and were able to see the blue sky and the clouds above me.

"I turned my head to the side so that I wouldn't get burned by the sun, as I opened my eyes once more I see a field of white lilies surrounding me. I quickly sat up and my head started to ache, it's a bad idea to get up fast. I rubbed the temples of my head until the headache became better

I opened my eyes as my headache started to fade away, all I could see was a large field of white lilies and a few tall trees randomly placed. What the hell am I doing here? Is this another weird dream?

I turned my head to look at the whole place, nothing but trees and flowers. I lazily got up and dusted myself off. I looked down at my clothes; I was wearing the same white dress that I wore in my dream with Rick. I moved my feet out and saw that I wasn't wearing any shoes or socks.

I had noticed that my left arm was partly tattooed. I could clearly see the shape of my tattoo, but not what it was yet. I looked up as I breathed heavily. How would the people that I know react to my new tattoo?

I closed my eyes and tried to breathe slowly, attempting to calm myself down. I opened my eyes and looked at the ground where I lay. I took a huge step back. There were black lilies that formed a silhouette of my body, none of the lilies were bent which was very strange.

I stepped on a black lily to see if it would bend, but it didn't. It seemed like nothing had happened to it, this was very odd.

I turned around to look at the field, trying to find something that might help me get out of there. I walked to nowhere in particular. I tried to forget the black lilies but it wouldn't leave my mind, it was no coincidence that those lilies were shaped in a perfectly human silhouette.

I clenched my teeth together and continued walking, my feet stomping on the white lilies, making them bend. I needed to get out of there. I looked at my right palm and saw the seal that Ken put on me.

"Shit," I said quietly to myself, I still couldn't use my powers here.

My feet became stained with dirty from the earthy ground. I looked up to see clouds in different shades of white slowly move with me as I strolled through the endless field. Everything at the moment became calm and nice. I wish my life would be this peaceful.

I looked straight ahead to see the endless field of white lilies. I wonder what's going to happen next. What will happen to me in this dream? Am I going to get shot by that yellow arrow again or something much worse?

I needed to wake up from this place. I held up my two hands up to my face and smacked the side of my face. I really need to wake up, I know this is a dream.

I turned around to see the field of white lilies changed to black lilies like a flood. I stopped walking and stood in the same spot not moving, maybe this was the way to get out of this dream. I waited for the flood of black lilies coming towards me, when it reached me the flood didn't stop moving.

Nothing happened for the moment. I walked straight in front of me, my arms feeling tingly like something was crawling under my skin. My mouth started to taste bitter. I looked up and saw no clouds in the blue sky. I started to feel an odd sensation in my body, maybe it's the unsettling atmosphere in this place.

As I was walking my whole body suddenly went through the ground, I let out a gasp as I fell into darkness.

I slowly opened my eyes to the bright light of a room, everything in my body feeling severely numb. I couldn't even turn my head, so I just stared at the white ceiling. How long was I going to be like this? Is this what people who are paralyzed feel like? This was horrible.

I heard a sink faucet turn on in the bathroom, I tried to talk but couldn't make any sounds. This is useless I hope I get better today or at least able to feel my limbs.

What happened in that laboratory? I remember that I got injected with two substances, started to get my tattoo, but nothing else after that. What's going to happen to me now?

The faucet turned off and someone open the bathroom door from down the hall. I heard the person's footsteps come closer to me. I slowly blinked my eyes; Ashton's head came to my view.

He made a smile. "I'm glad you're awake, you have been out for at least a day and a half. I have never seen anyone who got injected twice in the same day. I'm happy that you're alive and breathing," he said, relieved.

I tried to talk but I couldn't even feel my mouth moving. How long was I going to be like this? My last memory was when Ken was creating my tattoo with his powers. My eyes went wide as I looked at Ashton who gave me a confused look. I needed to see my tattoo right now.

I blinked my eyes because I could feel them becoming dry. Ashton placed a wet towel on my forehead. I felt the slight coolness of the towel against my skin.

He looked at my left arm and then back at me. "I know what you're thinking, 'I wonder what my tattoo look like' right? I took a picture of your arm so you can look at it without getting up to look at it yourself. I want you to be relaxed, please don't panic about it," he said as he took something from his back pocket. I can't believe I got another tattoo and I can't even get up to look at it because I'm temporarily paralyzed.

Ashton move out of my view for a few minutes, then he came back to my view. "I'm going to show you your tattoo, in my opinion I think it looks very nice and I hope you like it," he said in a nervous tone.

He held his phone over my face so I could look at the picture. My eyes slowly adjusted the screen, my vision became very clear. In the picture my whole arm was covered in red and black ink. I slowly examined my arm and noticed that the tattoo was a dragon like an Asian style drawing of a dragon. The dragon has multiple designs on its scales and some parts of its body it have multiple masks on it. Those masks are actually well drawn; it looks like the masks show a representation of different emotions. When I look at the dragon's face near my lower arm it has its mouth open, showing its sharp teeth. The dragon's body swirls around my whole arm; near my lotus tattoo the dragon's body surrounds the lotus tattoo. I thought it was a good thing because I don't want it to cover my other tattoo. I actually like my sleeve tattoo but I couldn't believe I had a whole arm sleeve tattoo. My eyes slowly relaxed, I blinked multiple times so my eyes wouldn't be dry once again.

I looked at Ashton who was still holding his phone in front of my face. I blinked at him and he put his phone away.

"Do you like your tattoo? Blink twice for yes and close your eyes for no," he said as he looked at me with suspense.

I blinked twice and he made a relieved smile. "I'm glad you like it too; I hope you get better so you can actually walk or talk." He moved out of my view, I wished that I didn't feel so numb so I could actually get up and talk to Ashton.

After I recovered we had to contact Rick. I tried to make a sound but nothing came out. We needed to get Rick right now. I couldn't wait another minute to be stuck here, especially when I couldn't even move a single muscle.

"I don't know how long your powers are going to take to fully develop. Ken said that we have to give it a few days to see your results. Just to remind you, after you get injected the beginning is always the hardest so don't be surprised that it is." In the corner of my eye I saw Ashton standing next to me, he leaned closer to my ear. "I know that we have to go with the plan but I want to wait until you fully recover..." He paused like he's contemplating about what he's going to say next. He shifted his eyes away from me and looked through the window in the room. I wonder what he's thinking about. Ashton's eyes met mine. I could see bits of gold in his green iris. I could hear myself breathing hard because he was so close to my face or maybe he was going to say something important. "Kai…" he said quietly, "I don't want you to die because of me. Don't try to save me from this place; I don't deserve your kindness." He sharply inhaled. "You don't know the real me. You don't know what I'm capable of," he whispered, his eyes searching mine, he pressed his lips together. We never looked away from each other's gaze. "I know that you can't talk but I have to tell you something, something bad that I did." He suddenly looked very ill; his skin turned slightly pale. "Something that I still regret to this day."

Ashton moved his head away from me and sat on the edge of my bed and looked at the floor in front of him. I could only see his back so I just looked up at the ceiling. "I need to tell you what happened to my best friend. It's okay if you don't like me after I tell you my story, I understand." I heard him take a deep breath and exhale. I wished I could tell him that I didn't care what he did in the past and that I only cared about what he did now. "During my time in this building I made enemies and friends, I was careful of who I trusted and who I didn't trust. I only trust a few people in this place and that says a lot, you're one of those people who I trust. There is one person who first became my closest friend and then turned into my best friend, well used to be. His name was Carlos Santos. We had been close friends for at least four years and we have been through a lot together. I thought I really knew him but I was wrong. I guess I was still naive at the time." I heard him make a sniffing sound. I wished that I wasn't paralyzed so I could tell him not to be depressed or sad about this. "All these years that I knew him I didn't know that he was against this organization, against me…" His voice faded. "How could I have known that he worked with the people who are against us? The two of us told each other our secrets that we never told anyone else about. How could he have kept this from me? When Ken found out that Carlos was giving our personal information to another group he was furious, I've never seen Ken act like that. I was there when Ken tortured Carlos, at the time I was angry at him because he lost my trust. I thought I had someone who I could actually trust but I was wrong, I still feel bitter when I think about it." Ashton ran his right hand through his hair and he turned his head to look at me. I tried so hard to make any noises or move any of my limbs but I couldn't do it.

He gave me a sad smile. I couldn't help but notice that his eyes were watery. It made me feel ashamed of myself for just listening to him and not doing anything. "After Ken and I interrogated Carlos to tell him about what exactly he was doing with the organization's information, Ken ordered me to…kill him after he got what he wanted from him." He looked away from my eyes and placed his left hand on top of my mattress. "Deep down inside I didn't want to kill him, but I had to obey Ken. You know that room where you got injected yesterday? It was the exact room where I killed him. I don't know which is more haunting: killing my best friend or that his last words were 'I'm sorry Ash.' It's hard to say, they both haunt me in the back of my mind." He bit his bottom lip as he closed his eyes.

Ashton opened his eyes, but he didn't look at me. "But it doesn't matter anyway. He's dead." He didn't say anything else for a couple of minutes. He held my left hand and looked at me. I could slightly feel the warmth of his hand. "I'll try to get you out of here even if it kills me. Don't think about saving me when you get out of here. I don't deserve to live for all the things I did to the people I killed and tortured." He made a pause. "I'll grab something for you to drink. I'll be back in a few minutes." Ashton let go of my hand and got up and walked out of my view. There were so many emotions swarming around my head and in my heart that it made me feel sick. My throat felt like it was burning and I let out a weird gasping noise.

I heard the fridge door open and close. I also heard his footsteps coming closer toward my bedroom, he entered the room. "I have water."

Ashton sat on the edge of the bed next to me. He opened a water bottle and placed it on a nightstand next to my bed. He positioned his body so that he was facing me.

I looked at Ashton who took out a yellow pill from the nightstand. "Kai, I need you to take this, this pill will help you recover faster," he said as he moved some strands of my hair out of my face.

He moved his right hand to hold the back of my head and tilt my head up. He moved the other hand to grasp my chin and slowly opened my mouth, and placed the pill on my tongue. He grabbed the opened water bottle and tilted the bottle on my lips so I could swallow the pill. I felt awkward that he had to take more care of me because I was very weak. I could see that my eyes were getting watery. I felt a tear trickle down my face.

Ashton saw that I was crying, he placed my head back onto my pillow. He capped the water bottle and placed it on the nightstand. He turned back to me and wiped my tears with his sleeve of his shirt, I avoided his gaze. "I'm sorry that I made you sad. I shouldn't have told you that story. But now since you took that pill you will get better by tomorrow, so you should rest," he said as he wiped more tears from my face.

I still couldn't feel my limbs but I could manage to make some noises. I slowly gained my voice just a little bit, but it hurt when I tried to talk. I wanted to tell him everything that I wanted to say to him, but I had to rest so I would recover better.

"I'm going to save you no matter what," I said in a frail voice, my voice burning when I talked, but I needed to tell him this.

Ashton looked at me with a frown. "I told you, don't even think about saving me."

"I don't care, you're too important to me to let you go." I slowly inhaled and exhaled, my throat stung but I pushed on. "I know you want me to get out of here safely as possible," I weakly inhaled, "but I don't care what's going to happen to me. You will get out of here, that's a promise," I said, looking at him.

"Not all promises are meant to be kept, I should know."

I immediately felt lightheaded and sleepy. I tried to open my eyes but I gave into the darkness.

In the city of New York, people walked up and down the sidewalk as they looked at their surroundings. Buildings of different sizes lined next to the sidewalk, loud chatter from people can be heard from afar. The light blue sky was cloudless; the only thing in the sky was pigeons flying left and right, and the bright sun beaming down on the city.

Rick walked down the quiet street passing shops, buildings, and people. He took out his phone from his jacket pocket and typed on it; he looked up and kept walking. He looks around the street until he stopped at a restaurant. Rick looked through the window. There were a few people sitting at different tables talking to someone and eating their meals. Rick looked at the address on his phone; it was the same address as the restaurant.

He put his phone in his jacket pocket and opened the restaurant door. As he was walking inside the restaurant he was greeted by a young waiter with light brown hair and brown eyes. He also was wearing a gray apron with a name tag on it that said 'Simon.'

"Hello welcome to Local Flavours, table for one?" Simon said as he grabbed a menu from the front desk.

"I'm here to see someone who works here, does the name Stefano Alfonsi sound familiar to you?" Rick said as he put his hands in his pants pocket.

Simon looked at Rick and put the menu back on the desk. "Yeah he's the owner of this restaurant, do you want me to get him for you?"

"Yes please. I'll wait in one of the tables here." Rick nodded at Simon and walked to a table near the window far away from the other people in the restaurant. He looked back and saw Simon walking to the door that led to the back room.

Rick look around the restaurant, everything seemed nice and clean as any nice restaurants in the area. He looked through the window, people walking down the streets, cars passing by, etc. A father and a young son talked to each other as they were walking down the street. Rick exhaled and looked away from the window.

Simon and a man who was in his late fifties walked side by side, Rick looked at both of them as they walked towards him.

Rick stands up. "Are you Stefano Alfonsi?" He looked at the man; the man looked a bit similar to Simon.

The man nodded and held out his hand. "The one and only, who's asking?"

Rick shook Stefano's hand. "I'm Rick Kago, I need to talk to you privately if that's okay with you?"

Stefano looked at Simon. "You can leave us son." Simon nodded at Rick and then at Stefano. Stefano looked at Rick and leaned closer. "I already know who you are from your older brother, why are you here?" he asked in a serious tone.

"I'm here to find that bastard and my father. Do you know where they are?"

Stefano snorted. He knit his eyebrows together. "I know where they are but I don't want to help someone like you. I don't want to ruin my business relationship with your father. Leave." He stared daggers at Rick, Rick's jaw tightened.

"No, you don't have to tell me willingly. I'll make you tell me." Rick's eyes flickered purple, Stefano's facial expression turned emotionless. "I guess I have to do this my way," Rick said to himself, he looked at Stefano. "Take me somewhere private where no one will disturb us."

Stefano turned around and walk through the restaurant. Rick followed him to the back of the restaurant and into a room where the door said, 'Manager's Office.'

Rick closed the door behind him as he walked into the room. Stefano stood in the middle of the room, waiting for Rick's next instructions. Rick walked towards Stefano, his hands glowed red.

Rick placed his glowing fingers on Stefano's forehead, Stefano didn't move. A few minutes passed. Rick moved his finger away from Stefano's head.

"Go have a seat on that chair," Rick said, pointing at the desk chair.

Stefano followed Rick's orders and sat on the chair, looking at Rick with a blank stare. Rick's eyes flash purple and Stefano instantly passed out on the chair. Rick looked at Stefano, his eyes hardening. He turned around and walked out of the office door leaving Stefano in the room.

As Rick walked through the restaurant Simon went up to him. "What happened?"

Rick looked at Simon, his face softened. "It's nothing serious, just regular talk. Stefano is taking a nap in his office, just to let you know. Will you excuse me, I have something to do." Rick looked at Simon and then walked toward the restaurant doors.

Rick walked out into the sidewalk, not looking back at Simon who was looking at Rick with a concerned look on his face.

CHAPTER 21

I slowly opened my eyes to the darkness. I let out a yawn and rolled to the side so I was looking at a clock that was in the front of the room. The clock read 3:38am. How long was I sleeping?

I lazily got up and stretched my arms and legs; I finally didn't feel numb anymore. I got out of bed. My feet touched the cold tile floor, giving me goose bumps on my arms and legs. I stumbled through the hallway and into the bathroom.

I stood in front of the sink and the large mirror as I washed my face with cold water. I looked at the mirror in front of me; I looked very pale and tired. I noticed that I had a different pair of clothes on me, I wore a gray t-shirt and black sweatpants. I guess Ashton or someone else changed my clothes for me.

My eyes moved down to my left arm that now had a big tattoo of a dragon all over it. I moved my left arm to my face so I could look at every detail of my tattoo. I felt calm about my new tattoo. Getting another tattoo doesn't bother me at all; I loved the style and everything about it.

I wiped my face with a dry towel and looked at myself once again. I couldn't believe all of this was happening to me. I placed the towel on the sink counter and looked at both of my arms; the veins in both were back to their original blue color. I wonder when I'll develop my other powers.

I scratched my head and looked at the shower through the mirror. I turned around to open the shower door and turned the shower knob.

After my nice relaxing shower I sat on my sofa watching a television show, I didn't feel like sleeping again. As I was watching television I was thinking about what happened with my conversation with Ashton. All the personal things he said to me, it made me feel sad for him. Maybe because he pitied me or that he needed someone to talk to about his problems. I needed to keep my promise to him, but he said that promises can be broken. I'm going to prove him wrong.

I turned off the television and grabbed my room card from my desk and walked to my mini fridge; I really needed something sugary to drink. I took out a bottle of soda and drank half the bottle. I eventually drank the whole bottle in one gulp.

I put the empty bottle in the trash bin and walked out of my room and to the long hallway. I closed my door and made sure it's locked. I looked down at my feet and realized that I'm only wearing socks. I don't care if I'm wearing socks or shoes as along my actual feet are not touching the floor.

No one was in the hallway, which was good, but also creepy since it was nighttime and I was the only person out there. At least the hallway lights were on. I turned to the right and walked three doors down where a door was labeled 219. I knocked on the door and waited for Ashton to open it.

After a minute I knocked again then I heard footsteps on the other side of the door. I heard the door unlock and then it opened. Ashton was standing on the other side of the door wearing a black tank top and black jogger sweatpants.

He moved out of the way to let me into his room. "I'm glad that you're awake now, come in," he said, yawning.

"That pill actually helped me feel much better, thanks for giving me that," I said as I sat on the sofa.

Ashton closed the door and locked it. "It's no problem; Ken gave it to me, if you need help recovering. I guess you want to talk about what we're going to do next right?" he said, walking to the sofa to sit next to me. "But first are you sure that you're fully recovered? Do you feel any numbness or pain anywhere?"

I looked at my arms and legs and stretched them. "I would say that I'm fully recovered, thank you for taking care of me. Now we have to talk about our next step in our plan." The two of us locked eyes. "We need to contact Rick," I said quietly.

Ashton raised an eyebrow. "You just woke up from your coma, could you just wait for a few days until you develop your powers to do this?"

"We don't know when exactly I will develop my powers or abilities; it could be days, weeks, or even months until I gain them. The substance is in my system for two or three days, there might be a chance that I might develop my powers today or tomorrow. I don't want to waste my time here. I want the two of us to get out of here as soon as possible."

"We're risking everything. What happens if Rick never shows up? Then we have to face Ken and the others by ourselves. If that did happen then we're in big trouble." Ashton began to look concerned as he said that.

"I understand you have doubts and so do I, but we need to have faith in Rick."

Ashton let out a long sigh. "If you want to contact him, then you should use my burner phone. This can buy us time, but I'm not sure if Rick will pick up the phone."

"He has to pick it up, I have a gut feeling that he will help us get out of here," I said, looking away from Ashton's stare.

"Okay we'll try to call him with my burner phone. No one will know where the phone is because I will completely destroy the phone after we make that call. We only have one chance to tell him where we are and to warn him about his father and siblings." He stood up and walked through the hallway.

He walked back to the living room holding a small flip phone. He opened it and it turned on, he walked back to the sofa and sat next to me.

"Are you sure you want to do this? It's early in the morning, I don't think he'll pick up," Ashton worried as he handed me the phone.

"Rick always gets emergency calls from his work during late night and early morning. He's always ready when someone calls him at any time," I said, looking at the phone.

I took a deep breath and typed in Rick's phone number. I looked at Ashton who was as nervous as me, and pressed the call button. I placed the phone at my right ear. I let out a shaky breath as the phone started ringing. The phone picked up; my heart was rapidly beating.

"Hello, Rick?" I said quietly. Ashton and I both exchanged looks. I put the phone on speaker so Ashton could hear Rick on the line.

The person on the other line laughed and it didn't sound like my Rick, my heart dropped. I gripped the phone tighter. "Who is this?" I demanded.

"Do you really think I would be that ignorant to let you and Ashton escape that easily?" said the person on the other line. Fear took over, it's over.

Aston quickly grabbed the phone and ended the call. He looked at me with widened eyes. I've never seen him look so scared. His chest was moving up and down and his skin turned pale white.

"Kai." He looked at the phone and then at me. "That was Ken."

I didn't move a muscle or said a word. I was still processing what had just happened. I looked at Ashton. "Are you really sure that's Ken?" I said nervously, laughing it off.

Aston looked at me with a serious look and his jaw clenched. "I'm positive that's Ken, who would say something like that?" He looked around his room. "We have to get out of here; Ken now knows that you and I are trying to escape." He got up and walked towards his closet.

I looked at the clock on the wall in front of me; it read 4:13 am. "We're so screwed." I put my face in my hands and let out a groan, this can't be happening. Where's Rick, is he even trying to find me or did something happen to him?

Ashton grabbed something inside of the closet and took out a large black duffel bag. He carried the bag, straps on his shoulders, and walked towards me.

"If Ken knows what we're doing, he'll try to get us or send people to do it for him. We need to get ready and we have to run." He placed the bag on top of the coffee table and walked back to his closet.

I opened the bag. Inside the bag was different varieties of weapons and gear. "Do you really expect me to use these weapons? I can't even use my own powers since Ken put this damn seal on me since I got here," I said, holding a small silver tube and looking closely at it.

"We have to find a way to defend ourselves from the people who are trying to get us or even kill us. I just wish that Ken would unseal you so you can use your powers to teleport us away from here." Ashton took out a black long sleeve shirt and black hoodie jacket. He turned around and looked at me. "Kai be careful with that, it's a collapsible bo staff, I don't want it to hit you in the eye." I put the tube back in the bag as Ashton walked into the bathroom.

I rubbed my temples and clench my jaw. I shouldn't have done that. I should have known that I wouldn't get out of here easily. I let out a frustrated groan. I could feel myself breathe hard, my lungs starting to hurt. I think I'm hyperventilating. I'm in over my head, what am I going to do?

Ashton got out of the bathroom wearing his new clothes. He noticed that I was hyperventilating and sat next to me rubbing my back. "Hey, don't worry, we just have to find a place to lay low. I know a few places to stay but you have to stay strong for me," he said, placing his hands on my shoulders.

I let out a quivery sigh. "What happens if it's too late, what happens if they already found us?" I closed my eyes, trying to calm myself down but that didn't help at all. "What happens if Rick never comes? There's a lot of buildings like this, it would take time to find out which building we're in."

"Kai don't panic, we're going to get out of here no matter what." I opened my eyes to see Ashton looking at me. "We made a promise to each other and I'm planning to keep my side of the promise."

I made a fist on top of my lap. "I know Ash, I'm trying not to feel overwhelmed." I looked around the room and then at Ashton. "I need to get changed," I said standing up.

"Wait, don't go outside yet, I need to pack some things and then we'll go to your room. I don't want you to go out there alone." Ashton took out a small gun and loaded it with bullets. He also checked all the weapons in his bag to make sure that they were in good shape.

After ten minutes of Ashton preparing his weapons and me panicking internally, we finally got ready to head out. I didn't think anyone would be out walking in the building at this time; at least we wouldn't get caught by anyone. Hopefully.

Ashton and I were standing at his door. I got my room card out and Ashton was carrying his bag. We exchanged glances and I opened the door and ran to my room sliding my card into the card slot. Ashton closed his room door and ran behind me. I open the door and quickly ran inside. Ashton closed the door behind him and locked the door.

I was breathing hard as Ashton set his bag down on the sofa. I walked to my closet and picked out a black t-shirt, dark blue jeans, and black and white sneakers. "Do you know where we're going to hide?" I asked as I got inside the bathroom.

"I know a hiding spot in the library; I don't think most people know about that spot so it's a good place to settle," he said as I changed into my newly picked clothes.

I got out of the bathroom and walked to my mini fridge to get a soda. I twisted the cap and drank the whole bottle. I dumped the empty bottle in the trash bin that was next to the door that led outside. I needed all the energy for the morning and for the rest of the day.

Then I remembered that I had put my photo of my parents in the desk drawer. I quickly walked into my room and to my desk, opening the desk drawer. Inside the drawer were a few office supplies and my photo. I took the photo and looked at it again. I exhaled and folded the photo, put it in my pants pocket, and closed the drawer. I walked back into the living room where Ashton walked left and right, thinking about something.

"Here's a question, do we need anything else before we're going on the lam?"

"We got all the things we need to defend ourselves, it's better that we go now before Ken sends more people to find us." Ashton got up, slung his bag across his back, and walked next to me. "Let me go first, then you follow me okay?" He took out two pairs of black gloves from his pants pocket. "It's better if we wear gloves so no one would find our fingerprints you know."

I took the gloves and put them on. "Thanks." We both walked toward my door and paused, listening to any noises from outside.

Ashton slowly opened the door and peeked his head out into the hallway. He opened the door wide and swiftly ran out. I quickly followed him as I closed my door carefully, not making any loud noises.

We quietly ran at the end of the long hallway then stop at an opening that was between the hallway and a small room that has two doors, one for an elevator and one for the stairwell.

Ashton ran to the door where the stairs were. He opened the door and looked out. "Looks like it's too early for anyone to be out. That's good; at least we have a chance not to get caught." Ashton pulled out his gun and checked it.

"Hopefully Ken and everyone else don't pop out of nowhere and get us," I said quietly.

Ashton opened the stairwell doors and ran down the stairs. As I ran behind him I looked down in the middle of the spiral stairwell and my stomach dropped. The stairwell looked like it would go on forever, it wouldn't be nice if I fell down and died right there.

I looked away from the center of the stairwell and ran against the wall. Ashton and I were running down the stairs for what felt like hours, until he stopped as he looked at the sign that said, 'seventh floor.' He raised his hand to signal me to stop and he opened the door and looked out.

He opened the door and walked out. I carefully closed the door behind me and walked into an opening, standing next to Ashton. We ran to the left and hid behind a row of potted plants and benches. Looking at our surroundings, some of the lights were still on, which didn't help us blend into our surroundings.

I heard footsteps coming to our left. I crouched down but looked through the plants; a lady in a white coat was walking across holding a stack of papers in both of her hands. Ashton and I stayed silent until we couldn't see the lady or hear her footsteps. Then we ran through the hallway where the lady came from. We made turns left and right until we stopped at a set of double doors that said 'library.' I tried to open the door but it's locked.

"Do you have a key to the library?" I asked Ashton who opened a small pocket that was on his bag and took out what looked like a pocketknife. He opened it and it popped up a couple different shaped picks. It wasn't a pocketknife; it was a lock pick.

He inserted one of the picks and an individual thin pick into the doorknob and slowly moved the two picks. His eyes focused on the door, not focusing on anything else. He moved the picks until we heard a small click sound. He removed the picks and put it back into his bag.

He looked at me and smiled. "That was easy, let's go." He opened the door and we walked in.

I followed him into the dark room, closed the door, and locked it. I looked at Ashton who was standing beside me. "I think we're safe here but not for long, follow me," he said as he walked to the right side of the library.

We stopped at a wall with a long row of bookshelves against it. Ashton ran his hand through the row of books. His fingers brushed the book spines until he stopped. He looked at the shelf and grabbed it; a creaking sound was made as he slowly pulled the shelf out. The wall that was behind the shelves had a thin outline of a small square. I softly pushed the wall and it opened. It was a secret door that led to a dark room or opening. That's a cool hiding place, I hope no one knows that we're in there.

I looked back at Ashton who held out a flashlight to me. I took it and turned it on and began to crawl through the opening. The secret room was much bigger than I imagined, it had enough room for the both of us, but there were no windows or an exit besides the one I just went through. There's a table and two chairs in the middle of the room, which was good because I didn't want to sit on the dirty floor. I stood up and wiped off the dust from my clothes.

Ashton slowly pulled the bookshelf back to its place and closed the door opening. He stood up, wiping off the dust of his clothes and looking at me.

"I guess we have to stay here until we get caught or until your seal is broken, so we have a lot of time," he said as he pulled out a chair and wiped dust from the seat. "Sit, it's going to be a long night." He gestured to the chair. I walked to the chair and sat on it.

I looked at the dusty tabletop in front of me. "We can't hide like this forever, it's useless." I doubted that Rick would find us in time. I should've told Rick how much he means to me before all of this had happened. I rested my elbows on the table with my hands on my cheeks. "You shouldn't have helped me; you're going to face Ken and risk getting killed. I don't want you to die because of me." I really don't want him to die for something that is my fault, if there were another way to get him out of here… "Ashton, is there another way to contact Rick?"

Ashton walked to the other side of the table, wiped the dust of the chair seat, and sat on it as he looked at me. "I brought my phone but I'm afraid the results would be the same as last time. But we can try if you want." He took out his phone from his jacket pocket and held it towards me. I took it and looked at it, thinking about multiple scenarios if I did call Rick.

I looked at Ashton, holding my stomach, feeling like I had been punched. "Don't do this to yourself; you can get out of this building easily. Just go and try to find Rick if you can, here." I reached inside my shirt and pulled out my note that was inside my bra and hand it to Ashton. Ashton's cheeks turned pink as he took my letter.

"I wrote Rick's address and his contact information on the paper if you need it. It's just in case if we got separated," I told him as he read the note.

"I'm not going anywhere without you," he said immovably as he placed the note in his pants pocket. "My goal is to get you away from this place and reunite you and Rick, that's all and nothing will ever change my mind." He gave me a determined look. "I want to do something that I would be proud of for once." His gaze softened. "We should rest, we're going to need the energy." He placed his gun on the table and took off his sweatshirt and held it out to me. "You should use this as a pillow. I don't want dust on you when you're resting."

"Thanks," I said as I took his sweatshirt, bundled it up into a ball, and placed it on the table in front of me.

Ashton lay back on his chair and crossed his arms. I looked down at the sweatshirt. "I just woke up; I don't feel sleepy at all. You should rest, you're going to need the energy more than me."

"Are you sure? We're in a hiding place where no one will look, we should both rest and get ready for tomorrow."

I laid my head on Ashton's sweatshirt. "Goodnight Ash," I whispered.

"Goodnight Kai," he said softly.

CHAPTER 22

The morning sunlight shined into Ken's office window, making the room have a warm glow. Someone unlocked the door from the outside. Ken walked in his office and sat on his desk chair letting out a tired sigh. He turned on his desk computer and logged in, looking up data and charts from multiple people, including Kai. He placed his right knuckles on his lips, his elbow resting on top of his desk. Ken clicked on Kai's data and looked at her results. He picked up his office phone that was on the left corner of his desk and dialed a phone number.

He placed the phone on his left ear. The phone rang for a few seconds. "Yes?" said a male voice on the other line.

Ken looked at his office door. "Sean, I want you to do something for me," he said in a low tone.

"What do you want me to do?"

"Kai and Ashton are hiding in this building and are trying to contact Rick. Ask Chrissy to help you and bring them to me if you do find them. I prevented Kai from getting out of this building, so take your time." His eyes hardened. "Make sure they're alive when you bring them to me, I want to teach Ashton a lesson about loyalty." Ken placed his phone back in the phone holder, not waiting for Sean to respond.

Sean was standing in the training room observing people doing their training. He held his phone and dialed a phone number. He placed the phone against his right ear.

"What do you want now?" said a female voice from the other line.

Sean looked at the people using their powers on individual training equipment. A man transformed into a lion and bit into a log, completely breaking the log in half. A woman shot a green substance from her hands at a wooden target from across the room, the target quickly dissolved into thin air.

"Dad wants us to find our niece and Ashton, Chris will you help?"

Chrissy let out a yawn. "Yeah whatever, did Dad say anything about asking other people to help?"

"No he only wants us to find those two ourselves, it's only the two of us looking for them."

"That's annoying; you know how big this building is? It would take us a while to find those two. When does Dad want them?"

Sean let out a sigh. "He said take your time, he really doesn't care as long as those two are alive."

"I'll look at the top half of the building and you'll look at the bottom half, bye Sean." Chrissy hung up the phone.

Sean's eyes narrowed, he looked at one of the spectators that was also observing the people training. "Make sure that they don't mess up the training room, I have something important to do."

The spectators nodded at him as he walked out of the room and down the hall, looking left and right for Kai and Ashton.

Chrissy looked at her phone after she hung up on Sean, she sat at a bench that was in front of a marble fountain. She began to dial a phone number on her phone.

Her phone rang. "Yes Chrissy?" said Ken from the other line.

"Hi Dad, do you know what room number and floor Kai and Ashton live in?" she asked as she tapped the bench seat with her fingernails.

"They're both on the ninth floor, Kai's room number is 216 and Ashton's is room 219. Is there anything else you want to ask me?"

Chrissy took in a deep breath. "Yes, who else knows about this problem?"

"Only you, Sean, and me. I don't want to make this a public problem. I already injected Kai with the substance so it's crucial for me to have Kai before she has the chance to do anything more idiotic. I'll teleport you their room cards."

Chrissy bit her lip. "Okay, thank you." Ken hung up the phone.

She let out a sigh and placed her phone on the bench next to her, staring at the fountain with a sad look on her face. A minute later two room cards appeared on the bench next to her. She took the room cards and stood up as she placed the cards in her jean pocket.

She walked out of the fountain room and into an elevator. She pressed a button and waited for the doors to open. A few people walked out of the elevator but some stayed inside. Chrissy walked into the elevator and pressed a button for the ninth floor.

After a few minutes Chrissy arrived at the ninth floor; the elevator door opened and she walked out. She walked towards a hallway that was on her left side. She walked down the long hallway, looking at the doors that each had their own room numbers.

She stopped at a door with the number 219 on it, and she inserted Ashton's card into the card slot on the door. She opened the door and put the card back in her pocket. As she walked into the room she carefully looked for anything unusual.

Chrissy walked to the closet and opened it. She moved Ashton's clothes to the side to see if there was something hiding in the back of his closet; nothing was there. She closed the closet door and quickly walked around the room opening drawers and thoroughly searching all of Ashton's belongings.

After she searched everywhere in the room she inhaled sharply. Sparks of light around her body started to appear out of thin air, making a crackling noise. She took a deep breath and the sparks slowly died down. She took out another room card and walked out of Ashton's room, slamming the door behind her

She turned left and walked towards Kai's room. She stopped at the room with number 216 on the door. She inserted Kai's room card into the card slot and opened the door as she put the room card back in her pocket.

She quickly walked to the closet and looked inside it. She rummaged through Kai's closet but found nothing. She closed the closet door, walking into the bedroom and opening all the drawers of the desk, searching each individual drawer carefully. She closed the drawers and searched everywhere in the room, but she found nothing.

Chrissy thrust her right arm angrily toward the sofa, and a loud static sound echoed through the room. Lightning shot out from her hand and into the sofa, making the sofa catch on fire.

"Shit," she said out loud with annoyance. She walked towards the burning sofa, grabbed a pillow, and hit the pillow onto the fire attempting to put it out. She kept hitting the fire until the fire was completely out.

She went to the mini fridge and took a water bottle, opened it and walked to the sofa and poured the water into the sofa, making sure the fire wouldn't start again. She placed the empty bottle on the table next to the sofa and left the room.

CHAPTER 23

Someone was poking me on the arm but I didn't want to wake up. I let out a sleepy groan but that person kept poking me.

"Five more minutes," I sluggishly said, not opening my eyes.

"Kai, I need you to wake up." A voice echoed in my head, that person pressed his hand to my back and patted my back with the palm of his hand. I opened my eyes to see Ashton, who was looking down at me.

He stood beside me. "It's about ten in the morning, we can still try to contact Rick by using my phone." He took out his phone from his back pants pocket, unlocked it, and handed it to me.

I took the phone and looked at Ashton, he nodded and I looked at the phone. I started to dial Rick's phone number and I placed the phone against my left ear, the phone kept ringing. My heart started beating really fast, I'm afraid that Ken will be on the other side again.

"Hello?" said Rick on the other line. My heart skipped a beat.

"Rick is that really you?" I answered. Ashton looked at me, surprised.

"Kai? Kai! It's me Rick, where are you? I'm in New York, do you know where you are?" said Rick with eagerness.

I smiled with joy; I can't believe it worked! "I have a friend who's going to tell you the address, don't worry he's helping me." I quickly handed the phone to Ashton.

He quickly put the phone against his ear. "Hello, I'm Kai's friend, Ashton. The address is the corner of West 77th Street and Riverside Drive, it's a large building with mirrored windows so it's easy to find," he said quietly.

Ashton also warned Rick about his siblings and the other people in the building. Ashton looked at me and handed the phone back to me.

I quickly took it and pressed the phone against my ear. "Rick, I didn't have the chance to say how much you mean to me in person. I just want you to know that I love you so much, if I die take care of Ashton, he's blonde and has green eyes just to let you know." My eyes started to water.

"Kai, don't say that, I'm going to save you and your friend Ashton no matter what, I'm on my way. I love you more than anything, you're my niece and I love you no matter what," Rick said, his voice breaking, almost crying. Then I heard a loud thumping sound from inside the library.

Ashton walked to the other side of the table to get his bag. "It's time to go. We have to move," he said quickly as he carried the bag over his shoulder, holding on to his gun.

I looked at the tabletop. "We have to go, please hurry."

"Okay Kai, I'll be there. Try to hide until I come into the building."

I pressed the end call button and gave the phone to Ashton. He put the phone in his bag.

I got up and wiped the excess dust off of me. "We can't go through the opening since someone is on the other side," I said, looking around the room.

Ashton walked to one of the walls and ran his hand against the wall until something clicked. A part of the wall opened up, revealing a small set of stairs that led into darkness. Ashton took out a flashlight and turned it on.

He looked at me. "Don't worry I'll be by your side. Just follow me and I'll protect you."

I felt sick like I'm going to throw up, but I had to be strong for Ashton and Rick. "Alright lead the way," I said, my hands shaking as I followed Ashton into the secret passageway.

Rick hastily ran out of his hotel room and down a hall leading to an elevator. He pressed the elevator button. The elevator immediately opened its doors; no one was there. Rick walked inside and pressed the lobby button. The doors closed; Rick tapped his foot impatiently as the elevator went down. He took out his phone to dial a phone number. He placed his phone against his right ear.

"Hello Mark's taxi services, who's calling?" asked Mark on the line.

"Hey Mark, it's Rick from yesterday. Are you available right now?" Rick asked as he walked around the inside of the elevator.

"Yeah, just tell me where you are and I'll be there."

"Meet me at Orchard Hotel."

"Okay I'll be there in three minutes."

Rick hung up the phone as the elevator doors opened. Rick swiftly speed walked through the lobby and out the hotel, stopping at a sidewalk waiting for Mark.

He looked at his surroundings as he waited for Mark, a few minutes passed. A taxi slowly parked in front of Rick.

Rick walked towards the taxi and looked through the window; Mark was in the driver's seat. He looked back at Rick and smiled. Rick opened the door and sat behind the passenger seat.

"Take me to West 77th Street and Riverside Drive and make it quick, I have to do something important," Rick said eagerly.

Mark nodded. "Hold on tight." He drove the car into the street driving quickly. He almost hit a car that was trying to move to his lane, but he missed that car by a foot.

In a few quick minutes Rick and Mark arrived at a tall building. Rick took out a twenty dollar bill and held it out to Mark.

Mark gingerly took the money. "You don't have too; the ride doesn't cost much."

Rick opened the door and looked back at Mark. "It's for your kindness. I want you to get out of this area, okay? I don't want you to get hurt." Rick got out of the taxi and walked toward the building without hearing what Mark had to say to him.

He looked at the double doors and then at a doorbell with a small card slot next to the doors. He grabbed the door handle and pulled, but the door didn't open. Rick looked left and right down the sidewalk; there were only a small handful of people walking by. He placed his glowing red hand on the doorbell until the door made a clicking noise.

He grabbed the door handle and opened it. As he walked inside the building a few people were walking in and out of the large lobby. He looked at a woman who had a lotus symbol on her right forearm in black ink. He looked at the front desk that was in the middle of the lobby and walked toward it.

A man was typing at his desk computer and looked up at Rick. "Hello, may I help you?" the man asked.

Rick's eyes switched from brown to purple. He looked at the man and the man's eyes flashed purple, his face turning emotionless.

"Where are my father and siblings?" Rick demanded.

"They're in the building, a few floors above us."

Other people in the lobby saw what Rick had done. They immediately ran towards him, he turned around and held out his hand. Everyone was forcefully knocked back into the wall by an invisible force, unable to move.

Rick looked at the man with a side glance, the man instantly dropped on the floor. Rick's whole body suddenly glowed red. He kneeled down to the floor, his hands pressed against the marble. A large circle with multiple symbols and shapes started to appear from his hand. The circle started to grow bigger until it covered the whole lobby floor. The circle began to glow white until the light was so bright that the circle on the floor had disappeared.

Rick stood up as the red glow around his body disappeared. He walked behind the desk and laid his hand on the computer, multiple pop-ups immediately covered the screen. After a few minutes he moved his hand away from the computer.

"Substance? What did my father do to these people?" he said to himself before he disappeared out of thin air.

Rick reappeared inside the laboratory. The scientists didn't move a muscle from what they were doing at the time.

Rick walked up to one of the scientists, standing near a desk. "Do you know where this enhancement substance is? And what does it do?" he asked.

The scientist looked at Rick with an empty look in his eyes. "The substance makes you stronger and more powerful; it can also lead to developing new powers or abilities. I'll lead you to it." The scientist turned around and walked to the back corner of the lab. A clear cabinet held multiple syringes in a syringe rack with different colored substances inside each individual syringe. The scientist unlocked the doors of the cabinet, opening the doors wide for Rick to see.

Rick moved closer to the cabinet, and the scientist moved out of Rick's way. He looked at the scientist. "What happens if I get injected with this?"

"It all depends on which substance you choose, most substances can likely make you develop powers, abilities, or it can increase your skills tremendously. It will either take days, weeks, or months to completely develop your powers or abilities."

Rick looked at the substance again, his jaw tightened. "Which one will give me enough power to kill Ken?"

"We have a substance that is specifically made for Ken himself, it's in a special room. Follow me." The scientist and Rick walked to a door in the corner of the lab and the scientist placed his hand on the touch screen that was beside the door. The light turned green and the door opened.

Both of them walk inside the small room. Inside the room there was a table that held two large syringes in a case. There was also a chair placed on the left side of the table. Both of the syringes were filled with a black substance. Rick walked closer to the table.

"What does this substance do?" Rick asked.

"It's the most powerful substance that we ever created. It can give an individual maximum power to do almost anything. Once this substance is in an individual's system they permanently become much more powerful than any being in the world, even Ken himself."

Rick gently touched one of the syringes. "Inject both of them in each of my arms." He took off his jacket, revealing his bare forearms, and sat on the chair.

The scientist obeyed Rick's order. He took one of the syringes and touched Rick's right arm. He slowly pushed the needle into Rick's arm and pushed down the plunger, injecting the black substance into Rick's veins. Rick's veins changed from blue to black, he let out a groan and shut his eyes as the scientist inserted all the substance into Rick's arm. Once there was no more of the black substance left the scientist pulled out the needle from Rick's arm and placed the empty syringe back on the syringe case.

The scientist picked up the second syringe and walked to Rick's left side to push the needle inside of Rick's left arm. The scientist push down the plunger of the syringe. All the black substance was slowly injected into Rick's veins, making them turn black as well. Rick let out another pain filled groan. The scientist removed the needle from Rick's arm and placed it beside the other empty syringe on the table.

Rick was breathing heavily; he slightly opened his eyes and looked at his arm. All the veins in his arms were black. Rick's right hand glowed red as he slowly closed his hand into a fist. The scientist who was in the room with him fell on the ground. The other scientists in the laboratory fell on the ground also.

Rick's hand stop glowing and his hand opened up from his fist. Rick gasped for air, his eyes slowly shut as his head tilted back, sitting on the chair unconscious.

CHAPTER 24

Ashton and I were at the end of the passageway. Ashton placed his hands on the bare wall, and I heard a clicking noise as he ran his hands against the wall. We looked at each other. Ashton pulled a part of the wall toward him; a light shone through the mini door. Ashton fully opened the hidden door and he crawled through it, I crawled behind him.

As we got through the door my eyes adjusted to the light. Ashton took my wrist and dragged me behind a cabinet. I rubbed my eyes and noticed that we're in the training room that I had been to before.

"Is anyone in here?" I whispered.

Ashton peeked through the side of the cabinet then looked back at me with a confused look. "There's only three people, but they looked like they'd been Paralyzed."

I looked at him with a confused look. "Paralyzed? What do you mean?" What the hell is happening here? Could Ken have done that?

He peeked through the side of the cabinet again. "It's like someone used some kind of power that stopped these people from moving. Maybe this was Ken's doing but at least we can get out of here without killing anyone. Let's go." He casually walked out from behind the cabinet and into the training room as I followed him.

We walked towards the door. I looked at the three people who didn't move an inch. I carefully examine them. None of them blinked or made a noise. They reminded me of mannequins, just standing there in place. It made me feel creeped out just by looking at them.

Ashton stopped at the door, opened it, and looked out. We ran into the hallway and crouched behind a row of potted flowers. I looked to the side of a flowerpot to see if anyone saw us, no one was out in the hall which was good.

Ashton looked at me with an uneasy look in his eyes. "Kai we have to go to the laboratory, I have to destroy this special substance that was made for Ken. If Ken ever injects that substance into him, he'd have the power to kill us in an instant. You have to go with me; I can't leave you alone here."

"Let's get this over with," I said. We stood up and ran down the hallway.

I saw the door leading to the stairway. We both went through the door and climbed up the stairs until Ashton stopped on the twelfth floor. He took a deep breath and opened the door, his gun positioned in front of him. We both ran out into the hallway. He stood back against the wall to see if anyone was walking our way. But there was a man that was standing still in the middle of the hall.

We cautiously walked toward the man who was standing very still. As we came closer to the man I noticed that he was phased out, just like the people from the training room. I guess Ken 'froze' everyone in this building so it would be easier to find us, great.

We both ran towards the lab, passing through people who weren't moving at all. We stopped at the double doors of the lab and opened them.

As we walked inside the lab people in white lab coats were laying on the floor. It seemed that they had been knocked out by someone or something. I kept my focus on Ashton who was walking towards a door that was in the corner of the lab. He placed his hand on a touchscreen that was next to the door. The light turned green and the door opened. We both walked inside the room.

Then as I walked into the room I saw Rick lying unconscious on a chair that was next to a table with two empty syringes on top. I ran to Rick and hugged him. I squeezed Rick so I knew he's actually there and it's not my imagination.

Rick let out a weak noise. I looked at him then at Ashton. "Did he inject that substance into himself?" I asked, poking Rick in the upper arm. Ashton placed his bag on the floor next to the chair.

Ashton observed Rick and the man in the white lab coat was on the floor. To be honest I didn't notice the guy in the white coat was in there. He looked at the table where the empty syringes were. "I'm positive he did."

He came closer to Rick and gingerly grabbed his left arm, moving it to show his forearm with the red lotus tattoo on it. Rick's veins were black. I turned his right arm to show his forearm. His veins in that arm were black also.

I let out a gasp and looked at Ashton. "What is in that substance? How long is Rick going to be like this?" I slapped Rick's face in an attempt to wake him up. It didn't work; he only let out a painful noise.

Ashton placed Rick's left arm on the chair's armrest. "That substance makes someone permanently more powerful than before; at least Rick got to use them before Ken could. We might have the chance to get out of this place since Rick has taken both of those substances." He turned around and walked to the door. "There's a substance that immediately makes a person wake up; I'll get it for Rick."

The door opened and Ashton walked out, his gun positioned in front of him. Then the door closed. I looked back at Rick who was still passed out. I took off my black gloves; I still had that seal on my right hand. I looked at Rick's arms again. I understand why he did this to himself. He knew that he couldn't defeat Ken by using his original powers so he injected the two substances into him to help him fight. If only I could help Rick and Ashton by using my powers. I felt helpless without them.

I took a deep breath and exhaled. The door opened and I immediately turned my head at the door. Ashton was walking through the door, holding a small syringe with a blue substance inside it. He walked to Rick and he positioned the syringe into Rick's neck.

Ashton looked at me. I nodded and he pushed the needle into Rick's neck and pushed the plunger down until all the substance was gone. Rick winced as Ashton removed the needle out of Rick's neck. Ashton placed the empty syringe on top of the table.

Ashton looked at Rick. "It will take only a few seconds. No one is inside the laboratory which is good. I also locked the doors so we're safe for now."

I held Rick's hand and held out my other hand to Ashton, he took my hand. I could feel the warmth from both of their hands and it made me feel a bit safer. I held both of their hands until I felt a bit of movement from Rick's hand. I looked at Rick. Suddenly he opened his eyes and gasped.

I let go of both of their hands and jumped back. Rick was looking at me then at Ashton with a confused look. Then his eyes relaxed, his facial expression looked relieved. He stood up and hugged me and Ashton.

"Oh my God! I finally get to see you again Kai! I missed you so much, I love you so much!" Rick said, sobbing, his chin resting on top of my head.

"And thank you so much Ashton for helping Kai, I owe you big time!" I looked at Ashton who had a surprised look on his face.

I could hear Rick still crying. "I'm gonna get you two home, but I have to do something first."

The three of us broke up our group hug after a few long minutes. Rick wiped his eyes with his arm and looked down at my left arm. His face turned into shock.

"When did you get that?" he said looking straight that my sleeve tattoo. His facial expression turned calm. "But I do like your tattoo though."

"It's a long story but that's not important right now, we need to get out of this building before Ken finds us."

He looked at Ashton and then at me. "Are you two sure you're just friends right?" Rick said, looking at both of his arms. I looked at Rick annoyed; this is not the right time to ask this but I'm gonna answer him anyways.

"We're friends," Ashton and I said at the same time. We looked at each other and looked away, embarrassed.

Rick chuckled. "Okay, good 'cuz my Kai is too young to date, just an FIY."

I looked at Rick, feeling embarrassed again. "It's FYI Rick," I corrected him; for someone who's a cop he should learn his acronyms better.

Rick looked at me with the same embarrassed look. "Uh okay." He looked at Ashton. "Kai is too young to date just an F-FYI," he stuttered.

Ashton smiled, his green eyes sparkled, but then his smile turned to a frown. "Wait. Kai can't get out of here; Ken placed a seal on her to prevent her from escaping the building and using her powers. In order to remove the seal Ken will have to unseal her willingly, but I don't think he would do that. Another way to remove the seal is to… kill him," he said with a nervous look.

Rick's expression changed from happy to serious. "Oh, I forgot my father was still in this building, and my siblings." Rick sighed and looked at me. "I regret saying this, but you and Ashton have to hide again, I don't want you two to get hurt. Also it's not a pretty sight when I have to fight my—" Rick immediately fell on his hands and knees, his hands gripped into fists and he let out a loud painful moan. Ashton and I tried to get Rick back up to his feet, but Rick swatted us away.

"No. Stay away from me kids, something in the substance did some—" Rick fell completely on the floor and rolled over on his back. His hands still gripped into fists; his jaw clenched tightly. All of a sudden Rick's whole body furiously shook like he's having a seizure. I let out a gasp, what happened to him?

Ashton walked in front of me, shielding my view of Rick who was still shaking. Ashton hugged me; my face pressed against his shoulder.

"Don't look. I saw the same thing happened to Ken once when he injected that substance into him. Rick will be like that for a few seconds, but it's the substance moving around his system and that's a good thing too. The substance is now completely developed for Rick to use after his episode," Ashton said still holding on to me.

Ashton had been hugging me for what felt like a while. I moved my head so I could look at Rick, and Rick stopped moving. I looked at Ashton, God he smells nice. Uh yeah, this isn't the time to act weird.

"I think Rick is dead." I told him.

"Wait. What?" Ashton let go of me and looked at Rick, still lying on the floor.

We both walked up to Rick gingerly. I knelt down to poke Rick in the cheek, he didn't move a muscle.

"I thought he would be fine after he had that seizure," I said to Ashton. He also kneeled down next to Rick, examining him.

"He should get back to his normal self, I have no idea what happened." Ashton placed his fingers onto Rick's neck. "He's still alive, but I don't know when he's going to wake up."

"Damn it, Ken, Sean, and Chrissy are looking for us right now and I don't think we can fight them off. We can't even fight off one of them without getting our limbs chopped off. Maybe Ken might come to the lab to get those substances but realize that all three of us are inside and he will kill us as soon as he sees one of us." I'm starting to panic now; Rick is out cold and it's only Ashton and me.

"Kai don't panic, we have to stay calm in this type of situation. We'll have to stay here until Rick eventually wakes up," he said as he stood up. An intense explosion echoed inside the lab.

I could feel my eyes grow wide as Ashton grabbed his bag and unzipped it, his facial expression turned serious.

He looked at me. "Kai, stay with Rick. It sounds like Sean found us." Ashton walked through the door and ran out. I could see a yellow and red light glowed from inside the lab.

I looked at Rick and slap him; he didn't wake up or move. I let out a frustrated sigh. Come on Rick wake up! I heard gunshots and explosions from inside the lab where Ashton was, I needed to help him.

I looked at Rick and I got up. "Sorry Rick I need to help Ashton before he gets himself killed." I got up and walked through the door, leaving Rick alone in the room.

As I walked into the lab, half of it was on fire. I ran toward a desk and hid behind it. Some of the fire was in black flames and some of them were regular red and orange flames.

"Where is she?!" I heard as Sean's loud voice echoed through the room. Another explosion erupted, making the lab equipment fly over my head. "It doesn't matter, I'll find her myself then."

A minute after he said that multiple explosions quickly exploded around the room. I got up and looked at where the noise came from. A few yards in front of me Sean was behind a wall made out of fire. Ashton was on my left side shooting his gun at Sean.

Sean's flames died down; his face filled with rage. Sean bolted towards Ashton, who nearly dodged him, but Ashton placed a small device behind Sean's back. Ashton swiftly ran away from Sean as the device exploded.

Sean let out an annoyed groan. "You of all people should know not to make me pissed off," Sean growled.

"Yeah I know, but I love to see you get angry, it makes the fight seem more... interesting," Ashton said as he threw more bombs at Sean, who swung his arm making a fire wall that made the bombs melt or self-destruct.

Sean's hands suddenly covered in flames. "I'm going to end you. You don't deserve to be here." Sean's flames turned black, that doesn't look good.

I stood up and took a deep breath as I grabbed a large book that was on a desk next to me. "Hey asshole, you came for me? Then come and get me if you're not afraid to get hurt by a girl!" I threw the book at Sean but he swung his hand to the side, making a wall of black flames.

The book disintegrated immediately. Sean looked at me with this scary look on his face. He got that crazy look in his eye that makes me want to put him in a mental hospital.

Sean lowered his hand and made a malevolent smiled. "There you are." He quickly thrust his hand toward Ashton who neatly dodged Sean's attack. Sean ran towards me and I ran to my right, trying to get away from him.

I yelled as I was jumping over knocked-down lab equipment. Rick, it's a good time to wake up now! I looked back and Sean was running after me. He thrust his arms towards me and shot flames in my direction. I turned right and knocked an empty cabinet onto a large computer as I ran.

The computer exploded next to Sean, who knocked the computers out of his way with his flames. "To be honest I didn't like you when you first came here, you remind me of your idiotic father and Rick!" he yelled as I kept knocking objects down.

I snatched another large book and threw it at Sean, who ducked as the book flew over his head.

"To be honest I don't like you either and everybody else in this hell hole, besides Ashton. Do I look like I care if you like me or not? You sir, can suck an egg!" I yelled from the top of my lungs, fearful of getting burned alive.

I looked to my left and saw Ashton was standing next to a cabinet on the other side of the lab, and it looked like he's injecting himself with another substance. Seriously what's with people and injecting themselves these days? Ashton winced and leaned against the cabinet, knocking over some other syringes.

I looked straight ahead because I didn't want to let Sean to take his attention off of me. I tried to run away from Ashton. I looked back at Sean who was still running towards me, I knocked down a file cabinet but Sean jumped and ran faster. Shit, that didn't work.

Sean was now a few feet closer to me, my legs felt strained. In an instant Sean was knocked down by Ashton, who was now on top of him punching him in the face, making Sean's face bleed. Sean's black flames disappeared. Ashton let out a loud grunt as he punched Sean. Sean grabbed a broken computer screen that was near him and slammed it into Ashton's head, but Ashton grabbed Sean's wrist and bent it until he let go of the computer screen.

Ashton kept bending Sean's wrist as Sean cried in agony. I ran toward them and I grabbed Sean's other hand, restraining him from doing anything else.

"I'm going to burn you two alive! You hear me? Alive! And I don't care what my father will say, I'll kill you two even if it's the last thing I'll do," Sean growled as Ashton and I pressed him against the floor.

"Yeah well you're going to die before that even happens, so don't get your hopes up," Ashton said, looking at Sean dead in the eye.

Sean closed his eyes. His skin started to feel very hot, now I'm getting worried. All of a sudden Sean's body was engulfed in flames. The force of the flames made Ashton and I fly across the lab.

My back slammed against the wall. I let out a groan as I fell on the floor. I felt like I got the wind knocked out of me. I let out a wheeze as I looked at Ashton, who was on the floor, looking at Sean with an annoyed look.

Sean got up, his body engulfed in black flames. He walked toward us with a wicked look on his face. I let out another wheeze, shit we're screwed.

The door of the room where I left Rick violently burst open. The door flew into the lab, making more of a mess.

"What the hell was that?" Ashton said as he sat up and looked at the room.

CHAPTER 25

Ashton and I looked at the room where we left Rick who was unconscious, I guess not anymore. Rick walked up to the door's threshold and slumped against it as he looked at the partly destroyed lab.

Rick winced and touched his head as he closed his eyes. "Ey Sean, if you mess..." He paused as he took a deep breath. "If you mess…with my kids, then. Then you have… to. To fight me first," he said breathlessly. Rick should've rested a bit more before he came out, he looked like he's going to pass out again.

Sean thrust his hands toward Rick, black flames spewed out of Sean's hand. Rick moved out of the way before the flames touched him. Rick stumbled as he ran behind a metal cabinet that was on the same side were Ashton and I were hiding.

Rick's back was pressed against the cabinet, I looked back at Ashton. "We should go to Rick; he doesn't look so good."

"You have to run to him; I'll make sure that Sean is distracted so he won't come for you or Rick."

"Just make sure you won't get hurt."

"I won't, make sure that Rick is conscious. We need him to help us fight your family." Ashton stood up

"They're not my family anymore," I said with no emotions in my voice.

He looked at me with a frown and ran toward Sean.

I peeked to the side of the desk and saw that Sean had his back towards me. He was thrusting his hands at a piece of lab equipment. He's going to set the whole lab on fire; I needed to get Ashton and Rick out of this room.

I quickly ran to Rick who sat on the floor, his back against the back of the cabinet. As I got to him I crouched down next to him.

Rick looked at me, exhausted from that seizure he had. "Kai," he said as he raised his hand and touched my cheek. "No matter what happens, remember that I love you more than anything. Your mom and dad must be disappointed in me." His voice broke as tears streamed down his face.

I placed my hand on his. I clenched my jaw, trying not to cry. This is no time to cry, I have to be strong and do what I have to do.

I closed my eyes as I moved my head and pressed it against his. "Don't say that you're here right? This is not the time to give up, we need to get out of here. I don't want you or Ashton to get hurt or worse." I opened my eyes. "Can you fight at all?"

Rick let out a grunt as he removed his hand from my cheek and sat up straight. I moved my head and look at him. "Kind of, I feel weak. I just have to wait until that substance takes on its effect." The two of us stared at each other. "You and Ashton should hide somewhere that is far away from the lab. Make sure that you two don't get spotted by anyone. Once you find a place to hide, stay there until I find you guys. Can you do that for me?"

"What happens if you need our help?" I asked as I heard a loud explosion on the other side of the room. I hope Ashton can distract Sean longer so I can talk to Rick.

"I can do this myself; I am counting on the two of you to hide and to stay safe. I'm sorry for everything, I should have told you about our family, about what happened to your mom and dad." Rick wrapped his arms around me and hugged me, I hugged him back. "I'm so sorry Kai," he whispered.

Instantly I got teleported outside the laboratory, and I fell on the floor. I looked to my side and saw Ashton almost running into the wall. He immediately stopped and looked left and right with a confused look. He saw me on the floor and ran to me, helping me get up.

"What happened to Rick?"

"He's weak but he said that he's still going to fight Sean. He told us to find a place to hide until he finds us." Then I remembered when Ashton injected himself with a substance as I got chased by Sean. "Back then when Sean was chasing me like a dog, you injected another substance into you. What kind of substance was that?" I asked as I place my hands on my hips.

He looked at my hips and then at my face. "It's just something to make my abilities permanently better, and thank God I tackled Sean before he got to you. We should hide somewhere." He looked around and walked towards the end of the hallway.

I followed him to the door leading to the stairwell. We walked down the set of stairs until we reached the fifth floor. We open the stairwell door and walked out into the hall as we looked around our surroundings. No one was there, which was a relief.

We carefully walked down the hall but then I heard footsteps behind us. I turned around to see Ken standing in front of me.

Rick slowly got up. He leaned against the cabinet as he breathed hard. Sean walked towards the cabinet Rick was hiding behind. Sean's hands ignited in black flames.

"Are you too weak to come out and fight me?" Sean shouted as he thrust his hand at the cabinet.

Black flame spewed out of his hand; the cabinet was completely engulfed in flames. Within minutes the cabinet had completely disintegrated, nothing was behind it. Sean gripped his hands into fists and looked around the room.

"Where the hell are you?" Sean growled.

To the left side of Sean, multiple red glowing spear-like objects shot at him. He swept his hand in front of him, making a wall of black flames. He thrust his hands at the wall, and the wall moved forward. As the spears touched the wall, they instantly disintegrated.

More spears appeared out of thin air and shot at Sean. He looked up at the spears that surrounded him. His eyebrows knitted together, he swiped his hand again and turned around making a large dome of black flames that surrounded him.

The red spears instantly shot at Sean's dome. The spears disintegrated. Sean's dome extinguished after all the spears had shot at it, and he looked around the room once more.

Rick appeared behind Sean, his fist curled as he thrust his hands at him. Sean swiftly turned around, glaring at Rick as he instantly thrust his hand at him, blocking the punch.

Rick and Sean's hands touched, it suddenly made large explosion of black flames and red light. The two were forcefully pushed back to opposite sides, crashing into yet more lab equipment. Rick crashed into a bookcase, completely destroying it as fragments of wood scattered around the area. Sean crashed into the wall, creating a large dent on it. He fell off the wall and lay on the floor.

Rick let out a yelp as he rolled out of the broken bookcase. There were a few small cuts on his face and hands, and parts of his shirt and pants were slightly ripped. He winced as he lightly touched his head and closed his eyes.

Sean lay on the floor as he placed his hand on his stomach. He looked up at the room and sat up. He wiped sweat from his forehead with the back of his hand, closed his eyes for a few seconds and opened them.

He took a deep breath and he stood up. Dust from the broken wall stained his clothes and skin. He looked down at his clothes and dusted himself off as he let out a dry cough.

After Sean dusted himself off, he immediately walked toward the direction where Rick was at. He pushed some lab equipment out of his way as he got closer to Rick.

Rick lay on the bookcase not moving at all. Sean crouched down near Rick and grabbed him by the neck. Rick immediately opened his eyes, his eyes changed to purple.

Before Rick could do anything Sean's hand ignited in red and orange flames. Rick let out a weak yell as the flames burned his neck. Rick disappeared out of thin air and reappeared on the other side of the room. He gasped for air and gingerly touched his neck, wincing as he did so.

"Running away from me? Why can't you come out and fight me like a man!" Sean shouted as he lit a desk on fire.

The burn marks on Rick's neck slowly healed. He stood up breathing very heavily. He look at Sean irritated, his body suddenly surrounded by a red aura. He thrust both of his arms at Sean, multiple balls of red light aimed towards him.

Sean looked back and dodged Rick's attack. The balls of light collided into lab equipment or into the wall, causing everything to fall apart.

Sean ran towards Rick as he thrust his hands at him. Balls of black flames appeared out of thin air, shooting at Rick's direction.

Rick held out his palm as the black flames came closer to him. As the black flames came towards Rick an invisible force field blocked the flames from touching him. The flames moved around Rick, objects that were touched by the flames instantly caught on fire and turned into ash.

Rick sighed. "Do you really want to waste your energy on me? I think we both know who's getting out of here alive," he said as the flames around him slowly died down.

Sean made a smirk. "I thought you're giving me the silent treatment," he said as he slowly walked towards Rick. "Do you really think that you can kill me? You have high hopes little brother, but you should know the most powerful person always wins the fight."

Sean thrust his hand at Rick. Large black flames from Sean's hands burst out of thin air. The flames surrounded Rick, trapping him inside a circle. Rick teleported himself beside Sean and landed a punch at the back of his head.

Sean moved his head out of the way, missing Rick's fist by only a few inches. Sean grabbed Rick's arm, fire from Sean's hand burned Rick. Rick let out a muffled yell as his whole arm was completely on fire. He swung his other arm at Sean's stomach but Sean blocked the attack with his hand.

The two landed punches and attacked each other with their powers for what seemed like hours, the two didn't want to give up. Both of them kept fighting as they destroyed more than half the laboratory, but they seemed not to care about it.

Sean and Rick punched each other with their fists. The two of them were pushed back from the force. Right before Rick made his next attack a bolt of lightning struck him, causing Rick to become paralyzed for a moment. Rick stiffly moved his neck to the direction where there was a clicking noise coming closer to him and Sean.

Chrissy walked over a knocked down chair as she headed towards Sean and Rick. As she stood between the two she crossed her arms. She looked at Rick who slightly moved. She pointed her finger at him. A bolt of lightning came out of her finger and zapped him, preventing him from moving once more.

"You finally showed up huh?" she said as she looked around the laboratory. "I can't believe you two destroyed half the lab, you know how much money we have to spend to restore all of this?" she said, irritated.

"Chris, we have something much more important to accomplish," Sean said, looking at Chrissy with a stern look.

Rick disappeared out of thin air and reappeared behind Chrissy. His left hand struck Chrissy's back, and her body was surrounded by lightning. She flew into a row of file cabinets, making all the cabinets fall on top of her.

She let out a cry, lightning sparked under the cabinets. All at once the cabinets exploded, making them crash into lab equipment and into the walls. Chrissy slowly got up, a trail of blood flowing from her forehead and down to her cheek. She touched the trail of blood and looked at it.

"You're going to pay for this!" she yelled as multiple lightning bolts struck at Rick. The remainder of the computers exploded at the same time.

Rick moved out of the way as lightning struck at the ground where Rick had been standing a few seconds ago. Rick looked at Sean, who was shooting fireballs at Rick without hesitation. Rick teleported, dodging the attacks.

He reappeared behind Sean who swiftly turned around and punched Rick in the stomach. His black flames grew intensely as he forcefully pushed Rick into a wall. Rick let out a groan as he crashed into the wall, making the wall fall apart. The broken wall material crumbled and fell on top of Rick.

Rick's hands pressed the rubble covered floor and got up. The red aura around his body grew brighter and larger, his pupils dilated as he looked at his siblings.

"I've had enough of this! Let's get this over with!" Rick yelled as he wiped the dust off of him and walked near Chrissy. Rick's iris turned back to brown. He closed his eyes and stumbled backwards; his body slumped against the wall.

Chrissy and Sean instantly sprinted to Rick. They both thrust their hands at the same time. Lightning and black flames hit Rick in the chest. Rick yelled as he slowly fell down on the floor.

The flames and lightning intensified as they came closer to Rick. He lay on the floor not moving.

"You're still weak; you can't defeat your older siblings even if you tried. After we finish you Kai will be ours," Sean said as he put more force into Rick. Fire started to burn through Rick's shirt and into his bare skin. Rick didn't react to the pain, he just lay there with his eyes closed shut.

"Just kill him already, he's already dead to us anyway," Chrissy said as she looked down at Rick with pity.

"I will Chris, I just want him to suffer to death," Sean said as his flames vanished. He walked next to Rick and made a fist. His hand lighting up in red flames, he struck his fist into Rick's stomach. Sean kept his flaming hand on Rick's stomach, making his stomach severely burned.

Rick's head rolled to his side, blood dripping from the corner of his lips. Chrissy moved closer to Rick. She grabbed his head; electric currents ran through her hand and into Rick's head electrocuting him.

Rick lazily opened his eyes and looked at Sean and Chrissy, his irises turned completely back. Chrissy added more power into Rick's head. He let out a wail and closed his eyes.

"Chris, get out of the way," Sean ordered. Chrissy obeyed him and walked next to him. Sean's hands engulfed in black flames, he held out his palm at Rick who was suddenly covered in black flames.

Rick yelled in agony as he violently shook with his eyes still closed. Sean and Chrissy stood back as they watched Rick having another seizure episode.

The flames in Rick's body burned more than half of his clothes. It also severely burned his skin, turning it white or light tan.

Rick had the seizure for a few minutes until he stopped. He didn't move or make any noises. He laid on the floor as the flames burned his entire body.

Chrissy looked at Sean with an uneasy look. "Is he dead?"

Sean looked back at Chrissy. "He should be dead now; my black flames are burning him alive." He looked back at Rick. "We should leave him; we need to find Kai and Ashton."

Chrissy ran her hands through her ponytail and walked away from Rick's burning body. Sean followed her without saying anything. He wiped a bead of sweat from his forehead with his arm.

Rick fully opened his eyes, his irises turned completely black. His body was still engulfed in black flames, but all the burn marks, cuts, and bruises had gradually healed or regenerated. After all of his wounds had fully healed his skin looked like nothing had happened to him.

Rick's black eyes changed to purple, flecks of black surrounding the outside of his pupil. His pupils dilated as the black flames disappeared from his body.

Rick blinked his eyes as he sat up. He licked his lips and made a confused look as he stared at his legs. He extended his right hand and wiped his mouth. He looked at his hand and the faint blood stain on it.

He let out a groan as he stood up and looked around the room. Sean and Chrissy were walking towards the exit doors. Rick's face hardened as he moved his hand in the direction of the two of them.

All the broken equipment and rubble from the room was moved in front of the door, preventing anyone from getting in or out of the laboratory.

Sean and Chrissy stopped walking. They exchanged glances, turned around, and saw Rick. The two immediately had their guard up and ran towards him, preparing to strike.

Rick also ran towards them getting ready to attack. As the three came closer to each other, Rick thrust his hand at Sean and Chrissy. The two were instantly slammed against the wall behind them by a strong force.

Rick looked at himself, his shirt almost burned off and his pants half burned off. Rick ripped off what was left of his shirt and looked at his muscular chest. There were multiple large scratches on the left side of Rick's stomach. Also, there was an Ankh tattoo on the left side of his chest.

He looked at Sean and Chrissy lying on the floor. His whole body was suddenly surrounded by a black aura as his eyes grew intense. He teleported to Chrissy and violently slammed her head against a desk, breaking it into pieces. She let out a wheeze as she lay on the floor. Rick looked at Sean, who looked at his sister.

Rick teleported himself and Sean to the other side of the lab. Rick grabbed Sean's neck and slammed him into the wall. Sean shut his eyes and spat out blood from his mouth.

Sean opened his eyes. He smiled, his teeth stained red. "Who knew you had it in you?" He let out a laugh, but Rick squeezed Sean's throat. Sean stopped laughing. "I guess it's the end little brother." Sean let out a humm sound. "I finally get to see you for the last time. When you left, it's like a part of me was gone. I missed you during these years but my sadness turned to pure hatred." Sean gasped for air. "And now...I want to see you die," he whispered as Chrissy electrocuted Rick on the back of his head.

The shock didn't affect Rick. He turned around and let go of Sean, who lay on the ground gasping for air. Rick looked at Chrissy. He walked towards her as she kept thrusting her hand at him. Lightning bolts came out of her hands and hit Rick.

Rick kept walking towards her as the lightning bolts struck at him, he wasn't affected by her attacks. Chrissy punched Rick near the face, but he grabbed her fist and pulled her towards him.

"Why are you doing this to me and Kai? Don't you see that our father is using you and Sean?" Rick said as he held her fist.

Chrissy landed another punch at him with her other hand, which Rick immediately grabbed. Both of Chrissy's hands were detained by Rick's hands, electric currents flowing through her arms and into Rick. Rick didn't flinch as the electricity touched his hands.

"Many people have different views about how they should live their lives," Chrissy said as her eyebrows knitted together. "You're a cop, aren't you? Then you should know how people are. Some people change, some people don't." She moved closer to Rick with a sly grin. "I'm the kind of person who's not going to change, I worked this hard to get to where I am and I don't want to lose everything to someone like you." Her voice hardened.

Large sparks from the computers and lab equipment quickly caught on fire. Chrissy's whole body was surrounded by multiple bright electric currents. The electric currents grew intense as they moved into Rick's body. Rick struggled to hold on to her hands and let go of his grip.

Sean sneaked up behind Rick and swiftly moved his arm around his neck, forcefully choking him. Sean's body ignited in black flames; Rick let out a gurgling noise as he stepped back.

Chrissy ran up to Rick, all the electric currents around her body moved onto her right hand. She slammed her palm into Rick's chest. The electricity ran all over his torso.

Rick gasped for air as he was choked and struck by electricity. He closed his eyes and let out a weak yell. He ran backwards and slammed Sean into a metal cabinet. Sean let out a groan as he let go of his grip. Sean fell on the floor and looked up at Rick.

Rick thrust his hand at him. Black energy burst out of his hand and hit Sean in the torso. Sean let out an agonizing yell as he spat out blood and lay on the floor, unable to move.

Rick turned around to Chrissy and ran up to her, pressing his palm on her stomach. Black light from Rick's hands went through Chrissy's stomach. Chrissy made a gasping noise, blood dripping from her mouth and onto the floor. She looked at Rick and fell. A pool of blood slowly surrounded her as she lay, dead. Her blood splattered the objects and floor behind her. Rick looked at his palm. There were blood stains on it.

"Chrissy!" Sean bawled weakly.

Rick turned around and walked towards Sean who was crawling away from him. Sean looked back at him with a frightened look on his face. His eyes grew wide as Rick came up to him.

"See you in hell." Rick crouched down to Sean and looked at him with pure hatred in his eyes.

Rick made a fist. He let out a grunt and drove his glowing fist into Sean's chest. Black light spread out onto his chest as he wailed.

Sean stopped moving. His eyes turned glassy, blood pouring out of his body making a small puddle underneath him. Rick removed his fist from Sean's body and he looked at it. His hand was completely covered in his brother's and sister's blood.

Rick's eyes turned back to normal as tears streamed down his cheeks. The black glow around his body disappeared. He let out a loud yell and started to sob as he knelt on the ground, his bloody hands on his head.

CHAPTER 26

I looked at Ken and made a weird smile. "Hey Ken, how are ya?" I said nervously. Ashton studied Ken as he looked at the both of us with a straight face.

Ken's eyes narrowed as his face hardened. "I'm not doing very well. You have two choices, either you come with me or you and Ashton will die," he said callously.

I stepped back, Ashton grabbing my shoulder. "We need to get away from him as possible," he whispered in my ear. I looked at Ken who was still staring daggers at us.

I turned my head to the side to look at Ashton. "We're going to run through that hallway until we find somewhere to hide."

"You two know that I can hear you. You children can try to hide from me, but I always know where you are." Ken gestured for us to leave. "Go ahead and hide, it will be a fun game for me. We all know what's going to happen at the end," Ken said in a low voice.

We turned around and sprinted through the hallway until we're in the big room that had the marble fountain in the center. I looked back; I didn't see Ken or hear any footsteps from that direction.

"Ash, I don't think Ken is following us, I can't hear his footsteps." I looked at the fountain next to me and then at my surroundings. There were a lot of flowerpots around the room, and wooden benches.

Ashton looked at the benches. "He wants us to think that, but he can sense that we're here." Ashton turned to the fountain and then pushed me out of the way. Yellow arrows shot at us from the fountain, one of the arrows cut Ashton on the arm.

Ashton looked at the cut on his arm. "We have to find something to shield us from those arrows." He took my arm and led me to a wall with multiple benches in a row. He flipped a bench onto its side and we hid behind it. I didn't hear anything else. I tried to look out, but Ashton grabbed my shoulder and shook his head.

"We can't risk it, Ken's already here." Ashton pressed his head against the bench. "Shit, if only I had a weapon or something to fight off Ken or distract him with." He looked at me with concern. "I'm sorry that you have to be in this mess."

I looked at him, my eyebrows raised. "To be honest I'm the main reason why this mess even started." I rubbed my temples. "If only we knew how to stop Ken ourselves, then we'd have a chance to survive this. I'm not sure what happened to Rick, maybe he's already dead." I felt all sorts of negative emotions throughout my body. I wish I could just relax but I can't, in this situation I'm freaking out. I'm starting to think that neither of us will make it out of here.

"Don't say that, Rick injected those substances into him that means it's hard for him to die from someone like Sean or Chrissy. We just have to wait until Rick shows up. We can distract Ken at the moment. This might buy Rick some time to get here." Ashton took a deep breath and looked at me. His eyes bore into mine. "Stay here; I don't want you to get hurt." Ashton suddenly got up and ran into the room.

What the hell is he doing? I can't believe he just did that; he's going to get himself killed! I let out an annoyed sigh and got up. I looked at the room. Ken and Ashton were on the other side of the marble fountain

"You have to fight me first before you get to Kai!" Ashton yelled as he gripped his hands into a fist.

Ken turned around, his eyes turning bright blue. "Hmm you sure about that? I know everyone's weakness, even you." Ken ran his hands through his hair. "Fine. After I'm done with you I'll get Kai."

Ashton took out a silver tube from his pants pocket and tapped the tube. It immediately expanded into a staff. He swung the staff around and walked towards Ken on the other side of the large fountain.

I quietly scurried to the other side of the room that was near a hall. I needed to find something to distract Ken before he hurt Ashton.

I ran to the hall and looked at a fire extinguisher that was in a glass case on the wall. I opened the door and grabbed the extinguisher. I looked at the tag on the extinguisher; it only showed the inspection record. I don't know how to use this; I should've paid attention to Rick when he tried to teach me how to use it. I held the extinguisher in one hand and closed the glass door.

I ran back into the fountain room to see Ashton and Ken fighting. Ken held up his palm, multiple arrows shot out of his hands and into Ashton's direction. Ashton dodged the arrows and blocked them with his staff.

Ashton saw me with the extinguisher and shook his head slightly as he quickly glanced at me. He grabbed his staff with both hands and twisted it to make two separate staffs. Both staffs extended. He spun both staffs with his fingers as he walked around Ken, who was still standing in place. I needed to find the right time to use this extinguisher or even learn how to use it.

Ken thrust his hand toward Ashton. A bright yellow beam of light shot out from his hand. Ashton moved swiftly towards Ken as he avoided the light beam. Ashton swung one staff at Ken, who blocked it with his arm. Ashton thrust his other staff into Ken's stomach, but the tip of the staff was an inch from Ken's stomach.

Ken grunted as Ashton was pushed back by an invisible force. I quietly sneaked on the edge of the fountain where Ken was right in front of me. I grabbed the tube from the side of the extinguisher and held it towards Ken's direction.

As Ken got ready to make another attack I pressed the handle. The white foam started to squirt out of the black tube that was attached to the handle. I kept squeezing the handle until I ran out of the foam. I looked at Ken who didn't get covered in foam. All the foam was a few inches in front of him like he was protected by a barrier.

"Shit!" I said out loud. Ken turned around and looked at me with an amused look.

Ken smiled. "You finally get a chance to fight. Sadly you've still got that seal on you. At least it will be much easier for me to kill you." He raised his hand towards me, a beam of light flashed toward me. I ducked and hid behind the fountain, barely missing the light beam. Parts of the fountain broke off and fell inside the fountain pool and on the floor.

I looked up and saw Ken looking straight at me. Ashton quickly struck at Ken's head with his staff and then at his neck with the other staff. Ken turned around and swung at Ashton who ducked and dodged Ken's attack. I got up and walked towards Ken and threw the empty fire extinguisher at him.

The extinguisher hit Ken in the back. As he let out a groan Ashton swung his staff at Ken's head and hit Ken in the side of his face. Ashton stepped back at least ten feet away from Ken. I ran next to Ashton.

"The fight has just begun," Ken said as he touched his cut cheek. Multiple arrows formed out of thin air in front of him. All at once the arrows shot at our direction.

Ashton grabbed my wrist and dragged me to the other side of the fountain. I'm so glad that we had a fountain between us so it could block most of Ken's arrows.

"I thought you left already, I saw you running into the hall," Ashton said as he gripped his staff.

"Well you thought wrong, I'm not going to leave you alone with Ken. Plus I found a distraction, and you took that opportunity to hit Ken," I said as I looked over the fountain. Ken was still standing at the same spot, not looking at us.

"But one hit isn't going to hurt him, that's just a small scratch anyway. It's going to be a very long time for me to even hurt him, it's impossible for me to even kill him." Ashton tapped his staffs together and sharp blades instantly shot out of each tip of the two staffs. "I want you to hide or try to find Rick if you can, just leave me here with Ken."

I made a fist with both of my hands, my eyes searched his face. "No, I'm not going anywhere. Rick can take care of himself, he's a grown man. We just have to stall Ken until Rick shows up, I hope." I looked at the flowerpots that surrounded the room. I walked towards them and took out the flowers and grabbed a pot for each of my hands.

I walked near Ken without looking back at Ashton. I moved my arms behind me, preparing to throw the pots at Ken. I threw a pot at Ken, who swiped his hand to the side. The pot flew against the fountain, shattering into pieces. I threw another one as I ran around him but a single arrow flew out of nowhere to smash through the pot and into my left hand.

I let out a yelp as the arrow pierced through my hand. Blood dripped from my hand through the yellow arrow and into the floor. My hand beginning to shake, I ran behind the tilted bench. I looked at the arrow that was stuck in my hand. I grabbed the arrow with my other hand and tried to pull it out. It's no use, it hurts too much.

I banged my head against the bench and got up slowly. I looked at Ashton, already attacking Ken with his staff. Ashton swung both of his staffs at Ken's throat, but Ken moved back and knocked the staff out of Ashton's grip.

I slowly moved towards Ashton who held his fist up at Ken, waiting for Ken's next move. Ken moved his right hand at Ashton who ducked his attack. Ashton got closer and punched him in the throat and then turned around and hit Ken in the face with his elbow. Ken stumbled back and touched his throat as his facial expression turned irritated.

"Is that all you got?" Ken said as a yellow aura covered his body, his eyes changed into an intense shade of blue.

Ashton wiped sweat from his forehead, his eyes furrowed as he glared at Ken. I was about a few feet from the two of them. I looked around to find some more pots. I grabbed one of them and threw it at Ken. He looked at me fiercely as he dodged the pot.

"Don't you only want me? You wanted to use my powers for your own selfish reasons, so why waste your time on him? Come and get me!" I yelled. Both Ashton and Ken looked at me with surprise.

I looked at Ashton and sprinted towards him, grabbing him by the shoulders, pushing him away from Ken. I pushed Ashton near a bench and tipped the bench, the two of us hiding behind it. Ashton was looking at me with an annoyed look.

"What the hell! I told you you're going to get yourself killed!" he yelled at me, but then he looked at my left hand and shut his mouth.

"I need you to pull it out. As long as you and Rick are alive I don't care if I die or not," I told Ashton, who gingerly took my left hand to examine the arrow. I winced as he touched it. He pulled his hand out as I made a noise. I looked at him dead in the eye. "Just pull the goddamn arrow out of my hand!" I yelled at him. He looked at me, his lips pressed into a thin line. Ashton grabbed the arrow with his hand and pulled the arrow out, apologizing to me. I let out a cry as my hand started to bleed. I covered the hole with the bottom of my shirt. My eyes started to water as Aston dropped the arrow on the ground. As it fell onto the ground a bright yellow beam of light shot at us over our heads.

Ashton pushed me out of the way as the beam moved down towards the floor. We were separated by the beam of light. I winced as I felt a weird sensation in my left hand. I ran away from the beam and hid behind a row of flowerpots. I looked at my blood covered hand, with the hole in it. My heart was beating really fast as I looked through the hole in my hand, I can't believe I just got impaled.

I wiped the sweat from my forehead with my right arm. I turned my head and looked at my surroundings. Ken was shooting arrows at Ashton but he didn't dodge most of Ken's attacks. Ashton's body was cut all over the place. There was a deep gash on his right cheek, blood flowing from his cheek to his jaw. Shit I have to do something; I don't want Ashton to fight Ken all by himself.

I carefully got up; my hand was still bleeding but I ignored the pain. I looked directly at Ken. I wished my other powers would develop sooner so I could actually fight Ken. I looked at Ashton's staff that was a few feet in front of me.

I took a shaky breath and ran towards the staff, grabbing it tightly as I ran towards Ken. I thrust the staff at Ken's back but he turned around and dodged my attack. I swung the staff at Ken but I kept missing. I stepped back and looked at him.

"You finally have the courage to directly fight me."

"Yeah, I just want to get this shit over with," I said, eyes watery from the pain of my hand. I looked at Ashton who swiftly swung his fist towards Ken's neck. I tightly gripped the staff and forcefully jabbed it at Ken's chest.

As Ashton and I struck at Ken a force prevented us from hitting him. I grabbed the staff with my other hand and pushed but it didn't do anything. Ken placed his hand on Ashton's chest. He instantly flew back into the wall, making a loud thud noise as the wall vibrated from his impact. Out of thin air multiple yellow arrows stabbed Ashton in both of his arms, pinning him onto the wall. He let out an agonizing groan as he tilted his head to the side, his eyes barely open.

I looked at Ashton with wide eyes. "No!" I yelled as I stepped back from Ken, still holding onto the staff. I quickly swung the staff at him. Ken thrust his hand at me. An invisible force knocked the staff out of my hand. It dropped on the floor and slowly rolled next to Ken.

Ken grabbed the staff from the floor and swung it at me. Quickly I covered my face with my arms. I could feel my arms being cut by the staff, the feeling was unbearable. I jumped back and moved my arms away from my face. Ken quickly sprinted towards me, as he drove the staff into my left thigh I let out a gasp. Ken punched me in the stomach and made the wind get knocked out of me. I bent down as Ken pushed the staff into my thigh, making a large blood stain in my jeans, and making me completely fall onto the floor. Blood was all over my hands and arms. I moved my head towards Ashton who had his head down with his eyes closed. The blood from his arms dripped down the wall under him.

"Such a shame, I had high hopes for you. Now you're nothing to me, it is no use for me to keep you alive," Ken said, crouching in front of me. "When I'm done with you I'm going to kill Ashton too. I thought he was on my side but I guess he's not."

I tried to get away from Ken but he clutched the staff that impaled my thigh and slowly pulled it out. I let out a shriek as my thigh started to bleed, making the floor turn red with my blood.

Ken crouched down and grabbed me by the neck. I gasped for air. My eyes felt like they had just been stabbed by pins. I grabbed Ken's hand with my right hand to try to loosen his grip by scratching his hand, but it didn't do anything.

Ken's eyes glowed a bright shade of blue that made me feel horrified. He got up, his hand still on my neck. He lifted me up to my feet. Sharp pain instantly poked my thigh as I managed to stand up. I looked down on the floor, a messy puddle of blood, as my eyes lazily closed. Ken shook me so I would open my eyes. I slowly opened my tired eyes and looked at Ken, who had a sinister look on his face.

Ken let out a deep sigh, his jaw clenched tightly. "I went through all this effort to make you become much more powerful than ever, but at the end you proved that my effort was pointless. You're just like your parents and Rick, you're all disappointments. Now I will tell you this, you're going to end up like them and I won't feel bad killing you with my bare hands," Ken said with hatred as his eyebrows knitted.

I managed to breathe a little bit. "Did. Did you kill my parents?" I said, wheezing as I gasped for air.

Ken made a frown. "I did. For someone who was more powerful than Sean and Chrissy combined your father wasn't easy to kill, but your mother was, poor thing," he said, making a tsk sound.

There's a strong pain in my heart, the feeling of hatred and despair mixed together. I could feel tears streaming down my cheeks as I looked at Ken. There's no point going on like this, this is the end.

I locked eyes with Ken and made a smirk. There's no need to cry now, I had to be strong and tell him what I wanted to say to him.

"Go ahead and kill me. I bet you will lose all the people you loved because of who you truly are; you're just a monster who never loved anything. I bet Grandma would say the same thing." I let out a weak laugh. "Who gives a shit anyway, we're all going to hell anyway so kill me; maybe you might feel accomplished after that." Ken tightly squeezed my throat then loosened his grip so I finally got to breathe.

Ken still held me by the neck, his hand glowing a bright yellow. Them he plunged his yellow fist into my chest where my heart is. The pain was nothing that I ever felt before. It was a million times worse than all the pain I felt in my lifetime combined. My head drooped down in front of me. I saw Ken's whole hand went through my chest. I looked to my side to look at Ashton one more time, but I couldn't manage to turn my head. My mouth instantly tasted like blood. Blood began pouring out of my mouth and from the hole in my chest. I felt my body go limp.

CHAPTER 27

K en slowly removed his fist from Kai's body. Kai's body went limp, her blood all over her chest, hands, and legs. There was a large hole where her heart should have been. Ken looked at his blood covered hand and then at Kai who was dead.

His blue eyes went back to their normal brown color, the yellow glow around his body faded as he still was holding Kai by the neck. He looked at the fountain and walked up to it dragging Kai beside him, making a small trail of blood towards the fountain. When he was in front of the fountain he placed Kai's body into the fountain pool. Most of her body was covered in water but her head wasn't. The water turned a light shade of pink but then changed to deep red. Kai's long dark brown hair calmly swayed underwater as all the water turned red.

Ken looked at Kai's body in the fountain and held out his right hand, his palm facing up. A white towel instantly appeared on top of his hand. He grabbed the towel and wiped up most of Kai's blood from his hands, still looking at her.

After he wiped most of the blood off him he tossed the bloody towel off to the side and turned around to look at Ashton who was still pinned to the wall. Ken walked up to Ashton and observed him, his lips moved into a smirk.

Ken let out a heavy sigh. "All these years I raised you when you had no one, at the end you betrayed me. I thought I'd raised you better." Ken made a tsk sound as he walked left and right, staring daggers at Ashton.

Ashton's fingers twitched and he let out a sore groan, his eyes slightly open as he tilted his head up. His bloodshot eyes looked at Ken and then at the trail of blood that led to the fountain. Kai's deceased body lay in the fountain pool. Her body from the neck down was submerged in red tinted water.

Ashton's eyes grew wide as he stared at Kai's lifeless body, his eyes starting to water. He looked back at Ken with rage. He moved his left arm, slowly getting his arm loose from the arrows.

As his arm almost got free, Ken thrust his hand at him. Two more arrows shot out of his hands. Ashton let out a weak yell as the arrows impaled him in the stomach. Blood from the wounds of his stomach soaked his shirt.

Ashton coughed up blood. "What happened to my parents that day? I know that you lied to me about it. Tell me the truth," he said as a trail of blood dripped out of the corner of his mouth.

Ken made a wicked smile. "I'll tell you the truth before I kill you. Your parents were a part of that rebel group with Kai's parents and Rick. Both of your parents planned to completely destroy all the formulas, data, and substances as part of their plan to attempt to end this organization. I had no choice but to kill them myself. It's a shame; they're some of the best scientists I have ever met." Ken made a pitiful smile as he observed Ashton's wounded body. "And now their child will face the same fate as them."

Ashton bared his teeth. "You raised a heartless hit man. I hope you die slowly and painfully for the things you did to me and to everyone else who didn't ask to be this way," he said fiercely and spat out blood.

Ken made a smirk. "You really think that I can die that easily? I could kill everyone in this building without thinking twice. It's an outrageous thing I hear you say." Ashton started to quietly chuckle. Ken's smirk faded. "Why are you laughing at?" Ken's eyes narrowed; his lips made a thin line.

"Rick took both of your secret substances. I don't think you have a chance against him." Ashton glared at Ken with icy eyes.

Ken's arrows disappeared. Ashton dropped on the floor; he let out a gasp as he tried to get up. Both of his arms barely moved from the pain of the arrows. He lay on the floor, covered with his own blood as he looked at Ken.

Ken stepped closer to Ashton, his hands glowing yellow, then Ashton disappeared all of a sudden. Ken stopped walking. He turned his head, looking around the room for Ashton but he was nowhere to be found.

All of a sudden a ball of black energy shot at Ken, but he moved his hand in front of him, making an invisible shield. The ball vanished as it touched his shield. He looked at the direction where the ball was shot from.

Rick walked out of the hall and into the room where Ken was. Rick's eyes glowed a powerful shade of purple and black. He wore a new set of clothes, a gray t-shirt and jeans, but his skin and hair were splattered with blood and dirt.

Ken lowered his hand and looked at Rick, making a smirk. "Look who showed up, you're too late son." Ken raised his hands sympathetically and then gestured towards the fountain with his eyes.

Rick looked at Ken and then at the fountain, his face turned from serious to fearful. Rick couldn't take his eyes off of Kai, who was lying in the fountain, her body covered in blood. Rick's whole body immediately flared with a black aura. He turned his head at Ken, he fought back the urge to cry but it was already too late, tears streamed down his face. Kai's body disappeared."

"I'm going to kill you. How could you hurt my Kai?" Rick said with clenched teeth. Rick wiped his eyes with his arms and glared at Ken with pure fury. "At least I have more reasons to KILL YOU!" He instantly thrust both of his arms at Ken, black energy beamed out of his hands and crashed into Ken.

Ken crossed his arms in front of his face, the beam of energy pushing Ken back against the wall with a strong force. Rick disappeared but then reappeared in front of Ken. He made a fist and struck Ken in the stomach. Ken blocked Rick's punch with his hands, making a blast of wind emanate from the impact. Flowerpots instantly smashed into the wall making a shattered noise. Water from the fountain made waves, and the benches were forcefully moved against the wall.

Rick swung his other hand at Ken's face but an invisible shield stopped Rick's punch. His fist was only a few inches from Ken's face. Rick's face tensed as he drove his fist into Ken's face, breaking the shield. Rick slammed his fist into Ken's cheek making his face forcefully move to the side. A trail of blood dripped down from Ken's nose.

Rick moved his hand back and struck at Ken's face again. Ken vanished as Rick's fist almost touched him. Rick's fist slammed into the wall, causing the wall to crumble down and making a large hole.

Ken appeared next to the fountain. He wiped his bloody nose with his right arm and looked at his arm. "I guess the real fight just had begun." Ken's whole body glowed bright yellow as he swing his right arm in front of him. Waves of yellow light appeared, smashing through benches, wall décor, and part of the wall.

Rick ran away from the light and thrust his hand at Ken. Black light blasted from Rick's hand but Ken dodged the light. Ken pulled back his left arm and pushed his hand out at Rick, a yellow beam from his hands shot directly at Rick.

Rick thrust his hand at Ken black light beamed out of his hand. Both beams of light collided into each other, making a huge explosion of colors that destroyed everything in the room. The collision pushed both Rick and Ken back in opposite directions. The collision also destroyed the top part of the fountain, making the red water splash onto the floor.

Rick and Ken instantly ran towards each other their arms positioned ready to strike with all the power they had.

Ashton and Kai lay on the floor in the middle of the lobby of the building. Other people that Rick encountered lay unconscious, not moving at all. The window of the lobby directed light at the floor, making the room brighten up.

Ashton grunted as his closed eyes squeezed shut. His arms weakly moved up to his head, but his hand touched someone's arm. He slowly opened his eyes and saw Kai lying next to him. His eyes were wide open, he let out a gasp and tried to get up but his arms gave way, making him lay on the floor.

There was a loud rumbling noise from a few floors above the lobby making the whole building vibrate. The vibration caused a few decorations to break instantly.

His lips moved a bit like he's trying to say something. His hands weakly moved on top of Kai's bloody arm. His arms were covered in his own blood; there were multiple holes in his arms and in his stomach from Ken's arrows. He closed his eyes once more, his head rolled to the side.

Kai's body was soaked in water and blood, her face was pale, her hair was all over the place. Blood was oozing out of hole in her chest, making a small puddle of blood under her.

Rick let out a yell as he sprinted towards Ken, his glowing fist positioned to strike. Ken clenched his teeth as the yellow aura that surrounded his body grew extremely bright. All the broken materials in the room started to shake from the vibrating floor.

Both men came at each other thrusting their fists in front of them, their eyes burned with rage. Their fists touched, a massive blast of yellow and black energy rapidly spread throughout the room, making the fountain instantly break. All the water in the marble fountain quickly spread on to the floor, making the floor have a tinted red color.

Both Rick and Ken were unaffected by the blast. They immediately threw punches at each other, dodging one another's attacks. Ken struck his fist at Rick's chest, but he blocked Ken's hand with his own hand making a small blast of colors. Ken repeatedly attempted to punch Rick, but Rick dodged and blocked all of Ken's attacks.

Both Rick and Ken backed away from each other. Ken let his arms drop to his side. Both of the men stared at each other as they were breathing hard, sweat dripping down their faces.

"I guess you weren't as weak as I thought," Ken said as he wiped sweat from his forehead with his arm.

Rick's jaw tightened, he instantly disappeared into thin air. In a few seconds Rick appeared in front of him, both of his hands forcefully grabbing Ken's hands. Ken tried to move away but he couldn't get away from Rick's grip.

Ken's yellow aura and blue eyes slowly faded; his eyes grew wide as his body tensed up. Rick let go of his grip as Ken fell onto the floor. There were two circle-like symbols on each of Ken's hands. Ken was unable to move at all; it was like he was paralyzed.

Rick casually walked in front of him with a vengeful look on his face. Rick's black aura faded and his eyes changed back to his normal brown color. Rick looked at Ken with a straight face as he lay helplessly in front of him. Rick crouched down and grabbed Ken by the neck. He got up and lifted Ken up by his neck so that both men were eye to eye. Ken made a gurgling noise as his hands clawed at Rick's hand.

"How could do this to me and my siblings? I never wanted to be like this!" Rick shook Ken so that he would look at him. "You did this to us! And this is all your fault!" Rick's voice broke, his eyes were watery. Rick tilted his head down for a few seconds and looked back at Ken, tears streaming down his cheeks. "You turned my brother and sister against me, you made them lose their humanity… I can't forgive you for that." Rick bit his bottom lip and tightened his grip, making Ken gasp for air. "If you weren't fucked up in the mind, we could have been a happy family… even if mother wasn't here. She would be happy if we had been a normal happy family, but you had to do this to us. Look what you've done, making all of us monsters and making this pathetic place so more people become like us. You caused all of this, you made me kill my own brother and sister, you killed my fucking niece!" Ken flinched as Rick screamed at him, tears streaming down his face. "Now it's your turn to die," He said in a low growl as be bared his teeth. Rick thrust Ken into a wall. Ken's collision caused the wall to break. He spat out blood onto the floor. Ken's back was against the cracked wall, cuts and bruises were all over his body. He looked at Rick with a weak stare.

Ken licked his lips and mumbled something as Rick walked towards Ken, his eyebrows furrowed. Ken thrust his right hand at Rick but nothing happened. Ken let out a dry cough.

"What did you do to me?" Ken said as he kept moving his hands at Rick, but nothing happened.

Rick made a dark smile. "Since I got injected by your black substance, I became much more powerful. I restrained you from using your powers so I wouldn't have trouble killing you." Rick crouched beside Ken who was sitting on the floor. "And this new power can help me end you and this goddamn organization," Rick said as he placed his left hand on top of Ken's head.

Ken attempt to move away from Rick but he swiftly clutched Ken's head. Rick took a deep breath, his whole body glowed black and his eyes glowed purple and black. All of a sudden Ken's whole body glowed yellow, all the yellow glow moved up to his head then slithered through Rick's arm and into his body. Rick's black glow slowly turned yellow; Ken let out a painful cry. Rick clenched his jaw and closed his eyes as all the yellow glow was absorbed into his body. Ken looked at Rick with fear in his eyes, but then his eyes turned glassy. Ken didn't blink his eyes or move a muscle; he just stared blankly at Rick.

As all of Ken's powers were absorbed into Rick's body, Rick opened his eyes and looked at Ken in front of him. Ken's head was pressed against the wall. Both of his eyes were open staring blankly at him, his body became stiff like he's becoming a statue. Rick's whole body was surrounded by a yellow glow but his eyes were still purple and black."

Rick let go of his grip on Ken and moved away from him. Rick stood up and looked down at Ken; he winced as he touched his heart. Rick leaned his body against the wall as his purple eyes slowly changed to blue. As his eyes turned completely blue Rick fell onto the ground.

Rick moved his body to his side. He made a fist with his hand and slammed his hand onto the ground, fighting with the pain. He let out an agonizing cry as the yellow glow around his body started to glow brighter. The glow became so bright that it looked white. The glow intensified but then it slowly died down. The glow was gone.

Rick moved his body so that he was lying on his back, he sharply inhaled and exhaled. He rubbed his blue eyes, his eyes dilated as he looked up at the ceiling. He let out a sigh his eyes changed back to brown. He turned his head to the side and closed his eyes.

CHAPTER 28

Inside a vet's office, Stella sat on her office chair looking through her phone. Her face showed concern as she scrolled down her call log; Rick's and Kai's names kept showing up in red. Stella turned off her phone and placed it next to her laptop on top of her desk.

Stella's office was any other ordinary office: her walls were decorated with photos of her friends and family, a few framed drawings of her patients' pets, and a degree in veterinary medicine. In one of her photos Rick, Kai, Stella, and Tobi were at Boston's waterfront, the city of Boston was in the background behind them. Rick and Stella were between Kai who was holding Tobi. Tobi was licking Kai in the face making her smile with her eyes closed. Rick made bunny ears with his hand behind Kai's head as he smiled at the photo, while Stella looked at Kai and Tobi, laughing at them.

Stella tapped her finger on her desk, looking anxious for something to happen. Someone outside her door knocked.

"Come in," Stella said out loud, she turned her head towards the door.

A woman in a light pink scrub uniform came inside the office and closed the door.

"Hey Stella, I got you a new patient today, maybe it might cheer you up." The nurse walked up to Stella and placed a folder on top of her desk.

Stella looked at the nurse and smiled. "Why do you think I'm sad?"

The nurse looked at Stella, embarrassed. "Oh, it's just you don't seem like your happy self these past few days. You can talk about your problems to me, it's okay if you don't; it's not my business anyways. I don't want to be nosy." She gave a shy smile.

Stella took the folder and opened it, looking at the paperwork. She looked at the nurse. "You're my best friend Beth, don't worry about me. You know how I can handle things on my own." Stella placed the folder back on the desk and stood up as she looked at Beth.

"Yeah I know, you're a tough cookie, but if something happens I'm always there for you. But I just have to know; did Rick say or do something to you? We both know how men are these days. I could get him rabies in no time, but that's between the two of us ya know." Beth gestured her pointer finger at Stella and to herself.

Both of them look at each other and laughed. Stella gave Beth a hug and Beth hugged back.

"He's a gentleman, he wouldn't say or do something bad to me or anyone else. What do you think he said to me?" Stella asked with a raised eyebrow.

Both women broke their hug. Beth placed both of her hands on Stella's shoulders and looked at her. "I thought he told you that he got a girlfriend or something. I thought…No, I know that you two would be a cute couple."

Stella's cheeks and ears turned red with embarrassment. "No, Rick and I are just close friends." She looked away from Beth flustered.

"Just you wait; I bet he has feelings for you. But I don't want to jump to conclusions, well… I already have." Beth moved her mouth to the side and tapped her fingers on Stella's shoulder. "I know you have feelings for him and as your best friend I'm telling you, go for it before some other chick gets to him first."

Stella looked back at Beth, her eyes sparkled. "I'm not sure how I feel about him; he's an amazing guy but…"

Beth nodded her head with curiosity. "But what?"

Stella took a deep breath and sighed. "It's complicated. Just don't worry so much about me; I just need some time to figure this out." She looked at the folder on her desk. "But the first thing I need to do is to take care of my patient."

Beth moved her hands away from Stella's shoulders. Stella grabbed the folder and nodded at Beth. Both Stella and Beth walked out the door.

Rick opened his brown eyes lazily. He let out a tired moan as he moved his hands up to his head. He rubbed his eyes and started to wheeze heavily, he moved his hands on the floor and sat up.

He adjusted his jaw as he looked around the destroyed room. The walls had large holes that allowed anyone to see through to the other room. Flowerpots, benches, and wall decor were completely destroyed, and small pieces of wall rubble were scattered around the room. Most of the floor in the room was wet from the broken fountain; the floor still had a slight tint of red on it.

He turned his head to face Ken who didn't move an inch; his eyes were still wide open. Rick glanced at Ken and stood up, dusting all the dirt and rubble off of his clothes. He walked next to Ken and crouched down. He placed his two fingers against Ken's neck. His eyes seemed to dull at the sight of Ken. He moved his fingers in front of Ken's eyes and carefully closed his eyelids.

Rick got up and walked towards the middle of the room, his left eye shifting to blue and black and his right eyes shifting to purple and black. He raised his right hand up to the height of his chest. Purple, yellow and black flames flared up around his hand. The colored flames swayed around his hand elegantly as Rick kneeled down on the floor. He forcefully slammed his palm into the floor causing a loud thud. A black circle with patterns and shapes formed under his hand. The circle grew wide enough it completely covered the whole floor in the room. The light of the circle instantly flashed white and disappeared.

In the lobby people who lay unconscious disappeared instantly. Ashton and Kai's body remained in the lobby. In the laboratory Sean's and Chrissy's bodies disappeared, everything in the laboratory disappeared as well. Everyone and everything in the building disappeared, leaving only Rick, Kai, and Ashton in the empty building.

As Rick got up he saw all the broken decor had disappeared. He looked at Ken and he too vanished. Rick let out a sigh as his colored flames died out. He disappeared and reappeared in the lobby where Kai's and Ashton's bodies lay.

In the lobby Rick instantly looked at Kai's and Ashton's bodies. He walked towards the two with damp eyes that never looked away from them, he had a look that could make someone pity him. His face turned colorless as he placed his right hand over his mouth and kneeled down next to Ashton. Tears streamed down his face, he closed his eyes and made a muffled scream as he leaned his head toward his chest. His muffled screams could be heard throughout the lobby, but no one outside the building would ever hear him cry in deep agony.

Rick's screams and wails slowly died out, it took time for Rick to compose himself once again. He opens his reddened eyes and looked away from the bodies, he removed his hand from his mouth and lay it on the tile floor. Both of his hands lay flat on the floor, his fingers curled up into a tight fist. He clenched his jaw and looked back at the bodies, his jaw softens as he let out a quivering sigh.

He wiped his eyes with the palm of his hand and looked down at Ashton, he raised his hand and stroked Ashton's sweat drenched hair.

"I-I should have come..." He wiped his nose with his arm. "Sooner," he whispered as he tilted his head down towards Ashton's pale face. He began to cry again, tears came rushing down his face and onto Ashton's forehead.

Ashton's eyebrow twitched as Rick's tears continue to drop onto his forehead. Rick noticed that Ashton is still alive and gasped.

Rick held Ashton's hand and patted it. "I'm going to heal you, okay? I'm not going to let you die." Rick said quietly as he placed Ashton's hand back on the floor. Both of Rick's hands are now covered with a black glow.

Rick held both of his hands on top of Ashton's body. Holes inside his arms slowly regenerated, cuts and bruises on Ashton's body fully healed. Ashton didn't move or open his eyes. Rick's hands stopped glowing.

"I'm going to let you rest kiddo." He patted Ashton's head and look at Kai, his smile faded.

"This is all my fault, if I was here earlier you would still be alive. I'm so, so sorry Kai. What would Veha and Jenna think of me?" He moved next to Kai and kneeled down next to her.

He brushed Kai's hair out of her face and gently moved her body to hug her, his chin pressed on top of Kai's head. He wrapped his arms around Kai and rocked back and forth, sobbing.

"You're going to be okay, you're going to be okay," Rick said repeatedly as he hugged Kai, not letting go of her.

He looked at Kai's right hand and gently grabbed it, turning her hand to show her palm, Ken's seal had disappeared. Rick kissed Kai on top of her head and softly pressed his cheek against her head. He slowly laid Kai's body on the floor. Both of his hands glowed black as he carefully held his hands on top of Kai's chest and head.

The black glow flowed from Rick's hands and into Kai's body as a dark circle that resembled a flower appeared on Kai's right hand. The glow was absorbed inside Kai's body. Rick stood up and all three of them disappeared.

Rick, Kai, and Ashton reappeared inside Rick and Kai's living room. Rick walked to the front door and took the paper off of the outside of the door and crumbled it up to toss it in the paper bin in the living room.

Rick stood next to Kai and Ashton. He lifted his hand at them, in an instant a black glow covered both of their bodies but then it disappeared. The glow that covered their bodies changed their clothes to a new clean pair of clothes. There were no bloody stains or marks on their bodies. Both Kai and Ashton disappeared once again.

Kai reappeared in her room lying in her bed, resting. Ashton reappeared lying on a bed in the guess bedroom. Neither of them moved or made a noise.

A black silhouette formed next to Rick in the living room. Rick looked at the silhouette. The silhouette transformed into an exact copy of Rick wearing the same clothes Rick wore this morning. Rick looked at his double. "I'm going to send you back to New York so you can get back to that hotel and check out, I don't want anyone to be suspicious of me. Also find the people who I've met and erase their memories about me."

Rick's double nodded then the double vanished in black smoke.

Rick raked his hair with his hand and walked up the stairs, through the hallway. The hallway walls were decorated with photos of Rick, Kai, and their friends. One of the photos was Rick in his officer uniform standing next to Chief Gray, smiling. A few other photos were of Kai and her friends when they were younger at a few different locations and events.

Rick stopped next to a door that had multiple stickers on the door. He opened the door and peeked inside. Kai was lying on her bed resting. Rick made a sad smile and softly closed the door. He turned around and opened the door next to Kai's room; Ashton was resting on the bed, sleeping. He closed the door and walked to his room.

In his room there was a black desk with a matching chair in the corner of his room, office supplies and folders were neatly placed on top of his desk. His bed was in the side of the room next to his large built in closet. The walls were painted light gray and were decorated with black and white framed photographs. His room was very modern with a dark color scheme that fit his style.

Rick walked up to his closet and picked out a white tank top and gray sweatpants. He turned around and walked out of his bedroom. He walked into the bathroom and placed his new clothes on top of the sink counter. The bathroom was a similar color scheme to Rick's room, gray colored walls decorated with stylish framed photographs. The sink counter was made with brown wood, while the tile floor was decorated with black and white patterned tiles. The walk-in shower was made with gray tiles. Rick opened the glass shower doors and turned on the knob.

He touched the water and then turned the knob again. He took off his shirt and tossed it on the floor. He looked at the wide mirror that was above the sink counter. He looked at his strongly built body with a frown. He touched his ankh tattoo on his upper left chest and looked down at his stomach. On the left side of his stomach there were large scratch marks that scarred his body.

Rick moved closer to the mirror and looked at his face, his hair was messy with blood and dirt, his cheeks were slightly sunken, and spots of dried blood were on his cheeks. Rick's left eye switched to blue and black and his right eye switched to purple and black. His facial expression changed to shock, he quietly observed his eyes fascinated with his new discovery. He took a deep breath and exhaled, his eyes changing back to brown. He placed both of his hands on the sink counter looking down at the sink, reflecting on what had happened today.

CHAPTER 29

"**C**ome on Stella we're going to Rick's house and I want you to tell him how you feel about him. I don't want you to be a loner. I'm doing you a favor, you can thank me later," Beth said as she and Stella were walking down the sidewalk. Stella was walking next to Beth; she looked at her with an annoyed look.

Beth looked back at Stella and raised an eyebrow. "What?" she said nonchalantly.

Stella let out a sigh. "Rick is in New York, there's no point going to his house," she said as she put her hands in her jacket pockets.

"Maybe he lied to you, he's probably sitting at his house doing whatever guys do. We're going to meet him and I'm going to force you to tell him how you feel or I will do it for you," Beth said, walking a bit faster.

Stella struggled to keep up with Beth. "Hey, quit walking so fast, don't you have something better to do? Like being with your husband?" she said as she almost tripped over a small rock, swearing in Spanish.

Beth looked back and stopped speed walking. She walks up to Stella. "Are you okay? You almost fell in public and that would have been embarrassing. And like I said, I'm doing a favor for you, Rick, and myself," she said as she helped Stella gain her balance.

Stella looked at Beth. "Thanks for your concern," she said sarcastically. "Like I told you, I don't know how I feel towards him."

Stella and Beth started to walk casually into Rick's neighborhood. Stella led the way to his house and stopped at a brick row home. Both women looked at each other; they both went up the stairs and knocked on the front door.

A few minutes passed; footsteps could be heard inside the home. Through the glass part of the door a silhouette of a person walked towards the door. The person unlocked the door and opened it. On the other side of the door was a shirtless Rick, wearing only his black jogger pants. His face looked shocked as he looked at Stella, hair still wet from his shower.

Both Beth's and Stella's face were red at the sight of Rick and both looked at him, not saying a word.

Rick made an awkward smile at them. "Hey Stella, I just got back from New York I was just about to call, you," he said, and looked at Beth. "Hey Beth," he said, still maintaining an awkward smile.

Both of the women took a few seconds trying to stay focused. Stella looked to the side as Beth looked at Rick's body.

Beth looked at Stella. "I knew that Rick was hot, but I didn't know he was that hot. Like wow. You better make your move before I do, and I have a husband," she said, blushing and smiling.

Stella elbowed Beth in the arm, Beth let out an 'ouch!' and looked back at her. Rick let out a playful laugh.

Both women looked at Rick, flustered. "That's funny, it's not the first time a woman said something like that to me." He looked at Stella his face turned serious. "But I have to tell you something very important, can you come in?"

Stella and Beth exchanged looks and Stella nodded. "You can leave us, see you tomorrow."

"Okay make sure you text me when you're done. Well I guess I'm leaving, good luck you two." Beth winked at Stella and Rick as she walked down the stairs and onto the sidewalk.

After Beth walked a house down, she turned around and cupped her hands and yelled. "You two are so cute together!" Then she turned around and walked away.

Stella looked back at Rick, both of them blushing. Stella pressed her hands against her cheeks. "Sorry about her, she doesn't know what she's talking about." She made a forced laugh.

Rick raised his eyebrow, leaning against the doorframe, his arms crossed. "You sure? I think I know what she meant by that." He tilted his head towards Stella. "And I also agree we look cute together." He made a smirk.

Stella removed her hands from her cheeks and walked inside his home. "S-Shut up!" she stuttered.

Rick looked back at Stella, still smirking. She walked through the hallway and into the kitchen, Rick following her.

Inside the kitchen Rick grabbed a kettle from a cabinet and turned on the sink. He placed the kettle under the sink, filling up the kettle with water. He placed the kettle on the stove and turned on the stove. A white tank top appeared on the counter next to the stove. Rick took the tank top and put it on.

Stella walked into the kitchen and took a seat at the kitchen table. Rick sat next to her, placing a mug with a teabag in it in front of her.

"Why didn't you answer my calls and text?" Stella said, looking at the mug.

"I think my phone got completely destroyed during my trip, so that's why I couldn't call or text you back," Rick said, holding onto his mug.

"What is this importing thing you wanted to say to me?" Stella asked as she took the mug, tapping her fingernail on it.

Rick looked at her without saying anything for a moment. Stella looked back at Rick. They locked eyes. "It's very complicated Stella. It's going to take a while for me to explain all of this to you or to anyone. I'm afraid that after I tell you what happened, you won't like me and won't be friends with me. I don't want to lose you; you're such a great person." Rick took Stella's hands and held them, still looking at her in the eyes.

Stella took a deep breath and exhaled. "Why would you think I wouldn't be friends with you? I already know that you have powers, is that what you're going to talk about?"

Rick bit his lip. "That's partly the reason I wanted to talk to you, but I have to start from the beginning…"

In about two hours of Rick explaining to Stella what happened during the situation about his family and what had happened today, Stella kept quiet and listened to Rick until the end. Her facial expression changed from calm to horrified to sad. When he was at the part where he found Kai and Ashton in the lobby after his fight with his father, his voice became quiet.

Stella's face turned pale when Rick told her that Kai was dead, but he told her that he resurrected Kai from the dead by using his new powers. He told her that Kai was in her room waiting to be completely revived. Stella instantly stood up, almost knocking the chair onto the floor. She ran up the stairs and into Kai's room, she walked into the room and towards Kai who lay on the bed.

Stella held Kai's hand and carefully stroked her hair with her other hand. Rick walked next to Stella and looked at Kai, his face saddened. There was a small glowing yellow dot in the center of the circle that was on her right hand. The dark part of the circle didn't glow yet.

"I thought you were joking about her getting a tattoo, I didn't know that it would be so… revealing. When is she going to be fully recovered?" Stella asked, not taking her eyes off of Kai.

"Kai suffered major injuries; it's going to be a while for her to recover. If I was there earlier Kai wouldn't have died in the first place. What will she say to me when she wakes up? She must hate me!" Rick made fists of his hands, his body tense.

Stella let go of Kai's hand and placed both of her hands on Rick's shoulders. "It's not your fault, don't bring yourself down. You have the power to bring people back from the dead, you're bringing Kai back. You should be happy that she's going to be alive again." Stella wrapped her arms around Rick's body. "I don't want you to be hard on yourself."

Rick hugged Stella back. "Don't worry I won't, are you sure you're still friends with me?"

"Of course we're still friends." Stella let go of Rick and looked at him. "Can I see Ashton if you don't mind?"

Rick smiled and nodded. Stella walked up to Kai and kissed her on the forehead and walked out of the room. Rick took Kai's right hand and kissed it; he rubbed his thumb on her hand as he looked at her. He made a sad smile and placed Kai's hand back on the bed and left the room.

Rick looked at the guest bedroom door, it was already open. He walked into the room; Stella sat on the bedside holding Ashton's hand. Rick stood on the other side of the bed looking at Ashton, who was sleeping peacefully.

"Are you going to be his guardian? I could take care of him if you like," Stella said as she hummed a tune. "He's quite handsome."

Rick smiled and nodded. "Yeah he's quite a looker. Once he wakes up I need him to tell me everything that my father and siblings have done during these past few years. I will take care of him so don't worry. We should let him rest, let's go to the living room," he said as he stroked Ashton's hair.

Stella looked at Rick and then at Ashton. "It's better if both of the kids are left alone," she said as she placed Ashton's hand back on the bed and got up.

Both Stella and Rick walked out of the room, Rick quietly closed the door. They walked down the stairs and into the living room. Stella opened the curtains making the room brighter. Rick sat on the sofa and looked at Stella who had her back to him.

"So do you want to talk about it?" Rick asked as he lay back onto the sofa, resting his right arm on the armrest.

Stella turned around with a raised eyebrow. "Talk about what?"

Rick rested his cheek on his hand and looked at Stella. "You like me don't you?" He paused for a second, thinking what to say next. He smiled nervously. "I like you too; we've been friends for about six years and…I was wondering if you want to be more than friends?"

Stella walked towards Rick and sat next to him. She held his hands. Her chest moved up and down, she looked at him fondly. Neither of them said anything, they just looked at each other.

Stella let go of Rick's hand to touch his cheeks. She took a deep breath and pulled his face into hers, kissing him. Rick's eyes were wide open with surprise but then they slowly shut, his left hand touched the side of Stella's neck and his right hand gripped her waist.

The two broke up their kiss and looked at each other with slightly pink cheeks. Rick touched his lips and smiled; his eyes sparkled with joy. Stella pressed her cheeks with her hands and cheerfully smiled.

"Wow that was a really good kiss." Stella lightly laughed.

"It was," chuckled Rick as he placed his hands on Stella's. "I guess I already know the answer to my question." He looked to the side and turned back. "Can I kiss you again?" he asked with a seductive look.

Stella smiled wide. "I thought you'd never asked." Rick instantly pressed his lips into hers.

It was morning, the bright sunlight shining into the guest room where Ashton was sleeping. Ashton's fingers twitched slightly for a few minutes, his eyes lazily opening. His pupils dilated as he looked up at the smooth ceiling.

He slowly rose up looking at his surroundings. The guest room had a dark brown wooden desk with a black desk chair. A large bookshelf was on the side of the room that was next to a closet. The room was painted in light gray to go with the brown wooden floors. A few framed photographs of a landscape decorated the walls, making the room seem cozy.

Ashton moved his leg off to the side of the room and touched his hair with his hands. His eyes grew wide as he looked at his arms, his arms seemed normal like nothing happened to them. He exhaled and got up, standing barefoot on the cold floor.

He opened the door and walked out the room and into the hallway, calmly stopped in front of Kai's door. He gingerly opened the door and walked in. As he walked inside the room, he saw Kai lying on her bed.

He quickly walked beside her bed. He looked at the circle on her right hand. He held her hand tenderly. His eyes started to water, he sat on the side of her bed looking at her with regret.

"It should have been me; I don't deserve to live. If only I was stronger I would've been able to protect you, this wouldn't happen. It's my fault that I'm weak." He wiped his eyes with his hand and made a sniffing sound.

"It's not your fault, don't be so hard on yourself," said Rick, who was leaning against the doorframe looking at Ashton. "She's going to live so don't worry about her too much. Let's talk in the kitchen, I made you breakfast."

Ashton looked at Rick, his emerald green eyes bright. "Okay." He placed Kai's hand back on the bed and got up. He turned around and started to walk out of the room.

Rick gave a friendly smile as Ashton walked into the hallway. He closed the door and walked down the stairs with Ashton.

The two went inside the kitchen, the kitchen table was filled with plates of scrambled eggs, bacon, toast, and bagels. Ashton took a seat at the table; Rick took a seat that was across from Ashton.

Ashton observed the food that was on the table and the empty plate that was in front of him. He looked up at Rick. "You don't have to be nice to me Mr. Kago. I don't deserve your hospitality."

Rick smiled. "You can call me Rick. I don't want you having an empty stomach, dig in!" Rick raised his glass of orange juice attempting to lighten up the mood.

Ashton blushed and looked down at his hands on his lap. "Thank you," he whispered.

He looked up Rick who was smearing cream cheese onto a bagel. Rick looked up at Ashton. "It's no problem kiddo." He took a bite of his bagel and hummed a tune.

Ashton gingerly took a plate of eggs and scooped some of them onto his plate. He put the plate back and grabbed a piece of toast and bit into it. He grabbed a glass of orange juice with his other hand and drank half the glass.

"You must be really hungry huh?" Rick chuckled as he wiped his lips with a napkin.

"I never had a home cooked meal before, it's really good." Ashton made a shy grin as he kept eating his toast.

"I'm glad you like my cooking Ashton. Let's eat all of this before the food gets cold," Rick said with a cheerful tone.

Ashton nodded at Rick and the two ate their breakfast as they talked, getting to know more about each other.

CHAPTER 30

After Rick and Ashton ate their breakfast the two sat on the sofa in the living room. Rick sat next to Ashton, placing his hand on Ashton's shoulder.

"I want to ask you if you're okay with me as your legal guardian, but it's okay if you aren't. You can live and explore the world by yourself. I can give you money if you like, or maybe you know someone and wanted to be with them?" Rick said, gazing at Ashton, who immediately turned his head to Rick with a surprised look on his face. His facial expression turned sad.

"I don't have anyone to be with, both of my parents are deceased and I only have you and Kai. I feel like I'm not welcome anywhere, if I were to live with you I would be invading your life. It's probably better if I was dead," Ashton said bitterly as he made a tight fist with his hands.

Rick wrapped his arms around Ashton and pulled him in, giving Ashton a loving hug, tears flowing down his cheeks and into Rick's shirt. Ashton wrapped his arms around Rick, hugging him back. He pressed his face against Rick's chest and began to cry.

"Don't say that kiddo, I will be here for you no matter what and that's a promise. I have only just met you but I want you to live with me and Kai. You helped Kai and took good care of her; I want to thank you for that."

Ashton turned his head to the side and wiped his nose with his arm. "I want to live here with you and Kai. I'm sorry that you have to see me like this Rick," he whispered.

"Don't apologize, this past week has been an emotional rollercoaster. I will take good care of you." The two broke up their hug.

Ashton's eyes were puffy and his cheeks were pink. "Thank you, I don't know how to repay you." He wiped his nose again with his arm.

Rick grinned and rubbed his hand against Ashton's hair, making it messy. "I want you to live a full life and enjoy it with us. I want you to go to school and work hard. Maybe you want to become something when you get older. Do you have any idea what you want to be?"

Ashton looked down at his lap thinking about Rick's question. "I'm not really sure yet, Ken raised me to become an assassin so I could do something like that."

Rick let out a slight laugh. "Your assassin skills will come in handy with some government work, maybe CIA or FBI? But I don't think you will use those skills now since you're still young."

Ashton looked up and smiled slightly. "You sure? CIA or FBI? I think it's a good start."

"You just have to work hard and actually enjoy what you do if you want any kind of job. It's not a bad idea, thinking about the future. You know Kai wants to be a detective? I'm glad she wants to become a detective, that way I can keep an eye on her during work. I'm afraid she will experience things that can change her life for the worst but I shouldn't think about those things." Rick paused and let out a sigh. "I'm getting off track. I also wanted to ask you about your time with Ken and the organization, I want you to tell me everything."

Ashton nodded and looked away from Rick. "Ken made this underground organization to make people develop powers or abilities so that he can make them become assassins. We all have different uses depending on our abilities or powers, I was Ken's go to assassin. Ken took me under his wing and he made me become the person I am today, he turned me into a killer. I'm just glad that I could get away from him and that place," he said in disgust. "What happen to Ken? Is he still alive?" He looked at Rick with concern.

Rick looked at Ashton as he bit his lip. "I fought Ken and killed him. I ended everyone and the organization for good. As long as that organization is gone there's no need to worry."

"Can you tell me what happened when you and Ken were fighting?"

"I'll tell you what happened after you tell me more about the organization."

Ashton nodded and continued the conversation. "Ken finds people and manipulates them to do underground work or tasks for him. He and his group of scientists created different kinds of substances and inject them into people.

After they get injected they can gain abilities or powers. Ken also sells those substances to other underground organization; it's unknown what the person may develop once they get injected with the substance."

"What do you mean by that?"

Ashton looked at the lotus tattoo on his right forearm. "When they create a new substance they don't know what powers or ability will develop, so it's random. Ken spent a long time perfecting his substance and then he finally injected himself with the final substance he made. Ken is the most powerful person in the whole organization, if you ever disrespect him or go against him he will torture or kill you without any remorse. I should know because I was there when he did all of that to many people. He also injected Kai with two power enhancement substances, one substance is made from her dad's DNA and the other is made from Ken's DNA. He wanted to see if she could develop her dad's superhuman strength and invincible skin and also Ken's supernatural abilities. He also made other different enhancement substances for only a small handful of people including himself, Sean, Chrissy, me, and a few other people. The people who were injected with this substance have to get a tattoo that represents that individual as a person. That's why Kai has a big arm sleeve tattoo because she got the tattoo from Ken himself. I hope I told you enough about this organization and that it helps you have a better understanding of this."

"It actually did, thank you for telling me all of this. But do you know when the substance that Kai was injected with will ever develop?"

"When injected with a substance the wait time for developing the new power or ability is random, so no one knows when it will actually develop. For some people it will take a few days, weeks, or even months. Maybe when Kai wakes up she might already develop her dad's powers and Ken's ability."

Rick nodded his thumb on his bottom lip. "So Kai will eventually gain her dad's powers huh?" he said thoughtfully. "You know that Kai's father, my older brother he had superhuman strength, but he also had an invincible body. That means if Kai gained at least her father's invincible body she can't get hurt or die again which is a good thing. I just hope she will develop her father's powers before she wakes up." He took a long pause before he said anything else.

"I hope she wakes up from her coma," Ashton said quietly. Rick placed his hand on his shoulder, comforting him.

Rick looked at Ashton. "Now it's my turn to tell you about my fight with my father. I was the person who teleported you and Kai to the lobby. Ken almost killed you right on the spot but I saved you just in time. I saw Kai lying in that fountain in the middle of the room dead and it made me very angry. I immediately threw punches at Ken but he blocked my attacks. Ken and I were just throwing punches and using our powers on each other. It was a really tough fight; Ken was really powerful but luckily I used up all that black substance and it help me keep up with Ken. The fight seemed like it lasted for hours and then I somehow managed to hurt Ken. For some parts of the fight I don't remember some of the stuff that happened, I just remembered that I had to kill him for what he had done to you and Kai. At the end we exchanged words and I used my new powers to extract all of Ken's power into me, so I now have three powers combined into one. When I gained Ken's powers I somehow sucked the life out of Ken, killing him right on the spot. I'm just glad that he's not going to cause any more trouble. I used my new powers to destroy everything inside the building and everyone in it. I know that it's a bad thing killing everyone in that building, but I had to do that so people won't be suspicious about that building and organization."

"I understand, it's better that way."

"After I did all of that I teleported myself inside the lobby and healed you. I used my powers to bring Kai back to life but it's going to take some time for her to fully recover," Rick said as he lay back on the sofa.

Ashton looked back at Rick. "Do you know how long until Kai's going to be fully recovered?"

"It's going to be a while. You know that circle on her right hand?"

"Yeah, what about it?"

Rick placed his arm on the armrest. "That circle indicates how long until she's going to come out of her coma. The light from the circle will slowly fill the part that was darkened; once the whole circle is fully covered by the light then we know she will wake up. Since she suffered major injuries the healing process will take a long time."

Before Ashton could respond the front door opened. "Hey Rick, I got some food for you and Ashton." Stella said as she walked into the living room carrying a few bags of groceries. She stopped as she saw Ashton sitting on the sofa. She placed the groceries on the floor and walk up to him. Tobi walked up to Ashton, smelling him, and then jumped up on the sofa to lie on Rick's lap. Rick petted Tobi on the head and looked at Stella.

"Hi Ashton! I'm Stella, Rick's girlfriend. Nice to meet you! I already know that he has powers so you don't have to hide that secret from me." Stella smiled. Ashton stood up as Stella took out her hand and Ashton took it, the two shook hands. After they shook hands Stella hugged Ashton lovingly.

"Aww he's so adorable with his beautiful green eyes," Stella said, still hugging Ashton who hugged back with a friendly smile.

"Rick you didn't tell me you have a girlfriend, and it is nice to meet you too Stella," Ashton said as Stella continued to hug him.

Rick scratched his head. "We just kissed yesterday, I don't want to rush our relationship," he said to Stella, blushing.

Stella looked at Rick, still holding Ashton. "Yeah, whatever Rick. We're officially a thing so you better get used to me calling you my boyfriend." Stella broke up the hug.

"I got some groceries for you guys, if you two didn't eat breakfast yet."

Rick got up and Tobi jumped from the sofa and walked towards Ashton. Ashton crouched down and petted Tobi. Rick grabbed the bags of groceries and walked into the kitchen, Stella following him, leaving Ashton and Tobi in the living room. Tobi licked Ashton in the face. Ashton smiled and laughed as he played with Tobi.

In the kitchen Rick and Stella unpacked the groceries and put them away in the cabinets and refrigerator.

"You don't have to buy this for us, I can buy all of this myself," Rick said as he put a jug of milk in the refrigerator.

"I want to help you and Ashton, plus it's the weekend so I really don't have much to do," Stella replied as she put a box of cereal in a cabinet.

The two were having a long conversation as they put away the groceries.

After two weeks of getting everything settled, Rick officially became Ashton's legal guardian. Ashton chose to keep his last name and Rick was happy with Ashton's choice, he told Ashton that he will never replace his parents and that he's happy that Ashton is part of his family. Rick helped Ashton fill out paperwork in order for him to go to high school. Ashton took a placement test that helped him find the right level classes to take. Rick was happy for him and longed for Kai to wake up.

During the time Kai was in her coma, Ashton and Rick became close. Both Ashton and Rick told each other stories about their lives and talked about general things that are happening in the world.

Ashton walked down the stairs and into the kitchen where Rick was sitting at the kitchen table eating pancakes. Ashton had gotten dressed up for his first day of school. He had a bright smile on his face as he sat at the kitchen table.

"Good morning Rick," Ashton said as he took a few pancakes from the plate and put them on an empty one.

"Good morning kiddo, are you excited for your first day of school?" Rick asked as he wiped his lips with a napkin. Rick was wearing his usual work outfit with his gun holster on his torso.

Ashton smiled. "Yes I am, but I'm also nervous. I'm not sure if I could make friends, maybe I would be a loner," he said as his smile faded.

Rick looked at Ashton with a reassuring smile. "Don't worry, you will make friends. Maybe you could be friends with Kai's friends, they're really good kids. When it's time for you to get on the bus, I will introduce you to one of Kai's friends who lives a few houses down. His name is Owen and he's a nice boy, I bet you two will become great friends."

"Really? You would do that? Thank you Rick I owe you a lot," Ashton said, his eyes lighting up.

The two finished their breakfast, Rick cleaning the dishes while Ashton was walking up the stairs. Ashton walked down the hall but then stopped at Kai's door. He opened the door and quietly walked in.

He sat on the bed where Kai was resting. He took her right hand and examined her glowing circle. The circle was one fourth away from being complete. Ashton patted Kai's hands tenderly.

"I'm going to miss you. I have to go to school now, goodbye." He placed her hand gently beside her and stood up, looking at her.

Ashton walked out of the room and walked into his. The guest room was slightly different from before; there were more decorations throughout the room and there is a large whiteboard on one wall that has neat handwriting on it. Ashton turned the guest room into his own room making it seem cozy to his liking.

Ashton walked up to his desk where he placed his gray backpack on his desk chair. He took his backpack and walked out of his room and into the kitchen where Rick was drinking his coffee out of a mug that Kai made when she was young.

Ashton noticed the mug. "Did Kai make that for you?" he asked.

Rick looked at the mug and smiled, the mug said, 'World's greatest uncle.' He looked back at Ashton. "It was a Father's Day gift from her; I guess I'm pretty lucky that I get a lot of gifts during Mother's and Father's Day." Rick chuckled. "Can't wait till my little monster wakes up so I can give her a big hug."

"I want to tell her how much I miss her," Ashton said, his hands in his jacket pocket.

Both of them smiled at each other. Rick looked at his black Rolex watch on his left wrist. "Well I guess it's time to go." He placed his coffee mug in the sink and walked into the hallway, grabbing his police badge, phone, and car keys. He put his phone in his back pants pocket and clipped his badge on his belt.

Ashton followed behind him, fishing for something in his bag. He took out his phone and zipped his bag up.

The two of them walked out the door. Ashton closed the door and tugged at the door to make sure that it was locked. Rick was out on the sidewalk waiting for Ashton. Ashton walked down the stairs and walked down the sidewalk with Rick.

A few feet ahead of them were students standing on the sidewalk waiting for their bus. One of the students was Owen, listening to music with his earbuds on. Owen looked at the direction where Rick and Ashton were walking. Owen's eyes grew wide he took off his earbuds and quickly walked toward them, almost tripping on his own foot.

"Rick! Where's Kai? And also how was your trip?" Owen said, looking at Rick with eagerness.

Rick smiled as he grabbed Ashton by the shoulders. "Our trip was quite an experience. Kai got into an accident during our trip and is resting in her bed right now. She's in a coma and it's better not to visit her for a few weeks. But don't worry she's fine, she will get better and she will see you and her other friends in no time," Rick said as he moved Ashton in front of him. "By the way this is Ashton Schutz, he's now Kai's adopted brother. I want you to show him around the school so he won't be lost. I also want you to show him Kai's other friends, I don't want him to be lonely during his time in school so be nice to him."

Ashton awkwardly took out his hand and smiled nervously. "Hi."

Owen smiled and quickly shook his hand with both of his hands. "Nice to meet you Ashton, I'm Owen Terrell. I already know we're going to be great friends!"

Ashton's facial expression turned from shy to relaxed. "You seem like a cool person to hang with, pleased to meet you Owen."

Rick removed his hands from Ashton's shoulders. "I have to go to work now, and don't cause any trouble," he said as he patted both Ashton's and Owen's shoulders, then he turned around and walked to his car parked in front of his house.

Ashton looked back and Owen who was still smiling. "We should head back to our bus stop."

Ashton nodded and walked to the bus stop with Owen. Cars drove by on the street, people walked through the sidewalk on their way to school or work. The sky was slightly cloudy, birds chirped as the two were talking to each other.

"So where are you originally from Ashton?" Owen asked as they stopped at the bus stop. Other students gathered at the spot, looking at their phones and listening to their music.

"I was originally from New York City. New York is a great place to be depending on the time of year."

Owen nodded and asked a few more questions about Ashton, the two were having a conversation until the bus arrived. Everyone at the bus stop lined up to get on the bus.

As Ashton took a seat by the window, Owen sat next to him, continuing their conversation. The bus door closed and the bus started to move on to the street.

CHAPTER 31

Rick opened the doors that lead inside the police station. A few citizens sat on the chairs on the other side of the room waiting to report a problem or issue. A man in an officer uniform at the front desk nodded at Rick, he nodded back at the officer. Rick opened the door that led inside the building. Police officers, detectives, and civilians were all over the large room. A few officers glanced at Rick as he continued to walk towards Fred's office.

Rick tapped on the glass door. Fred looked up from his paperwork and gestured with his hand for him to come in. Rick opened the door and walked inside.

"So how was your trip to New York, Rick?" Fred asked as he got up and walked towards him giving Rick a hug.

The two men broke up their hug. "It was quite a life changing experience since I had to kill my father, siblings, and other people with superhuman powers like me. My father killed Kai but I brought her back to life with the newly developed powers that I gained from my father and some black power substance. I have another kid now, his name is Ashton and he's the same age as Kai so I won't have to worry much about him, he knows how to take care of himself since he's a teen. Also I got a girlfriend now so everything seems to be looking up for me." Rick said as he looked around Fred's office. Fred's desk looked like it had been replaced with a new desk. "I like your desk, is it new?" he asked as he looked at it.

Fred's made a baffled look "What?"

"I like your desk, is it new?"

Fred shook his head with confusion. "I meant the other thing you said."

Rick leaned closer to Fred. "I have a girlfriend now." He made a silly smile.

Fred's eyebrow twitched. "Yeah that's the only thing that made sense, quit smiling like a crackhead. You got another kid?" His eyes grew wide. "Wait, is Kai really dead?"

"Well, she was, but I'm bringing her back to life like I did to you that one time." Rick gestured to Fred's right hand which had the same circle tattoo as Kai's.

"Oh my God. Tyrone kept asking me what happen to the two of you; all I told him was that you two went to New York for personal reasons. How am I going to tell him his best friend is coming back from the dead?" Fred rubbed his temples with his hands as he walked back and forth.

"Just tell him that Kai's been in an accident that made her have a long term coma, she'll be fine in a couple of weeks. Don't worry about her too much Fred," Rick said as he fixed his tie. "It's going to get better."

Fred stopped walking and looked at Rick with an annoyed look. "God have mercy."

At school Ashton and Owen were walking to the cafeteria where Kai's friends were gathered at a table. Everyone at the table was taking to each other. Ronnell and Tyrone were talking about their history homework. Tyrone looked up at Owen and then at Ashton and smiled at them.

"Hey guys this is Ashton, he's Kai's brother." Owen patted Ashton on the back as everyone said their hellos and introduced themselves. There were seven people at the table including Ashton. Those seven people were Owen, Tyrone, Ronnell, Dawn, Jake, and Ronny.

"Wait where's Kai?" Tyrone asked as he looked around the cafeteria, searching for her.

Ashton put his hands in his jacket pockets. "Uhh she got into an accident during her trip to New York and went into a coma, I really don't know how long until she's going to wake up. The doctor said that she should be left alone for a few weeks until she's completely recovered. But she's doing well right now."

"What kind of accident she got into?" asked Dawn, who was swirling her cup of iced coffee as she looked at him.

"She uhh, got into a car accident," Ashton said as he looked at the people who were at the table.

Ronny tapped his fingers on the tabletop. "Damn that sounds scary. Is she recovering well?" Ronny asked, concerned.

"Yeah she's doing fine, she might come back to see you guys when she wakes up," Ashton answered.

Everyone at the table mumbled 'okay' and 'yeah,' everyone seemed a bit sad at the news.

"I'm sorry that I ruined all of your mornings," Ashton said as he looked down at his shoes.

Ronnell made a smile. "It's alright, at least Kai might see us again, that's something that I look forward too."

Tyrone nodded. "I agree with her, do you need help finding your classes?" He turned on his phone to look at the time. "We still have at least fifteen or so minutes until school starts, I could help you find your classes."

Ashton looked up and smiled. "I would like that, this school is very big and I'm afraid that I might get lost," he said as he made a light laugh.

Tyrone smiled back. "Once you get used to this school it doesn't seem as big. But you have to be careful of the people who go to this school. Some of them are not what you think they are, just to let you know." Tyrone got up from his seat and put on his backpack.

"That's totally true. Some people in this place are kinda fake so watch out who you talk to, but don't worry about us we're the coolest kids you'll ever meet," Dawn said as she took a sip of her coffee.

"Advice remembered, see you guys later." Ashton waved at the group of kids and walked out of the cafeteria with Tyrone.

As the two were walking Ashton took out a piece of paper that had his class schedule on it. Ashton handed the paper to Tyrone. Tyrone looked at the paper and led the way to Ashton's classes. Tyrone also talked about what school is like, what clubs or sports to join, what college and career Ashton might be in.

The two engaged in their conversation until the bell rang for the first class. Ashton looked around the halls, students walking left and right.

Tyrone looked at Ashton. "Luckily some of your classes we have together, so at least your classes won't be boring."

Ashton smiled at Tyrone. "I think we have the same first period class together."

"You're right, let's go to class." Tyrone smiled back.

The two walked through the halls talking to each other until they arrived at their first class of the day.

It was the end of the school day. Ashton was finishing writing notes for English class. Ronnell sat next to Ashton trying to finish her notes also. The teacher sat at her desk grading yesterday's homework. Some students were already finished taking notes and were on their phones, some were just talking to their friends.

Ronnell turned her phone on and looked at the time. She turned her head to face Ashton. "Hey Ashton, it's almost time to go, I don't want you to miss the afternoon bus on your first day."

Ashton looked up at Ronnell. "Thanks for the heads up." He closed his notebook and put it inside his backpack. He took out his phone and looked at his notifications.

Rick had texted him a few minutes ago, the text read. 'Hey how was school?'

Ashton texted back. 'It was really great, it's almost time to come home now.'

The last bell had rung, everyone in the room started to get up and leave the room. The teacher said her goodbyes and a few of the students replied back. Ashton turned off his phone and put it in his jacket pocket.

Ronnell and Ashton walked out the class and outside the school. She led Ashton to his bus and both of them said their goodbyes.

Ashton walked inside the bus and saw Owen at a seat. Owen made space for Ashton to sit. The two talked about their day and other things going on in their lives.

About two more weeks went by. Ashton had become close friends with Kai's friends; he had become best friends with Tyrone. Ashton had been doing very well in school; he even joined the school's basketball team with Tyrone. Everything in his life seemed normal and calm. Every morning before he leaves the house, he visits Kai in her room sitting on her bed, talking to her about his thoughts and things that are happening in his life.

It was late afternoon; school was done for the week. Ashton was in the bathroom soaking a small hand towel in the sink. He squeezed the towel so it would be damp. He turned off the sink and walked out of the bathroom.

He walked into Kai's room and sat on the edge of her bed. He folded the towel and placed it on her forehead. He held her right hand and looked at the glowing circle, the circle was almost complete.

Kai's chest was slowly moving up and down, the hole in her chest was healed and her heart was restored. She had been in a coma for about four weeks; her body took a toll on her. Her body and face were pale and skinny, she didn't look like herself.

"Just another day and you will wake up," Ashton said as he patted Kai's hand. "I will be here by your side."

The front door opened as Rick walked in, carrying a cardboard box filled with files and papers. He set the box on the floor that was next to the stairs. He poked his head inside the living room and then walked in the kitchen.

He looked around; the kitchen table was already set with plates, glass cups, and eating utensils for three people. In the center of the table there was a large baking dish that was filled with chicken casserole. Rick looked at the dish and smelled its aroma, he let out a delighted hum.

"I already guess you like my cooking," said Ashton as he walked into the kitchen, placing a damp towel on the counter. "But don't eat it just yet, I invited Stella and Tobi to come over and eat with us."

"Thank you for making this, once Kai wakes up, she will enjoy your home cooked meals. I believe she might wake up any time tomorrow, are you excited?" asked Rick.

Ashton looked up at Rick as his smile faded. "I'm thrilled, but I just wonder what she's going to say to us. I'm afraid that she won't like me anymore because of what happened to her."

Rick made a sympathetic look. "Don't say that kiddo, she still likes you. She has to, since you're her brother now. I know you two will get along just fine as before."

Ashton didn't say anything, he just looked to the side. Rick patted Ashton's shoulders. "Don't think too much about it, I'm going to get ready for dinner. You can watch the television in the living room, okay?"

"Okay." He said glumly.

The two walked out of the kitchen. Ashton walked into the living room. Rick picked up the box filled with files and walked up the stairs. He got into his room and set the box on top of his desk. He took off his holster and his badge and placed them inside his desk drawer.

He walked into Kai's room and examined her room. The walls in her room were decorated with Polaroid photos, maps, and decorative stickers. There's a black wooden desk and a matching bookshelf next to it in one corner of the room. The bookshelf was filled with books on one level, papers on the other, and other things that Kai carelessly placed. Her built in closet was on the left side of her bed. Clothes were neatly hung on the rack, her shoes were at the bottom of the closet, accessories and a shoulder bag were placed on the side of the closet on a shelf. Her black wooden bed was a storage bed with two drawers in the front of the bed and one large drawer on each side.

Rick sat on the bed and brushed her hair with his hand, he looked at the yellow circle on her right hand. The yellow glow was a few centimeters away from completely covering the dark part of the circle.

"Can't wait to see you again." Rick kissed Kai on the forehead.

The front door opened and Tobi ran into the house. Stella walked in and closed the door. She was holding a brown paper bag on her arm. She went into the living room and saw Ashton watching a college basketball game on the television.

"Hey honey, where's Rick?"

Ashton turned around and looked at the bag. "He went upstairs but I think he might come down in a few minutes. You can put that bag in the kitchen. I made chicken casserole for dinner." He got up and followed Stella in the kitchen.

Stella set the bag on the counter and took out the contents, a wine bottle, chocolate cake, and a large Kit Kat bar.

"I got something for the two of you," she said, giving the Kit Kat bar to Ashton.

"Are you sure you want to give this to me?" he asked, taking the Kit Kat bar.

Stella placed the wine bottle and cake on the table. "I'm sure, I hope you like it. I don't think Rick wants you to eat too much sugar but whatever, you should treat yourself once in a while."

Ashton put the Kit Kat bar inside the refrigerator as Rick came inside the kitchen and hugged Stella. Tobi followed Rick into the kitchen. He strolled under the table and sat on the floor.

"I'm glad you're here," Rick said as he kissed Stella on the cheek.

Stella laughed and then sat at the table. "Let's eat and enjoy this food as a family."

Ashton and Rick glanced at each other and smiled. Both of them sat at the table and started eating dinner.

CHAPTER 32

Why does everything in my body feels like it's on fire? What is happening to me? Where am I?

It took me what felt like hours of just trying to open my eyes. Once my eyes had slightly opened, all I could see was brightness. I closed my eyes again so I wouldn't go blind.

What is happening to me? I need to do something but I can barely feel my body.

I tried to turn over but I don't think my body moved an inch. God this is so difficult, I needed to get out of here.

I lay on my back with my eyes closed for a while, waiting for something to happen. Nothing happened, so I was lying on the ground like an idiot. But during that time I started to feel my hands and feet, which was a good sign.

I attempted to roll over on my side and somehow I managed to do it. I carefully opened my eyes and looked in front of me. I was in the field of lilies again, great.

But this time the lilies were black instead of white and that gave me the shivers. I can't remember what had happened to me before I got here. I tried to think hard, but the last thing I remember is that I was in the fountain room with Ken and Ashton.

Oh God what happened to Ashton and Rick? I need to see them again; I need to get out of here.

I made a weird tried noise as I tried to move my arms and legs. I could feel my body again, but there's this weird sensation inside my chest. Like someone had punched my chest really hard.

I slowly sat up, my hands pressed into the dirt, as I looked at the endless fields of lilies. There was a slight jab in my left hand but it didn't feel painful. I turned my head around looking at my surroundings to see if something had changed. The trees that were in the field looked dead; by dead I mean really dead, like they hadn't been watered in years. As I looked out into the field all I could see was dead trees and black lilies.

I looked up at the bright blue sky; the odd thing was that there was no sun or clouds. I took a deep breath and tried to calm myself down.

I touched my chest with my left hand. When I pressed the area where my heart is my fingers went through my chest. My eyes grew wide open as I jolted and looked down at my chest. There was a medium sized hole that went through my chest, blood oozed out of my chest as it stained my white dress. I wore the same dress that I wore from my last dream about this place. I looked down at my feet, and once again I wasn't wearing shoes or socks. My dress and my skin were spattered or partly stained with my blood.

I looked at my left hand; the tips of my fingers were covered in blood, and there was a very small hole that went through my hand. I still had my dragon tattoo and my lotus tattoo. I looked at my other arm and saw a circle that had a flower inside it on my right hand and it was glowing yellow.

"What the–?" I said to myself as I raised my right hand up to my face to look at it closely. The flower circle wasn't that bad, I guess I gained another tattoo for some reason.

I placed my hands on my lap and did nothing for a few minutes. I just need to relax and wait for something to happen like last time, I hope. I can't be here forever, right?

I carefully got up and dusted off some dirt on my clothes, I could feel the dry dirt staining my feet. I looked down at the area where I lay and saw a silhouette of my body filled with white lilies. This time I wasn't as shocked or startled by whatever this was, I somehow felt relaxed by the sight of this.

I stretched my arms and legs; I could finally feel my body again. Now I got that problem out of the way I need to get out of this place. I started walking, not knowing where exactly where I was heading.

I was casually strolling through the field and looking at the place, trying not to freak out. I was just walking in the field for what felt like a very long time, but it wasn't a bad thing since I could finally move on my own and get some energy into me.

As I was walking, I noticed that the sky had quickly changed colors into a sunset color. It was very pretty but it bothered me that there's no sun in the sky. I stopped walking and looked at the beautiful sky.

Then I felt something touch my hands. I looked down and saw the black lily petals broke off from their stems and started to float up. I was shocked because I knew that something is going to happen and I'd never seen such a thing like this until now.

I took a petal and rubbed it between my forefinger and thumb, the petal was soft and smooth and it made me feel slightly relaxed.

I turned my head around and saw all the petals floating up into the sky, they reminded me of balloons. It was a pretty view, if only if I had my camera I could take a picture of this. But then I had to remind myself this was a weird nightmare or dream so I couldn't be off guard.

I continued walking to nowhere. The soft petals brushed my skin as I was looking at the sky. How long am I going to be in this place?

As I looked at the sky and the floating petals, the black petals instantly turned white and that made me jump with surprise. I knew it! Something is going to happen.

The white petals stopped moving and they were suspended in space. I touched one of the petals with my forefinger and it just moved while staying in place. All of the sudden the petals started to plunge down instantly.

"What the—" My whole body was sucked into the ground.

All of a sudden everything that happened to me during my stay at Ken's building rushed into my mind. I instantly remembered every single thing that happened to me. I also remembered that I died. As I gained all my memories everything started to go black.

I jerked up, hitting something with my hand. Someone made a noise and fell. I looked around at my surroundings, I was in my room. Everything seemed dark but the white tree lights I put up on my bed headboard showed some light, which helped me adjust to the darkness of my room.

I peered down at the floor where the noise came from and saw Ashton lying on the floor, his hands on his nose.

My eyes grew wide. "Oh my God! Ashton! I'm so sorry," I said with a weak and dry voice as I stumbled off my bed to crouch next to him.

Ashton rolled over onto his back and looked at me. "I missed you Kai, don't worry about me. I want to tell you what happened during these past few weeks, I even met your friends at school." Ashton let out a moan as he removed his hand from his nose; his nose was bleeding and his cheek was a light shade of red.

I teleported a small hand towel onto my hand and gave it to Ashton. Wait. I just realized that I could use my powers again, what a relief!. I teleported next to my light switch and turned it on, my whole room was now lit up. I could fully see everything in my room including Ashton who was still lying on the floor.

I teleported next to Ashton. I looked at my right hand and saw a flower tattoo. The flower circle was the same one as in my weird dream just a few moments ago.

I looked at Ashton who sat up holding the towel on his nose. I made a huge grin and immediately hugged him as hard as I can.

"Oh my God! I missed you too! Where's Rick? No I can meet him later but you have to tell me what happened while I was out. Wait. How long have I been out?" I said excitedly, but then my voice faded. What exactly happened to me?

"Ahh, Kai you're hurting me," Ashton said weakly. I instantly broke up my hug and held his hands. "I think you've now gained your dad's super strength."

I took a deep breath; my body was feeling a bit numb but at least I could move my body. I looked around my room; everything seemed the same as always. I looked at the window. Looks like it's about nighttime. As I looked back at Ashton I could feel my facial expression change from happy to sad. How did I get here? Didn't I just get killed by Ken, my own grandfather?

My heart started to beat very fast as I kept thinking about what had happened to me. I let go of Ashton's hand, he made a worried look as I got up. I sat on my bed and lay down.

Ashton stood up; he touched my hand. "Hey are you okay? Just a minute ago you were so happy, but now you seemed depressed. Let me go get Rick." He squeezed my hand and walked out of the room.

I lay on my bed not doing anything. I need to know what exactly happened to me. I need to know how I am still alive. My eyes grew wide as I touched my chest. There was no hole, it's like nothing had happened to me. I looked at my right hand where Ken's arrow stabbed me. I moved my fingers and looked at my palm, everything seemed fine. It's like somehow I fully recovered from my injuries, maybe Rick healed me with his powers.

I let out a sigh and looked at the ceiling. I heard two sets of footsteps run towards my room. I stood up and looked at my door, Rick and Ashton came rushing in.

Rick made a huge grin as he ran to me giving me a big hug. He also grabbed Ashton, making a group hug. I could feel Rick's tears fall on top of my head as I hugged Rick and Ashton.

"Oh Kai I missed you so much. I'm so, so sorry that you had to go through all of this. I think about you every day and I wanted to tell you how sorry I am, I could've saved you and Ashton from my bastard father but I was too late. If only I came sooner I could've saved you from your death." Rick began to sob on my head and I started to cry onto Rick. I could hear Ashton make sniffing sounds.

All three of us hugged in silence for at least a few minutes. I built up my courage to say something without crying but it took me many attempts to do it. I'm just relieved that I get to see everyone again.

"You two need to tell me what happened to me after I died." I wiped my nose on Rick's shirt. "And don't leave any details out, I want to know everything."

"Before we do that I want to make sure that you're fully recovered, do you feel any numbness in your body?" Rick asked as he broke up our hug. His face was slightly red and his eyes were puffy from crying.

I looked at Ashton who wiped his eyes with the clean part of the hand towel. I think his nose stopped bleeding but I want to make sure he's okay.

"Hey Rick, can you heal Ashton? I slapped him in the face and I made his nose bleed," I said as I turned my head at Rick and looked at his shirt. Ashton's blood stain was on his shirt. Geez how hard did I hit him?

"When Ashton woke me up he told me not to worry about his bloody nose, so I obeyed him and came to see you. But now I'm going to make your nose better," Rick said as he looked at Ashton and held his glowing black palm in front of Ashton's face. Rick's hand stopped glowing, he moved his hand away from Ashton's face.

Ashton touched his nose. "I think Kai already developed her new powers since I just witnessed her super strength."

Both Rick and Ashton looked at me, I raised an eyebrow. "Why are you guys looking at me like that?" I said nervously, if they make me test out my new powers now I might as well slap both of them.

"I guess she already gained both her father and Ken's powers," Ashton said as he moved his arms around my shoulders. I looked at Rick and then at his left forearm, he had the same red lotus tattoo as me and our family. I guess there's no need for him to hide that tattoo from me.

I looked at both of them. How long have I been out?"

"It's been about four weeks since you died. Rick told me that he brought you back to life using his new powers, but you went into a coma afterward," Ashton told me.

"Seriously? Four weeks? Wait. Ashton you told me that you met my friends at school, did they say anything about me?"

"Everyone was worried about you and wanted to see you but I told them not to since I don't want to expose our secret. Since you woke up from your coma you can finally see everyone in person."

"I can't wait to see them again," I said glumly. I just realized that I have to go back to school, but it's worth it because I can see my friends again.

Rick placed his hands on our heads. "I'm just so happy that I got my kids back, and since you gained your father's invincible body you can't get hurt or die so that's some good news."

"You're right, at least I can't feel pain when I stub my toes or get a paper cut. All I want to do now is to take a shower because I feel horrible right now," I said. Ashton removed his arm from around me and I walked up to my closet to pick out a new set of clothes. I took out a tie-dyed t-shirt and sweatpants.

"We'll wait for you in the living room, are you hungry?" asked Rick who was near the door.

"To be honest I don't feel hungry, I just want to relax and take a shower," I said without turning around. I looked at all the clothes I had in my closet. I might as well clean out my closet.

"Okay see you downstairs," Rick said as he and Ashton walked out of my room.

I turned around and walked out of my room, turning off my bedroom light, and walked into the bathroom.

I slightly opened the cabinet door that was next to the sink but it was jammed. I tugged on the cabinet door once again and I instantly broke the door. I let out a gasp as I looked at my hand that was holding the broken door. I have to get used to my super strength powers.

I took out a bath towel and place it on the sink counter. I carefully turned on the sink knob and splashed my face with cold water. I patted my face with the towel and looked at myself in the wide mirror that was above the sink. I could tell that I didn't eat; my face and arms were very skinny, my eyes were dark and tired, my face was pale and sunken. I guess being in a coma for weeks made me look like a living skeleton.

I turned the knob of the shower and looked at myself in the mirror again, thinking what's going to happen next.

I walked into the living room. Rick and Ashton were sitting next to each other watching a television show while drinking tea. Both of them looked at me and made space on the sofa for me to sit. I took a seat between Rick and Ashton; Rick was on my left side and Ashton was on my right side. I lay back onto the sofa as I watched the television show with them.

"I'll tell you what had happened to you after you…died." Rick began telling the whole story about him fighting with his siblings. He started to talk about his encounter with Ken. "When I came into that room I saw your body lying inside that fountain with a large hole in your chest. I instantly broke. I started to fight Ken because of what he had done to you and to Ashton. Our fight was intense and it felt like it lasted for hours. Since I injected those black substances into me it helped me fight Ken, eventually I killed him by absorbing all of his powers into me. After that I destroyed everything and everyone who was inside the building so it wouldn't raise any suspicion for the public. I don't want to expose what really happened inside that building. During that time I was fighting with Ken I teleported you and Ashton, who was also severely hurt, to the lobby where you two would be safe. I healed Ashton from his injuries and then used my newly developed powers to make you become alive again. Now my powers have been more potent than ever. I know it's a lot to process but I hope you understand what happened during the time you were gone."

I didn't look at Rick or Ashton; I just stared at the floor in front of me the whole time Rick told the story. All I was thinking is how crazy all of this is and somehow I got used to this craziness. I remembered the picture of me and my parents inside my pants pocket that day.

"What happened to the clothes that I wore during that day, I have a photo in my pants pocket," I said without looking up. "I want to see that photo, it's very important."

Ashton took a small pillow from the sofa and wrapped his arms around it. Rick put his right arm around my shoulders, his left palm facing up. A folded photo that was stained in blood appeared on top of his palm. Rick held his palm toward me and I took the photo.

Ashton and Rick leaned closer to me as I unfolded the photo of my parents and me when I was a baby. Rick pressed his cheek against my head as all of us examined the photo in silence. As I looked at the photo I wondered what it'd be like if all of us never had powers. Would I live a happy normal life and enjoy what it feels like to have a complete family? Would things end up different if I did something different during my time in that building with Ken, Sean, Chrissy, or even Ashton?

"Is there a place we can put the photo in?" I asked as I placed the photo on my lap. I'm glad things ended up like this, I wouldn't change any choices I made during that time. Plus having a family with superpowers makes my life less normal and boring.

"I can frame the photo for you," Rick said as the photo on my lap disappeared.

I teleported the television remote to my left hand. I turned on the television and changed the channel to the news channel. All three of us watched the news for an hour or so. I checked the time on the television: 2:32 am.

"Sorry that I woke the two of you up. You guys should go to bed, I'll stay here and watch some TV shows until I go back to sleep."

"It's alright, I'll stay here with you, don't worry about me," Ashton said as he leaned back onto the sofa.

"I'll stay here with the two of you, it's the weekend so we can stay up as long as we like," Rick said as he teleported a light gray fuzzy blanket to his hand and wrapped it around all of us. The three of us watched a random show until we fell asleep.

CHAPTER 33

I lazily opened my eyes; the television was turned off and the whole room was bright from the natural sunlight that went through the windows. Everything seemed pure and clean, like all the bad energy had left the home. Ashton's head was resting on top of mine and it sounded like he's still sleeping. I slowly turned my head to the left to see if Rick was sleeping with us, but I didn't see him on the sofa. I turned my head back towards Ashton and closed my eyes once more, feeling relieved and happy that I'm alive again.

I heard faint footsteps walking through the hallway and into the living room. The footsteps became louder as they came into the living room. I opened my eyes and Rick came into my view.

Rick was looking at the bookshelves in the room, his back towards me. He placed a framed photo on a shelf and turned around. Rick looked at me with surprise and walked towards me, he was already dressed for today. I looked at the photo on the shelf. It was the photo of my mom and dad.

Rick stood in front of me. I could feel Ashton's head slightly shift, as he made a tired grunt and rubbed his head against mine.

"I made breakfast, you two can come in the kitchen any time you like." Rick planted a kiss on top of my head and gently patted Ashton on the head. "I'll let the two of you rest." He walked out of the kitchen.

I teleported my phone onto my hand, luckily it didn't get destroyed. I unlocked my phone and looked at all my notifications and I have a lot of them to go through. I looked at the time on my phone, 8:49 am. I poked Ashton on the arm to wake him up, what time did he get to sleep?

I poked him repeatedly until he finally woke up. He moved his head from mine and lay back on the sofa. He stretched his arms and let out a yawn.

"It's about nine. Do you want to eat breakfast?" I asked as I turned my head to look at him.

Ashton rubbed his eyes. "Sure."

"Alright then," I said as I grabbed the blanket and moved it to the side of the sofa.

The two of us stood up and walked into the kitchen where Rick was sitting at a table, typing on his laptop.

Rick peered at the two of us. "Are you guys hungry? You should wash up before you two eat," Rick said as he smiled.

I teleported Ashton and I into the bathroom on the second floor, he made a surprised face and looked around the bathroom. I walked up to the sink and washed my face and hands, Ashton did the same thing as I wiped my face with a towel.

"It would be fun if I could teleport anywhere in the world," Ashton said as he wiped his face with a different towel.

"It is, I didn't forget about our promise," I said as I hung my towel on the drying rack.

Ashton moved the towel away from his face. "What promise?"

"The one that I made to you that we get to travel around the world," I said as Ashton's face turned a slight shade of light pink.

"You still remember that?" he said, embarrassed.

I looked at him and nodded. "I did and I'm going to keep the promise. Let's go and eat, not eating for weeks makes me severely hungry."

Instantly I teleported the two of us back into the kitchen. Ashton and I sat at the table across from Rick. Already made scrambled eggs, toast, bacon, and sausage sat on a few plates at the table. We began eating our breakfast as Rick typed on his laptop.

"So when am I going to go back to school? I want to see my friends again," I said after I took a gulp of orange juice.

"Maybe in a week or so, I want you to get used to your body since you've now gained different abilities. I don't want you to expose your powers to the public. I don't think the public will handle it if everyone knows that a few people in the world have superpowers. Also you have make-up work to do but don't bother reading your textbooks, I'll just transfer some information into you with my powers. You'll do fine in school, but you still have to make up your classwork, tests, quizzes, and projects by yourself."

I let out an annoyed groan. "You know how much work I missed? It's going to take a very long time for me to finish it. Why can't you do it for me?" Seriously, most of my classes are honors and those classes give you a ton of work. I wonder how people in AP classes handle school; it must be hell for them.

"My part of the deal is that I give you all the information you need for school and you'll do all your schoolwork. Bada bing bada boom you'll ace your classes kid," Rick said with a bad New York accent.

Ashton made a choking sound after Rick made that accent. I could feel my eyebrow twitch as I cringed. Rick made a goofy smile as he looked at us. Yep, he's a typical goofy uncle.

"Don't make that accent again, you can't make a good accent to save your life so don't even try it buddy," I said as I bit my bacon.

"Well you're just jealous that I have supa wicked good accent," Rick said in a Boston accent. I tried not to laugh because I was still eating my food and didn't want to choke. "Aye my Boston accent isn't bad since I learned it from my coworkers," he said, still having an accent and winking.

Ashton laughed out loud and had a huge grin. "You got sum cawfee or wawda with dis breakfast?" he said in a New York accent. Rick began to laugh loudly at Ashton's accent.

I could seriously feel my eyebrows twitching but I can't help but laugh at my two guys being goofy. I laughed so hard that I made a snorting sound. Ashton laughed harder after I made that snort, which made Rick laugh even louder.

"That was a bloody awful accent you two mates got there," I said in a horrible British accent as I was still laughing. I hope British people don't get offended by my awful accent. All three of us were laughing our butts off.

It took a while until we composed ourselves from whatever this was. I'm glad that I'm back and can enjoy life with my family. I ate my breakfast and teleported all our empty plates into the sink; I'm also glad that I got my powers back.

As all three of us were talking about all the things that happened to me when I was out, I started to feel something odd inside my body. There's this very weird sensation inside my stomach. I think I'm going to get sick! I wrapped one of my arms around my stomach and put my other hand over my mouth. Both Rick and Ashton noticed me gagging and looking sick.

"Hey Kai, are you okay?" Rick said with a worried look.

Before anyone said anything else I could feel my stomach burning like it was set on fire. I could feel myself starting to vomit! I instantly teleported myself into the bathroom and ran to the toilet and vomited into it. It's a gross feeling when you have to vomit in the morning. Rick was right, I have to get used to my body until I go to school.

After I completely threw up my lungs and flushed the toilet, I rinsed my mouth with mouthwash two times to get all that gross stuff out of my mouth. I splashed my face with cold water and dried myself with a dry towel. I teleported back into the kitchen; the whole table was clean of plates and food. Rick was placing the wet plates on the drying rack. Ashton was sitting at a table typing on Rick's laptop.

Ashton looked up from the laptop. "Do you feel better?"

I sat on a chair next to him. "I guess I do need a week to get used to my body."

"You two should take a shower and get dressed, we're going out today," Rick said as he wiped his hands with a dish towel.

"You can go first Ashton, I'll just sit here recovering from my vomit incident," I said as I lay my head on the table.

"Okay." Ashton got up and walked out of the kitchen.

Rick leaned against the counter. "You know that Fred's sixty-eighth birthday is two weeks away?"

I looked at Rick. "It's May already? I already missed the beginning of my new trimester. Geez I've been gone for a long time."

"I know how much work you got. I placed all of your missing classwork next to your desk just to let you know."

"You asked me about Fred's birthday, why do you ask me about it?"

"His birthday is two weeks away and it's on a Saturday, we all need to buy new clothes for his party. His party's at some formal venue and everyone has to dress nicely, so I'm going to take you and Ashton to my tailor to make you two outfits for the party. I just want to get everything prepared for the party so that we all look nice during that evening," Rick said excitedly, his eyes sparkled with joy.

"Huh, I guess that would be cool getting a custom outfit for me, can I choose any type of clothes for myself?" I want to look nice especially since I get to choose what kind of outfit I want and it's specifically made for my liking.

Rick beamed. "You can get an outfit that you want, if it gets my approval just so you know."

My phone appeared on the kitchen table and I took my phone and looked at all the messages. Most of the messages were from Ronnell, Owen, Tyrone, and some of the school's messages that send students information about weather and other boring stuff.

I looked up at Rick who was still looking at me. "Hey Rick, you think it's a good time to text my friends since they're worried about me?" I wanted to see them and talk to them about what had happened to me. I don't know how well they're going to handle this crazy situation that I have been in.

"I already talked to your friends and their parents about you, it's better if you see them in person rather than texting them. Talking in person would be better for the both of us."

I looked down at my phone. "I understand, can't wait to go back to school and see everyone again."

Ashton walked into the kitchen wearing an outfit for today, his outfit seemed like the type of thing that I would wear.

"Cool outfit Ash, I might borrow that shirt someday though," I said jokingly as I got up and walked towards the hallway. I looked at his right forearm and saw his lotus tattoo. Maybe I don't have to cover my arm tattoos since my whole right arm is covered by them so there's no point trying to use my concealer.

"That's what siblings are for sis," Ashton said, smirking.

I stopped at the threshold between the hallway and the kitchen. I turned around and looked back at Ashton. "Wait. Did you call me 'sis?' So that means that Rick adopted you, and now you're my brother?"

Ashton looked at me with an embarrassed look. "You don't want me to be your brother or to live with you?" he asked quietly.

I walked up to him. "No, it's not that. I'm just shocked that you're my brother now, I finally have a sibling and it's my best friend. Thank you for trying to protect me back then, I'm sorry that you had to see me die. I'm just glad that you're living a better life, I couldn't be any happier for you." I looked around the kitchen and then looked up at him. "I should get ready," I said as I walked through the kitchen and into the hall.

"Thank you for changing my life for the better Kai," Ashton said. I looked back as I kept walking; he was still looking at me.

"No need to thank me. It's fate that we became friends, isn't it?" I said, turning back around and climbing up the stairs.

I climbed to the top of the stairs and walked down the long hallway, passing the bathroom and Rick's room. I turned my room's doorknob and walked in. I looked at my desk to see a large stack of papers and a few textbooks on the floor next to my desk.

I let out an annoyed groan as I walked up to my closet. All my shirts and jackets were hung on the long rack. My pants, jeans, and other junk I have were placed inside a shelf that was on the side of the closet. My shoes were placed at the bottom of the closet. I grabbed a white graphic t-shirt, light blue ripped jeans, and black and white high top shoes.

I teleported myself into the bathroom then I closed and locked the door. I placed my new clothes on top of the sink counter and turned on the shower knob.

CHAPTER 34

I walked out of the bathroom wearing my new clothes. I touched my wet hair. I should get a haircut; maybe I should ask Rick if he ever lets me. I just realized that my birthday was in three weeks. I'm going to turn sixteen this month and that means that I have to do a lot of things this year. I have to figure out what college or career I'll be in, I need to learn how to drive, and all that stressful pre-adult stuff. Thinking about this hit me because I'd started to realize that I'm going to grow up and become an adult, and it's stressful and scary.

I tried not to think about it and walked into my room. I placed my old clothes in a clothes basket next to my closet and teleported into the living room. Ashton sat on the sofa looking at his phone, next to him was Rick was watching the television. He looked at his black watch on his left wrist to check the time.

I sat on the floor my back pressed against the sofa. My phone appeared next to me on the floor. I tapped on my phone; the time read 10:37am. I looked up at Rick.

"Hey Ricky, when do we get to go outside and get to the tailor's?" I asked. Rick smiled as he looked down at me.

"We'll go at eleven; we're not in a hurry. Since your sixteenth birthday is going to be a week after Fred's birthday, do you want to go somewhere special for your birthday? You can invite some of your friends to go out and eat or do whatever you teens do," he said lying back onto the sofa.

"To be honest, I didn't think much about what I'm going to do for my birthday."

"Hmm, I didn't even bother to ask Ashton when his birthday is." Rick turned his head to face Ashton. Ashton looked back at Rick.

"My birthday isn't that important," Ashton said as he moved his eyes to glance at me.

"What? You're part of our family now; we need to throw you a birthday party. I bet this is the first time someone threw you a birthday party huh?" I said, thinking of the times when Ashton had never celebrated his birthday. I don't think he'd ever been to a party at all. Maybe when he's on a mission like in those spy movies where spies go to these extravagant parties, but that doesn't consider a party that is meant for him.

"I have never been to a birthday party before or even celebrated my own birthday. You guys don't have to do this for me, my birthday already passed," Ashton said. His cheeks turned pink.

"When is your birthday kiddo?" Rick asked.

"It's on January 24th. There's no point in having a party for me, aren't birthday parties for little kids?"

"Depends on the decorations and the food, maybe location too," I said. I wanted to throw a party for him. It made me feel sad that Ashton didn't have anyone to celebrate his birthday with. I'm going to make his birthday the best birthday he ever had, maybe we can celebrate our birthdays together.

"After we're done with the tailor's, we all could go to a store and buy something for Ashton," Rick said as he pressed a remote button. The channel switched until it played The Golden Girls. I actually like those older kinds of shows, they're much better than some reality television garbage in today's world.

"Maybe Ashton and I could celebrate our birthdays together and have a small party at the house." It would be fun to have a party with Ashton. I should plan out what gifts I should buy for him.

"That's a good idea kiddo, we should plan out the party before the week of," Rick said.

"You don't have to do this, it's just a birthday party," Ashton said as he placed his phone on his lap.

"Come on Ash, it's your first party and I'm going to make it the best party you ever witnessed," I said confidently.

Ashton lips curved into an embarrassed smile. "Thank you guys for doing this."

We all watched television and talked until eleven. I can't wait till I go to the tailor's; I want to have a nice suit outfit for myself. I should ask Rick if I could get a haircut, my hair is too long for me.

"Hey Rick, can I have a haircut? I don't want to have super long hair anymore," I asked. Rick looked at me, his eyes widened a bit.

"What? Why would you want to cut your beautiful long hair? I like you with long hair and so does everybody else," Rick said surprised.

"I just told you why I want to cut my hair, plus I want to look nice for the first day back to school and for Fred's party," I said. I'm positive that I want to cut my hair. It's just hair, it will grow back.

I took my phone and looked at the photos of women with long haircuts. I want it to have layers. I found a picture of what I want my hair to have and showed it to Rick and to Ashton.

"That's too short, maybe a little longer?" Rick said, his eyebrow twitching.

"I think you will look amazing with that haircut; you should get it. Maybe I should get a haircut too," Ashton said thoughtfully.

I smiled. "You should, hopefully Rick will allow us to get it."

Rick glanced at me then to Ashton, his hands on his chin thinking about our decision. He closed his eyes for a minute and opened them. He raised his hands up.

"What the hell, let's do it!" Rick said loudly in a joyful way.

Ashton and I exchanged looks as we smiled at each other. I scratched my left arm. What would people say about it, especially my friends? To be honest I could care less about them, I like my tattoos a lot and why not show them off? Some people at the school already have tattoos so it's not a big thing to worry about.

Rick looked at his watch. "It's time to go kids, make sure you two get your phones just in case one of you gets lost or something bad happens." Rick got up and teleported a black arm cover. "Here Kai I don't want you to show your tattoos out in public, put this on your left arm, you can use a concealer for your right hand." He handed me the arm cover.

"Seriously? An arm cover? Why can't I just show off my tattoos, it's not as big of a deal!" I said, taking the arm cover.

"You just woke up from your coma, I want you to get used to your new lifestyle. If you show off your tattoos, people will have mixed feelings towards you and might think badly about you. I don't want people to get the wrong impression of you." Rick said as I put on my arm cover. The arm cover wasn't that bad, at least it wasn't itchy.

"I only need to cover my lotus tattoo, my back tattoo isn't going to be a problem." Ashton said.

"Oh, I didn't even bother to ask you about your other tattoo from that enhancement substance. May I ask what it is?" Rick asked.

"I have a centipede tattoo on my back. It's not really that important, it's just a tattoo," Ashton replied.

"May I see it, if you don't mind?"

Ashton's cheeks slightly turned light pink. "Sure." He turned around and lifted the back of his shirt so that Rick and I could see his tattoo.

Rick leaned closer to Ashton, observing his red and black tattoo. I carefully looked at every part of his tattoo. I still liked his tattoo; the centipede's body was colored in some kind of patterns and shapes which looked very abstract. His tattoo suits him very well, maybe that's because the centipede represents him as a person.

"I can't believe that my father forced my kids to get these tattoos. Did it hurt?" Rick asked as Ashton pulled his shirt down.

"I passed out when I started getting it," I said.

"It didn't hurt at all, Ken used his powers to give us those tattoos," Ashton replied.

Rick made a thoughtful look as he looked at the two of us. "At least you two like your tattoos, right?"

"Yes."

"Hell yeah."

Rick also teleported two bottles of concealer with two different shades, one lighter than the other. I guess that was for Ashton. Rick handed the lighter shade to Ashton and the other one to me.

Ashton opened the lid and spread the concealer on his tattoo on his right forearm. I opened the lid of the bottle and spread it over my right hand, covering my large circle flower tattoo. The two of us completely covered our tattoos and handed the bottles to Rick who took them. The bottles disappeared.

"Let's go to the tailor's first, then go get a haircut, and then do whatever we want during the time we have left." Rick turned off the television and walked out of the living room.

Ashton and I followed him. Rick took his keys and his wallet from on top of a small table that was near the door. He put his wallet in his pants pocket and held his keys with his left pointer finger through the key ring. He opened the door and walk out.

I let Ashton walked ahead of me; finally, I get to go outside. It had been at least a month or two that I was trapped from the outside world. I got to breathe the fresh air again! Ashton walked through the door as I followed behind him. As I walked out of the house I closed the door behind me and tugged at the door, making sure it was locked.

I looked around the street. A few cars drove by, some people were walking down the sidewalk, the sky was bright blue, and the smell of fresh air made me feel relieved. I had waited a while for this moment. Everything at this moment made me forget all the craziness that I had been through. It makes me want to fully live my life and enjoy every small thing in life.

I walked down the stairs; Rick and Ashton were already inside the car. I quickly speed walked towards the car. I opened the back doors and sat inside the seat. Ashton sat on the left side of me while Rick was up front, turning on the car.

Rick drove down the street and made a left turn. I looked through the window looking at the shops, houses, and people as they passed by.

CHAPTER 35

The three of us went to the tailor's where we met Rick's tailor, Vinny, who helped us picked out the materials for our outfits and the types of clothes that we wanted to wear. In my opinion I had fun picking out my outfit and my materials for my outfit. Once we finished with everything I didn't even notice we spent at least two and a half hours in there.

After we went to the tailor's, Rick, Ashton, and I walked into a barber shop that was somewhere in Back Bay. The barbershop was large; different sized pictures were plastered all over the walls, chairs were lined up at one wall. There were at least five barbers doing someone's haircut. All three of us sat on the chairs waiting for the next available barber to do Ashton's hair.

Rick raked his thick and long hair with his hand and looked at himself in the large mirror that was across from us. I looked at myself and wondered what am I going to do when I get older? Will I do something in the future that I will regret? I quickly zoned out from thinking about my future and what kind of adult I will become.

"Hmm, maybe I might need a haircut too," Rick said. I instantly snapped back into reality.

I looked to my left. Ashton was flipping through a photo book of hairstyles that the barbershop had done over the years. He stopped at a page where a guy had his hair cut short on the sides but had medium length hair on top. It's not bad for Ashton I think he'll pull that look off.

"Hey Kai, do you think this will look good on me?" Ashton asked as he moved the book towards me so I could look at it closely. Ashton's hair was becoming quite long since the last time I saw him, but that's when we were in New York.

I looked at a photo then at him. "This hairstyle will look really nice on you, you should get it," I said confidently. It's good that we all get new haircuts. It's like new year new me, but it's with haircuts. I'm just happy that I can get rid of my annoying long hair.

One of the people who sat in a barber chair got up. The barber looked at us. "Who's next?" he asked.

Ashton took the book and placed it on a table next to him. He got up and sat on the chair, he talked to the barber who nodded and grabbed a pair of clippers. The barber was dressed in a casual outfit: t-shirt, jeans, and sneakers.

I looked at the other barbers and they wore casual outfits under their aprons. I looked at the other people in the shop who were sitting on the row of chairs with me. Mostly everyone was on their phones or looking at a magazine. I looked at Rick who was looking through the window of the shop with a worried look on his face.

"What's wrong?" I asked.

Rick blinked and looked at me. "Oh it's nothing, just thinking what will happen if Ashton got a bad haircut. I might well threaten that barber to death," he said as he made a playful smile.

I looked at him, silently observing his face. Even though Rick was smiling I could tell that he was sad just by looking at his eyes. It's funny how Rick looks quite similar to my dad, but of course it was because they are brothers. I looked at his eyes and saw lines and a little dark spot under his eyes; it looks like he didn't sleep well at all. I could slowly see that he was tired and sad; it made me feel awful about myself. I felt like I was the reason, that I made him this way.

"Hey kiddo you look sad, I guess because you have to wait for us to get our haircuts first huh."

"That and I wish I could go to school this week to see all my friends." I didn't want to tell him about how I feel right now, especially since it was about him.

"I know how that feels, but when you do go to school, make sure that you don't tell anyone what actually happened to us. And also make sure that no one can see your tattoos so it won't raise any suspicion. The legal age limit for kids to get a tattoo is fourteen to seventeen years old if they have a legal guardian's approval, so if anyone somehow sees your tattoo and asks about it, just say that you had my approval to get it," he said, winking.

"I bet no one would care about my tattoos even if I show them off. It's the least of my problems."

"That's good to hear, I'm happy as long as I have you and Ashton here with me," he said quietly.

Rick and Ashton finally got their haircuts done and I must say they both look really nice. Ashton got the haircut that he wanted and he looks totally different from before. I think he looks much better with his new cut. Rick got a medium length slicked back haircut. The hairstyle suits him; it reminds me of one of those characters from spy movies like James Bond.

All of us were in the car driving to a hair salon to get my hair cut; I'm excited to get rid of my very long hair. I can't wait to see my friends again next week but I have to stay home and finish all my boring schoolwork.

Rick parked in a medium sized parking lot that was next to a large building. Everyone got out of the car and stood on the sidewalk. I looked at Ashton who was touching his hair as he looked at the street.

"Do you like your hair?" I asked as we followed Rick towards a building. The building was an average suburban building with large windows that people could see inside.

Ashton smiled. "Yep I like it a lot, I feel like a new person." I smiled back at him; I'm glad that he's enjoying himself.

Rick opened the door for us, we both walked into the hair salon. The salon was like any other nice looking salon. Chairs were placed in the corner of the room where the entrance was, a flat screen television was mounted on the wall so that everyone can watch a show that was on. Five styling chairs were placed in a row, each in front of a large mirror.

There were not many people in the salon which was nice. I looked at the styling chairs and there was one empty chair. All three of us sat down on a chair in the corner of the room.

A lady wearing a black sweater and light blue jeans came walking through the back door. She tied her hair back and looked at us with a smile.

"Welcome to Josey's Salon, do you need time to find the hairstyle you want?" she asked, looking at me.

I looked at her. "No I'm good, I just want a medium layered haircut," I said as I stood up.

The lady smiled and walked up to the empty chair. "Okay, you can sit here," she said as I walked up to the chair and sat on it.

The lady put a black nylon cape around me so I wouldn't get hair on my clothes. She walked up to the mirror and grabbed a pair of scissors from the table. She walked back behind me and began cutting my hair.

Rick, Ashton, and I were sitting on a bench in Boston Common Park eating ice cream on a cone. Rick got vanilla, Ashton got strawberry, and I got cookies and cream. It is nice to be outside again eating ice cream and enjoying the city of Boston.

I grabbed my hair that was in a low ponytail and moved it towards my face; my hair was now short, which I like. I licked my ice cream as I looked at people walking in the park and at birds walking on the ground in front of me. A group of tourists was walking and taking pictures at the state house in front of the park. The group was led by a guy wearing a patriot costume who was talking as the tourists were talking pictures.

I finished my ice cream and looked at Rick and Ashton who were already done. I wiped my lips with a napkin as I looked at the blue cloudless sky.

"We spent the whole day together; do you guys want to go home?" Ashton asked as he looked at the tourist group.

"It's almost dark out, we should head home. Ashton has school tomorrow and I have work. I have to go over a case so I need the energy for tomorrow," Rick said as he got up and stretched his arms.

Before I got up someone yelled. "Kai!"

I looked to my side to see Owen running towards me his arms open wide, getting ready to give me the biggest hug. I got up and smiled as Owen tightly hugged me, the two of us almost fell but thank God we didn't. He pressed his face into my shoulder and we hugged each other.

"Oh my God! I missed you; you never answered my texts or calls. I thought you were mad at me for something." He removed his face from my shoulder and looked at me face to face. "Are you mad at me?" he asked as his brown puppy eyes bore into my eyes.

Rick made a fake cough. "Little touchy Owen."

Owen looked at Rick and withdrew his arms from around me. "Oh sorry I'm just excited to see Kai again." He looked back at me. "What happened to you?"

"I got into an accident while I was away, did Rick and Ashton tell you about it? I thought they did," I said calmly. It's difficult to lie to my best friend but I just got back. I had to think about what to say to him and to my other friends about my so called 'trip.'

Owen nodded. "Yeah they told me what happened to you. I'm sorry that you got into a car accident and went into a coma."

My eyes moved to the side. "Everyone feels sorry for me about that accident but I'm back, good as new," I said lightly to make my situation sound not as bad as it actually was.

Owen's dad, Seth, and his younger brother, Mason, walked up to us. Seth patted me on my shoulders. "I'm glad that you're back, Kai. Owen missed you a lot while you were away. Are you feeling any better since the accident?" he asked.

I looked at Seth. "I feel much better, thanks for asking Seth."

Seth walked to Rick and talked to him as Ashton walked up to us. "Kai still needs to rest and recover from her injuries for another week; you still can visit us if you want," he told Owen.

Owen made a grin and hugged the both of us. "Okay, can't wait to tell Ronnell and the others the good news. I'm just glad that Kai is back, I missed my best friend."

I smiled as Ashton and I got squished together in a group hug. "I missed you and everyone else, can't wait to see everyone," I said.

"You guys want to hang out someday this week?" Owen said as he broke up our hug.

Ashton looked at me and then at Owen. "We can hang out after school at our house if you want, we can bring Tyrone and Ronnell."

"That would be a good idea. I still have to make up my classwork so I need some help with that."

Owen still kept a smile on his face. "That sounds like a good idea Ash." His eyes looked down at my left arm. He looked up at me with a raised eyebrow. "What happened to your arm?"

I looked at my arm that was covered by the black arm cover. I looked back at Owen. "I got some deep scratches from the accident; it will heal in a few weeks."

Owen nodded thoughtfully. "I hope your arm gets better, at least you didn't lose a limb."

Owen's little brother Mason grabbed his hand and held it as he looked at the two of us, smiling.

Owen held Mason's hand as he was telling us what had happened during school while I was out. He told me all the gossip and rumors happening at school and it was really interesting. He also told me that Ronnell and Kyle broke up but he said he doesn't know why. I wonder what will happen to them, Ronnell must be sad about the breakup. I wish I was there when it happened so I could comfort her or beat the life out of Kyle.

Seth walked up to us. "It's time to go home. I have to make dinner before Mom comes home. Say goodbye you two," he said to Owen and Mason.

"Bye guys," Owen said walking away. Mason turned back and waved at us. Ashton and I waved back.

Rick walked up behind us and put his arms on our shoulders. "I guess it's time for us to go too."

The three of us walked through the park as the sun began to set, painting the sky in a beautiful sunset color.

CHAPTER 36

I woke up inside a building. I got up and looked around the place. This place seemed so familiar but I couldn't place my finger on it. There was a huge blurry wall on one side of me, the other walls were not blurred.

I walked closer to the blurred wall and touched it with my hands. Can't go any further. Maybe if I punched the wall it could possibly break and I could see the other side. With super strength I had a chance to break this wall and see what's on the other side of it.

I looked through the blurred wall, the only thing I could see were three silhouettes. As I saw those silhouettes everything came back to me, I have been in this dream before. The two adults wanted the kid to leave this place with their baby, the kid doesn't want to leave the adults, but he has no choice.

I looked all over the blurry wall as I gripped my right hand into a fist. I stepped back and ran to the wall, thrusting my fist into it. The wall made a very loud vibrating sound after I punched it. I closed my eyes and placed my pointer fingers inside my ears to block out the painful noise.

After the noise had faded I opened my eyes once again, there was a small crack in the wall where I had punched it. I walked closer to the wall and carefully touched the crack. I needed to punch the wall more until it broke.

I gripped my right hand into a fist once more and pulled back. I took a deep breath and slammed my fist into the wall as I yelled. The crack on the wall was becoming bigger. I repeatedly punched the wall until I heard a cracking noise.

I stopped punching when I heard that noise. I looked at the wall. Every part of it was cracked, but it didn't break. I looked straight in front of me and punched the wall once more.

The wall immediately shattered into small pieces; the shiny glass pieces fell down onto the floor in front of me. I looked straight in front of me; the room behind the wall looked similar to the fountain room where I had died. There were two adults in their late twenties and a kid who was about thirteen or fourteen years old and was holding a baby in his arms.

I instantly knew those three people were my parents and a younger version of Rick. I quickly jumped over the shattered glass and ran towards them; they were only about twenty feet away from me. I looked at my mom and dad, they both looked very heartbroken. I looked at the younger Rick and he was holding a baby, and I already knew the baby was me.

My mom looked at the younger Rick with a sad frown. "Please take care of our daughter, we trust you to look after her…" said my mom as she wiped her eyes with her shaking hand.

As I came close to them I opened both of my arms wide to give them a hug. I ran into them as I closed my arms, and I somehow went through them! I almost fell but I stopped in time. I looked back and slowly walked up to them.

My dad wrapped his arms around my mom to comfort her. "Run as fast as you can away from this horrible place, we will take care of this, just protect our baby," he said tensely as he looked at Rick and the baby.

"Dad…" I quietly said as I stood next to him. I looked like both of my parents and it made me feel weird but happy at the same time. I get to see them with my own eyes but it's in a dream.

I gingerly raised my hand and tried to touch my dad's arm. My hand and arm went through him. It's just a dream. My parents aren't really here with me. I couldn't even touch them or talk to them.

I felt disappointed because I couldn't even interact with them or with younger Rick. But I have to look at the bright side; at least I get to see my parents and younger Rick together.

I could hear other people shouting in the background. I looked at the direction where the noise came from. There were two hallways that were at the opposite sides of each other. I looked at the center of the room; there was a white marble fountain that had a few designs on it. I looked away from the fountain and looked around the room, a few paintings and benches were placed throughout the room.

The baby started to cry. I quickly looked back at Rick and the baby version of me. Rick was shushing and rocking the baby to make the noise stop. I couldn't help but notice that Rick's facial features haven't changed significantly; he still has a slightly sunken face, full lips, and almond like eyes.

"Don't worry she will be safe with me, I would do anything for her," Rick said, looking at the baby in his arms lovingly.

I heard yelling in one of the hallways on the left side of the room, there was a bright red light that glowed at the end of it.

"If we're dead can you find our bodies and bury them somewhere nice for me, please brother? Tell our baby that we love her so much. Tell her the truth when it's the right time. I love you," my dad said walking up to Rick, hugging him and the baby.

My mom went up and hugged both of them, she started to cry as she said how much she loves her baby and how she wishes things could be better for me and the three of them.

I walked up to them but I know it's no use trying to touch them or try to interact with them. I turned around and walked towards the fountain. I touched the fountain with my hand to see if I could or could not touch it. My hand touched the marble fountain. At least I have a place to sit on and watch how this dream turns out. I sat on the edge of the fountain pool and looked at the three of them, who were about ten feet away from me.

"You're the only person who we can trust, please be safe. I couldn't thank you enough for doing this for the two of us," my mom said as the three of them kept hugging each other.

People's yells and screams in the hallway became louder. The three of them broke up the hug. My mom and dad hugged and kissed like it was the last time they'd ever see each other. I had already known this would be the last time any of them saw each other alive.

Rick looked at my parents with a scared look on his innocent face. "You can't fight them all, you need my help, I don't wan—"

"No! You make sure the baby is safe. Leave now before it's too late," my dad said, his voice breaking. His eyes started to water as he looked at the baby.

"But-But I can't leave you two to die here, you two are my family. The only family I can trust, I don't want to lose you." I could hear the pain and fear in Rick's voice. He looked down at the baby in his arms who was making noises. He looked up at my parents with a bold look in his eyes. "Be careful. I love the two of you, don't ever forget that."

"We love you and our child very much, but we have to end this before it gets worse. Please don't ever come back to this place ever again," my mom said as she walked up to Rick and kissed the baby and him on the head.

She walked back and stood next to my dad. The two exchanged glances and nodded at each other with determination. Before Rick could say anything else he suddenly disappeared into thin air.

Just as Rick disappeared someone ran into the fountain room. The person was a boy who was at least a few years older than Rick. The boy had a red lotus tattoo on his left forearm. I think the boy was a younger version of Sean.

My parents looked back at Sean who had red and orange flames on his hands. "Is it true that you, Jen, Rick, and a few other people are fighting against Dad?" he asked with a confused look on his face.

My dad closed his eyes and frowned. "You're still too young to understand what our father has done to us, to this organization. Our father made us have powers so that he could use us to do these horrible missions for him." He opened his eyes and stared at Sean. "Sean, we're fighting him so that we can be free from him and from this place. I want you and Chrissy to come with us. We could live together and become a happy family for once. You don't have to fight me or Jen. You can come with us and live the life that you want."

Sean's flames disappeared as he walked towards my parents. "Are you sure that you will be able to get out of here? You know how Dad is when he's mad," Sean said nervously.

My mom looked down at Sean. "We have to fight your father until our group destroys most of those substances and the whole building, we need to end this organization for good," she said as she placed her hands on his shoulders.

I could hear a faint sound of footsteps down the hallway where Sean just came from. I looked at the hallway but didn't see anything down there. I looked back at Sean just when his eyes flashed blue. That doesn't look like a good sign.

Sean's body instantly ignited with bright flames. My mom let out a yelp as she jumped back and looked down at her hands. Her hands were red.

I got up with shock, what had happened to Sean? Could this be Ken's doing? This can't actually happen, right? It all seems fake but everything seems too real, why am I having this dream for the second time now?

Sean ran up to my mom but he was caught by my dad, who wasn't harmed by the flames that surrounded Sean's body. My dad lifted Sean and ran towards the fountain and dropped him into the fountain pool. The fire around his body was extinguished as he was submerged by the water.

Sean was throwing punches and scratched my dad but he didn't look hurt at all. My dad restrained Sean from attacking by wrapping his arms around him.

My dad looked back at my mom. "Jen, teleport him somewhere safe. My father got to him." His voice lowered.

Sean suddenly disappeared into thin air. The footsteps from inside the hallway gradually coming closer. I could tell that my parents heard it too; all three of us looked at the hallway waiting to see who was coming in the room.

My dad looked at my mom. "Jen get out of here be—" A yellow arrow struck my mom's stomach. She let out a gasp as the arrow impaled her.

Both my dad and I ran towards her, my mom was still standing as she placed her hand on the arrow. The arrow went through her body and fell on the floor making a ping sound. She placed her hand on her wound and looked up at my dad who stood behind her and placed his hand on her hand. I stood next to them and watched helplessly. My dad made a frightened look as he held onto her hand that was on her wound. Both of them looked at each other, she moved her other hand and laid her hand on his face.

"I can already tell that I won't have trouble killing you, Jenna," said a male voice at the other side of the room.

I turned to look who it was, and it was Ken standing thirty feet away from them. He, like everyone else looked younger. His hair was fully brown and his body looked much more muscular than the last time I met him.

My dad pressed his head against my mom's head. My dad kissed her head. "I'll get you out of here no matter what, please stay alive for me. I love you so much, I don't want to lose you," he whispered into her ear.

Tears started to stream down her face, she looked up at him. "I don't want to lose you too; I love you so much." She started to cry. "I know I can't get out of here, but you can. Leave this place, I'll teleport you wit—"

Ken thrust his hand at them. My dad moved him and my mom away from the arrow's path. Ken's eyes glowed blue as his body glowed yellow.

Ken thrust both of his hands at my parents, beams of yellow light shot out of both of his hands. I ran into the beams' way trying to protect my parents, but it was no use. The beams went through me.

"Shit!" I said out loud as I turned around and saw my parents dodged the beam.

"Jen please teleport yourself with Rick, I want you to be with our baby. Let me fight my father," my dad said as he fiercely glared at Ken.

"No. I'll stay here with you no matter what, I trust Rick to take care of our child and he'll someday tell her the truth about our family and this horrible place. As long as this place is destroyed and Ken dies I will be happy."

"Why do you have to be so stubborn? I want you to live and be with our daughter. It's too much to bear for her if she knows that both of her parents died because of her own grandfather."

"She will be strong enough to handle the truth when the time is right, I know it," she said confidently.

The beams had disappeared. I looked at Ken who stood there looking at my parents with a malevolent look in his blue eyes. The sight of his eyes made me have goose bumps. He's scary now and still was back then.

"One day when your daughter, my granddaughter is getting older, I will come and find her. I will see if she's able to develop one of your powers, maybe she will develop both of them. Who knows? But I do know that I will find her no matter what and you two will do nothing about it. She's my grand-daughter after all," Ken said in a low voice.

Ken instantly disappeared and reappeared in front of my parents. His right hand glowed bright yellow and he thrust his hand at them. My mom closed her eyes shut and held on to my dad. My dad looked at Ken with pure hatred in his eyes. Both of them were prepared to die, right in front of me.

I ran to my parents my left hand reaching for them as I let out a loud scream. Everything slowly turned white.

CHAPTER 37

I opened my eyes to see Rick and Ashton looking down at me. I blinked a few times and sat up. My head ached, my eyes were blurry and strained. I sat up and leaned my back against my headboard.

"Good morning, did you sleep well?" Ashton asked as he sat on the edge of my bed.

"Not really, I just had a weird dream," I said as I rubbed my eyes. I couldn't forget the look on my parents' faces right before my dream ended.

Rick sat on the other side of my bed and pushed some of my hair out of my face "What did you dream about?" he asked. I looked at them; they're already dressed for the day.

"I don't want to make you two late because of my unimportant dream," I said as I scratched my head. I don't want the two of them to worry about me but my dream that felt so real. That dream, what would happen if my dream had happened in real life?

Rick looked at his black watch. "We still have at least thirty minutes until it's time to go, I want to hear what happened in your dream."

I lay back against my bed's headboard and looked at Ashton and Rick. "I woke up in a room; there was a wall that blurred most of the room. The other three walls weren't blurred so I could see the decorations on the walls. I walked up to the wall and saw three silhouettes on the other side of the blurred wall. I tried to go through the wall but I couldn't, I punched the wall and it ended up shattering into pieces." I looked at Rick. "On the other side of that blurred wall, the room was similar to that fountain room where I had died. In that room, my parents and a younger version of you were talking to each other, you were holding a baby in your arms. My parents told the younger you to take care of that baby which I know was a baby version of myself." Rick's face slowly turned pale, I looked at my hands to avoid his stare. "You wanted my parents to go with you but they didn't let you, they wanted the two of us to get away from the organization and Ken. My parents said something about becoming free from the organization and from Ken; they were trying to destroy the organization for good. My mom teleported you and me somewhere because they heard noises in one of the hallways that led to the fountain room. The person who was in the hallway was a younger version of Sean, he wanted to be with my parents and to become free but something had happened to him. Sean started to fight my parents and use his fire powers on them. My dad said something about Ken 'got to him' and restrained him by dumping him into the fountain pool. My mom teleported Sean away and she was shot by a yellow arrow. Ken was already in the room with them. My parents exchanged words with each other as Ken attacked them by using his powers. Ken said that one day he would get me and take me to see if I'd gained both or one of my parents' powers. The scary thing is that he actually did that." My hands gripped my blankets as I remembered the part just before Ken killed my parents. "Ken teleported himself in front of my parents as he moved his glowing yellow hand at them. After that moment I woke up."

Ashton and Rick didn't say a word. I looked up and saw that Ashton was looking at me with widened eyes and a slightly opened mouth. I looked at Rick who was staring at me with a terrified look on his face. The two looked like they're still processing what had happened in my dream.

I opened my mouth to say something but Rick slowly fell back out of my bed and lay on the floor. I looked at Rick's body on the floor. Holy shit I just made him pass out!

"Holy. Shit," was all Ashton managed to say.

I looked back at Ashton who still had a shocked look on his face. "Ash, I think we should help Rick, then we'll say what we want to say about my odd dream."

I teleported myself next to Rick. Ashton stood up from my bed and walked next to me, looking down at Rick. Rick laid there on the floor with his eyes closed. I felt bad for him. I crouched down and placed my arms around his body, lifting him up. When I lifted him up and placed him on my bed his weight didn't feel heavy at all, it was like carrying a full box of papers.

Ashton moved Rick's legs on the bed so that he would be comfortable. I teleported an icepack to my hand and placed it on Rick's forehead.

Ashton sat on the bed across from me. "Do you think he'll wake up?"

"I have no idea. Was my dream that strange?"

"It seems very real, maybe Rick got PTSD or something that relates to that event. I hope he wakes up," Ashton said as he patted Rick on top of his head.

"Maybe if I lightly slap him he'll wake up," I said as I looked down at Rick's pale face.

I held up my right hand on the side of Rick's face. I took a deep breath and swiftly moved my hand towards his face. Rick's eyes immediately opened as I slapped him on his right cheek, making a smacking sound.

His head moved to the side as his cheek began to turn red. "What the...? Kai! Why did you do that?" he asked as he looked up at Ashton.

Ashton and I helped Rick sit up, the icepack fell on top of my bed beside him. He took the icepack and placed it on his slapped cheek.

"You passed out. We thought you would wake up if Kai slapped you, but you woke up before she did that," Ashton said.

Rick adjusted his jaw and winced. "At least I'm fully awake thanks to that hard slap in the face." He turned his head to look at me. "Kai, did you really dream that?"

"Yes I did. What about it?" I replied.

"All those things that happened in your dream were real. That day was the last time I saw your mom and dad."

I could feel my eyebrows rise in shock. "What? That was all real?"

"It was. I'm sorry that you saw that. Somehow you got to see that event even if you weren't there at that time, maybe Ken's powers in you made you dream of that event."

"But that wasn't my first time dreaming the same dream. The day I got in trouble with that lady in the car, that night I had the same dream but I couldn't get through that blurry wall. This could or could not have been Ken's powers, but it's something."

Rick closed his eyes and placed the ice pouch on his forehead. "It's better if we all think of something else, the past is the past. I just wish I could say goodbye to your parents one more time." He moved the ice pouch away from his head and the pouch disappeared. "You should wash up, I made breakfast for you. Ashton and I will wait for you in the living room," he said, making a groan as he stood up.

I looked at Ashton who looked back at me. "It's better if you don't think about the past. Trust me, the feeling slowly gets better," he said getting up from my bed.

Both Ashton and Rick looked back at me waiting for me to get up. I pressed my hands on my bed and got up. We all walked out of my room, I walked inside the bathroom as the two walked downstairs.

I looked at myself in the mirror and took a deep breath, what a dream. I turned on the sink knob and washed my face with cold water. I turned off the knob and wiped my face with a towel. I placed the towel on the towel rack and I looked at my right hand.

I flexed my fingers and pressed my hand against the wall, my hand started to go through the wall and then my whole body. I walked through the bathroom wall and into Rick's bedroom. I just want to make sure that my intangibility powers were still working. I looked around Rick's room, nothing out of the ordinary. I teleported into the kitchen.

I reappeared in the kitchen. No one was there. I looked at the table where Rick made breakfast for me; he made chocolate chip pancakes. I don't feel like eating right now, I'm worried that I might vomit again.

I walked down the hallway and into the living room. I took a deep breath and exhaled. Ashton sat on the sofa tying his shoes. Rick was standing with his arms crossed, watching the television. I sat next to Ashton who flashed a smile at me after he finished tying his other shoe.

"So I have to be stuck in this home for another week, great," I said stretching my arms and legs.

Rick turned around, already wearing his holster and his badge. "I know that you don't want to be stuck in here but I want you to get used to your new powers and your body. You just got back from your coma so you should relax before you go to school." He walked up to us and sat on the sofa armrest. "Ashton and I were talking about letting your friends visit you after school. I'll allow you kids to let your friends visit you as long as you tell me that they're coming to the house." Rick looked at me. "Also when your friends visit the house you make sure you cover your tattoos. Don't tell them what happened to you or to us during these past few weeks, can you do that for me Kai?"

I looked back at Rick lacing my fingers together. "Don't worry Rick. You and Ashton should get to work and school now."

"Oh that reminds me, I'm going to transfer all the information you need for your classes, it will only take a few seconds." Before I could say anything he raised his pointer finger and pressed it on my forehead.

I blacked out; colors started to quickly zoom into my view. The colors turned to image of pictures from the civil war to chemical formulas to mathematical equations. My head felt tingly as I kept looking at the images. Suddenly my eyes went blurry and I closed my eyes.

I opened my eyes and saw Rick looking back at me. "Are you alright?"

I rubbed my eyes. "What the hell? That felt weird."

"Now you can breeze through your classwork and still have time to hang out with your friends and with us." He looked at his watch. "It's time to go, make sure you eat and do your work." He kissed me on the head and stood up.

I looked at Ashton who gave me a hug. "I can help you with your classwork when I come home."

Ashton and I stood up. He grabbed his backpack off the floor and slung it on one of his shoulders. The two of us walked out of the living room and toward the door where Rick was standing outside on our porch.

Rick looked back at us. "I'll come home at six so I can make dinner for you guys."

Ashton walked out the door and look back at me. "Bye Kai."

I waved at Ashton and Rick as they walked down the stairs and to the sidewalk. "Bye guys see you later."

I closed the door and locked it. I walked into the living room and sat on the floor in front of the wooden table. Books, stacks of papers, and my backpack appeared next to me on the floor, my laptop appeared on top of the table. I opened the laptop and turned it on. I looked at one of the stacks of papers and grabbed a small section of them.

I grabbed the television remote and turned the television off, going to my music playlist on my laptop to begin playing music. I took a pencil and a notebook out of my backpack and began doing my work.

It was already Friday and I made it through the whole week, the work that I missed wasn't as bad as I thought. That was a lie, I had missed at least three projects and I had to do it all by myself. I think I did at least two or three all-nighters which made me feel overwhelmingly exhausted, but I don't really care as long as I finish my work.

When Rick did that transferring thing in my head, I had a better understanding of what I'm learning in my classes. I'm just glad that I don't have to read my textbooks; it would take me weeks to learn the things that I missed in class. Plus reading the big textbooks bores me to death.

Ashton had told me that he's in AP and honors classes; he even told me that he's in some of my honors classes, which was really good. I told Ashton that I'm very proud of him of joining the AP classes. He's a very smart guy and I know he's going to do very well in those smart people classes.

Stella and Tobi came for dinner for most of the week; she was very relieved that I came out of my coma. One day she made me chocolate cake for dinner and I was very happy that she did that. The most surprising thing about this week was that I learned that Rick and Stella are dating. When the four of us were having dinner on Thursday, Stella and Rick kissed and I was shocked when they did that. But I got over it, I'm grateful that Rick and Stella are happy together.

Ronnell, Owen, and Tyrone visited me on Wednesday, and today they helped me with my classwork and we talked about my trip and the 'accident' I got into. Dawn and Ronny couldn't make it but they called me and said that they'd be happy to see me next Monday. Jake called me to say that his dad was in the hospital. I told him to tell his dad that I hope he feels much better.

Everything was going great; everyone was happy that I was back and I couldn't be happier to see my friends again. We all talked about what had happened when I was away. I learned that a teacher got fired because he was smoking weed with his students and also learned about some drama between some people in school. So I guess I didn't miss anything much.

Ashton had told me that he made the school basketball team and that he and Tyrone won every single game. I told him and Tyrone that I was proud of them; someday I'd go to his basketball game and be there to support them.

It was midafternoon. All of us were in the living room talking about classes and other school drama. Tyrone, Ashton, and Ronnell sat on the sofa while Owen and I sat on the floor going over the classwork that I finished. It took me a long time to finish all of my missing work, but I still had to take my tests and quizzes when I went back to school which I wasn't looking forward to.

Ronnell tapped my shoulder. "I want to talk to you about something, can we go to your room to talk about it privately."

I looked back at her. "Sure." What does she want to ask me? I hope it isn't about my 'trip.'

Ronnell and I stood up and walked up to my room. I looked back and Ashton looked at me with a concerned look. I gave him a shoulder shrug as I left the living room. Ronnell and I walked into my room. I sat on my bed and Ronnell sat next to me.

"I guess you're going to tell me what happen between you and Kyle huh?" I said as I ran my hands on my bed.

"That and the real reason you left; I know that you wouldn't leave without saying goodbye to your best friends. You would have told me where you're going or how long you're going to be out before you left. You were gone for at least a month; you never returned my calls or my texts. I know you wouldn't ignore me or your friends just like that," she said with a serious tone.

I couldn't tell what'd happen, not yet anyway, I just needed time to find a way to tell her and everyone else what happened to me. I needed to make up something fast so she wouldn't be too suspicious about me.

I looked at my best friend dead in the eye. "I'll tell you and everyone else the truth when the time comes. I just need to figure out when."

Ronnell's expression changed from serious to worried. "What? I need to know what happened to you. After you came back...you seem different from before, I can tell by the look in your eyes."

My heart was beating fast, I shouldn't have said that. "It's better if I tell you and everyone my story when the time is right, right now isn't the time. I need to think about it first, don't be mad at me," I said quickly as I looked down at the floor.

"I'm not mad, just concerned. I was worried sick about you, we have been best friends for about seven years now. I thought you would tell me what had happened to you or something. But I understand that this is a personal matter and I shouldn't force you to tell me this."

I made a frown and put my hand on her shoulder. "Don't worry so much about me, I'm alive aren't I? You and everyone else have to wait for me to find the right time to tell my story. But all I can do is show you my tattoos under this stupid arm cover." I grabbed my arm cover and pulled it completely off revealing my dragon and lotus tattoo.

Ronnell's eyes grew wide, her mouth was open from shock. "When did you get that? Why do you have that? Rick wouldn't let you get that tattoo."

My eyebrows twitched. "It's just a tattoo and I think it's pretty badass. Plus I didn't choose it and it didn't hurt when I got it, well maybe because I passed out before I got my tattoo," I said casually.

Ronnell looked at me like I was crazy. "How can you be so calm? It's a whole sleeve tattoo, people will say things about you. You know how people are."

"I don't care what those irrelevant people say about me. I have been through some crazy stuff more extreme than getting this; it's not a big deal."

"Who else knows about your…tattoo?" she asked quietly.

"Rick, Ashton, Stella, and you. I was going to show you my tattoo sooner or later, but now you know that I have an arm sleeve tattoo."

"So is this the reason you left or is there something more to it?" she asked me observing my arm tattoo.

"Yes."

She looked up at me. "No seriously, is this the reason you left? To get a tattoo?"

"No it's a small part of my very long story; it's not even that important now."

"Okay then, tell me about how Ashton became part of your family," she asked still looking at me.

"It will all make sense when I tell the story about my trip. Rick legally adopt him, Ashton's a good guy."

"I know that he is, he's a really nice guy, but is he the reason you and Rick went to New York?"

I looked at her, my lips pressed together in a line. "No he isn't, it's complicated. When the time is right I will tell you the truth of what happened, but you have to be patient."

Ronnell let out a sigh. "I know."

"Why did you and Kyle break up?" I asked as I put my arm sleeve back.

She looked away from me. "He cheated on me with Lexi," she said quietly.

My eyes hardened. "What? He cheated on you? Oh come on!" I said loudly as I threw my hands up. "He's just like those typical guys who don't want to have a real relationship. But to be honest, you're too young to get into a relationship that quickly," I said as my voice went back to normal.

"I know Kai. I was in the moment, he made me feel special." She looked up at me, her eyes watery. I could feel a prick in my chest, I felt so bad that I wasn't there for her back then.

"I'm so sorry that I wasn't there for you. I feel like a horrible best friend. I'm here if you need a shoulder to cry on," I said as I opened my arms wide.

Tears started to stream down her cheeks. She moved towards me and hugged me as she pressed her face onto my shoulder. I wrapped my arms around her as I pressed my cheek on her head. I looked at nothing in particular in my room.

I felt my breathing becoming shallow. When I find Kyle I will break him.

CHAPTER 38

I woke up looking at the ceiling lying on my bed, feeling tired and lazy. I lay on my side so I could face the wall that had a digital clock on it. 5:37am. I let out a groan as I gripped my blanket and sat up.

Gosh, it's my first day back to school. I have to take so many tests and quizzes. I just have to suck it up and go through all that. I already know that I will bomb my tests and quizzes so screw it.

I got out of my bed my bare feet touched the cold floor. I walked up to my closet and picked out a new set of clothes for the day. I walked out of my room and through the hallway. I walked up to the bathroom door; the door was closed.

I sat on the floor; my back pressed against the wall. I looked at my arms and legs; they still looked skinny since I woke up from my coma.

The bathroom door opened. I looked up and saw Ashton walking out of the bathroom; he was wearing black jeans but he was shirtless. He was still muscular as always, I guess being in a sports team makes you really fit.

Ashton looked at me and blushed. "Oh hey Kai, I should wear a shirt." He looked down at his chest.

"No don't worry about that, we're siblings now. I might as well get used to you doing whatever guys do, it doesn't bother me," I said as I got up, standing next to him.

"I'm so happy that you're here with me and Rick. And now you're finally coming to school with me." I could smell a lavender scent from him; it smelled like the body wash that I used.

"I know and I'm happy too. Did you use my body wash?" I asked.

Ashton looked off to the side. "Oh that? I didn't know that was yours, I should have asked before I used it."

I let out a laugh and patted his arms. "It's alright Ash. I guess the two of us already got used to sharing our stuff huh. Just so you know I use your long socks sometimes when I sleep," I said smiling at him.

Ashton looked back at me and made a shy smile. "You can use my stuff as long as they aren't lost. You should get ready, see you downstairs." He turned around and walked down the hall.

I looked at his back as he walked towards his room. I looked his centipede tattoo again. At least he won't be judged by other people in public by his tattoo.

I picked up my clothes from the floor and walked into the bathroom.

I teleported inside the kitchen where Ashton and Rick sat at the table as they were discussing Fred's party this Saturday. I sat at the table and listened to their conversation as I poured myself a glass of orange juice.

"When do we get to see our outfits for the party?" I asked and took a gulp of orange juice, lucky now I can eat and drink without vomiting afterwards.

"I was just about to tell you guys about that. Yesterday Vinny called me and told me that our outfits are done. We can go to the shop after I'm done with work which is about six or seven in the afternoon. We can try our outfits to see if they look good on us, maybe we could add something to them," Rick said as his eyes lit up.

"I can't wait to try them on," I said with a smile.

Ashton nodded, agreeing with me. "It sucks that we have to wait a whole week until the party, I hope the party will be exciting. By the way, what did you get for Fred?"

A small green box with a small golden crown at the bottom lid of the box appeared on the table in front of us. Rick took the box and opened it for Ashton and me to see. Inside the box was a black and gold Rolex watch.

I could feel my eyes widen; Rolex watches are very expensive. Rick owns a black Rolex that cost about thirteen thousand dollars, but it was a gift from

Fred. I looked at Ashton who had his mouth in amazement. I looked back at Rick who smiled at us.

"Isn't it a nice gift for Fred? He and I go way back, maybe about nine or ten years since we first met each other. He's like a father to me; he even babysat you a few times. All the things he did for me and you, I couldn't find the right words to tell him how much he influenced me to become the man that I am today," Rick said wholeheartedly.

"You should tell him that in person when we're at the party, I think he would like hearing you tell him how much he means to you," Ashton said.

"It's a really beautiful watch; do you think that Fred will like it?" I asked, thinking how much money that watch is worth. That watch is worth more than all my clothes and shoes combined.

"You know that black Rolex watch I have? That watch was originally his but he gave it to me as a gift when I became a lieutenant. This gift will show him how much I have grown into a good person because of him," Rick said as he carefully looked at the watch.

"I'm glad that you got something special for Fred," Ashton said as he looked at his phone.

Rick closed the lid. The box disappeared into thin air. He took his mug that I made when I was little and took a sip of coffee.

"We should get ready; I don't want my kids to miss the bus." Rick stood up and placed his mug in the sink.

Ashton and I stood up. I took both of our glasses and placed them in the sink. I walked out of the kitchen and into the hallway. My backpack appeared lying against the wall next to me. I picked up my bag and slung it on my shoulder. My backpack was filled with missing paperwork, it should've been very heavy but it felt very light. I put my hands out in front of me and two textbooks appeared on my hands. The weight of all of those large textbooks didn't feel heavy at all.

Rick grabbed his keys and fixed his hair. "Ready?"

"Ready as I'll ever be," I said carrying my books in one arm.

All three of us walked out of the house and down the porch stairs. Rick stopped at the sidewalk and gave us a bear hug.

"Good luck," Rick said as he broke up our hug. Ashton and I said our goodbyes and walked the other way towards our bus stop.

Owen smiled at us as we walked to him. "Finally you get to go to school again, I missed you so much."

"I know Owen, I missed everyone while I was away. Glad that I'm back."

In the morning everyone sat at our usual table in the cafeteria before classes started. Dawn and Jake gave me a hug and Ronny told me that he was happy that I came back from my 'trip.' It looked like nothing much had changed in the school, which was good.

I had to go to my teachers and give them my missing work so that they can grade them. I already knew my grades were going to be bad, so be it. Ronnell and I walked through the school, delivering my papers and textbooks to my teachers before class started. We both talked about our normal stuff like clubs that we go to and other school related stuff that I missed.

The whole day was the same as any other day in school, boring and depressing. Whatever Rick did to me last week made me understand what is happening during my classes which was good for me. My teacher told me that I had to stay after school during the week so I could finish my tests and quizzes. I stayed after for Geometry since I wanted to get the most boring subject out of the way first.

Ashton stayed after for writing club with Tyrone, maybe if I finished my tests early I could walk home with them. It took me about two hours to fully finish all my Geometry tests and quizzes. That was harder than I thought.

After I had finished my very long and stressful tests and quizzes, I left my papers to my Geometry teacher, and walked out of the classroom. I walked through the halls to go to the bathroom. I spent two whole hours focusing so hard on my tests and quizzes that I didn't feel like going to the bathroom, but I did now.

As I walked through the empty hallway I heard Kyle's voice in one of the classrooms near the bathrooms. I looked up and down the hallway; there was no one in the hallway with me. I looked up at the ceiling; there were only two cameras at each corner of the long hallway.

I walked up to the classroom where I heard his voice and poked my head through the door. Kyle was with Lexi; the two of them were hugging and kissing each other. I couldn't forget how sad Ronnell was when she told me that Kyle cheated on her with Lexi, thinking about this made me pissed off.

I removed my backpack and placed it outside the classroom. I took a deep breath and walked inside the room as I closed and locked the door. I turned my head to look at Kyle and Lexi, the two of them stopped kissing and looked at me with an annoyed glare.

"What the hell are you doing here?" Lexi said in a very rude tone.

I didn't say anything as I walked up to them. Kyle and Lexi broke up their hug and glared at me. I stopped a few feet away from them. I observed each of their faces and let out a scoff.

"So you cheated on Ronnell just to be with that? Huh?" I said as I crossed my arms.

Kyle looked up and down at me. Lexi opened her mouth with shock. "So? She didn't seem like she wanted to be with me, I want to have a real relationship with someone and that person is Lexi. She's better than her! Ronnell doesn't even want me to kiss her! We'd been dating for about a month," he said.

"You should know that Ronnell wanted to take time in the relationship, you were moving too fast for her. I'm glad that the two of you are done because I don't want her to be with someone like you," I said, tilting my head towards him. "People like you should go to hell," I said in a low voice.

Lexi walked up to me; she was only a few inches taller than me. She's very annoying and the worst part is that she's a preppy cheerleader just like some of the people in this school.

"A little girl like you shouldn't say those things to people who are more popular than you." She made a smirk and leaned closer to me. "You're just a shabby nobody."

I raised an eyebrow. "Says a slut; is he like the fourteenth guy you have been with this year? What happened to that senior guy? Oh, maybe he dumped you when he heard that you're pregnant." I looked down at her stomach and then back up at her punchable face. "Judging by that little bump on your stomach," I said with a fake smile.

Lexi's beady blue eyes glared into mine. I wasn't even that scared of her. "You have a lot of balls to say tha—" She moved into my face as I took a step back and punched her in the face. Hard. Lexi moved to the side and fell onto the floor. She lay on the floor not moving at all. Her cheek had reddened from the impact of my fist and she started to have a bloody nose.

I looked up at Kyle with his eyes and mouth wide open. He looked down at Lexi and then up at me. "What. The. Hell." His face turned angry, he lunged towards me with his hands reaching at me.

I took a step to the side and let him fall onto the floor. "You know, after I kick your ass make sure that you won't be a snitch and tell everyone, especially the teachers and principal about this little incident."

Kyle got up and ran towards me. As he was a few feet from me I kicked him in the stomach. I kicked him so hard that he flew to the other side of the room. He let out a yell, but the door was closed so no one could hear him. I could feel myself make an evil smile as I walked up to Kyle who sat against the wall gasping for air. I'm starting to realize that I somewhat act like Ken, being evil, sinister and all that, but I don't care at all.

I stood in front of him as he looked up at me with a smirk. "You know what Kai? When I told my friends about Ronnell, I told them that I was going to slowly turn her into a freak," he said, making a weak chuckle.

My body tensed as he said that horrible thing. I crouched down to him. He thrust his hands at me and grabbed me by the neck. I could feel his hands squeeze as he looked at me with an irritated look in his eyes.

The thing is, I can't feel pain or get killed. I could only feel a slight pressure to my neck, but I still could breathe and talk.

I made a wicked smile as the two of us locked eyes. I swiftly moved my left hand onto his neck and slowly squeezed his neck. His face turned from irritated to horrified within seconds.

I let out a laugh as his hands moved away from my neck. He moved his hands onto my hands that held onto his neck. He kept scratching my hands as he gasped for air.

I moved him closer to me so that we were eye to eye. "If you ever look or even talk about her or any of my friends in a negative way, then I will make sure that I will break your other limbs." I stared daggers at him. He moved his eyes away from me but I shook him so that he'd look at me. "Don't you ever say such a thing about Ronnell ever again!" I growled at him.

"What other limbs?" he said in a strained voice.

"The ones that I'm going to break after I break your leg," I whispered as I pulled him away from me.

I held him so that he was able to stand up. I looked up at him as he looked down at me with pure fear in his eyes. I made another wicked smile as he let out a weak yell. I lifted up my right leg and slammed it towards his leg. He made a muffled scream as my foot almost touched his leg. I quickly stopped just when my foot was a few inches from his lower leg.

I looked up at him and laughed. "Do you think I'm that evil? Well, I could be but I don't go around and break people's limbs. But I'm very serious about this; don't ever mess with me, my friends or anyone innocent ever again," I said, moving him towards me once again. "And don't ever tell anyone about this, tell your slutty girlfriend not to tell a soul about this. You hear me?" My voice grew louder as Kyle shook his head quickly. "Okay that's good. Next time if you ever talk shit to anyone especially when it's about my friends, I will be happy to break your legs in order for you to know that I'm not the type of person to be messed with." Before he made any noises or said something I slammed my right fist into his face. Kyle immediately passed out right after I punched him.

I dropped his body onto the floor. I looked at Lexi, who watched the whole thing. I walked up to her and crouched down to her. There was a dry trail of blood from her nose to the side of her face.

"Like I said to Kyle, don't ever tell anyone about this or you'll be wearing a cast. If I hear anything about this incident anywhere, I will personally hunt you and Kyle down and will make you regret being in this school or having even met me," I said. Lexi's eyes grew wide with horror as she made a quiet whimpering noise.

I stood up and looked at her once again, then at Kyle. I turned around and walked out of the classroom with silence.

I guess Ken and I aren't so different after all.

I met Ashton and Tyrone outside the school. They were sitting on the benches doing their homework. I sat next to Tyrone and looked at the two of them.

"You want to walk to your house, or should we go get something to drink?" Tyrone asked as he put his dark blue binder inside his bag.

"We should grab something to drink at a coffee shop," Ashton said as he stood up and slung his bag on one shoulder.

"That's a good idea, I'll pay," I said, standing up and stretching my arms and legs.

All three of us walked out of the school's property and into the center of the city. I didn't realize how much I missed hanging outside with my friends. I took a deep breath of fresh air and closed my eyes, enjoying life.

We stopped in front of a coffee shop in Newbury Street. All three of us walked into the shop. There were a lot of people in the shop. The three of us ordered our drinks and sat at an empty table that was next to the shop window.

Ashton got iced coffee, Tyrone got vanilla ginger latte with a blueberry muffin, and I got a chai latte. I paid for everyone's orders, which wasn't that expensive, at least it's less than twenty dollars.

The three of us talked about Fred's party this Saturday. Tyrone told us that he already got a gift for his granddad. He told us that he got Fred a custom made pen set, a Whiskey test tube set, and a one hundred dollar gift card to his favorite restaurant IHOP. To be honest I would love to get a hundred dollar gift card to IHOP.

Ashton and I told Tyrone that Rick got Fred a Rolex watch, Tyrone told us that he wouldn't tell Fred about Rick's gift. We told him that we're going to a tailor shop to try our custom made outfits for the party in a couple of hours. Tyrone told us that he already had his suit ready and how excited he was about going to the party.

The three of us talked about school, politics, and other things that had happened around the world. I enjoy how the three of us can go into a deep conversation, unlike some people who don't care about real world problems.

We'd been talking for a while. I looked through the window; I could tell that the sun was slowly setting. I turned on my phone, 5:37pm. I looked up and saw Ashton and Tyrone talking about sports.

"Hey Ash, it's almost time to go home."

Ashton and Tyrone stopped talking and both looked at me.

"I guess it's time for me to go home too," Tyrone said as he glanced at Ashton who was sitting across from him.

Ashton looked at Tyrone and then at me. "We should get ready before Rick comes to pick us up."

Tyrone collected all of our trash and tossed it into the trash bin. The three of us put on our backpacks and walked out of the shop and into the cool breezy afternoon. Tyrone asked if Ashton and I could walk him to his apartment and we yes, at least his apartment is about six blocks away from our home. The three of us walked down the sidewalk as we talked to each other.

Ashton and I sat on the floor doing our homework on top of the living room table as we waited for Rick. Ashton helped me with my homework and classwork that I didn't finish today. As the two of us were doing our homework, I began to think about Ken and his organization.

"Do you think there's more people like us somewhere around the world?" I asked without looking up from my homework.

Out of the corner of my eye I saw Ashton's head turn towards me. There was a long pause before he could say anything.

"It's better if you don't think too much about that; it's the least of our worries."

"You didn't answer my question." I stopped writing and placed my pen down on my notebook.

Ashton let out a sigh and placed his arm on the table. "I have no idea how many people have powers or abilities, but I do know that there's people like us somewhere in the world. Like I said, don't think too much about this."

I turned my head and looked at him. "Yeah, I guess you're right," I said quietly.

Ashton made a sad frown as he looked at me. "I know what happened to us was really difficult, but we just have to move on. You should think more about the future and what kind of person you're going to be when you're an adult."

"I know Ash, but now I don't have much motivation to do anything, but don't let me get in your way of doing what you want to do."

I heard the front door open. Footsteps came closer, heading towards the living room. Rick walked up to the threshold between the living room and hallway holding a box of paperwork.

"Make sure you two get ready in a few minutes okay?" he told us as Ashton and I were putting away our school supplies.

"Okay," I said as I stuffed my notebook into my bag.

Rick nodded and walked up the stairs. Ashton had already finished packing his school supplies in his bag.

"Are you excited?" Ashton asked as I took out my wallet from my bag.

"Yes I am, are you?" I opened my wallet and count how much money I had, only twenty-two dollars left. I put my money in my pants pocket.

"I've been waiting for us to try on our custom made outfits for a while."

I zipped my bag up, both of our bags disappeared. I stood up and sat on the sofa, Ashton sat on the floor with his back against the sofa.

Rick walked down the stairs and into the living room. "Okay, it's time to go," he said smiling with excitement.

Inside a dark warehouse men dressed in black suits holding guns were scattered around inside and outside the property. It was now late afternoon; lights inside the warehouse began to turn on. A man dressed in a police uniform casually walked toward the entrance of the building. Two men in suits were standing side by side by the door.

The man in the police uniform took off his hat and nodded at the men, who nodded back as he walked inside the building. On his uniform a label on his left chest read 'H. Reed.' Inside the building large wooden crates were stacked on top of each other; all the crates were branded with an Ankh symbol.

Multiple men in suites surrounded the area, all of them quietly watching the officer walking through stacked crates and towards a room at the back of the building. A man stood in front of the door.

"I'm here to talk to Liam. Is he around?" the officer said standing in front of the man in black.

"He's in his office, what is your name?"

"Henry Reed."

The man turned around and opened the door, poking his head inside the room. He said something quietly and then turned his head back and looked at Henry.

"You can come in," the man said, pushing the door wide for Henry to walk in.

Henry nodded at the man and walked inside the room. Inside the room there was a desk, a chair in front of the desk, bookshelves, and a wide window that viewed the city from afar.

Liam sat at his desk. He had a large scar over his cheek and down his neck. He looked up at Henry and gestured him to take a seat in front of the desk.

Henry sat down and placed his hat on top of the desk. The two of them looked at each other for a few seconds before one of them said something.

"I have information about Rick Kago," Henry said as he twiddled his thumbs together and gawked at Liam nervously.

Liam opened his cigarette box on his desk and put one between his lips. He grabbed his lighter from his shirt pocket and lit his cigarette.

"What kind of information?" Liam asked.

"This Saturday Chief Gray will be throwing a party in a building called 'State Room' on the thirty-third floor. I know that all of Gray's closest friends from around the state will be there, including Rick. This could be a great opportunity for you to kill him, he's a threat to all of us," Henry said as he wiped his forehead with his hand.

Liam sat back on to his chair as smoke blew out of his mouth. He looked at Henry up and down. "He wouldn't be a threat if you did a better job keeping your secret away from him. Rick is a smart and dangerous man. I can't believe you're still alive today, I thought he would've ended you by now."

Henry frowned. "But he and everyone else don't have a clue that I'm leaking out information from the department and also destroying evidence that leads to your group. I'm the one who's trying to protect your group."

"I know but next time you have to be careful. I will make use of your information about Gray's party. You're dismissed," Liam said waving his hand, dismissing Henry from his office.

Henry stood up, grabbing his hat from the desk. "Do I get a reward for the information I shared with you?"

Liam looked at Henry and then opened his drawer and took out a stack of twenty dollar bills. He took out five and handed them to Henry.

"Thank you," Henry said as he took the money and left the office.

Liam sat back and tapped his fingers on top of his desk deciding what to do next.

"Luke, get in here!" Liam yelled loudly, gray smoke from his mouth clouded around his face.

The door quickly opened. A man in a black suit speed walked in.

"What do you need sir?" Luke asked.

"I want you and everyone else to learn more about Chief Gray's party this Saturday at the State Room. Make sure that all my men will replace all of the staff members in the building for the night. I don't want anyone to leave the whole building until I have successfully killed Kago." Liam looked down at his desk. "That reminds me; when are my special bullets going to be shipped in?" he asked.

"They're going to come here tonight, sir."

Liam took his cigarette and discarded it on his ashtray on the corner of his desk. He reached inside one of his desk drawers and took out a small silver bullet with a skull symbol etched into it.

"Good, I'll need more when the big day comes."

CHAPTER 39

In my room I was getting ready for Fred's party. Ashton and I got him a shaving kit and a bottle of red wine, we both made Rick buy the wine for us and it wasn't cheap. I just hope that Fred will like our presents, especially Rick's.

I buttoned up my black shirt as I looked at myself in the mirror. I was wearing maroon dress pants and the matching jacket that goes with my black button up shirt. The outfit that I chose actually looked nice on me. At least Rick, Ashton, and I got to try our outfits the week before the party.

Rick made my hair into a single French braid; I'm glad that he can do my hair when I'm too lazy to style it myself. I wore gold stud earrings with matching gold rings. My pants and jacket were fitted nicely as well as my buttoned shirt, and I was also wearing my black and white slip-on shoes. I know I could wear something else besides those shoes but I don't like wearing high heels or flats, plus my slip-ons are very professional looking and comfortable.

Someone knocked on my door, I turned around. "Come in," I said walking to my bed and sitting on the edge of it.

Ashton walked into my room, already dressed. He sat next to me on my bed. He was wearing a white button up shirt, dark gray slim vest and matching pants, pink and white tie, and black dress shoes.

He looked at my outfit. "You look very beautiful," he said, his lips curved in a smile.

"Thanks you look handsome as always, where did you put our presents for Fred?"

"I've put them on the kitchen table. I hope he likes our presents."

I looked at my hands. My right hand was wrapped in white bandages so no one would look at my hand tattoos. I actually liked using bandages to hide my tattoos better than using an arm or a hand cover. I didn't use bandages for my left arm since I was wearing a long sleeve shirt. I just had to remember not to roll my sleeves up.

"So your birthday is next week, do you want anything for your birthday?" Ashton asked.

"It's our birthday and I don't want anything. I have everything I need and that's good enough for me," I said nodding to myself.

He raised an eyebrow. "Are you sure? I owe you and Rick everything for what you did for me, it doesn't feel right if I don't do anything for the two of you."

I lightly punched him on his arm. "Here's something you can do for me. Live your life and become someone great, I will always be here to watch you grow up and that's all I need from you. Promise me you will do that."

He placed his head against my shoulder. "I'm afraid that I won't keep that promise Kai. I'm not sure that I will be someone great."

"Don't doubt yourself, I know that you will be a great person in the future, trust me."

"I'm not sure. I'm a cold-blooded killer, I don't deserve your and Rick's generosity. I would be better off dead."

I grabbed his warm face with my hands and looked at him. We locked eyes; his eyes were wide open. I lightly slapped him on both sides of his face. He closed his eyes as I slapped him for a few seconds. I stopped slapping him but my hands cupped his face, he opened his eyes and stared at me. His green eyes gazed into mine.

"Don't you ever say or think of something like that, okay? I know that you're going to become a great person in the future. Rick and I already know that you have potential and we wouldn't give up on you, we're a family and we won't give up on you no matter what. Will you keep your promise to me?" I said still locking eyes with Ashton. "Promise me that you'll look up to the future and live a life that you want."

He blinked his eyes and made a frown. "What happens if I kill someone again?"

"You won't, if you're attacked by someone you can always fight back but do not kill that person. You can always break their legs or arms so they wouldn't hurt other people, the police will understand that you're defending yourself from that attacker. But the main thing is to remember to not kill anyone; hurt them until they can't move or cause any more harm."

He nodded and made a sniffling sound. "Okay, I'll keep your promise."

I smiled at him and lightly slapped his face once more. "That's my boy."

I moved my hands away from his face and placed them on my lap. I looked outside the window; the sun was beginning to fall into the horizon.

"Well, do you want anything for your birthday?" I asked.

"Nothing at all, I have everything that I need and that's good enough for me. For me family is the best thing that I will ever have, nothing can be much better than that."

"Nothing can be better than family," I said as I smiled to myself.

"By the way we should plan our party since it's in a week."

"I guess you're right, we both know that our party will be at our house and that Rick is getting the food. We should make invitations for all of our friends, maybe in our party we could watch a movie or play a game. But I want you to plan it out the way you like, I'm open to anything."

"We could use Owen's gaming consoles for our party and watch a funny movie. I don't know how to throw a party, but that's all I came up with."

I stretched my arms and legs. "That's a good idea, after Fred's party we can fully plan out our party."

Rick walked into the room. His hair was slicked back and his outfit perfectly fit him, which made him look like those cool spy agents from those movies. He was wearing a white button up shirt, navy blue pants, black suspenders, black tie, and dark brown dress shoes.

The three of us look like a cool and stylish family. I wonder where Stella is; I guess she's on her way here. I felt bad that Tobi couldn't come; he was staying at Stella's parents' house for the night.

"Are you two excited for tonight?" Rick said as he stood in front of us with a smile on his face.

"Yeah I can't wait to eat some good food," I said as I tucked my bangs behind my ear.

"Is Stella coming?" Ashton asked.

"She just texted me, she's going to be here in ten minutes since traffic is a pain in the ass. Other than that your birthdays are next week, do you two want anything in particular?" Rick asked as he placed his hands in his back pants pockets.

"Nothing at all," Ashton said and I nodded my head, agreeing with him.

Rick made a puzzled face. "You two sure you guys don't want anything? You know that I would do and get anything for the two of you, right?"

"We know Rick, but we have decided that family is the best gift of all," I said as I patted Ashton on the shoulder.

Rick's eyes twinkled and he made a sad smile, he lifted his arms up. "You two are going make me cry, come here and give me a hug."

Ashton and I exchanged glances as we got up and hugged Rick. I missed this feeling, being loved and being happy. I pressed my face against Rick's chest. I could feel Rick's and Ashton's arms wrapped around me as we all gave each other a group hug.

"I love my kids, I would do anything for you two," Rick said as we kept hugging each other.

Rick gave us a squeeze and let go of his grip, he looked at me and then at Ashton.

"You need to gel your hair Ashton; I want you to look even more dashing for the party." Rick held his left palm out, a container of hair gel appeared on top of his hand.

"You don't have to do that for me Rick," Ashton said as Rick opened the lid and placed the lid on top of my bed.

"I want my kids to look their best. I want us to look better than most of the people in the party, I want to show off my family to my other friends and make them jealous," he said as his face lit up with confidence.

That's Rick alright, he gets over his head about looking better than most people but I can see why.

Rick used his right pointer and middle finger and scooped up the hair gel after placing the container on top of my bed. He slathered the gel on his left palm and rubbed it with both of his hands. He moved his hands onto Ashton's hair and rubbed Ashton's hair until it was the way Rick liked it.

Rick removed his hands from Ashton's hair. His hair was slicked to the side which was a good look for him.

"Now you look like a million bucks kid," Rick said proudly.

"Not bad," I said observing Ashton's hair.

Ashton walked up to my body mirror and looked at himself. He lightly touched his hair and fixed his vest.

"Thanks Rick," he said without looking away from the mirror.

Rick grabbed the gel container and put the lid back on, the container disappeared. I don't have to use hair gel, but Rick used hairspray on me just an hour ago.

"We should go down to the living room and wait for Stella," Rick said as he turned around and walked towards the door.

Ashton turned around and walked towards the door, I followed him out of my room. I closed the door walking down the hallway and stairs.

All of us were inside the living room; I sat on the sofa and Ashton sat on the sofa armrest. I teleported our presents, packed in a gift bag. I peeked inside the bag; everything was neatly wrapped. Gold tissue paper was placed on top of the presents inside the bag, which was my idea, and it looked pretty.

I teleported my phone to the sofa next to me. I turned on my phone and saw that I had multiple notifications from a group chat with Tyrone, Ashton, and me. I went to my messages and looked at the text messages that were sent.

From Tyrone: 'Are you guys ready?"

From Ashton: 'Yeah we're just waiting for Stella to come, where are you?'

From Tyrone: 'I'm already at the party, a few people showed up early. Our tables are all already set up, we're sitting at the same table which is a good thing.'

From Ashton: 'At least we get to sit with each other, is there food?"

From Tyrone: 'Yeah there's a lot of servers walking around the floor offering food, I try some of the food that they have and it's really good.'

From Ashton: 'You're making me hungry; I really want to eat something.'

From Tyrone: 'Just wait until the real food is coming, I bet it's going to be better than those finger foods. BTW where's Kai?'

From me: 'I'm here, I'm just reading your texts.'

From Ashton: 'Can't wait to go to the party. Do you know if anyone else we know is coming?'

From Tyrone: 'Just some other people I don't talk to or like, but it's alright, you guys are coming so I won't be bored to death.'

From me: 'IKR at least we can all hang out together.'

I heard the front door open, must be Stella. I texted Tyrone that we're going to the party now and I turned off my phone.

I heard Stella's high heels click against the floor as she was walking into the living room. Ashton got up from the armrest and placed his phone in his back pants pocket. I got up and wiped lint from my pants.

Stella looked at Ashton and I, she walked towards us and gave us a hug.

"You two look so adorable! Aw, I love you two so much!" Stella said as she squeezed us.

"You look very beautiful Stella," Ashton said.

"You look like a model," I said.

Stella broke up our hugs and smiled at us. "Thank you for the compliments."

Stella was wearing a light purple cocktail party dress with a long lace skirt. She wore gold earrings, bracelets, and high heels. Her makeup was neatly done and wasn't too much. I didn't wear makeup because I'm the kind of person who likes to be all natural.

Stella walked up to Rick and gave him a hug, the two of them kissed on the lips. It made me feel awkward when the two of them kissed and I think Ashton felt the same. I looked to my side to see Ashton looking down at the floor.

"You two get a room," Ashton said jokingly as he looked up.

Rick looked at him blushing. "I just want to show everyone that I finally have a girlfriend," he said making a silly smile.

"You look even more beautiful than ever," Rick said to Stella, his hands holding her waist.

Stella smiled. "You look handsome as always," she said, her arms around Rick's neck.

"Okay you two love birds, we have a party to go to," I said holding my gift bag.

"Kai's right, we should go now." Rick let go of his grip from Stella's waist, a small dark blue bag appeared on top of the table.

Rick walked up to the table and carried the bag towards the door, everyone followed Rick. He took his car keys from the key holder near the door and opened the door. Everyone else walked through the door and down the porch stairs while Ashton closed and locked the door.

Rick sat in the driver's seat, Stella sat in the passenger seat, Ashton and I sat in the back. I placed our gift bags on the seat between Ashton and me.

Rick turned on the car, everyone wore their seat belts. Rick drove the car out of the parking spot and toward the city.

CHAPTER 40

T he four of us got out of the car that was parked in a parking lot next to a tall building. I looked around my surroundings, people walking left and right down the sidewalk, birds flying up in the sky, cars driving through the street.

Rick locked his car and walked toward the tall building as he placed his car keys in his pants pocket. Ashton was carrying our gift and I was carrying Rick's gift. Stella, Ashton, and I followed Rick inside the building.

Inside the building, people were in the lobby talking to each other and mingling. Rick walked up to the elevator and pressed a button. The elevator doors opened and the four of us walked inside.

Rick pressed the thirty-third floor button and the elevator doors closed; I could feel the pressure of the elevator as we went up. There was a window that was on the opposite side of the door. I looked through the window and saw the city view of Boston.

After a couple of minutes inside the elevator we finally reached our floor. Once the door opened, the four of us walked out of the elevator and into a large room. In the large room multiple tables were scattered around the whole space. Plant decorations were placed everywhere and servers wearing a black and white uniform walked around the room holding trays of food. I could hear classical music playing on the ceiling speakers, people were standing in groups conversing.

One of the servers walked up to us holding a tray of meatballs on a toothpick. Rick turned down the offer but Stella and I took the meatballs. I took two for Ashton and me to eat. I said thank you to the server and looked to my side to find Ashton looking around the room with a fascinated look on his face.

I handed one of the meatballs to Ashton who took and ate it as we looked around the room once more. There was a wide and long window that viewed the city and everything within the city. Tables were covered in white cloth and decorated with a flower centerpiece; the dining ware was already set on the tables. This place is very fancy and formal; this is the kind of thing Fred likes.

"Can we take a picture all together?" Stella said as she took out her phone from her hand purse.

"We need someone to take the photo for us," Ashton said as he looked around the room.

A man wearing a dark green button up shirt with black pants walked by, Rick tapped him on the shoulder. The man turned around and looked at Rick with surprise.

"Sorry to bother you, can you take a picture of the four of us?" Rick asked as he took Stella's phone and held it toward the man.

"Sure thing," the man replied joyfully as he took Stella's phone. Ashton took Rick's gift bag from me and placed our bags on the floor next to our impromptu picture taker.

The four of us stood side by side posing for the photo. As the man was taking the photos I could hear multiple clicking noises from the phone. It seemed like the man was talking a lot of photos. I hope I look good in most of them.

"All of you are an adorable family, have a great evening," the man said as he handed the phone to Rick and walked away.

"You too," I replied as I looked at the photos on the phone. All the photos turned out very well.

"I will send these pictures to all of you later," Stella said as she zoomed in on one of the pictures. Ashton grabbed the bags and handed me Rick's.

"Hey, I think I see Fred down there, we should all go up to him and say happy birthday," Rick said as he looked to his left.

"Okay let's go," I said looking at Rick's direction. I could see Fred talking to his other friends that were in a group. I gave Rick his gift bag as the four of us walked toward Fred.

Fred looked at our direction and smiled at us. "Welcome to my party! I'm so glad that all of you made it." Fred walked away from his group of friends and stood in front of Rick.

Rick smiled and the two hugged each other. "Happy sixty-eighth birthday Fred, I got you a gift that I put so much thought into it. I hope you like it," Rick said as the two broke up their hug. Rick handed his bag to Fred who took the bag and looked up at Rick.

"Thank you son, I will be opening up my many gifts near the end of the night. I wonder what's inside the bag." Fred chuckled as he patted Rick on the shoulders.

Fred looked at Ashton. "So you're Ashton, I heard many things about you from Rick who never shuts up about his kids, and also from my grandson, Tyrone, who always talks about how cool you are. It's a pleasure to finally meet you in person." Fred held out his hand toward Ashton who took his hand, the two shook hands.

I laughed when Fred said that Rick never shut up about us, I think it was really cute. I could hear Rick letting out a forced laugh and it made me laugh even more.

"The pleasure is mine, Kai and I got you a gift as well," Ashton said after the two broke off their handshake and he gave Fred our gift bag.

"You two kids don't have to buy me anything, but thank you," Fred said as he took our bags.

A male staff member walked up to us. "Mr. Gray, may I take your gifts and place them in the gifts area?"

Fred nod at the staff member. "Yes you may, thank you," he said as he handed the two bags to the staff member who walked away carrying the bags.

Fred looked at me and hugged me without saying anything to me. I hugged him back. I bet everyone is looking at me, this is awkward.

"I'm so glad that you're alive now, I'm sorry that all of that happened to you. A child shouldn't have gone through that," Fred said still hugging me.

"It sounds like Rick already told you about my incident. Also the past is the past and I chose to forget about it," I said as I moved my head to the side so I could breathe.

Fred let go of his grip and held me by my shoulders. "That's my girl; you're strong as your uncle."

"Thanks Fred," I said with an embarrassed smile. Rick and I are fairly similar, we both can be stubborn, we're both sassy sometimes, we laugh at the dumbest things, and we both care about people depending on the situation.

"I have assigned all of you to my table so we all could be together, isn't that great?" Fred said.

"That's good news Fred, I can't wait until you open my gift," Rick said.

"I can't wait too. Let the kids find Tyrone, you and Stella could mingle with some of my other friends whom I have known for a long time," Fred said as he patted Ashton and my shoulder.

"I think Tyrone is up in the indoor balcony." Fred looked up at the balcony in the room where a lot of people were standing.

"Okay let's go Kai, see you soon Mr. Gray," Ashton said looking at me.

"Call me Fred, we're friends aren't we?," Fred said with a wink.

Ashton smiled. The two of us left the adults to do whatever they do and walk up the stairs.

The stair's railings were wrapped in shiny ribbons and materials. People stood on the stairs talking pictures or talking to their friends. I wonder how much money booking a place like this would cost.

Ashton and I walked around the area absorbing every detail of the party, many servers walk around the area offering finger foods. I took a few finger foods and ate them as we tried to find Tyrone. Ashton only ate one finger food which was a cheese ball with a slice of tomato on it. As the minutes went by I could tell that more people were showing up at the party judging by the noise of people talking.

Ashton stopped at a small seating area that was in the corner, the two of us sat at a bench.

"Do you want to text Tyrone or should I?" I asked as I took a bite of my mini turkey wrap. These foods are so good and the whole place is so nice, no wonder Fred picked this place.

"I should, I'll let you finish your wrap," he said as he took out his phone and went to his messages. He typed something on his phone, then I heard a ding sound from the phone.

"Looks like Tyrone just came out of the bathroom, he should be here in a few minutes," Ashton said as he turned off his phone and placed it on his lap.

I finished my mini wrap and wiped my hands and mouth with a napkin. I looked at my right hand; my bandages were still tightly wrapped. I looked at the other people who were in the balcony with us, everyone was dressed in formal clothing and they seemed to enjoy the party.

I look at the servers and other staff members. I couldn't help but notice that all the members were all men. I thought that some of the staff members would be women employees, I found that odd. I looked at Ashton who was observing a group of people talking to one another.

"Hey guys did you two eat anything yet?" a person said. I looked to the side and saw Tyrone standing in front of us.

Tyrone was wearing a light purple dress shirt with gray dress pants and a gray tie. Tyrone sat next to Ashton who looked at him and smiled. The two of them wore similar outfits, which made me feel like they have some best friend telepathy kind of thing.

"Kai ate a lot of those finger foods but I didn't eat much, how about you?" Ashton replied.

"I only ate a few, I'm waiting for the actual food that will come later," Tyrone said as he looked at the people walking by us.

"Do you know some place where there isn't much noise?" I asked, the noise from other people at the party was getting louder and it made me a bit lightheaded.

Tyrone looked at me with a worried look on his face. "Kai, are you okay?"

I looked at him. "Yeah I'm just lightheaded that's all. Do you know where I could get something to drink?"

"We could go to a bar and get a drink. Are you able to walk?" Tyrone asked as he reached his hand toward me and patted my back.

"I can walk, somehow now I feel uneasy at the moment. Let's go to the bar," I said as I got up. I could feel my cheeks becoming very warm. I needed something cold to drink.

Tyrone led the way to the bar, the three of us walked down the stairs and through a crowd of people. I could see large shelves on the wall filled with many varieties of alcohol. There was a large bartender desk where people sat and drank their drinks.

The three of us walked up the desk. A strongly built man wearing a white buttoned shirt with suspenders stood behind the desk serving drinks to the guests.

The man looked at the three of us. "What can I get for you?" the man asked politely as he grabbed three glasses.

"I'll order for the two of you okay?" Tyrone said as he looked at us.

"That would be good thanks," Ashton said as I nodded at Tyrone.

Tyrone turned his head to face the bartender. "Can I have one pink lemonade, one lemon berry spritzer, and one tropical punch; all of them with ice please?"

"Alright coming right up," the man said as he took out multiple large bottles of drinks and began pouring them into our glasses.

The man poured different colored drinks into the glasses and add fruit and herbs into our drinks before he finished. The man slid our drinks towards us. I took out my money and put three dollar bills into the tip jar.

"Thank you miss," the man said as Tyrone and Ashton took our drinks.

"No problem," I said flashing a smile at the bartender.

I turned around and followed Tyrone and Ashton through the crowded area and up the stairs again. Ashton looked back at me and handed me a glass of lemonade. I took a big gulp of my lemonade. It made me feel so much better; I placed the cool glass against my cheek to cool down my warm face.

As the three of us were walking we were stopped by Kalie. Her father and my uncle are coworkers at the police department. I don't like her because she's a snobby type of person. I usually don't like to judge people, but Tyrone and I had known her for a while now and learned that she never changes at all. She only gets more annoying each year; lucky I don't see her that much since she's in some preppy private schools.

"Hey guys, how are you?" Kalie said checking us out, her other group of friends were somewhere in the back observing us from a distance. I can tell that they're talking to each other about us and it makes me annoyed. Those kinds of people can be two-faced and become backstabbers if you say anything bad to them. I'm glad that I don't have friends who are like that.

"Same as always, you?" Tyrone said taking a sip of his drink.

"My volleyball team is going to a competition in two weeks, isn't that great news?" she said with a bragging tone. Kalie was wearing a very revealing two piece dress that didn't even look nice on her at all. She also wore too much makeup on her face; it made her look like a slutty clown.

"Oh that's cool," I said quietly, unimpressed.

Tyrone looked at me with a concerned look. Ashton look at Kalie and then at me, and Kalie stared daggers at me. I guess I didn't talk very quietly.

"Says a person who has never been on a sports team. It's a big deal for my team; your school will compete against mine. I bet our team will win," Kalie said confidently.

"You seem cocky for a person who always sat on the benches every game in the season… bi—" As I said the last word Ashton's hand covered my mouth preventing me from saying anything else. I'm glad I had him so I didn't make this conversation worse.

"Isn't my sister so cute and sassy? Just ignore her, she just came out of an accident, she's still a bit woozy," Ashton said as he kept his hand covering my mouth. I could feel his head pressed against mine as he talked to Kalie.

She looked at me and then at Ashton with observing eyes. "So you're her brother?" she asked with a raised eyebrow.

"Yes I am. I'm her adopted brother. You got a problem with that?"

"I do, why would a guy like you become siblings with that? I would move out immediately if I had to live with her," she said rudely with her hands on her hips.

I could feel Ashton's grip on my mouth tighten, he moved his head away from mine and looked straight at Kalie. He moved his hand away from my mouth. As I looked up at him, his eyes hardened. I could feel my chest burn from what Kalie said. I'm so close to doing the same thing that I did with Kyle and Lexi.

"No one says that to her. You and everyone else don't know what kind of mess we have been through." He made a cold wicked smile as he checked her out. "I've now learned why selfish and ignorant people like you never become anything but a waste of life. I don't even know why I'm talking to you." He gestured his hand toward Kalie. "You're not even worth my time talking to."

I could feel my jaw drop from what my not-so innocent brother said, I couldn't be any more proud of him. My eyes shifted to the side where I saw Tyrone had his mouth open and his eyes wide. My eyes shifted to Kalie who had the same expression as Tyrone.

Ashton turned his head to face Tyrone. "Let's go, I have better things to do than talk to someone like that." He walked away from Kalie. He grabbed me by the shoulders, pushing me in front of him as we walked toward a group of people.

Before I went through the group of people I turned around and yelled. "Slutty clown!" Ashton looked at me and smiled as we walked through the crowd. I know it makes the situation a bit worse but who cares?

We stopped in front of a door. Ashton let go of my shoulders and I turned around to look at Ashton and Tyrone.

"Damn, I can't believe you just did that. Who knew that you could be like that?" Tyrone said as he playfully punched Ashton in the arm.

Ashton smiled with embarrassment. "To be honest, most people don't know what I'm capable of, also no one talks shit about my friends and family."

I walked next to Tyrone. "Thanks for standing up for me, if you didn't I would have fought her and it wouldn't look pretty," I said, drinking my pink lemonade.

Ashton looked at me, his eyes softening. "I would do anything for you guys. Telling that girl off makes me have more energy for some reason and it felt really good." He made a grin.

I laughed. "Lucky she doesn't go to our school so that's good news."

Tyrone opened the door that the three of us stood in front of and he walked in. Ashton and I followed him into the room. Inside the room there was a large window that looked over the city, there were two crystal chandeliers that hung from the ceiling. Multiple benches were arranged on the side of the room. The room wasn't too large but wasn't too small which was good for me.

I sat on one of the benches and drank my lemonade as I looked through the window. Looking at the city from this viewpoint is really lovely and relaxing. Ashton and Tyrone sat between me, the three of us talked as the sun set into the horizon.

CHAPTER 41

A server carrying an empty tray walked through the double doors with a sign that said, 'Staff members only.' Inside the room there was a large kitchen where people were preparing the guests' dinners. The server placed his tray on a table as he walked through the kitchen and into another room that was on the other side of the kitchen.

The man opened the door and walked in. Inside the room Liam was sitting on top of a desk cleaning his gun. There were large crates full of different types of guns, bullets, and other weapons. A few other staff members were inside the room filling guns with bullets.

Liam looked up at the man. "Is he here?"

The man nodded. "Yes, he's with a group of people, do you want to start now?"

Liam moved the gun closer to his face and examined his gun. "In a few more minutes, tell all my men to get ready."

"Yes sir," the man said as he turned around and walked out of the room.

Liam unloaded his empty magazine and replaced it with a new magazine. He placed his gun on the desk next to him.

I sat on the floor eating my ice from my drink as I listened to Tyrone and Ashton arguing about if burgers are better than tacos for at least ten minutes straight. I know right? How did those two even get into that topic? I have no idea who even started this weird conversation. All I had learned from this was that Tyrone likes tacos and Ashton likes burgers.

"Tacos can be serves soft shell or hard shell; it's great for any kind of person who prefers one over the other. You can even make a burger taco," Tyrone said as he slapped his hands onto his lap making a loud smacking sound.

"Seriously? There's a thing called a burger taco?" Ashton said as his face moved closer to Tyrone's.

"Yeah there's a thing called a burger taco; my mama can make the best burger taco you've ever had.. You should try it someday, it's really good," Tyrone said loudly as he stared at Ashton.

"That would be great, thanks best friend," Ashton said loudly.

The two of them stared at each other not saying a word for a few long seconds. Then all of a sudden the two of them hugged each other.

I could feel my eyebrows twitching. "What is happening?" I said as I could feel my face cringe from whatever this was.

"This is the power of bromance Kai, you wouldn't know," Tyrone said as he patted Ashton's back, still hugging him.

"I don't even want to know," I said, feeling weirded out.

The two of them broke up their hug and patted each other on the back. I could feel my whole face cringe as I looked at the two of them and their weird 'bromance.'

"I need to go to the bathroom," Ashton said as he got up and wiped dust off of his pants.

"I guess your heated argument with Tyrone made your bladder weak," I said as I pressed my back against the bench.

Ashton turned his head to look at me. "You wish! I just drank too much." He turned his head back and walked towards the door. He opened the door and walked out closing the door behind him.

I stood up and sat next to Tyrone. "Do you and Ashton always argue about something crazy like that?" I asked.

Tyrone smiled at me and placed his arm around my shoulders. "Of course, we do this all the time, it's really fun."

I laughed. "You two are something else." I'm glad that Ashton became best friends with Tyrone. At least I get to see the two of them having a great time together.

Ashton closed the door, leaving Kai and Tyrone to chat. He walked through the crowd of people in the balcony. On one side of the balcony Kalie and her group of friends were whispering to each other as they glared at Ashton walking towards the stairs. People were standing on the stairs looking down at the main floor observing the whole party from a different view. Male servers were walking around the place offering different varieties of finger foods.

Ashton straightened his vest as he walked down the stairs. He looked to his side where the large window was. The sun began to set behind multiple tall buildings. Ashton walked down to the main floor of the party. He looked around the large room trying to find the bathroom.

A server was standing by a group of people who were taking the finger food from the tray.

Ashton walked up to the server. "Excuse me, do you know where the bathroom is?" he asked.

The server looked at Ashton. "If you go towards the entrance of the floor take a left, you'll see a hallway on the right side of the wall. Go down that hallway you'll see the bathroom door."

"Thank you." Ashton said, the server smiled at him.

Ashton walked towards the entrance and then turned left walking through people as they talked and ate their finger foods. Ashton looked to his right and saw an opening in the wall, as he was at the opening he looked down the hall. People were standing next to the wall. Maybe there's a line for the bathroom.

Ashton walked down the hall and stopped behind a man who was on his phone. He turned his head to the side and looked at a line full of men waiting for the bathroom. There was an even longer line for the women's bathroom, most of the women in the line were either looking at their phones or talking to one another. He let out a sigh as he took out his phone.

Rick and Stella sat at the bar talking to each other. Multiple people sat at the bar talking to their friends or to the bartender. As the bartender finished other people's orders he looked at Rick and Stella.

"You two want anything?" the bartender asked.

Rick looked up at the bartender. "I would like an Old Fashioned."

"I would like a Negroni please." Stella said.

The bartender nodded. "Great choices, coming right up."

The bartender took out two glasses and placed them on the table, poured bottles of liquor into the glasses. He moved swiftly as he poured different colored liquid into each glass.

Rick looked at Stella. "So how was work this week?" he asked.

Stella looked back at Rick with a pleasant smile. "Same as always, you?"

"I just got assigned a new homicide case earlier this week, everything seems to be going back to normal after that trip. That reminds me, the kids' birthday party is in a week."

Stella grabbed Rick's hand and rubbed her thumb against the top of his hand. "I know, I've already got the two of them their presents."

"Oh really? What did you get them?"

"I'm not going to tell you, it's a secret," she said playfully.

Rick made a pout. "Always playing hard to get." He smiled seductively. "I like that." He chuckled as Stella blushed, turning her head to the side.

The bartender placed Rick's and Stella's drinks in front of them.

"Thank you," Rick said as Stella smiled at the bartender.

Stella took her glass and drank it. She placed her glass on the table. "Did you get them anything yet?"

"I asked them earlier today if they want anything specific for their birthday, the two of them said that family is the best present they'll ever get. The way they said that, it made them look so cute and so precious." Rick smiled wholeheartedly.

"I'm glad the kids said that, the three of you should be happy together."

"You know that you're part of our family too? I and the kids love you very much. I would do anything for my family no matter what."

Inside the kitchen a dozen staff members were holding guns and checking if their guns were loaded. Liam walked out from a room and walked in the middle of the kitchen.

"I want all of you to gather all of the party guests and move them downstairs. I and a few of my men will find Rick. When I find him I will end him permanently," Liam said bitterly.

All the staff members stormed out of the large kitchen and into the party. As the staff moved into the party the guests saw them holding guns. People started to scream and make loud noises as they tried to run away from Liam's men.

Lights on the floor flickered. The elevator lights suddenly turned off, a few lights in the floor turned off as well. There were still a few lights turned on, but it made the room slightly darkened. People piled up at the elevator but the elevator didn't work at all, people screamed as they ran to the stairs at the corner of the whole floor. A few men holding guns blocked the stairway, preventing anyone from leaving.

All the staff members surround the guests making them huddle into a large group. A few guests resisted the staff by fighting them and yelling at them. One of the staff members was attacked by two men, one of the men knocked a staff member on the ground and the other one grabbed the gun.

The two men punched each other, the man holding the gun positioned the gun at the staff member. Multiple staff members surrounded the three men. The man holding the gun looked around him and made an annoyed look as he dropped the gun.

The group of staff members grabbed the man and forced him to the ground then they stopped the man fighting with a staff member by hitting the man with their fists and feet. The man fell on the ground; the other staff members grabbed the wounded staff member and dragged him away.

A man who was wearing shades and a staff uniform pointed his gun at the ceiling and pulled the trigger. Everyone screamed as the ceiling material fell onto the floor.

"All of you will listen to me, if you disobey me everyone else will end up like him." The man with shades pointed his gun at one of the men and shot him in the leg.

A woman cried; a few others shrieked as the man let out a painful howl as he touched his bleeding leg. Two staff members dragged the man out of the area, leaving a trail of blood towards the hallway.

CHAPTER 42

Ashton was inside the men's bathroom washing his hands, there were a few people in the bathroom but it wasn't crowded. The bathroom was large and was decorated with abstract paintings and tall flowerpots. A few men walked out of the bathroom until there was no one left in the bathroom except for Ashton.

He looked at himself through the sink mirror, silently observing himself. A tiny cut was on his left eyebrow. He had light pink lips; his cheeks slightly skinny showing off his high cheekbones.

As he looked at himself in the mirror, there was a loud noise of gunshots from the main floor. A faint commotion was heard through the hallway. Ashton turned around and walked up to the door. He locked the door and took out his phone. He turned his phone on but there were no service.

"Shit," he said to himself as he placed his phone back in his pants pocket. He looked around the bathroom to find something to defend himself with.

He walked to the stalls and looked inside, nothing in there was useful. Heavy footsteps could be heard walking down the hallway and towards the bathroom. Ashton quickly unlocked the door and grabbed a pot of flowers and hid behind one of the three stalls. He quietly and carefully closed the stall door; he made a disgusted look as he stepped on top of the toilet seat.

The bathroom was silent. The only thing that could be heard was a pair of footsteps walking towards the bathrooms. The men's bathroom door burst open like someone had kicked the door very hard. Ashton kept quiet. His

chest slowly moved up and down, his eyes stared at the stall door with antici-
pation.

"Who's in here? You better come out or you will get hurt," a man's voice
boomed throughout the room.

The man slowly walked up to the first stall; he made a grunt as he forcefully kicked the stall door. Both Ashton and the man were silent. Ashton's
hands tightly gripped the pot as the man moved to the second stall, the stall
where Ashton is in.

"I guess you want to do this the hard way," the man said.

The man's shadow was in front of the second stall. Ashton knitted his
eyebrows and clenched his jaw. Suddenly the man behind the door kicked the
door open, his gun pointed at Ashton. Ashton instantly smashed the pot on
the man who shot the pot with his gun. He jumped at the man forcing the
two of them onto the ground. The man let out a groan as Ashton swiftly
punched the man in the face. The gun slid inside the first stall, Ashton looked
at the gun and reached toward it.

Ashton was a few inches from the gun's reach but the man grabbed Ashton by his left leg and pulled him back. The man clenched Ashton's leg and
pulled him back once more. Ashton looked back at the man. He moved his
body so that his back was against the floor. As the man pulled Ashton he
lunged at the man and punched him on the neck.

Ashton drove his other fist into the man's stomach making the man lay
on the floor, gasping for air. Ashton got up and grabbed the gun that was
inside the first stall. He examined at the gun checking if it had any bullets left.

The man got up as he pressed his neck with his left hand. He glared at
Ashton and lunged towards him. Ashton had his back towards the man, the
man's hands reached out towards Ashton.

Ashton turned around and looked at the man calmly as he pulled his arm
back and slammed the gun into the man's face. The man collided against the
side of the stall and slumped against it; a trail of blood came out of the man's
nose. Ashton moved up to the man and delivered a swift uppercut. The man's
head instantly tilted up as he stumbled backwards. He fell onto the tile floor,
blood dripping from his nose and from the corner of his mouth.

Ashton moved towards the man lying on the floor. He placed his foot on
the man's neck as he positioned the gun at the man's forehead.

The man made a groan and he looked at Ashton. "Who knew that I got
my ass beat by a kid. Go ahead kill me if you have the balls to do it."

Ashton's eyes narrowed. "What's going on here?"

The man made a toothy smile. His teeth were stained with blood. "I guess you didn't know; we're crashing the party. There's someone particular that we need to find and kill." He turned his head to the side and spat out blood.

"We? Who is we?" Ashton asked.

"A gang called the Pharaohs," the man said as he moved his arms to Ashton's legs attempting to knock him off balance.

Ashton grabbed one of the man's arms and slammed his leg onto it, breaking the man's arm. The man cried out and swore at Ashton who stomped his foot onto the man's chest.

"Tell me who's the target. I'm not afraid to kill you if I have to," Ashton threatened.

"Some guy named Rick Kago. You should go to hell for what you've done to me." The man spat at Ashton. Ashton's eyes grew wide after the man told him that his gang was after Rick.

Ashton's fingers curled around the trigger of his gun. "Why are you after him?"

"He's an ex-member of ours, our leader has some grudge against Rick and wanted to kill him," the man said wheezing.

"That's all I need to know," Ashton said as he forcefully kicked the man in the face, knocking the man out cold.

Ashton placed his gun behind his belt and walked up to the mirror. He took off his necktie and stuffed it in his pants pocket. He unbuttoned the two top buttons on his shirt. He ran his hand through his hair as he walked out of the bathroom.

Rick and Stella were in the middle of a conversation when the loud sounds of gunshots mixed with general commotion were heard in the main area. Everyone at the bar looked at the direction where all the noise came from.

Stella looked at Rick. "What's going on?" she asked. Her eyes grew wide, her eyebrows raised.

Before Rick could say anything staff members holding guns ran into the bar area pointing their guns at people. The bartender took out a large gun from inside the desk and pointed his gun at Rick.

"There's someone who wants to meet you, follow me and don't do anything stupid," said a man who was behind Rick, also pointing his gun at him.

Rick looked at Stella and made an apologetic smile. "It's going to be okay. I'll handle this myself, just follow what they say. If you see the kids make sure they're with you, promise me that."

Stella's eyes started to water. "Okay," she whispered as Rick got up and kissed her on the head.

Rick got up from his stool, he looked at the man. "Let's get this over with."

The man walked out of the bar area. Rick followed him not making any sounds. Another man holding a gun walked behind Rick as the three of them went through the main room.

Rick looked at the large group of people clustered together looking at him and also the two men walking on either side of him. He noticed there was a trail of blood leading to the far side of the room. He turned his head so that he wouldn't see the horrified stares of the group. He looked straight ahead. He clenched his jaw as the three of them walked into the emergency stairs. All of them walked up the stairs to the floor above the party.

The man in front of Rick stopped at the door and looked back at Rick. "Liam wants to see you, go through that door."

Rick obeyed the man's order and opened the door to see Liam sitting on a wooden table. Rick walked into the large and half-empty room; the two men closed the door behind him. Rick walked up to Liam until he was about a few yards away from him. The two glared at each other in silence.

The large room was similar to the room under them but without a balcony. There was a large window behind Liam that looked over the city. The sky was now in different shades of dark blue and purple. Tables and other decorations for the room were pushed to one side.

"What do you want?" Rick said as he placed his hands in his pants pockets.

Liam made a fake smile. "I just want to see you just because."

Rick's eyes narrowed. "Why are you doing this now? In front of all these people?"

"I just want them to know who you really are, a bad guy, a man who only knows how to kill. Back then when you were just a young teen I took you in, I made you part of the family. I taught you things about surviving in this cruel world, but now you've turned your back against us." Liam raised both of his hands up to the side. "Now you're a threat to the gang. We both know what happens next, don't you?"

"That's the old me. I was naive as any other kid back then, especially with what I'd been going through before that. You don't know anything about me.

I did those things for the gang in order for my niece to have a good life. I promised my older brother and my stepsister to make sure that their child was going to be okay, but I broke their promise a while ago." His voice quieted down; he took a deep breath still glaring at Liam. "As I got older I realized this way of living my life isn't worth it at all," Rick said as he got teary eyed.

"You're my right hand man; we've been through so much chaos together. Why did you leave?"

"I met someone who changed my life for the better. And that person is the one who threw this party that you and your pathetic gang ruined. I was about to tell Fred how he was like a father to me and how he made me a better man, unlike you. If I could only tell him before this."

"You can, I'm right here," said a male voice. Rick turned around to his left and saw Fred tied to a chair. Nylon ropes were wrapped around him multiple times making sure that he wouldn't escape. Fred was against the wall looking at Rick with a frown.

"What the hell?" Rick looked at Liam. "You brought him here for what?"

Liam moved his hand inside his jacket and pulled out a gun. "To see you die in front of him. Now!"

Instantly men in black suits came rushing in surrounding Rick, pointing their guns at him. Rick looked at the large group of men surrounding him. Fred sat still on the chair as his eyes grew wide with panic, gazing at the men in black suits and Rick.

"You have no idea what I'm capable of do you?" Rick said as his left iris turned blue and black and his right iris turned purple and black.

Rick walked toward Liam who aimed the gun at him. His eyes glared at Liam fiercely. All the men in suits started shooting at Rick but none of the bullets hit him. The noise of multiple gunshots was loud enough that the noise could be heard from the floor below. An invisible shield that surrounded Rick prevented the bullets from going through him.

The circle of men walked closer to Rick, but he wasn't affected by the bullets. Fred was shaking violently trying to untangle himself from the chair, but he wasn't successful. He tried multiple times to untangle himself but all he could manage to do was fall onto the floor.

Rick opened his glowing hands and squeezed them closed. All the guns that the men in suits were holding exploded in front of them. The men yelled as they were wounded by the explosions and fell back on the ground. Multiple men had deep cuts and burn marks on their bodies and faces.

Rick swiped both of his arms to the side; all the men that surrounded him were forcefully pushed into the wall. The collision created multiple vibrations throughout the room. All the men in suits lay unconscious, not moving at all. Rick was now only about a few feet in front of Liam, who pulled the trigger.

Two gunshots were heard, Rick stepped back as the bullets hit him. The whole room went silent. Fred's eyes grew wide with shock.

Rick looked at his chest where the bullets had hit him, no blood came out. He looked up at Liam and smiled sinisterly.

Liam knitted his eyebrows with frustration. He pulled the trigger until he had no more bullets left in the magazine. As the bullets hit Rick he didn't move, he let the bullets hit him until Liam stopped shooting. Small holes dotted Rick's shirt but he didn't seem concerned about it.

Liam pulled the trigger once more but nothing came out. "What? I thought these bullets would work! They should have killed you! Shit!" Liam yelled as he got off of the table.

Rick and Liam disappeared into thin air but reappeared on the other side of the room. Rick grabbed Liam's neck and pushed him against the wall, causing a loud thud noise.

"Nothing can kill me," Rick said. His eyes glowed intensely at Liam who never looked away from Rick.

"Kill me," Liam said as his hands grabbed something underneath his belt. Liam jabbed his knife into Rick's neck, the attack didn't do anything to Rick. The knife bent as Liam pushed the knife into Rick's skin.

Liam dropped the knife, the knife made a metal clang sound as it hit the hard floor. Liam's hands started to shake as Rick looked at him, his face annoyed.

"I'm a nice person. I'm not going to kill you. I'm just going to make you mentally insane so you will kill yourself for me." Rick locked eyes with Liam who stopped shaking.

Liam's eyes flashed purple; his eyes looked like a deer in headlights. The two of them stared at each other, not saying a word. Liam began to violently shake; he began to scream and wail as he kept his gaze at Rick. Liam's spine chilling screams could be heard throughout the room. Fred scrunched up his face his eyes squeezed shut, trying not to hear Liam screaming in terror.

Rick and Liam locked eyes for only a few minutes. Only the few minutes Rick needed to destroy Liam's mentality. Rick's eyes turned back to normal as he dropped Liam onto the floor; he started to sob as he lay on the floor in a fetal position.

Rick took a step back and looked down at Liam who was curled up in a ball, his face pressed onto his knees. Rick placed his right hand on his neck, no dents or blood was in sight. He placed his right black glowing hand on his chest. The holes in his shirt quickly repaired themselves.

He turned around and looked at the mess. Unconscious men in suits lay on the side of the room; decorations, along with the wooden table, were destroyed by their impact. Rick moved his eyes and saw that Fred was lying on the floor still tied onto the chair. Fred had his eyes closed; he didn't say anything. Rick's eyes widened as he ran towards Fred, hoping that he wasn't hurt.

"Fred? Fred! Wake up! I'm sorry that this had happened, it's all my fault," Rick said as he patted Fred's cheeks with his hands.

Fred opened his eyes and looked up at Rick. "I'm not dead, just untie me."

Rick made a relieved smile as he untied Fred. He helped Fred get up. Fred looked at the room and then at Rick with a raised eyebrow.

"I can't believe you did all of this. What did you do to that man?" Fred asked.

"First of all they started it and I ended it. I used my powers and made Liam mentally unstable, he's not a threat anymore so don't worry about it," Rick replied as he scratched his arm.

Fred's eyebrow twitched. "How can you be so calm? You just made someone become mentally insane."

"Well Fred, you too don't know much about me do you? I killed my own father and siblings and I even saw one of my kids die in front of me, nothing fazes me anymore."

Fred made an odd look. "I hope you fix this mess Lieutenant. I hope no one else innocent got hurt."

Rick made an awkward look. "Yeah…about that." He made a forced laugh and turned his head away from Fred's direction.

Fred's eyes widened. "You gotta be kidding me, someone got hurt already? Well no wonder, some of the people I invited to my party are from the military, navy, or in law enforcement. You have to use your powers and heal them."

Rick turned his head back to Fred. "I know Chief. I have something to say to you since we're here together." Rick held out his palm. His gift bag appeared on top of it. Rick held the bag towards Fred who took it. His face turned from strange to relaxed.

"Do you want me to open it?" Fred asked as he examined the outside of the bag.

"Yes, it will all make sense when you see my gift," Rick said as Fred took out the tissue paper on top of the bag and let it fall onto the ground.

Fred placed his hand inside the bag and fished out a green box. He placed the bag on the floor and opened the box. In the green box there was a black and gold Rolex watch.

"Rick you didn't have to buy this for me, Rolex watches cost a lot of money." He looked up at Rick. "Why did you buy this for me?"

Rick made a genuine smile as his eyes brightened up. "I was thinking long and hard about what to get for your birthday, and decided that this year's birthday present for you would be meaningful. You know that black Rolex watch you gave me when I became a lieutenant?" he asked.

"I remember. I was so very proud of you that I gave you my special watch. People back then looked down on you and doubted you because you're an infamous ex-gang member. I and a few other people supported you no matter what, you worked hard to be the man you are today and I couldn't be more proud of you son," Fred said wholeheartedly.

"I got you that watch because I want to show you how I became a better and much more diligent man. You made me and Kai part of your family; you even take care of Kai when I'm too busy to take care of her. There's no words or actions to express what that meant to me and how you impacted my life. You're like a father to me, I couldn't be any more grateful to have you in my life." Tears streamed down his face. "Thank you for being my best friend and a father figure to me. You already know how my real father was and know what happened between us." Rick made a laugh and made sniffing sounds as he cried. Rick wiped his eyes with his shaking hands.

Fred made a sentimental smile as he walked up to Rick, hugging him with teary eyes. Rick looked at Fred and hugged him back, his tears falling from his face and onto Fred's shoulder.

CHAPTER 43

I was sitting on the floor facing the wide window looking at the lit up city. Planes flew left and right, neighboring building room lights turned off and on, streetlamps turned on as people walked down the sidewalk enjoying the night.

Tyrone was lying on the bench staring at the window with me. We both talked about our usual stuff like what shows to watch, videogames to play, and we also talked about Ashton and my birthday party next week. Everything seemed normal and peaceful until I heard gunshots from the main floor.

I quickly looked at Tyrone who instantly sat up. His eyes darted at the door. I got up and looked at Tyrone.

"You heard that right?" I asked.

"I did, you want to wait here or go outside?" he asked as he stood up and looked at me with widened eyes.

"I should lock the door, you call Ashton. Something isn't right here," I said concerned. My mind started racing as I thought of multiple scenarios of what could be happen at this moment. Thinking about it made my body feel tingly.

I walked up to the door. I heard another gunshot and a faint noise of people screaming. I could feel my heart race, where was Ashton?

I opened the door just a little bit so that I could see outside of the room. A large group of people were gathered in a cluster, they looked terrified. I looked around and saw a handful of staff members holding guns. I let out a gasp as I kept looking at the group of people. What is going on here?

I could hear one of the staff members yelling at the group of people to go down to the main room and walk down the emergency stairs until they reached the floor below the party. Then three staff members escorted the group of people down the balcony stairs, moving them to the floor below us.

I carefully closed the door and locked it. I looked back at Tyrone. "Holy shit," I whispered.

Tyrone's face turned panicky. "I have no service. Oh my God we're gonna die, we're gonna die!" he said as he started pacing back and forth, breathing heavy.

I walked up to him and grabbed him by the shoulders. "Ty, calm down we're not going to die."

Tyrone looked at the door ignoring me. "We're gonna die." He looked at me; I could see the fear in his eyes. "Kai I don't want to die; I need to tell my mama that I love her." His voice started to break.

I felt bad for him. Tyrone is just a kid, at least he didn't go through the things that I'd been though. I pressed my right hand on his cheek and looked at his brown eyes.

"Ty I will protect you no matter what, I want you to know that you're not going to die okay?" I told him with assurance. I guess today is the day when I'm going to expose my powers to him and possibly to everyone in this party.

Tyrone's lips quivered. "O-Okay." He wiped his nose with his sleeve.

I patted him on the cheek. "That's my boy."

I removed my hands off of Tyrone and lifted one of the benches, dragging it towards the door and jamming it against the door handle. Tyrone stood at the same spot looking at me as he fidgeted with his fingers.

"You should sit down on one of the benches," I said as I wiped my forehead. I needed to get ready for what's going to happen.

Tyrone followed my order and sat at a bench tapping his foot. I have known him for a long time; whenever he gets scared or really nervous he gets very jittery. I need to protect him no matter what. I just wish Ashton was here with us, but I know that he could handle this kind of thing by himself.

I sat next to Tyrone, he turned on his phone. "There's no service. We can't call for help," he whispered.

"Maybe it's just your phone, let me check mine." I took out my phone from my jacket pocket and turned it on, no service.

"Shit, no service," I said to myself. I could feel my jaw tighten.

"How are we going to get out of here? We're at least thirty floors up," Tyrone said as he looked at my phone then at me.

"We have to fight them," I said as I got up and took off my jacket, placing my phone in my jacket pocket.

"Fight them? I know you're crazy but not that crazy. They have guns and we have nothing." His eyes blinked in disbelief.

I placed my jacket on the bench, though I teleported my phone to my room so it wouldn't get destroyed. I unbuttoned the first button on my shirt as I looked at Tyrone, debating if I should tell him about my powers or not.

"This past month I've changed, you'll see sooner or later," I said. I was worried he wouldn't be my friend if I showed him my powers.

I heard yelling outside the door, the two of us froze. I looked at Tyrone and motioned for him to come to me. He stood up and slowly walked towards me. Tyrone was next to me, I could hear his breathing becoming shallow. I stood on my toes since he's at least a half a foot taller than me. I could hear his heavy breathing as the noise grew louder.

"I need you to go to the left side of the wall, hide behind that potted plant. Don't move or make any noise, okay?" I whispered into Tyrone's ear.

I pulled my head back. Tyrone nodded at me and quietly walked towards the potted plant. I watched him hide behind the plant before I looked at the door and slowly walked towards it, my heart beating faster and faster. I took a deep breath and exhaled as I stood at the edge of the door.

I could see the door handle turn from the other side, but the benches prevented the door from opening. The door began to shake violently. I took a step back. I don't know what to do; this is the first time I'm going to fight someone using my new powers.

Multiple voices could be heard on the other side of the door. I heard one person telling someone else to shoot the door handle. I held my fist up ready to fight. I could feel myself getting sweaty from anxiety.

I could hear a gunshot as the door handle broke off. Someone kicked the door so hard that the benches flew back. I held my breath as three men ran into the room, pointing their guns around the room.

I instantly ran up to one of the men. All three men saw me and pointed their guns at me, yelling at me to stop but I didn't. I heard multiple shots and saw bright lights as I lunged at a man and slapped his gun. The gun flew to the other side of the room. The other two men kept shooting at me but I didn't feel any pain, only a slight pressure from the bullets.

My right hand made a fist as I swung my hand at the man punching him in the face. The man flew back and lay on the floor, letting out a moan. It seemed like the man was unconscious which was good for me.

I felt better, like my anxiety had disappeared. No wonder people like to fight, it makes them feel alive. I looked at the man and smiled at myself, amused at my super strength.

The two men stopped firing their guns. I punched one of the men's hands and kicked at his leg, but I missed by a foot. That's embarrassing.

The man ran towards me but I rammed my fist into the man's stomach. The man flew back onto the wall making the wall vibrate and also making a loud thud noise. I started to like my super strength better than my teleportation powers, depending on the situation.

There was only one man left. I turned around and looked at him; the man reloaded his gun and started shooting at me. I ran at him tackling him into the wall and destroying the wall. The two of us fell into the other room.

I stood up and dusted myself off as I looked at the empty room that I was in. I turned back and looked at the three men, either passed out or unable to move. I let out a sigh of relief as I smiled to myself, I felt really good after fighting those bad guys.

I walked through the hole in the wall and walked towards Tyrone who was standing in the middle of the room looking at me with widened eyes. I guess it's a good time to tell him about my powers.

"I can't believe you just did that. How are you still alive? You literally got shot at, you even have a bullet hole in your shirt," Tyrone said as he ran his hand over his head.

I looked down at my clothes; there were multiple small holes in my shirt and a few in my pants. I really liked this shirt too, why does it have to be ruined? I looked at my left, my shirt sleeve was so ripped that it showed most of my arm tattoo. I looked at my right hand, it was still covered in white bandages but it had some bullet holes in it.

I let out a sigh. "I need to tell you something, something important." I made a pause, my heart started beating rapidly again. "I have superpowers." I paused again.

Tyrone looked at me and made a slight smile. "Yeah I know. At least you admitted that you do have superpowers, it's all good. I just wish you had told me sooner, like a few years ago."

I could feel my eyebrows twitching and my nose flared up in confusion. "What? When did you know?"

"Owen told me when we were kids; I thought he was joking at the time. As time passed by I started to notice little things, things like the time when we're at your house and you went to the second floor bathroom but came out of the kitchen. Or the time in gym class a ball was aimed at you but it didn't hit you; it seemed that the ball went through you like a ghost. Why didn't you tell me about this? Are you afraid of me?" he asked as his eyes bore into mine.

"Uhhh…" I kept saying out loud because I was shocked that he already knew. Can't believe Owen had told him but I'm not mad at him, at least Tyrone has an idea that I have superpowers.

I licked my dry lips and looked at him. "It's not that I'm afraid of you, it's that I'm afraid that you won't be my friend anymore." I really meant that, I have no idea how people would react to people with superpowers besides my friends and family. There's at least one scenario in my head that someone found out about my powers and contacted the government, and let me say, things escalated quickly.

"You think if you hid your powers from me we would still be friends? Kai," he placed his hands on my shoulders, "I wouldn't stop being friends with you because of your powers, we're still going to be best friends no matter what. I'm just glad that you told me the truth."

"I'm so sorry that I didn't tell you my secret sooner, I'm just afraid that something would happen to Rick or Ashton because of me."

"Why would something happen to Rick and Ashton? Do they have superpowers too? If they do, then your family is the coolest family I have ever met!" he said as he made a huge grin.

I looked at the mess I made. "They do, but just don't tell anyone else about our secret."

"I promise that I won't expose your family. What kind of powers do you, Rick, and Ashton have? Maybe Rick has fire powers and Ashton has invisibility," Tyrone said as his eyes widened with joy. Tyrone looked like an excited puppy and I think that's cute.

"Not quite." I looked around the room; all the men were still unconscious. "Ashton doesn't technically have superpowers; he has these abilities. I know one of his abilities is reading people's movements a few seconds ahead of time; he has really good agility, better than most people in the world. To sum it up he's like a really good assassin or fighter, whatever you call people who can fight good."

"Oh my God, that's so cool! Both of my best friends have amazing powers and abilities!" Tyrone said, still maintaining his grin.

"I have teleportation powers so that means that I could go anywhere in the world and even into space, but I would rather not go into space in my lifetime, that's an awful way to die. I can go through objects, which you've already seen me do before. I also just recently gained new powers and abilities, one of them is super strength and the other one is invincibility so that means that I cannot die or get hurt. Rick on the other hand, he has to my knowledge three different powers, but it's a long story. His original powers are like dark magic, you know powers of the devil and all that type of thing. He just recently gained two different powers. One of them is light power, opposite from his original dark power, and the other one I have no idea what it did to him, all I know is that it made him more powerful than before. I know that's a lot of information to process, one day I will tell you the whole story about all of this but I don't know when."

Tyrone moved his hands away from my shoulders and wrapped them around my neck and hugged me. I wrapped my arms around his waist and hugged him back.

"I'm geeking out! I can't believe I'm best friends with a superhero! You're so cool! You're like Wonder Woman, but prettier and more badass."

"Don't dis on Wonder Woman she's the coolest chick I know, I'm not even on her level," I said laughing. I'm so relieved that Tyrone is okay with me and Ashton having powers and abilities.

Tyrone and I broke our hug and looked at each other. Then I remembered that Rick and Ashton were somewhere. They might need my help.

I looked at Tyrone. "We should go and find Ashton or someone who needs our help." My eyes darted to the gun that was a few feet away from me, I looked back at Tyrone. "Do you know how to shoot a gun?"

"Yes I do, why?" he asked but then he raised his eyebrows. "You want me to kill someone?"

"What? No. It's for self-protection, but if you do have to shoot someone just don't kill them. You know, shoot them in the leg or in the arm so they won't move or cause any more harm. Can you do that for me?"

Tyrone looked me dead in the eye and nodded with a bold look on his face. "Let's do this."

I walked to the gun and grabbed it and handed it to Tyrone, who examined the gun and checked its magazine for bullets.

"Do the other guys have any bullets left, I'm out," he told me.

I walked up to one of the men and checked his pockets; there was nothing I could find. I went to the next man and searched his pocket. I found one magazine but I didn't think it was enough for Tyrone. I took all the bullets out of the magazine, only five bullets left. I put the bullets inside my pants pocket. I walked up to the last man who was in the other room. I walked through the wall using my powers and went into the next room where the last guy lay on the floor. I searched his pockets and found another magazine. I instantly teleported out of the room and reappeared next to Tyrone who jumped back.

"Whoa, you scared me with your teleportation power," he said as I gave him the magazine I had found.

Tyrone tossed the empty magazine and took one of the new magazines and inserted it in the gun holder. I gave him the five bullets I found and he put them inside his pants pocket.

"Did you get that tattoo during your trip?" Tyrone asked as he flipped the safety switch on the gun.

I looked down at my left arm once again and saw that my sleeve had been completely ripped. One half of the sleeve was hanging on my wrist. I grabbed that half of the sleeve and yanked it out making a ripping noise as the material fell onto the floor. My arm was completely visible; anyone could see most of my tattoo.

"About that 'trip,' it's a very, very long and complicated story. I will tell you everything when the time is right," I told him as I examined my tattoo. Huh, I do look kind of badass showing off my cool tattoo.

"You don't have to tell me, it's none of my business anyway."

"It would take the weight off my shoulders better if I tell you and the people I trust about what happened to Rick, Ashton, and me."

"Don't feel pressured by doing this," he said quietly.

"I know but now we have something much more important to do, follow me," I said as I walked to the edge of the door, Tyrone followed behind me.

I peeked my head to the side of the door looking out. There were five people walking up to the balcony.

I looked back at Tyrone. "Let me handle this, don't let me out of your sight and try to hide from those bad guys."

Tyrone nodded and the two of us walked outside. I gestured behind a sofa where Tyrone could hide. Tyrone quickly walked behind the sofa and crouched.

I casually walked to the group of men, feeling more confident than I'd ever felt before.

"Hey losers!" I yelled at the men. All the men instantly looked at me pointing their guns at me.

"Where did you come from?" One of the men walked in front of the group, aiming the gun at me.

"None of your business dingbats!," I continued to yell; all of a sudden all my anger and rage just lashed out of me.

I ran at the man who started shooting at me, the other men started shooting me as well. All the bullets went through me; I didn't want to damage my outfit more so I used my intangibility powers. All the men walked back as I tackled the man; the two of us fell onto the floor. I instantly punched the man in the face until he blacked out.

I looked up as the other men walked up to me reloading their guns and shooting at me. I disappeared into nowhere and appeared behind one of the men and karate chopped the man's neck. The man fell forward onto the floor not moving at all. I should feel bad, but I truly don't.

A man behind me hit me with the butt of his gun, that hit didn't even hurt at all. I turned around and kicked him in the stomach making the man collide with another man. The two of them crashed into a table, breaking the table completely.

I could feel myself smile with joy as I looked at the two men passed out on the broken table. My powers are so freaking cool!

Suddenly someone smashed a chair on my head and I fell onto the floor.

"What are you?" the man asked, breathing hard as he placed his foot on the back of my neck.

"Get away from her you bitch!" I could hear Tyrone shriek as I heard a loud shattering sound. The man lost his balance and fell on the floor. His face fell next to me, his head facing away from me.

I could feel a pair of hands helping me sit up. Tyrone crouched next to me smiling and laughing.

"That felt really good, are you okay?" he asked as he took my hand and pulled me up.

I wiped the dust and dirt off of myself. "I'm okay. I can't get hurt so that's good. Thanks for hitting that guy for me, what did you hit him with?"

"A flower vase," he replied.

I looked down at the guy and the broken pieces of the vase that surrounded him. "Huh." I looked back at Tyrone. "Let's go downstairs."

The two of us were at the top of the stairs. I looked over the area below us; more and more men with guns were still here. A few men saw us and yelled at us to come down, I looked at Tyrone.

"Stay up here, I don't want you to get hurt," I told him.

"Okay," he said as I walked down the stairs observing my surroundings. I looked back and saw that Tyrone was standing away from the edge of the balcony holding his gun.

"Where's the other kid?" a man asked me as I walked the last steps of the stairs.

"Don't be concerned about him, he's not a threat," I told the guy. "I'm the one you should be worried about." My lips curved into a sly smile.

The guy clenched his jaw and attempt to hit me but I grabbed the man's wrist. I pulled the man toward me and bent his arm so that he hit himself with his gun. I slapped the man in the face, the man instantly fell.

All the other men began to yell at me and order me to lay on the ground but I refused. Instantly all the guns the group of men was holding disappeared. I unwrapped the bandage that was on my right hand.

All the men made a confused look as they looked at their hands and the other people beside them. I ran towards the man who was closest to me and I wrapped my bandage around his neck and swung him at another man, knocking the two of them onto the floor.

More men came at me. I swung my arm at a man who fell back, another man thrust his fist at me but I grabbed his fist and stomped on his lower leg. The man's leg snapped as he let out a loud cry, swearing at me.

I could feel myself made a disgusted look. "Ugh, that's gross, never going to do that again," I said to myself as I gagged.

I grabbed a man by the collar of his shirt and lifted him up and slammed him into a nearby table. Another man ran at me. I looked at a table next to me and ran towards it. I flipped the table so the tabletop was facing me and I kicked it hard. As I kicked the table there was an intense boom sound from my kick.

The table crashed into three men knocking them off of their feet. The table broke from its impact with the men. I looked at the remainder of the men, there's still more to go.

CHAPTER 44

Ashton walked out of the bathroom and looked down the hall to his left; there was a thin trail of blood leading toward the kitchen. He looked at the other end of the hallway, no one was there. He took out his gun. He slowly walked towards the kitchen. He stopped at the double doors and then slowly opened the door.

He poked his head between the kitchen doors to see if anyone was in there. He moved into the kitchen and closed the door behind him. He looked around the kitchen and saw a person's leg sticking out behind a large stove.

Ashton gingerly walked towards the person behind the stove. The man looked at Ashton with bloodshot eyes; there was a bullet hole in the man's leg. The man had cuts and bruises on his face and neck. Blood from the bullet wound had seeped into the man's pants and onto the floor creating a small puddle.

"Can you help me?" the man asked as he tried to sit up straight but couldn't.

Ashton grabbed a hand towel from the stovetop. He placed his gun in his belt and knelt next to the man.

"What happened?" Ashton asked as he carefully moved up the man's pant leg. Blood oozed out of the hole; the man made a muffled moan as Ashton pressed the towel against the wound. The towel quickly changed color from white to red.

"This big group of men impersonating the staff members started storming into the party holding guns and ordering us to go down to the floor below us. My friend and I tried to fight off one of the men holding a gun, but as you can tell things haven't gone well on my side." The man looked up at Ashton. "How did you manage to hide from those men?"

Ashton got up and looked at the man. "I was in the bathroom, I guess I was lucky," he said with a straight face.

Ashton looked away from the man. He got up and walked up to a cabinet, opening the cabinet doors. There was plenty of kitchen cookware and utensils neatly placed inside different boxes. He rummaged around the cabinet until he took out a thin pair of kitchen tongs.

He walked up to an alcohol and wine cabinet that was next to a prepping area. He opened the cabinet door and examined each bottle before he took out a bottle of whiskey. He closed the cabinet door and grabbed another towel as he walked towards the man who was slumped against the wall.

Ashton knelt on the ground next to the man's leg. He opened the bottle of whiskey and placed it on the floor next to him.

"Try not to make any loud noises okay?" Ashton told the man as he held the tongs.

"Don't worry kid; I'm a major general of the U.S. Army. I've handled more pain than this. You do what you need to do, but first can I get a sip of that whiskey before you use it?" the man asked.

Ashton handed the bottle to the man. "By the way I'm Ashton, what's your name sir?"

The man took the bottle and took two large gulp of whiskey. He held the bottle towards Ashton who took it.

"I'm Daniel but most people call me Dan, it's a pleasure to meet you Ashton." Dan weakly smiled at Ashton.

Ashton smiled back, his eyes softening. "It's a pleasure to meet you too Dan."

Ashton turned his head so that he was facing Dan's wound. Ashton held the tongs in his right hand and held a towel on his left. He began inserting the tongs inside Dan's bullet wound. Dan pressed his lips together as he made fists with both of his hands. The tongs went deeper into the wound. Ashton kept his eyes locked on the wound.

Ashton slowly pinched together the handle and carefully pulled the tongs out. A small blood covered bullet was between the two metal bands. He placed both the bullet and tongs on the floor. He wiped the wounds with a towel gently.

"Thank you," Dan told Ashton.

"Don't thank me yet, I have one more thing to do." Ashton grabbed the bottle of whiskey and poured it onto the open wound. Dan made a muffled groan as Ashton wrapped a new towel around Dan's leg, attempting to stop blood from oozing out.

Ashton looked at Dan; the two looked at each other. Dan wiped sweat from his forehead and lazily smiled at him.

"Your father must be proud of you," Dan said as he sat up straight.

Ashton's eyes looked down at his blood covered hands, he made a sad frown. Dan looked at him and made a regretful look.

"Oh I'm sorry, I shouldn't have said that," Dan said quietly.

"No need to apologize, I try to forget the past and look at the future," Ashton said quietly.

"Wise words for someone who's so young, how old are you?"

Ashton moved next to Dan and sat with him; his back pressed against the wall. "I'm sixteen."

Dan looked to the side at Ashton, one of his eyebrows raised. "Seriously? Sixteen? You're quite talented for someone your age. Not many kids today know how to treat a wound with the things in their surroundings or even know how to treat a wound by themselves without help. You know what? You're not too young to think about joining the military. We need people like you to help us fight the most challenging battles in the world."

Ashton looked at Dan and made a slight smile. "You think? I'm not sure what I want to do in the future. Rick told me that he would like to see me working with the FBI or CIA."

"Who's Rick? Is he your uncle or brother? Or a family member?" Dan asked.

"Rick is my adoptive uncle, he's a great guy. He's the lieutenant of the police department and very close friends with Chief Gray. Rick has a niece who's my adoptive sister and my best friend." Ashton paused. "Shit. Kai and Tyrone might be in trouble, I have to go and help them." He looked at Dan. "Can you walk at all? I could help you," he said hastily.

"Can you pull me up? I think I could walk with your help."

Ashton helped Dan get up, placing Dan's arm around his shoulders. Dan leaned against Ashton gaining his balance. Ashton grabbed his gun from his belt and held it as he and Dan walked towards the kitchen doors.

"Ashton, can we walk to that large table over there?" Dan pointed at the large table at the other side of the kitchen. On the tabletop there was a gun and multiple bullets scattered over the surface.

The two of them sluggishly walked to the table. Dan placed his arm on the table, holding his weight. Ashton unloaded his gun and filled his magazine with new bullets and reloaded it. He placed his gun on the table and took the other one. He checked the magazine on the other gun; there were no bullets in it. He filled the magazine with bullets and reloaded it into the gun. He gave that gun to Dan who took it and flipped its safety switch.

Dan looked around the room and stared at a room that was at the back of the kitchen. The room door was halfway open. There was an open crate with something in it, but it was too far to know what it was.

"Ashton, can we walk up to that room back there? It seems like there's something odd in that room," Dan said as he placed his gun behind his belt.

Ashton looked up at Dan and looked at the back of the kitchen. "It's better if I go check it out, you should stay here and wait for me."

Dan removed his arms from Ashton and placed them on the table. Dan held his weight on the table. "You should go, I can handle this myself."

Ashton walked to the back of the large kitchen. As he got closer to the room he realized the items in the crate were multiple types of guns. He opened the door and looked at the room; inside, there were multiple small boxes that were placed against a wall.

Ashton walked up to the crate and took out a large sniper gun. He examined the gun and put it back in the crate. He looked at the desk and saw multiple sheets of paper and a few photos of people.

He walked to the desk and grabbed one of the photos of his eyes suddenly grew wide open. In the photo was a picture of Rick, Kai, and Ashton sitting on a bench in a park.

"Damn it Rick, what did you do?" he said to himself as he spread all the other photos on the desk.

All the photos were of the three of them, but also a few of Fred and Stella. Ashton took one of the sheets of paper and looked at it. It was a blueprint of the whole building. He quickly grabbed another sheet of paper; it had a blueprint of the floor where the party took place. Ashton placed a sheet of paper on the desk and walked out of the room and towards Dan.

"What was in that crate?" Dan asked as he held his weight on the table.

"There were multiple guns in that crate. I also found blueprints of the building and photos of my family and Fred."

There were multiple rounds of shots fired outside the kitchen, and the noise seemed to be coming from the main floor. The two exchanged glances.

"We should go, there might be more people who need our help," Dan said as Ashton moved Dan's arm around his shoulders. The two walked towards the kitchen doors.

"Are you ready?" Dan asked as the two stopped in front of the double doors.

"Yes I am, don't worry I'll protect you Dan," Ashton said as he kicked the doors wide open and quickly stumbled through the hallway.

One man was at the front of the hallway pointing his gun at the two. Ashton swiftly pointed his gun and shot the man. The man dropped his gun and fell.

"Good aim," Dan said as he took deep breaths.

"Thank you," Ashton said confidently.

The two walked out of the hallway and towards the main floor. A few men with guns looked at the two and pointed their guns at them.

Dan quickly shot the men as they kept walking. They walked up to the corner and stopped at the edge of it. Ashton poked his head around the side of the wall, observing his surroundings. Men were running towards someone but at this angle he couldn't tell who it was. Ashton noticed that all the men had no guns at all. He looked back at Dan.

"Can you sit here? I'll go fight off the remainder of the people on this floor," Ashton told Dan as he slowly placed Dan on the floor, his back leaning against the wall.

"You sure about that? You need my help, don't say it's because I'm wounded."

Ashton unbuttoned his vest and took it off. "Well it is because you're wounded. I don't want you to get hurt more than you have to be," he said as he tossed his vest off to the side.

"Before you go, just make sure that you won't get hurt," Dan told Ashton as he nodded and walked around the corner leaving Dan alone.

He looked around the room to see Kai fighting multiple men at once. Her left sleeve was completely ripped and anyone could see her tattoos. Multiple bullet holes were on her shirt, strands of hair were in front of her face.

Ashton ran out and started shooting at the men. Kai looked up at Ashton and made a bold smile.

"I thought you were taken with the other people," she said as she kicked a man in the stomach. The man flew back a few feet and crashed into a potted plant.

Ashton spun around high kicking a man in the face, the man fell back and passed out on the floor. Ashton made a smirk as he placed his gun behind his belt.

The two ran beside each other, their backs touching each other. Kai looked to the side at Ashton and Ashton looked to the side at Kai.

"You think I would surrender that easily?" he said grinning. Kai rolled her eyes as the men scattered around them.

"Shut up and let's show them who's boss, shall we?" She smiled mischievously.

The two of them walked away from each other. Ashton walked up to a man and snatched a man's necktie pulling it towards him. Ashton made a fist with his right hand and thrust his fist up to the man's neck, upper cutting the man. The man stumbled back and fell down, blood dripping from his nose.

"I should have known; you're tough. You know what? I am too," Kai said as she repeatedly punched a man in the stomach.

A man was a few feet behind Kai; he was preparing to run towards her, his hands holding a steak knife. Ashton ran toward a table and grabbed multiple silver knives. He threw the knives at the man's hands. The steak knife fell onto the ground. Ashton grabbed a plate and smashed the plate onto the man's head, causing him to fall.

Ashton looked at the stairs and saw Tyrone shooting a man who was running up the stairs towards him. Three more men were heading towards Tyrone. Ashton looked at Kai.

"I need to help Tyrone; can you handle these guys?" Ashton asked.

"Of course I can, go help him," Kai said as she punched a man in the face.

Ashton ran towards the stairs. Up the stairs Tyrone pointed his gun at a man who was coming closer to him. Tyrone pulled the trigger but he missed. Tyrone shot his gun again and it hit the man on the arm, but the man kept moving towards him.

Ashton grabbed the first man in front of him by the back of his shirt and threw him over the stair railings; the man let out a scream as he fell three yards to the floor. He ran up to the second man, the man turned around and swung his arm at Ashton. Ashton dodged the man's attack and grabbed the man by the collar of his shirt. He yanked him down the stairs.

Tyrone shot the man who was closest to him in the leg; the man kneeled down. Tyrone ran up to the man and kicked the man in the chest. The man fell backwards, tumbling down the stairs as he yelled.

Ashton watched as the man rolled down the stairs and to the bottom. Tyrone walked down the stairs holding a gun in his left hand.

"Hey," Tyrone said as he was breathing heavily. He was a few steps away from Ashton.

Ashton smiled. "I didn't know that you could shoot a gun."

Tyrone looked at his gun and made an embarrassed smile, not looking at Ashton. "My dad and Grandpa Fred taught me how to shoot a gun earlier this year, I'm kind of rusty."

"You're really good at shooting. I didn't think that you could fight someone dead on. I'm proud of you."

Tyrone walked up to Ashton and hugged him. He made a surprised look and hugged Tyrone back.

"I know you have abilities," Tyrone said as the two were hugging each other.

Ashton flinched causing Tyrone's gun to go off. The two jumped and stumbled back falling down the stairs, still holding onto each other. Tyrone let out a shriek while Ashton yelled as the two went down. Tyrone's gun fell from his hand, leaving the gun on one of the steps above.

Once the two fell to the bottom to the stairs they let go of each other's grip. The both of them had landed on top of the three men they'd fought. Ashton got up and held out a hand to Tyrone. Tyrone took his hand and got up. The two looked at each other and started laughing.

"Sorry that I scared you," Tyrone said as he laughed.

"No it's okay, you'd eventually know sooner or later," Ashton said placing his left arm around Tyrone's shoulder as the two began walking towards Kai.

Kai was standing looking at the two boys with her hands inside her pants pockets. The men she'd fought lay on the floor either badly hurt or passed out.

"Are you two hurt?" Kai asked as she walked up to Ashton and Tyrone.

"No not really, don't worry about us," Tyrone said looking at Kai.

"Ashton what happened to you, your hands and parts of your clothes are covered with blood. Did you kill someone?" Kai asked.

"I didn't kill anyone; I was helping Dan with his injuries that were caused by those bad guys." Ashton looked around the room. "Oh crap, I forgot about Dan."

Ashton removed his arms from Tyrone's shoulders. He ran to the corner of a wall where Dan was at.

Kai and Tyrone exchanged glances but then ran behind Ashton. The three of them walked around the corner and saw Dan sitting at the edge of the wall.

"Hey kids, I see all of you fought those men. The three of you are so brave, I wish my kid was like that," Dan said as Ashton helped him stand up.

"This is my sister Kai and my best friend Tyrone. This is Major General Dan of the U.S. Army," Ashton said looking back and forth from Dan to Tyrone and Kai.

"Nice to meet you Dan," Tyrone said as he shook hands with Dan.

Kai and Dan shook hands. "What happened to your leg?" she asked.

"A bad guy shot me in the leg when I tried to fight him. Good thing that Ashton helped me with my wound," Dan said as he looked at Ashton.

"My brother is very talented," Kai said as she closed her eyes and made a wholehearted smile. Ashton looked at Kai and made an embarrassed smile.

A faint sound of a single gunshot was heard from the floor below the four of them. Kai opened her eyes and looked down at her feet. Tyrone looked around the room. Dan made a hardened face.

"Those innocent people don't deserve to be in this mess, those bastards." Dan's voice deepened.

"Why are they attacking us? Of all places why here?" Tyrone asked.

"Maybe it's because of Fred's many well-known friends. One of them might be a target. At least we know Dan isn't one of them but who is it?" Kai said as she moved a strand of hair behind her ear.

"It's possible that they're after all the government personnel, some people have the nerve to kill people like us," Dan said.

Ashton looked at the three of them talking about why the group of men attacked Fred's party. Ashton made a frown and looked down at the floor.

"They're coming for Rick," he said quietly.

The three of them stopped talking and looked at Ashton. Kai's eyebrows knitted with confusion.

"Rick? Our Rick? Why him? Wait, how do you know if they're actually targeting him?" Kai asked.

"I fought a man and he told me that Rick's an ex-gang member of a gang called the Pharaohs. The guy told me that their leader had a strong grudge against Rick and he wanted to kill him. The leader of the gang set up this attack in order to kill him," Ashton said as he looked up at Kai, staring at her.

"Holy shit," was all Kai managed to say.

"Wait what?" Tyrone said, blinking his eyes in disbelief.

"He's the reason why those people attacked us and crashed the party," Dan said, glancing at Kai and Tyrone.

"We need to find him." Kai's eyes grew wide. "But first we need to find everyone else and see if they're hurt, also find a safe place for Dan."

"Don't worry about me, it's just a scratch," Dan said.

"You must be blind! You literally got shot in the leg!" Tyrone said, pointing at Dan's leg with his hand.

Kai walked up the Dan and Ashton. "Let me carry Dan," she said gesturing her fingers at Dan and then at her.

"Are you sure? I don't want to be a problem for the three of you," Dan said as Ashton removed Dan's arm from around his shoulder.

"No it's alright Dan, I can handle this myself," Kai said as she held Dan by the waist and lifted him up. Dan made a yelp as she carried him on her right shoulder.

"How can you do this? This is impossible for a petite girl like you," Dan said as he looked at Kai, but he could only see the back of her head.

"People should've learned by now that a woman can do what a man can do, but better," Kai said with a confident smile.

"You're quite different from other young women that I have known, that's for sure," Dan said as he looked away from Kai. "Let's go downstairs and find the rest of the people."

Ashton was the first to walk to the emergency stairs, Kai who carrying Dan walked behind Ashton, and then Tyrone was at the end of the group. The four of them walked down the quiet and empty stairwell and down to the floor below them.

CHAPTER 45

The weight of Dan on my shoulder didn't feel like anything at all; at least I know that I could carry him or anyone with ease. Tyrone was behind me and Ashton was in front of us leading the way down the stairs. I could hear Dan's breathing, I felt bad for him because he got shot. I couldn't forget the fact that Rick was an ex-gang member, another secret he had been keeping from me. What other secrets had he been keeping? The thought of this made me annoyed as hell.

Ashton stopped in front of a door, slowly opening the door and peeking through it. He turned his head back looking at the three of us.

"There's a lot of bad guys in there, can you get rid of their guns?" Ashton asked, looking at me.

"You're good to go," I said, teleporting all the guns someplace else.

Ashton opened the door wide. I could hear a few men talking out loud about their guns disappearing. The three of us ran at the men and everyone that was held hostage looked at us with a shocked or a confused expression.

The men charged at us, their fists raised up, ready to fight.

"Don't do anything, I'll handle this," I said before Tyrone or Ashton made a move.

As the group of men ran towards us all of them suddenly fell through the floor gasping and yelling. The group of hostages gasped and made a commotion after all the men completely fell through.

I looked at the group and saw Stella walking quickly towards us her face concerned.

"Stella can you help Dan, he got shot in the leg," I said as I carefully placed Dan on the floor. Dan sat up and winced as he tried to move.

"I already took the bullet out and poured whiskey into his wound, but he needs to get to a hospital, or we could find Rick so he can heal Dan's wound," Ashton said.

"I'll go and find Rick, he could heal Dan and fix this crazy mess," I said as I walked to the door.

"Kai get back here," Stella ordered.

I stopped and turned around. "I got rid of the bad guys, they're not anyone's problem anymore," I told her. A first aid kit appeared on the floor next to Dan.

Stella walked up to me and put her hand on my shoulder. "You just exposed your powers in front of everyone here, what will someone say about that?" she whispered.

"Once I find Rick he can use his powers and erase these people's memories about this situation. He has to fix this because he's the reason the bad guys are crashing the party," I said disappearing out of the room without waiting for Stella to say anything back to me.

I appeared in the floor where the party was at. The only people on the floor were me and the men that were unconscious. I walked around the whole floor searching for Rick or anyone else. It was no use; no one was on the floor with me.

I teleported my phone and turned my phone on, there was still no cell service. I teleported my phone away and walked towards the stairs that led to the balcony. I stepped over the unconscious men on the bottom of the stairs, continuing up the stairs.

Halfway up the stairs I heard a door open. I immediately stopped. I heard two sets of footsteps walking to the main area of the floor. I teleported to the top of the balcony and watched the floor from above. I heard two people faintly talking to each other. I looked over the balcony railings and saw Rick and Fred walking into the area.

"What happened?" Fred asked as Rick kneeled down next to a man passed out.

Rick held out his right pointer and middle finger and placed them against the man's forehead. Both of Rick's fingers glowed black. It seems like he's already familiar with his new powers.

"It seems that my kids and Tyrone were fighting these men. I must say I'm impressed with the three of them," Rick said as he stood up and looked at Fred.

"Are they hurt?" Fred asked.

I teleported next to them; Fred jumped back. Rick looked to the side at me, his eyebrows slightly lowered as he frowned.

"I'm sorry that this happened to you and to everyone, I'm going to fix this," Rick said, his eyes searching my face. I made a straight face not saying anything to him. He looked at me with a raised eyebrow.

"What?"

"You know what, keeping more secrets from me," I said, my eyebrows knitted together.

Rick glanced at Fred then at me. "I will tell you and Ashton the truth after I fix this situation okay?"

I pressed my lips together and gazed at Rick blankly. I can't believe he didn't tell the truth sooner.

"Do you know where the rest of my guests are?" Fred asked me. I noticed that he was wearing the watch that Rick had bought him for his birthday. I guess Rick couldn't wait to give him that watch.

"The floor below us," I replied. Fred walked towards the emergency stairs.

"I'll promise that I will tell you the truth. Don't be mad at me," Rick said, his eyes pleading for forgiveness.

I ignored him and followed Fred. All of this had happened because of Rick! Tyrone almost had a panic attack, Dan got shot in the leg, other people's lives were in danger, and I learned that he was keeping another secret from me. A big secret. He's in a gang!

"Okay, let's all go downstairs and we'll let Rick explain why this happened later, after he fixes this problem," Fred said as he opened the door and walked downstairs.

No one else talked as the three of us walked downstairs and stopped at a door. Fred opened the door and peeked out, but then walked inside the room.

The three of us walked into a big area where the rest of the people were, including Stella, Ashton, Tyrone, and Dan. Everyone looked at us and started talking all at once, questioning about this situation.

Rick's eyes flashed purple. All the guests' eyes flashed purple and they immediately fell on the floor at the same time. The only people who didn't get affected by Rick's powers were Ashton, Tyrone, Stella, Dan, Fred, and me.

I looked back at Rick. "You have to heal Dan," I told him.

Rick walked towards Dan who was lying on the floor. Someone had replaced the towel that was around Dan's wound with a tan colored bandage.

Rick crouched next to Dan and held his hands over the wound as his hands started to glow black. Dan's expression turned to shock as he saw Rick's glowing hands, but then his face slowly relaxed.

Rick held his hands over Dan's leg for a few quick seconds. Rick pulled back his hands as the black aura faded away. He unwrapped Dan's bandage carefully. Dan's leg looked like it was good as new. Dan made a relieved smile as he sat up and pat Rick on the back.

"Wow, you have powers too? Thank you for healing me, I appreciate it," Dan said as he stood up.

Rick stood up as well. "It's no problem but I have to make you forget about this. I can't risk anyone telling my family's secret about our powers out in public. I don't want my kids and myself to get into serious trouble that we'll never get out of, I hope you understand," he apologized to Dan.

Dan made an understanding smile and nodded. "I do understand; just make sure that everyone else isn't hurt."

Ashton moved up towards Rick and Dan. He stood next to me, looking at the two men with a concerned look on his face.

"Ashton, is that blood on your clothes and hands?" Rick asked as he observed him with a raised eyebrow.

Ashton's eyes knitted. "No Rick, this is ketchup."

"Okay that's good I don—"

"No shit Sherlock! This is blood from Dan who I helped by taking the bullet out of his leg! I want to be his friend, I don't want him to forget about me," Ashton said as his voice slowly died down.

"Don't worry Ashton; once I forget about what happened, you and everyone else is always welcome to talk to me anytime," Dan said, reassuring him.

"I won't erase the moments when you and Dan met, I'll just alter those moments so that Dan still remembers you but not in this way. There's no need to worry," Rick said looking at Dan. The two locked eyes. Dan's eyes flashed purple, he suddenly fell onto Rick.

Rick held Dan and gently laid him on the floor. He got up and looked at the rest of us. Rick made an embarrassed smile and scratched the back of his head.

"So when are you going to tell us the truth?" Ashton asked, glancing down at Dan with a frown.

"It's better if you tell us the truth now before we get very pissed off," I told Rick.

Rick made a frown as he looked at us. "Okay. The reason why these guys crashed the party is that they're part of a gang called the Pharaohs. Their leader

Liam had a grudge against me because I was an ex-member of the group. Back then when I was younger, like about fifteen or sixteen years old, I became part of that group. My job was to kill people just like a hit man would. As a few years passed by I was one of the most notorious members in the group, I was even Liam's left hand man. About the time I became eighteen I realized that this way of life wasn't good for me and Kai so I just left the group and tried to make a living without doing anything illegal. A year after I met Fred, who came to my home to talk about the group. He learned that I wanted to become a better person and told me that I should become a cop. I know that most people in the academy and the whole department don't fully respect me because of who I am, but that was the old me. It took me a very long time to gain most people's respect and show them that bad guys like me can change to become good guys. Liam didn't like the fact that I became a cop, his hatred towards me grew so much that he tried to kill me. This is the third time he attempted to kill me. I used my powers on him today so he wouldn't cause any more problems to us and anyone else in the future. I made Liam mentally unstable so he would either get locked up or he would kill himself," he said, his hands in his pants pockets.

"You did what?" Ashton said. His eyes grew wide.

"You made that guy kill himself?" Tyrone quickly asked.

Rick looked at the two. "I used my powers to make Liam go insane so he would possibly kill himself. This is my revenge on him. I didn't actually make him kill himself right on the spot," he said, making two quotation marks with his fingers as he said, 'kill himself.' "He will do that when he can't handle what's going on in his head anymore."

"You're one shady cop Rick. But I understand that Liam is a bad guy and did some messed up things, you got revenge on him because of that," I said rubbing my left arm.

"I knew you'd understand," Rick said smiling with relief.

"How can you smile in a time like this? You used your Devil powers or whatever crazy powers you have on that man and made him go crazy!" Stella said then spoke in Spanish afterwards. I have no idea what she said; my Spanish teacher would be disappointed in me.

"I got used to doing those types of things way back then, I'm numb to torturing and hurting people. I was nicknamed the 'Devil' for a reason," Rick said as he looked at the five of us. "Anyway let me get back to what I've been saying. During that time after I left the group, I tried to hide the fact that I was an ex-gang member that killed people and did a lot of very illegal things. I hid my secret because I don't want my kids and all my closest friends to hate me," he said quietly as he looked at each of us.

"So you're an ex-gang member who wanted to change your life for the better so you became a cop?" Tyrone asked, his eyebrows raised in confusion.

"That's another way to summarize my backstory," Rick said nodding.

"Fred was the only person who knew what you are capable of and tried to make you become a better person," Ashton realized. Stella walked up behind Ashton and me and placed her hands on our shoulders.

"You're right; he's one of the few people who knew what I am and what I'm capable of. Now all of you know what kind of man that I am and what I can do with my powers."

"You almost made my grandson have a breakdown because he thought his mama was going to die. You better fix this mess before I beat your ass boy," Fred said in a scary and serious tone. I jumped from his loud voice.

Rick's face turned pale and he looked at Tyrone. "I'm so sorry Tyrone. I didn't think that you would feel that way. Let me make it up to you, I would do anything for you," he pleaded.

"I want you to fix this and get me an ice cream cake with extra sprinkles and whipped cream," Tyrone said as Fred placed his arm around him. I noticed that Fred's right hand had the same flower circle tattoo as mine, this seemed unusual.

Rick nodded his head. "Okay I'll get you an ice cream cake, will that make up for this?" he asked.

"Fred, when did you get that tattoo on your right hand?" I asked, curious about Fred's tattoo.

Fred looked at his hand and then at me, his eyes glanced at my right hand.

"I guess it's time to tell all of you about my incident. Kai, you and I have something in common, we both experienced death once," he said as Tyrone looked at his grandpa.

"What do you mean?" Stella asked.

"It was a few years ago. I was working on a case with Rick, a very dangerous case involving the mob in the south side of the city. The mob already knew that we were cops, so the two of us were fighting against the mob. I was shot two times in the chest and died. I don't remember much about that day, but I do know that Rick brought me back to life by using his powers."

"I killed all the members of that mob and used my powers to make Fred become alive again. So that's why he has that same tattoo as you, because I resurrected the two of you," Rick chimed in.

"Did you resurrect anyone else besides Kai and Fred?" Ashton asked.

"I have not. Fred is the first person who I brought back from the dead," Rick answered Ashton's question.

Everyone went quiet. The only sound I could hear was the noise outside from the city. I need some time to process what I have been told. I can't believe Fred had died.

"Rick, if Fred got resurrected that means that he has another chance of dying again," I said.

"There's a possibility but I won't let that happen, I want him to live his life to the fullest and die in a natural way," Rick said.

"You mean when I'm getting too old?" Fred raised an eyebrow.

Rick made a forced laugh. "Are you guys hungry? Cuz I am," Rick said attempting to lighten up the mood.

"Shut up and fix this," Stella ordered. Rick looked at Stella and made a pout.

"Okay honey," Rick pouted.

He held out his right hand, his palm facing up. Purple, yellow, and black flames ignited on his hands. The colored flames twirled together as Rick moved his fingers up and down, he didn't seem concerned about the flames. The flames mesmerized me with their strange beauty.

Rick kneeled down and pressed his flaming hand on the floor. The colored flames flowed onto the floor as a black circle with patterns and shapes formed under his hand. The circle grew until it had covered most of the floor. The edges of the circle's outline glowed bright white, but the main outline of the circle was still black. I could suddenly feel a slight vibration from the floor as the white light from the circle grew brighter and brighter. The light was so bright that everything went completely white.

CHAPTER 46

I opened my eyes. My vision was a bit blurry, but I could tell that I was sitting in front of a wide window. I rubbed my eyes and blinked once more; my vision cleared up. I turned around and saw Tyrone sitting up on a bench and looking at me, his eyes wide open.

Tyrone opened his mouth to say something but nothing came out. He's shocked as I am; I can't believe Rick fixed all of this mess within a few minutes.

I looked down at my clothes; there were no rips or cuts, like I hadn't been in a fight before. I got up, dusting off my pants still processing what just happened.

"We need to find Ashton," Tyrone said as he wiped his forehead with his sleeve.

Tyrone got up and walked up to me and hugged me, I hugged him back. I'm glad that he knew about how Rick, Ashton, and I have powers. The weight on my shoulders now felt lighter than before. I just needed to tell Ronnell and Owen about my new powers.

Tyrone broke up our hug and placed his arm around my shoulders and the two of us walked out of the room. Outside on the balcony people were talking to one another, eating snacks and walking left and right. I had noticed that the servers were not only men but women also, it seems like everything went back to normal.

The two of us walked down the stairs, everyone seemed like they were enjoying themselves. Tyrone tapped me on the shoulder. I looked at him.

"What is it?" I asked.

"Over there, Ashton is talking to Dan. We should go to them," Tyrone said as he started walking, pushing me with him.

I turned my head to see Ashton and Dan on the other side of the floor. We walked through a crowd of adults. Tyrone removed his arm from my shoulder. He started to walk in front of me, leading the way.

As we both walked up to Ashton and Dan, Dan turned his head and looked at us smiling.

"Hey Kai and Tyrone, where have you two been?" Dan asked as he patted us on the shoulders.

I looked at Ashton who gave a look that showed he knew what was going on. I looked back at Dan and try to act like nothing had happened.

"Up in one of the rooms on the balcony. It seems like you two were in a deep conversation," I said nodding.

Dam chuckled. "It's true Ashton is such an intelligent young man. I couldn't help but think that he could be something important you know? He could even become one of us; any armed force would appreciate someone like him." Dan patted Ashton on the back.

"Yeah he's a really smart guy, but we're still teens. We need time to think about the future, right?" Tyrone said.

I nodded my head in agreement and Ashton smiled at Tyrone.

Dan made an understanding smile. "I'm always thinking ahead, forgive me if I pressure you Ashton."

"No worries Dan, I still have time to consider what I'll be when I'm older," Ashton replied.

"Hey kids," said a male voice from the left.

All four of us looked towards the direction of the voice. Rick and Stella were standing in front of us. Stella walked up to Ashton and placed her hands on his shoulders, pushing him towards Tyrone and me. Ashton was between the two of us. Stella looked at the three of us.

"We'll talk about what happened a few moments ago, but now I'm relieved that everyone and Dan are back to normal. It's almost time for dinner now, we should take a seat," she whispered.

"Okay," I said as I walked up to Rick who was talking to Dan.

"Fred told me so much about you, you're quite a character you know," Dan said as he shook hands with Rick.

"So I've been told, I hope we could become good friends since you know Ashton."

Rick glanced to the side and saw me; he turned his head as he let go of Dan's hand. Rick walked behind me and placed his hands on my shoulders.

"I guess you already know Kai, isn't she a good kid?" Rick said.

Dan nodded and held out his right hand. I grabbed his hand and the two of us shook hands. Dan had a strong grip so I gripped his hand harder. Dan's face slowly turned concerned as he looked at our hands.

"Wow Kai, you got a strong grip there. It seems like you're the type of young women that can handle a fight," Dan said as I smiled. If he only knew.

"To be honest I can beat anyone in a fight, if I try," I said with a bold smile.

The two of us let go of our handshake. Dan looked at his slightly red hand with an astonished look. I could see the outline of my hand. I love my super strength.

"You're like your brother, you two seem quite…different." Dan said.

"I guess everyone has something unique in them," Rick said as he moved his left arm in front of me and pulled his sleeve back, revealing his black watch.

People started to walk toward the tables on the main floor. I looked to the side and saw that Stella, Ashton, and Tyrone had left.

"It's almost time to have dinner; we should find Stella and Ashton. It's been a pleasure to meet you Dan," Rick said.

"It has been a pleasure to meet you and your wonderful family, I hope we'll meet again Rick," Dan said walking towards the tables.

"We should go," Rick said as he moved me towards the tables still holding my shoulders.

At the table Ashton, Stella, Tyrone, Tyrone's parents, Fred, and Fred's wife sat at the large circular table. There were only two seats empty, one next to Ashton and one next to Stella. Rick sat next to Stella and I sat next to Ashton.

I looked at the table; all the dinnerware was neatly placed, a large transparent vase filled with flowers was on the center of the table. I looked around my surroundings, people started to take their seats, servers walked towards tables carrying multiple plates of food. Tyrone sat next to Ashton and the two started talking to each other. I looked at everyone at the table, they all seemed happy.

When am I going to tell Ronnell and Owen the truth? I think it's selfish of me not to tell them about my crazy experience. I need Ashton and Rick's approval about what I'm going to do; Ronnell already knows something is up. I just have to think about this carefully. Maybe I should invite the people who already know about my powers to my party.

There are so many scenarios going through my head about this situation. Fred and Tyrone already know about our powers, but what happens if they accidentally say something about it in public? I don't care if I get exposed; I'm more worried about Ashton and Rick, I don't want anything to happen to them. What will happen if all my closest friends don't like me anymore because of my family problems? I still have Ashton and Tyrone but I don't know how I'd feel if I saw my friends turn into strangers. The thought of this made me feel nauseous. I don't even know what their reactions will be like. What will go on in their heads when I tell them the whole awful story?

Someone poked me on the arm. I snapped out of my crazy thoughts and looked to my side. Ashton looked at me his lips pressed together; his eyes scanned my face.

"You looked stressed, what's wrong?" he asked.

"Nothing, just thinking about stuff." I tried to make it seem like it was not a big deal.

"You sure about that? It seems like something important," Ashton said, his eyebrow raised.

I looked in front of our table; servers were placing our plates on the table. I looked back at Ashton who kept his gaze on me.

"We should eat, all that fighting made me hungry," I said trying to change the subject.

"You can always tell me anything, you can trust me," Ashton said as he looked away from me.

I feel bad; this isn't a good time to tell him. Plus I don't want to ruin his first birthday party by telling our friends about our 'big' secret. Maybe I'll have the courage to tell him tomorrow, but I have to think about him too. I don't want to change Ashton's relationship with our friends because of what we have been through. I need to think about this and hope the outcome won't be as bad as I think.

A female server placed my plate of stuffed salmon with a side of salad. I said thank you and the lady smiled at me. Before everyone grabbed their eating utensils, Fred stood up.

"Before all of my wonderful guests eat their delicious dinner, I would like to thank everyone who came to my party. As all of you know I'm turning sixty eight this year," Fred said in a strong loud voice. "I know, I know, I look like I'm still in my fifties." He chuckled.

A group of people let out a laugh and talked quietly to their friends. A few people at our table also laughed, but I didn't laugh. I was still thinking about the time in New York with Ken. I wouldn't call Ken my grandpa, he's just some person who I met, and who killed me. I'm just relieved that all of this is over now, no more trouble for now.

"I appreciate that everyone came to the party and gave me these wonderful gifts. Most of the people I had invited to my party are my closest and most amazing friends. We all have been through tough times and somehow made it. We all should relax and enjoy the night, but don't enjoy it too much, you know who you are. Thank you," Fred said, smiling as he sat back onto his seat.

Everyone on the floor clapped their hands and cheered at Fred's short speech, I clapped my hands as Fred looked at everyone at our table. The noise slowly died out as everyone started to pick up their forks and knives. I took my glass of water and took a sip. I didn't realize how thirsty I was until I drank the whole glass of water.

Everything seemed calm and relaxing. People were talking quietly to each other, little kids played with each other near the stairs, servers refilled people's drinks, people were enjoying their dinner. A server poured cold water into my glass. I said thank you and the server nodded and left.

I took my silver fork in my right hand and my knife in the other. I looked at my covered hand. I just need to find a way to tell my story to my friends.

I shouldn't think about this now, all I need to do right now is to relax and enjoy the party. I looked at my utensils hovering over my salmon. I could feel myself ease up as I cut my salmon into small cubes.

CHAPTER 47

I opened my eyes and stared at the white ceiling. I turned to my side and teleported my phone on top of my bed and checked the time. It was already nine in the morning and I have school tomorrow, great.

I let out a lazy groan as I slowly sat up, rubbing my eyes. I swung my legs to the edge of my bed and looked at my room. I looked at nothing in particular, I started to think about my own birthday party and how I needed to plan it out with Ashton. I need to ask him and Rick about telling our story to my friends.

I planted my feet onto the cold wooden floor and teleported myself into the kitchen. In the kitchen there was a fresh aroma of cooked eggs and toast. I looked around the room and saw Rick at the stove cooking scrambled eggs.

"There's my little monster, did you sleep well?" Rick asked as he moved the eggs with a spatula.

"Meh, I still feel like shit," I said as I walked to the fridge and open the door.

"Language Kai. What are you going to do for you and Ashton's birthday party?"

I looked in the fridge. I moved a few bottles of drinks and grabbed a bottle of sparkling lemon water. I closed the fridge and raked my hands through my messy hair.

"I'm not sure, I need to ask Ashton. But I have something I wanted to ask the two of you, something important."

Rick looked back at me with a raised eyebrow. "If you're going to ask me to get a wizard or a mime for your birthday, that won't happen. I couldn't let a stranger into my home, you know that."

"To be honest Owen got a wizard costume; he could be a wizard for the party and do some magic tricks. He's not a stranger, plus he could put his magic skills to the test," I said with my hands raised.

Rick let out a sigh. "This is out of the question. I could get you anything else that doesn't involve people dressing up as characters."

"I don't really want anything particular for my birthday. Where is Ashton?" I asked as I walked to the kitchen table and sat on one of the wooden chairs.

"He's taking a shower; he might be out in a few minutes. Do you want scrambled eggs or an omelet?" Rick asked as walked up to the table and poured all the scrambled eggs onto an empty plate.

"I would like an omelet with a lot of cheese, thanks Rick," I said as I opened my bottle of sparkling water.

The bottle let out a sizzling sound as the bubbles in the bottle rose up, I could smell the citrus scent as I took a sip. The bubbles fizzed in my mouth as I looked around the kitchen. The kitchen had a nice modern look to it. Most of the kitchen appliances were black which matched the kitchen's color scheme: black, sliver, and white.

Ashton walked into the kitchen, his hair wet from his shower. "Good morning."

"Morning kiddo," Rick replied.

Ashton walked up to the refrigerator and took out a bottle that had some green stuff in it. It looked like those healthy smoothies he has been drinking for a while. He sat next to me at the table, I looked at him. "I need to ask you something, it's about our party next week."

He unscrewed the lid of the bottle and looked at me. "You can tell me anything, what is it?"

"I should wait until Rick is finished cooking, this involves him too." My heart started to beat faster. I hope they won't be mad at me for even thinking about what I'm about to tell them.

Ashton drank the green smoothie. I could feel myself gag because that smoothie looked gross. He'd been making these healthy smoothies for a week now and was trying to make me drink them. Some of the smoothies he makes are actually good but some of them are just either tasteless, have a weird texture, or just have an odd taste to them.

"I'm almost done cooking your omelet," Rick said as he flipped the omelet and turned off the stove. He turned around and walked towards the table holding the hot pan. An empty plate appeared in front of me. Rick carefully placed the lightly browned omelet onto my plate.

The pan disappeared out of Rick's hands and appeared in the sink, making a thud noise. Rick sat in front of Ashton and I and grabbed a piece of toast and a knife that was next to a tub of butter.

"What were you going to say Kai?" Rick asked me as he buttered his toast.

It took me a few minutes to think on what I was about to say. "I was wondering if the two of you would be okay if I tell my friends about what happened to me at our party."

Rick was about to take a bite of his buttered toast but stopped midway after I said that. No one said anything for what seemed like an hour.

Rick looked at me and placed his toast on his plate. He wiped his hands with a napkin and laid his hands on the table.

"I know what you two are thinking: 'she must be really crazy to say something like that.' But just letting you two know, I've been thinking about this for a while now, telling everyone about our story. Rick can erase some of our guests' memories so that they forget about it. We all know that Tyrone, Fred, and Stella know about our powers so you don't have to use your powers on them. I didn't tell you guys that I had already told Owen and Ronnell about my original powers." I looked at Rick and then at Ashton, they both kept the same straight face. I took a deep breath. "All I want for my birthday is to tell the people who I completely trust about my experience. I couldn't even bear the weight of my shoulders; I need to tell the truth or I won't feel like I've moved on."

Rick tapped his finger on the table thinking about what I had said. Ashton didn't move he just stared at the table. What are they thinking right now?

"I want to tell all my friends about our experience too, I want to start fresh and relieve all my stress from my past," Ashton said as he looked up at me.

Rick let out a sigh. "I guess the three of us feel the same thing, we should all tell our part of our story. At least I could just use my powers and erase people's memories, so there's no harm done."

I could feel myself smile. "I'm happy that the two of you agreed to do this, I love you two so much," I said with a relieved grin.

I sat at my desk in biology class, Ronnell sat in front of me. I looked at the classroom. The whole room was covered in posters of superheroes and characters from television shows. This is one of my favorite class-rooms in the school; I like how this room has a superhero theme. It re-minds me of myself and my family, maybe I could be a superhero in dis-guise.

My biology teacher, was passing out our classwork for today. We're learning about genes and genetics. I like my class mostly because Ronnell is here with me.

The teacher passed out a stack of papers in my row. Ronnell grabbed the papers from her and handed them to me. I grabbed the papers and took one for myself and handed out the papers to the person behind me.

"Hey Ronnell, are you excited for the party this weekend?" I said as I took my pen and wrote my name on my paper.

She turned her head to the side. "Yeah I can't wait for you and Ashton to open my gifts, I really hope you two like them. Is anyone else coming to your party?"

"I invited Tyrone, Owen, Ronny, Dawn, and their families, some of Ashton's friends from the basketball team, Stella, and Fred."

Ronnell turned around and placed her paper on the top of my desk. The two of us worked on our classwork. The paper seemed pretty easy since I had to figure out which gene matched with which characteristics.

"Rick and Ashton agreed to tell our story about our 'trip' at our party. You, Owen, and everyone else will finally know what exactly had hap-pened while I was out."

Ronnell looked up at me. "All three of you shouldn't have to do that, I'm sorry for what I said to you back then. I shouldn't have said that, I realized that I'm a really nosey and selfish best friend. I shouldn't put my-self into your personal business. I was so worried about you since you left because I thought something really bad had happened to you and to Rick. And I was right." "I wish I could help you in some way but I can't."

I stopped writing and set my pen down on my desk. "Don't say that. I know that I'm not the same as before, it will all make sense after I tell everyone what happened during my trip. I learned that I like myself more now than I did before, so don't worry about me."

"I'm grateful that I got my best friend back," she said with a genuine smile.

After school, I sat at the school's indoor gym watching the boys' basketball team train for a game. I was with Owen and Ronnell, the three of us talked about our classes and my party this weekend.

On the court the team was doing their practice drills. I don't know about sports but I did know that the team was practicing their shooting and dribbling skills. Ashton and Tyrone were passing the basketball to each other as they ran from one side of the court to another. I'm impressed by how fast those two are, I'm happy that Ashton is enjoying himself.

Owen took out a bag of Sun Chips from his backpack. "I can't wait for your party; it's going to be fun. Are you excited?" he asked with a grin as he opened the bag of chips.

I looked at the court. "I guess so, I'm just happy that Ashton gets to celebrate his late birthday. I've already gotten him a few gifts; I hope he likes them."

"What did you get him?" Owen asked.

"I got him his favorite book, a blue duffle bag, some clothes, and some other things that I bought for him."

"I hope Ashton likes your gifts. Do you think he bought something for you?" Ronnell asked.

I looked at the two of them. "To be honest I don't care if he buys me something or not, the gifts are not as important to me as family."

"Aww that's cute, I wish I had a sibling," Ronnell said, smiling.

"Having siblings can be annoying especially when you're the oldest. I should know, I have a younger brother," Owen said as he took a bite of a chip. "But once you get used to them it seems the new normal, so it isn't that bad. Kai is lucky, Ashton is the same age as us so she won't get annoyed that easily."

"That's partly true, Ashton keeps using my bath products and eating my food in the fridge but I'm cool with it. But he can be a pain in the ass sometimes. He always makes me drink these healthy smoothies that I sometimes don't like, he even made Rick drink them. Overall I still love him no matter what," I said, taking a piece of chip from Owen's bag of chips.

I looked down at the court and realized that the team had finished with their drill. I heard the coach telling the team that they should practice more for the game next weekend. I guess practice had ended; all the team members walked to the side of the court or to the bleachers to get their belongings.

Tyrone and Ashton walked up to the bleachers talking to each other and punching each other in the arms. The two of them laughed as they walked up to us.

"You guys were great out there," I told them.

"Thanks sis, coach told us that we're two of his favorites. Hey, can you get my bottle of Gatorade from my bag?" Ashton asked.

I looked to my left and saw Ashton's black gym sack. I took the bag and reached inside, grabbing a bottle of Gatorade. I tossed the bottle at Ashton who caught it and unscrewed the lid.

"Coach even said that we're his all-star duo, he also said that the two of us work better together than anyone else," Tyrone said sitting next to me, placing his arm around me as he laid his head on my shoulder.

I could feel Tyrone's sweat seeping into my clothes and skin. "Ty, you know that you're really sweaty right?"

"Yeah, I know, and I'm wearing a sleeveless t-shirt so you might need to change," Tyrone said as he rubbed his head on my shoulder laughing.

"So where do you guys want to go after practice?" Owen asked.

Ashton sat on the steps in front of us drinking his Gatorade. Owen gestured his bag of chips at him. Ashton reached inside the bag and took out a few pieces of chips and started eating them.

"We could eat at Owen's parents' diner, I miss eating there," I said, patting Tyrone on the arm.

"I agree. We should go to the diner, I want a vanilla milkshake and some loaded fries," Tyrone said.

"I don't think I have ever been to the diner before," Ashton said scratching his head.

"You haven't been to the diner since you got here? I thought Rick would take you to the place since he and Kai are regulars. In my opinion, you're missing out on a great food experience. We have to go to my parent's diner for Ashton's sake," Owen said as he crumpled up his chip bag.

"We should get changed and then we could leave, I don't want to wear my sweaty clothes outside," Ashton said to Tyrone.

Ashton grabbed the bottom of his t-shirt pulling it up to his face. The back of his shirt was lifting up. I could see the bottom of his centipede tattoo showing. I quickly grabbed the bottom of his shirt and pulled it down to cover the tattoo.

Ashton looked back at me making a confused look. I nodded my head at him gesturing that his tattoo was showing. Ashton opened his mouth and nodded, remembering that he might expose himself. I let go of his shirt.

"You know what? Screw it, everyone will know eventually," Ashton said looking at me.

I raised an eyebrow but then realized that he was going to expose his tattoo. Ashton took off his shirt exposing his back. He reached his arm toward his gym sack and took out a blue and white knitted hoodie that I bought him at the mall. He stuffed his t-shirt inside the bag and turned around, looking back at the four of us.

I look at Owen and Ronnell; the two of them had shocked looks on their faces. I can tell that Ronnell was blushing like crazy because she kept staring at Ashton in an odd way. I turned my head and looked at Tyrone who had his mouth slightly open. You know what? Screw it, I don't care what anyone thinks or says about my tattoo.

I took off my arm cover revealing my arm tattoo. At least I'm wearing a t-shirt so it was easier to take my arm cover off. Everyone looked at me and then at my arm, still maintaining the same shocked expression.

"Holy shit, you two got some cool ink," Owen said as he took my left arm and examined my tattoo.

"Damn you're ripped Ash," Tyrone said as he looked at his own arms.

"Is your tattoo a centipede?" Ronnell said her voice slightly quivered as she looked away from Ashton.

Ashton scratched his head and made an embarrassed smile. "Yeah it is, do you guys like it?"

"Hell yeah that's so cool, I wish my parents would let me get a tattoo like the two of you. Did you guys get it during your trip?" Owen asked as he turned my arm. As he turned my arm he looked at my lotus tattoo and then looked up at Ashton's right arm that also had a lotus tattoo.

"Why do you two have the same tattoo but in different ink and on different arms?" Owen asked.

"It's quite complicated, soon you will learn the reason why the two of us have tattoos in the first place," Ashton said as he put on his hoodie.

"You just have to wait till the party, that's when we're going to tell all of you what really happened during our crazy trip," I said as I looked at Ashton.

Tyrone removed his arm from around my shoulders and grabbed his gray hoodie and tugged it on over his shirt.

"We should head to the diner now, I'm a bit hungry from all that practice," Ashton said as he looked at the four of us.

"He's right we should eat something, maybe my parents might give us a discount," Owen said placing my arm on my lap before he stood up.

All five of us stood up and put on our backpacks. We all walked down the bleachers and towards the door that leads outside of the indoor gym.

As we walked through the exit door Ronnell walked next to me, looking at me and making a smile. I looked back at her and made a smile, letting her know everything was okay.

Outside was cool and fresh. I looked up; there were a few clouds floating in the sky. I took a deep breath and exhaled, taking in the sunlight on my skin. I'm turning over a new leaf and everything is going to be much better than before. Maybe it's a good thing that Rick brought me back to life, maybe it isn't.

CHAPTER 48

Today was the day of our party. Rick was out getting food for the party, Ashton was in the living room decorating the room with party decorations, and I was on the stairs wrapping the handrail with colored streamers. The party started in about two hours so it left us plenty of time to get ready.

"How is it going in there?" I asked.

"I'm almost done, how about you?" Ashton said out loud.

"I'm done, I have something for you," I said as I finished wrapping the colored streamers at the end of the handrail.

I walked down the stairs and inside the living room where Ashton was on a step ladder, tying paper pompoms on the curtain rod. The room looked really decorative and nice. I sat on the sofa and watched Ashton finish tying the pompoms.

"You did a really good job decorating the room, I'm impressed," I said as I teleported a can of soda onto my hand and open the tab.

"Thanks, I hope everyone enjoys our party," he said as he stepped down the ladder and walked to the sofa sitting next to me.

"I got you a present. Rick told me that he also got you a present but he wanted to give it to you later," I said drinking my soda and looking at Ashton.

He looked back at me and made a warm smile. His cheeks turned pink. "You guys don't have to do that for me."

"We both wanted to buy something for you for your late birthday, don't worry so much about it. You're part of our family and we want you to be happy. I can give you my present for you right now."

A blue duffel bag appeared in front of us. Ashton looked at the bag and then at me, his eyes grew wide.

"You seriously don't have to do this for me, how much money did you spend?" he asked as he grabbed the bag and dragged it towards our feet.

"Don't worry about that, open the bag there are more things inside it."

Ashton unzipped the bag and revealed neatly stacked clothes, a basketball, some other sports gear, a mug, and a book on top of all the other gifts.

Ashton took the book and looked at it, it was a book called To Kill a Mockingbird. I could see his lips curve into a smile.

"I know that's your favorite book so I got it for you if you ever want to read it again or do something with it. I hope you like your gifts," I said as I placed my can on the coffee table in front of me.

Ashton placed the book on the sofa next to him and looked at me with a huge grin. He suddenly hugged me his face buried in my neck and shoulder. I hugged him back, smiling to myself. It's been awhile since I felt truly happy with myself, it made me feel complete.

I could hear quiet sobbing noises coming from Ashton. I quickly became concerned. "Hey Ash, what's wrong?" I said quietly patting his back gently.

I could feel his head turn to the side. "It's nothing. I'm just so grateful to have you, Rick, and everyone else in my life," he said making a sniffling sound. "Thank you for saving me from that place and from those horrible people before I completely became one of them. I owe you and Rick everything." He pressed his face onto my shoulder. "Thank you for being in my life in the first place."

I could feel tears streaming down my cheeks. I tried my hardest not to cry but I couldn't help it. I felt bad for him, I'm just happy that he finally has a life that he wanted. I could feel myself make a sad smile as I patted his back. I pressed my head against Ashton's shoulder and closed my eyes, letting my tears run down my face.

"No need to thank me, I'm glad that you're not the one who got killed. Thank you for being there for me when I need you. I would do anything for you and everyone else, even if it breaks me," I said quietly.

All our party guests showed up to the house. Ashton was in the living room talking to his friends, and I was in the kitchen eating crab Rangoon out of a catering tray. Everyone seemed like they were enjoying themselves. All the adults including Rick, Stella, and Fred were at one side of the kitchen talking to other parents. I kept eating crab Rangoon as I looked around the kitchen and at the group of adults laughing and talking.

Rick looked at me and yelled jokingly. "Kai don't eat too much of that, you won't have the appetite to eat your cake!"

Most of the adults in the group looked at me and smiled, I kept eating the Rangoon. It's not my fault that it tastes so good. I looked back at Rick, grabbed a paper bowl and took a big fistful of Rangoon, and dumped it into my bowl.

Rick raised an eyebrow at me. I raised an eyebrow back trying to be sassy. I turned around and walked out of the kitchen and into the living room where the rest of my friends were. Ronnell and Owen sat on the sofa talking to each other. Ashton, Tyrone, and a few of Ashton's friends were at one side of the room talking. Owen's little brother, Mason, was sitting in the corner of the room playing with Tobi.

I walked up to Ronnell and Owen. "Hey guys, how do you like the party so far?" I asked as I sat on the floor.

"It's fun, I like how you and Ashton decorated the place," Ronnell said.

"I like the food, it's really good," Owen said as he took a Rangoon from my bowl and ate it.

"I'm glad that you guys like the party. I'll get to tell you guys about my trip near the end of the party or when most of my guests leave," I said.

"Don't worry about it too much, you don't have to say anything if it's too hard for you or your family to tell. Plus there's a lot of people here, I'm afraid that one of them, even my own parents might get your family in some big trouble," Ronnell said.

"Don't worry about it, the three of us know what to do. Rick got his ways," I said eating a piece of Rangoon.

Ashton walked up to us. "You're still eating that? You ate like half of the whole tray; leave some for our guests."

I lifted my plate up to Ashton who took a piece of rangoon and ate it. All the adults came into the living room. I placed my bowl under the table and stood up. I stood next to Ashton and the two of us glanced at each other, everyone was in the living room except Rick.

In a few minutes Rick came into the room holding a large cake with a lot of colored candles on it. Rick began to sing the birthday song, then everyone else began to sing along. I could feel my face cringe as everyone huddled around Ashton and me. I looked at Ashton who had an awkward look on his face.

As Rick walked toward us Tobi ran up to Rick barking at him. Rick stopped singing and started to sway left and right. Everyone else stopped singing and made a gasping noise. Tyrone's dad grabbed Rick by the shoulders, helping him gain his balance. Stella crouched down at Tobi and picked him up, carrying him in her arms. Tobi stopped barking.

Rick looked back at Tyrone's dad and made an embarrassed smile. Tyrone's dad smiled back, the two continued to sing, everyone else chimed in.

Rick stood in front of Ashton and me. He had a huge grin on his face that made me feel happy for him. I looked at the cake. It was covered in whipped cream and it had writing on it that said 'Happy Birthday Ashton & Kai' in blue cursive icing.

"Happy birthday you two, I love you two so much," Rick said as he moved the cake in front of us. The song had ended.

Ashton and I exchanged glances and turned to the cake. We blew out the candles at the same time. Everyone cheered and made a whooping sound. I felt my lips curve into a grin.

Rick placed the cake on the coffee table and wrapped his arms around the two of us, I could feel his face pressed against our heads.

"I'm sorry for what you two have been through. I promise that I won't keep any more secrets. I would do anything for my kids," Rick whispered.

"I love you guys so much," Ashton said as he tightened his grip.

"We love you too," I said as I pressed my face against Rick's chest.

"Okay who wants some cake?" Rick said breaking up our group hug and then looking around the room.

The guests came up to the table waiting to get a piece of cake. Rick let Ashton cut the cake and I got to hand out plates of cake to the guests. Everyone began to talk to one another and also began eating their cake.

I got my own plate of cake and started eating it. The cake was a sponge cake with fruit and cream inside it. Ashton got his own plate and we both began eating our cake as we stood next to our friends.

Outside my home I lay on the porch stairs looking at the street as I listened to my music blasting from my phone's speakers. It was already late afternoon, most of my guests left to go back home or somewhere else. Owen,

Ronnell, and Tyrone's parents had left the party but said that they'd come back to pick their kids up around eight or nine. I'm glad that my friends are still here so Rick won't have to use his powers on their parents.

I looked up at the sunset colored sky, my hands laced together as I lay my head against them. I took a deep breath and closed my eyes, taking in a new feeling of peace. The cool breeze lightly touched my face I exhaled slowly as I opened my eyes.

I heard the front door open and close. I didn't turn my head to see who it was. The footsteps began to come closer. I could see Ashton walking down the steps and sit next to me.

I turned my head to the side and looked at him. He was looking at the street in front of us. The two of us didn't say anything. I turned my head so that I was looking straight at the sky.

"Do you believe in God?" Ashton asked quietly.

I didn't answer his question right away because it was a kind of question that made me really think about it. It was also a question I didn't think Ashton might ask me.

"No, I do not believe in such things like that. Why do you ask?"

"I'm just curious about your response."

"Do you believe in God?" I asked as I observed a pink and yellow cloud drifting away.

"Sometimes. Back then when I was a kid I prayed to whoever would listen to me, maybe it was God or some spiritual being. I prayed that I would leave Ken and that place for good. I was still naive back then, thinking that someone like God would help me. Back then I used to pray every night that I could become free, as months became years I slowly lost faith in myself and everything else." He looked at me with a frown. "I became the person that I didn't want to become, I had lost complete faith in everything." He wiped his nose with his jacket sleeve. "I even attempted to kill myself so I wouldn't have to live this kind of life. I'm a kid who had nothing in his life; no parents, no siblings, or even other family members that I know of. Ken thought that he treated me like a son or whatever the hell he thought of me as. I've known since I could grasp the concept of life that Ken was using me all along." He let out a bitter laugh as he turned his head to look at the street.

I sat up and looked at him, I felt a prick in my chest. I sat up grabbing him by the shoulders, my watery eyes stinging. I don't want Ashton to be depressed, I don't want to be depressed, not today anyway.

Ashton looked at me. "I don't want you to feel this way. Today was supposed to be a happy time for us. I know that your past was extremely harsh even for a little kid, but you have to look at the future with Rick, myself, and everyone else," I said, my voice breaking. "You're my brother now, I'm proud of what you've become at this moment and as you grow up. Don't ever forget that."

Ashton made a sad smile. "I know and I'm so grateful for everything you and Rick have done for me, but you didn't let me finish what I was saying. When I saw you died in front of me I prayed that you'd somehow become alive again, it's been a long time since I prayed and I knew that my wish wasn't going to happen. After I woke up from that day Rick healed me he told me that you were in the process of being resurrected, and I felt relieved that you were going to be fine. That's when I suddenly gained faith. It made me feel like I have a purpose to live, it was all because of you and I want to thank you for that," he said as he placed his arm around my shoulders. His sad smile turned into a genuine smile.

I placed my arm around his shoulders as I smiled, looking at the street.

"There's no need to thank me, it's faith isn't it?" I said as I watched a gray pickup truck drive through the quiet street.

The two of us didn't say anything for a few minutes. I wonder what would happen if I didn't get resurrected by Rick, would everyone that I cared about become different or stay the same? Would my 'permanent' death affect anyone's lives for the better or worse? What would Rick feel or act if he didn't have the ability to make me become alive again? Would he become a broken man or become someone who was much worse than that? All these questions filled my head and made me feel awful about myself and the people who I cared about. Everything that had happened was because of Ken and I was his intended target. I shouldn't think too much about the past and the what-ifs, I should just look at the present and the future.

"Kai, may I ask you another question?" Ashton asked as he kept looking down at the street.

"Sure, you can ask me anything."

"What happened after you died? Did you see anything or feel anything?"

I removed my arm from his shoulders and placed both of my hands on my lap. I didn't answer his question right away; I kept looking down at my tan hands as I thought more about his second, debilitating question.

Ashton turned his head to look at me. I didn't move. I kept staring at my hands. "Did I say anything wrong? I'm sorry if I asked you a tough question, you don't have to answer it."

I straightened my back and looked at the sunset sky. "Don't apologize. I'm just carefully thinking about your question. All I could remember right after my so-called death is darkness. I didn't feel anything, like my senses had been numbed. But I clearly remember what happened before I woke up from my coma. I woke up in a field of black lilies and dead trees with no clouds and no sun in the blue sky. On the field where I lay there was a silhouette of my body that was covered in white lilies. I was wearing a white dress but I was partly covered in blood from my wounds during that day with Ken. I didn't feel pain but I could feel numbness throughout my body. Luckily within a few minutes I could feel my body once again. I began walking through the field because I didn't want to stand there and do nothing. As I walked to nowhere the sky began to change from blue to sunset colors. Petals from the black lilies started to float up into the sky. I haven't forgotten how beautiful that moment was, I wish that you could have seen it yourself." I glanced at Ashton who made a slight smile.

"I wish I could have seen it too," he said quietly as I looked down at my hands once again.

"As the petals floated up the black petals suddenly turned white. All the petals stopped moving, all of them were suspended in space. The white petals instantly fell onto the ground as I somehow went through the ground. After that I instantly remembered everything that happened to me and I woke up."

"What a strange dream you had, maybe the black and white lilies represent something that involves you or your past experiences. I'm happy and relieved that you woke up from your coma. That's the only thing that matters now."

The two of us watched the cars drive by left and right as the sun slowly dove into the horizon. Everything in that moment seemed calm and peaceful. I hoped the feeling could last a bit longer.

I was in the kitchen eating some of the leftover cake from my party. Ronnell walked up to me and handed me an unopened can of soda.

"Thanks," I said as I took the can of soda and placed my plate of cake on the kitchen counter.

"You and your family don't have to share your experiences from the trip. We all shouldn't get into your personal problems."

"Don't worry so much about it, we want to do this. Plus, all the people who we want to tell our story to are here, so it's a good time to do this. By telling this story it will help me move on and it will make me feel better about myself." I opened my can of soda and drank it.

"Okay, if you really want to do this, I won't stop you. You should finish your cake. I think everyone is in the living room."

I scooped my cake with my plastic spoon and shoved it into my mouth. I wiped my mouth with a napkin that Ronnell gave to me and dumped all my trash into the trash bin. Ronnell and I walked into the living room. Ashton and Owen were standing next to the bookshelf, Stella and Rick sat on the sofa, and Tyrone and Fred were petting Tobi.

The two of us walked up to Ashton and Owen who were talking about Ashton's tattoos.

"Do you ever regret getting your back tattoo?" Owen asked.

Ashton glanced at us, but then looked back at Owen. "I don't regret it at all, I got used to having that tattoo. I've had that tattoo for at least two years now so it doesn't bother me at all."

"That's good to hear, plus your tattoo makes you look badass," I said as I rolled up my sleeves.

"Me badass? How about you, miss 'I got a whole arm sleeve tattoo?'" Ashton said as he took my left arm and held it up so that all four of us could see it. "But overall I like how our tattoos represent us as people."

"I'm glad that the two of you like your tattoos and are comfortable with them," Ronnell said.

"I agree with her, I wish I could have cool tattoos like you guys," Owen said as he took my arm and carefully looked at it.

"I don't think your parents will approve of that. Also I don't want you to have any tattoos on you, you look better without them," Ashton said as he patted Owen on the shoulders.

Owen looked up at Ashton. "You sure about that?"

"I'm positive," Ashton replied.

"We should start now Ash," I said looking at him.

Ashton nodded at me. I walked towards the sofa where Rick and Stella sat.

"Hey Kai! Happy birthday, I hope that you and Ashton enjoyed your party," Stella said as I sat between her and Rick. She placed her arm around my shoulders and smiled at me.

"I did, I hope that you enjoyed the party as well," I said. Ashton walked up to the sofa and sat between Rick and me.

"Are you two sure you guys want to do this?" asked Rick.

Ashton and I exchanged glances. "We want to do this," I said.

Rick made a reassuring nod at us and looked around the room. Fred sat on the single sofa chair and Owen, Tyrone, and Ronnell sat on the floor behind the coffee table. I closed my eyes and took a deep breath.

I truly wonder where I'm going to end up in life but now I realize that I should live my life to the fullest and actually enjoy every bit of it. No matter what the future holds, I'll try to become a better person than I was before. I know that was kind of a cliché, but it does have some meaning to me. There are no words for how much my true friends and family mean to me and it makes me feel complete.

I opened my eyes and looked around the room. A dozen eyes stared at me with curiosity. I felt for once determined to express how I felt about my experience with the people who I strongly care about. I guess I could say that dying made me somewhat a reformed person.

I raised my head up high with determination as rolled up both of my sleeves, showing off my arm tattoo and my hand tattoo. The more I look at my tattoos, the more I like having them; they make me remember my life changing experience with my other family members and that organization. I just hope somewhere in heaven or someplace else my parents are proud of what Rick and I have become.

I looked to my left and right, looking at my real family that I'm so happy to be part of. My lips curved into a confident smile. "It all started when I was walking with Owen and saved a kid from getting hit by a car…"

ABOUT THE AUTHOR

Sovina Sey is open to new adventures and enjoys living her life with her friends and family in the state of Massachusetts. Throughout her life, she becomes inspired by the people in her community and looks forward to learning new things from her own experiences or from others. This is her first novel.